THE 38TH YEAR

L. EDWARD PEACOCK

PAGE PUBLISHING, INC.
New York, NY

First originally published by Page Publishing, Inc. 2017

Cover art by Rashad Gay

This novel is a work of fiction, names, characters, places, and incidents are the product of the author's imagination or are used fictitiously. Any resemblance to actual persons living or dead, events, or locales is entirely coincidental.

ISBN 978-1-68409-107-2 (Paperback)
ISBN 978-1-68409-109-6 (Hard Cover)
ISBN 978-1-68409-108-9 (Digital)

Printed in the United States of America

To Enrique,

Do not be afraid to step beyond your comfort zone.

J. Edward Peacock

DEDICATION

To my father Gerald Houston Peacock.

A victim of an unsolved murder in 1964, may
God judge those responsible most harshly.

PROLOGUE

I never thought to be one year older would make any difference.

My father told me that time is an enemy to man, for everyday that he lives, puts him one day closer to the grave. That concept no longer applies to me anymore.

I have looked into the face from whence evil originated, a powerful force that even death itself cowers away from.

James Houston Farnsworth Jr.

CHAPTER 1

As I sit here, waiting for my baby to be born, I wouldn't have ever imagined that I would be under protective custody by the FBI. Two agents are attached to me, one in the room and one outside the door. Most expectant fathers would be sitting in the waiting room with the general public or with their wives in the delivery room. Due to my certain predicament, the situation wouldn't allow either of the latter. It has been almost a year since I was made privy to what was hiding behind the curtain. I can assure you that it wasn't the wizard.

Time and events have a way of catching up with people; with me it was more like a planned hit-and-run by a cosmic semi. Even as a child growing up, I had some crazy-assed dreams and even incidences beyond comprehension happen to me. I had been prompted by them, but I chose to bury the weird shit into the deepest crevice of my mind. I knew as a kid, something was on the horizon and that something really began to accelerate after my thirty-seventh birthday. It initiated with the deaths in my immediate family, which occurred within six months from each other. The first deemed as accidental was my grandfather. He died from a reaction to a vitamin supplement, ninety-six years old and smoked a pack a day of Camel cigarettes from sunup to sundown. I never heard him cough. I don't remember the guy ever being sick a day in his life. And just like that, Grandfather was put in the ground eight months ago. Then it wasn't long before my dad too was gone. My father succumbed to lung cancer at the age of sixty-one, just two months ago; he too was an avid smoker. He always had one of the two things in his hand, a cup of coffee and/or a cigarette.

Unlike my grandfather, my dad had the ever-present smokers cough or hack. He refused chemo treatment. He told me that everyone has to go at some time or other. He said that you can't cheat death like people cheat on their taxes. For now, I'm running my father's business, which is a production company called Red Sand Productions. I worked for my father while going to high school, then I went to college and got a degree in business and marketing. I didn't realize the pressures on my father until a couple a months before he became ill when he was approached by a mobster from Chicago.

My father coproduced a very talented group from Rough Rock, Arizona, called Desert Reign. Their career didn't really take off until their video hit the media. My father and I worked together to come up with a video and soundtrack that earned the band considerable exposure. In doing so, the exposure put Red Sand Studio in the spotlight, and on the radar screen of a mobster. Despite my father's illness and his having to go in and out of the hospital with bouts of pneumonia, he was at the studio every day. When the band was voted by MTV as the best new rock artist of the year, that moment was the pinnacle in my father's life.

Well, as I mentioned before, this guy from Chicago showed up and introduced himself as Vincent Serlinni. He owns a couple of recording studios in the upper eastern states. He offered my father a considerable amount of money to buy out the business. My father knew that he wasn't going to make it much longer, and he asked me about the sell-off. I told him that he had built the business and that whatever he decided to do that I would accept it. He then told me that he knew what Mr. Serlinni's motives are. My dad told me that some acquaintances within the recording business were forced to sell or experience hostile takeovers by the mob.

Dad told me that the decision was mine to make because he was handing me the business. He then told me that he had been withholding information about his condition and that the doctor told him that since he refused the chemotherapy, it was a matter of months or weeks before the inevitable was to happen. I knew deep down inside that my dad's days were numbered, so I swallowed down the news, and he told me not to tell Mom or anyone else. He said that he wants things to go in a normal daily manner, and he plans to carry himself accordingly until. So I promised that I wouldn't tell anyone, and I also told him that I didn't want to sell the business either. He told me that men like Serlinni are ruthless and will go to any length to pressure me to sell the business. I told him to stop thinking about the business and concentrate on staying above ground with me.

That conversation took place one month before my dad left the world of the living. I would forsake all the wealth, big house, and fancy cars just to have my dad and my grandfather here with me now. An overly used phrase stated by many that their loved ones are in a far better place. Well, I've been to the place that exists between the good place and the bad place. I'll will get to that part. So now let me start, when I took the helm at the studio. Serlinni has called me and offered me a price for the business. Instead of me telling him flat out no and to go and fuck himself, I told him to let me finish production on Desert Reign's newest CD and video. He agreed with me, and by doing so, it would buy me some time to think about my next move.

During this time I have been carrying on a normal life, trying to balance my life with my fiancée, Nicole. She helps me to stay grounded. I don't know what I'd do without her; it's as if we knew each other from a past life. I haven't told her or Mom about the Serlinni situation because they would go ballistic on me. I'm good at keeping secrets, a trait that I inherited unknowingly from my father's family. For the moment I got several things staring me in the face. First, I'm getting married, which is only three weeks away. I already got honeymoon destination plans worked out, which is the minor of my situations. I got to finish a video shoot on location in Arizona on a Navajo reservation this week with the group Desert Reign, come back to the studio and splice in the sound track, and do the final editing to the video. Then I've got to meet with some new clients from Atlanta, an all-female group called Trailer Dolls. I know I won't have any problems coming up with ideas for CD artwork or video shoot locations with a group name like that.

I think the first thing I'll do is burn one to calm myself and get in a creative mode. I'll go tell my secretary that I'm going to get a bite to eat since it's almost lunchtime anyway, except I won't be eating lunch. Well, I might as well go in the bathroom and build one for the drive. I wonder if Dad ever got high because of the exposure around him. I never saw anyone using while my dad was around the studio; musicians always went out back between the building's alley or got into their limo. I don't allow it openly because I can't afford for anyone to use it against me or possibly draw attention from the man, you know, the heat. So I got it built and told Trina, my receptionist, that I'll return in a few minutes. On the way out, I stopped to tell her to call Edwin, Desert Reign's manager, to tell him that I'll be leaving for Flagstaff–Arizona Municipal tonight and that I'll call him once I touch down in. I asked Trina did she want me to bring her some lunch? She told me that she had brought a salad for lunch and that it's in the fridge. I told her okay and that I won't be gone for long, about a half hour or so.

I made my way to the car. As I was getting closer to the vehicle, a stray dog crawls from underneath the car. I didn't know what to think. *Am I going to get dog bit or what?* The animal wasn't posturing in anger with his ears laid back; the dog nervously wagged his tail and stopped in front of me. I reached down to pet the animal, and it licked my hand, and I heard an audible voice say, "Watch your ass today, James." The dog scurried off behind the dumpster. *Did that dog just say something, or am I losing it?*

I just got in the car, pulled out into the street, turned on some tunes, and made a visual sweep of the scenery. The coast was clear, so I fired up a chronic stick, took in a long inhalation, and enjoyed. The weather is nice, a beautiful late spring day in Georgia. As I make my way down the street, I had only gone a few blocks or so, and I looked to my left, and there on the sidewalk was that same dog that licked my hand, and he had a friend with him, another dog, and they were both looking at me. I put the chronic down in the ashtray; that stuff was better than I thought. *I better go and get something to eat.* I didn't eat breakfast this morning. I pulled into the Burger King drive thru, ordered my food, paid the attendant and parked in the parking lot. As I began to get ready to eat my food, my cell phone rings. I looked at the incoming call and it is Nicole. I answered the phone saying, "hello". She replied "hey baby. What are you doing?

I told her that I'm eating a burger in the Burger King parking lot. She then says that she's got my things packed for the trip to Arizona. I told her that I had a few things to finish at the studio, call the sound and film crew to see how close they are to being set up for tomorrow, confirm my charter flight from Flagstaff to Rough Rock, have a quick dinner with her before I have to leave. I told her that I loved her and I would see her later. As I put the cell phone down, I looked in my rearview mirror, and a black Lexus pulled up behind me. Two men in street clothes walked up to the car. One guy continues into Burger King, and the other stops at my window and told me that Mr. Serlinni sends his greetings and then handed me a sealed envelope. It looked like it could contain stacks of money. I handed the envelope back to the guy and said to him, "Tell Mr. Serlinni thanks for the gesture but keep the gift."

The guy kept on insisting to take the gift because it would be an insult to not to accept the gift, and I told the guy to leave me the fuck alone. About the time the guy's partner came out of Burger King, a police car drove up, and the guy that was hassling me withdrew and left. I started thinking about what my dad told me about those people. I got maybe two bites off the burger. I couldn't eat anymore. What am I going to do? Do I sell out to this hood so he can just take over the East Coast music business, or do I something to combat it? I have to fulfill my obligations to my clients and the people of my company first of all. My dad built this company from nothing. Fuck these bastards! So I might as well head on back to the studio and focus on what I do best.

I opened the ashtray and retrieved the remains of the chronic and hit it a few times on the way back to the studio. I pulled into the studio parking lot and parked the car, put the roach into the burger bag, and proceeded to the dumpster. Out of the corner of my eye, I see some movement. It's the same dog that licked my hand earlier. I took out the partially eaten burger and gave it to him and watched him disappear behind the dumpster. I walked into the office, and my secretary told me that I had a message from Mr. Serlinni. I asked her, "What did he have to say?" She said that he told her to tell me to have a good trip to Arizona. So I shrugged off the message and walked toward the sound room to check things out and make sure the techs didn't leave anything behind. As I entered the room, I started thinking about what Serlinni could be planning while I'm gone. I could call Nicole and get her to stay with her friend while I'm Arizona. That would ease my mind knowing she's fine and out of town. I'll call my cousin to come over to watch over things at Mom's and Grandma's also. If I didn't have this moron Serlinni bastard trying to give me an ulcer, I also have to think about the music side to my life that urges me forward.

Dad took a lot of shit from Serlinni right up to the end when cancer won. So it looks like the crew has gotten what it needs from the studio. I think I'll start up a disc by Desert Reign and try to focus on the music than to dwell on my personal problems. As the music is playing, I get the script for the video shoot and go over it to see if I need to make any alterations before I get to the shoot on location. I like to visualize myself behind the camera, setting up the scene, so to speak, without actually being there. Just as I was getting into the moment, my secretary comes into the studio and tells me that I have a phone call. I asked her if she couldn't have just taken the message. She said the caller's name is Vincent Serlinni, and he was insistent to talk to me. So I figured I'd go ahead and take the call just to see what this guy wanted now.

So I picked up the phone and answered, "What is it now, Serlinni?"

Serlinni answered, "Why did you turn down my peace-offering gift?"

I told Serlinni the only gift that he could give me is to just leave me the hell alone and stop bugging me, then I hung up the phone. My concentration at this point is shot to hell. So I shut off the music, grabbed the script, and made my way toward the front office. I stopped at the secretary's desk and told her that she could take off early since it's Friday, and quitting time is only two hours away. I told her to have a good weekend and that I would lock up. She said, "Have a good trip and hope the weather will be favorable for the video shoot." I said thanks as she was picking up her things to leave.

So I made my way back to the back door of the studio to check to see if it's locked, and then I went back up front and set the alarm on my way out. I locked the front door and gave it a shake and made my way toward the parking lot. As I walked toward my vehicle, I heard this dog barking his head off. I walked toward the barking noise; it seemed to come from the other side of my vehicle. As I made my way to my car I heard a vehicle turn into the parking lot. A voice said, "You better come over to this side, there's trouble coming." It's a good thing that I did. On the other side of my car there was safety because some of Vinnie's boys sprayed my car with bullets and left. The dog that was doing all that barking was the same dog I saw earlier that day. He saved my life, and he had company with him.

The dog said, "You're not going crazy. You did hear me talking to you. You have a gift that you don't realize yet. Those guys that are causing you this trouble will wish they never fucked with you."

Before I could say anything, the dog and his companion had turned and disappeared behind the dumpster and into a patch of woods. I got in my car and called the police and told them that I was a victim of a drive-by. As I waited for the police, I was completely in shock of what transpired. Who would ever believe me if I told someone that a dog spoke to me twice today and saved my life. What the fuck is going on? What does that dog know that I don't?

The police got there in about ten minutes or so. They asked if I got shot and if I saw the shooter. I told the police I saw the vehicle, black car with the windows tinted out, and I didn't get a tag number either. They asked me if I had an idea who was behind this shooting. I told them that it was probably some gang members that were about to carjack me. When I ducked down behind my vehicle, they probably thought I was carrying heat, so they shot up my vehicle. The cop said it was luck that I decided to take cover on the other side of my vehicle. The cop took down some more information and took pictures of the car. He asked me if I had tried to crank the vehicle to see if it was drivable. I told him that I hadn't tried the ignition yet. I got behind the wheel, and the engine turned over okay. I got out and looked, and judging by the bullet holes, most of the bullets went into the driver's door and the left rear quarter panel. One or two went into the front quarter panel but didn't damage the engine as far as I know.

I sat listening to the engine; it was running fine. I thanked the cop and asked him would insurance cover drive-by shootings. The cop suggested that I say that I was a victim of a carjacking attempt. I thanked the cop, and he said that he would have a report written up, and I could pick it up at the station tomorrow. I took out my cell and called the insurance agent, and she told me to get the police report once they have written it up. I told them what the policeman suggested to me. I called a friend of mine that owns an auto-body shop and told him that I was bringing my car by for some cosmetic repairs. I did not want Nicole or my mom to see the car with the bullet holes in it. On the way over to Mike's Body Shop, I called my cousin and told him to meet me at Mike's shop. He said that he would meet me there in a few minutes. I thought about Nicole, and I decided it might be a good idea to see if she wants to go to Arizona with me. She usually doesn't like to go anymore because she says that she gets bored on the set. Maybe I can come up with something before I have to leave tonight.

Well, I'm pulling into Mike's. I might as well tell him the same story that I told the police; it worked with them. I parked my car and walked into the office.

Mike said, "What happened to the car, a fender bender?"

I said, "No, go take a look at it."

So I followed Mike out to the parking lot.

He said the passenger side looks good. I told him to look at the driver's side.

He said, "What the fuck happened? Who's mad at you, James?"

I told him the same story as I told the cops and told him not to do anything to it yet until after Monday.

Mike said, "Sure thing."

And he asked if I needed a ride home. I told him my cousin Chris was coming to pick me up and told him not to say anything to Nicole about this. Mike told me that he would move my vehicle to the back and lock it up in the fence. Well, before Mike could ask me any more details about the shooting, my cousin Chris pulled up. I told Mike that I would let him know something Monday. I got in Chris's car, and we headed for my house.

Chris said, "What's up, cousin?"

I told him to keep what I am about to tell him between us only. I told him that Serlinni sent some of his boys to see me and shot up my vehicle.

Chris said, "Why don't you go to the cops?"

I told him that I can't prove it's Serlinni, don't have a recording of any threats.

Chris then said, "What are you going to do about this?"

I told him that I'm going to Flagstaff, Arizona, tonight then shoot a video at a Navajo reservation. I told him to keep a watch over Mom's house and Grandmother's just in case. I told him that I'm going to try and persuade Nicole to go to Rough Rock with me. By this time we had pulled up in my driveway, and lo and behold, there's Nicole, coming out the house, going to her car.

I told Chris as I was getting out of his car, "Remember, not a word." And I handed him the number to my motel in Flagstaff, Arizona. "Thanks for the ride, Chris."

Then he backed out of the drive.

Then Nicole said, "Where's your car, baby?"

I told her some old lady rear-ended me in traffic, did a little damage to the car. I told her that I'm glad the old lady didn't get hurt, and the damage to her car was minimal.

Nicole said, "Did she have insurance?"

I told her yes, and I dropped my car off at Mike's for repairs. She said that she had all my things packed for the flight.

I said, "Nicole, why don't you go with me to Arizona?"

Nicole said, "Well, since it's Arizona and you know how I love Indian art and turquoise."

I said, "Well, that was easy. Now go pack your stuff."

I looked at my watch, and it says four thirty. My flight leaves at eight o'clock. That means I've got about two hours to rest a little before we head to the airport for a hop flight from Macon to Atlanta. So I'd better call the local airport and check to see if everything is a go. I don't need any more surprises today. So I made the call, and everything is set.

I said to Nicole, "I'm going to take a shower while you pack your things."

She said, "I'm almost finished, I'm only taking a few things."

I jokingly said, "There's a weight limit on that small aircraft. I don't feel like pulling pine tree limbs out of my ass."

Nicole came into the bathroom as I was taking off my jeans and entered the now steaming shower.

She said "Let's work off a few pounds so I can take more room for clothes."

So she gets in the shower with me and starts kissing me and fondling me and getting me excited. We made love in the shower. If I had only known that it would be the last time. We got out and dried off. I headed for the bedroom to get dressed. I looked at my watch.

I said, "Nicole, you may want to speed up a little, we've got to be at the airport in an hour." I said to myself, *You know she takes forever to get ready. I know one thing, I'm getting me something comfortable to wear for the trip, ah yes, blue jeans, my favorite.* So I go into my closet to get my clothes, made my selection, and as I slide on my jeans, I could feel someone was looking at me. I thought that Nicole had slipped in behind me. I turned around, and in the mirror behind me, I briefly saw my grandfather in the mirror. I felt the hairs on my arms stand up; his image was there only for a moment. I wasn't experiencing a feeling of fear, more of being startled. Actually, he was smiling at me. So I asked myself, *Did I really see what I thought I saw? Is my mind playing tricks on me because I've been thinking about my grandfather and my dad a lot lately?* This on top of the incident with the talking dog is just too much. Maybe it's just the pressure of being muscled around by that thug Serlinni.

I continued to get dressed. I didn't dare tell Nicole about my experiences of the day. So I made my way over to my hidden stash location and built one. Maybe that will calm my nerves and give me an appetite. I didn't eat my lunch today because of the encounter with Serlinni's gorillas. At least that dog that I gave the burger to had something to eat today. Nicole walked in as I was rolling one and sat down on the edge of the bed.

She said, "You've must have had a rough day today. You usually don't smoke this early in the day."

I said, "I guess it's the video shoot, and I didn't eat lunch today either."

She said, "Do you want me to fix you a sandwich or something?"

I said, "No thanks, we'll get a dinner on the flight to Arizona."

Nicole said, "Since you're wearing jeans, so am I."

I told her, "Looks like you've set a new record for getting ready."

She said, "Well, don't hit the stopwatch yet. I've got to decide on a blouse and shoes."

I said, "Why don't you wear some tennis shoes for comfort, that's what I'm wearing."

So she leaves to finish getting ready, and I fired off the doob and took a couple drags. I started thinking about the total picture of what happened today. What in the fuck is going on here? Is someone trying to tell me something? Nicole walked back into the room and reached out for the doob. I handed it to her, and she hit it hard just like a pro, then she gave it back to me.

Nicole said, "When are we going somewhere to have fun for a change, just you and me, without the business interrupting?"

I said, "We'll have some time together when we go on our honeymoon."

Nicole said, "Is that a proposal?"

I said, "Not yet, I may still trade you in on a newer model."

Nicole said jokingly, "Just for that you can take your ass to Arizona without me."

I said, "Okay, but if you don't go, you won't get to buy any turquoise."

Nicole said, "You are going to keep right on, and I'm going to have to cut you off. On the other hand, that wouldn't work either, being that you like money more than you like pussy."

We both laughed and finished off the joint. She went in the bathroom to finish putting on her makeup, and I finished tying my shoes. I put the roach in the toilet and gave it a burial at sea. I went into the living room and turned on the tube to check the weather channel to see what the weather is going to be like in Flagstaff. As I was flipping through the channels to get to the weather channel, Nicole said, "We've got to get a move on if we are to get to the airport on time." So I got the luggage and carried it to the front room.

I said, "Nicole, is this everything before I lock up the house and turn on the alarm system?"

Nicole said, "Yes, that's everything, go ahead and lock up the house."

I went through the house to check all the doors to make sure they're locked, turned on the alarm system, and locked the front door. I shook the door to make sure the lock was engaged and headed for the car. I got into the car, and as I turned over the ignition, I told Nicole, "Make sure that you don't have any contraband in your purse or in the luggage. You know we'll be going through the airport, and we don't need any trouble."

She said, "I didn't put anything in the luggage. I just have this one doobie that we can smoke on the way to the plane. I'm calling the airport to tell them that we are on our way in."

So she gets out her cell phone and calls the airport.

"Hello, this is Nicole Adams calling to let the flight charter service know that myself and James Farnsworth are on our way to the airport and should be there in ten minutes or so." Nicole says, "Thank you, and we are on our way in." And she folds up her phone.

Nicole says they are expecting us, and she said the receptionist said that Bruce Stevens, our usual pilot, has our plane waiting on us.

I said, "Good, I trust Bruce, he's a great pilot and friend."

As we made our way through town, we were listening to the radio, and as usual the stations in this area tend to run popular songs in the ground, so I hit the CD button, and then the music came on. I knew automatically that it was one of Nicole's CDs, you know, chick music. I switched it back to the radio as quick as I could.

Nicole started laughing and said, "What's wrong, baby?"

I said, "You know what's wrong."

I scrolled over to the classic rewind channel, and they were playing "Fool in the Rain" by Led Zeppelin. I said to myself, getting XM radio was one of my best decisions. Local radio has the tendency to run certain songs into the ground. As we were making our way toward the airport on the other side of town, I made a left on Highway 49, heading to the airport, and lo and behold, there was that same stray dog, and this time he had a couple of friends with him. As we passed them, they all turned to look at us as we passed by.

Nicole said, "Looks like the gang is on the prowl."

I said, "Yep, I gave the ringleader a hamburger today in the parking lot. But he was by himself and didn't have the posse with him. Then I started thinking to myself, *What does this dog mean? Is he some kinda four-legged messenger from God? He saved my life today.* Well, we are almost at the airport. I can see the wind sock. It's drooping a bit; a calm breeze is blowing. I parked the car and got our bags and proceeded to the airport building.

Nicole said, "Did you lock the car."

I said, "Yes, the keys are in my pocket."

She said, "Give me one of the travel bags."

I said, "They're not heavy, I have them."

We then walked inside the airport lobby and to the receptionist desk.

I placed the bags on the floor and said, "I'm James Farnsworth."

The receptionist said, "Hello, Mr. Farnsworth, we've been expecting you. We have Ms. Adams's tickets ready, just need to confirm her identity."

Nicole took her ID from her purse.

She then said, "You two go ahead and sign in. Your plane is waiting, and do you want me to do the usual procedure and send you the bill, or do you want to take care of it now?

I said, "Send me the bill cause I didn't bring my checkbook."

The receptionist said, "Yes, sir, Mr. Farnsworth. I will call the pilot to alert him that you are here and see if he's ready for you to board." The receptionist then picked up the radio mike and talked to the pilot.

We heard the pilot say, "Tell them to come on out to the plane."

The receptionist said, "I guess you heard the pilot, he's ready. I will see you guys when you get back. Have a great flight."

I turned to Nicole as we were heading to the door and said to her, "Do you need to go take a leak before we get in the air?"

She said, "I'm fine. What about you?"

I said, "I feel like I need to go take a piss. I'll be right there."

I dropped the bags down and told her to go ahead and that I will bring the bags with me.

She said, "I'll wait for you."

So I headed to the bathroom and took a piss. I stopped at the sink to wash my hands, and I was reluctant to look in the mirror because of what I saw at home. So I looked up, and I just saw me, James Farnsworth, what a relief. So I headed for the door and picked up the bags, and we made our way toward the plane. We would be flying on a Gulfstream V executive jet. The pilot was standing in the doorway and proceeded to walk toward me.

He said, "You two ready to go?"

I said, "I guess so, Bruce."

He stood by the stairway and offered his hand to Nicole to assist her in the plane. She said, "Thank you, Bruce," and walked into the plane.

Bruce said, "Okay, you guys, have a seat and make yourself comfortable."

So Nicole and I sat down in our seat and put on our seat belts. Bruce went to the cockpit and prepared for takeoff. We heard the whirring of the engines, and Bruce came on over the intercom system and said, "Please fasten your seat belts if you haven't already, and I will let you know when you can unfasten them We will arrive in Atlanta Hartsfield International in thirty-five minutes."

I said to Nicole, "Bruce must have someone up front with him."

Nicole said, "Yes, I believe you're right. He doesn't normally go through the airline formalities with us because we're veterans."

The plane was climbing to altitude. I looked out the window and watched the ground get farther and farther away. Within a minute or two we were in level flight, and Bruce's voice came over the intercom and said, "You two can unfasten your seat belts, and I'm sending my girlfriend back there to serve you two some drinks if you like. Her name is Angela, and she will be your flight hostess on this flight, and thank you for flying White Dragon Charters."

We had unbuckled the seat belts, and from the cockpit emerged Bruce's girlfriend, Angela. I said to myself, Angela is definitely eye candy.

Angela said, "Hello, Mr. Farnsworth, I'm Angela."

I said, "Stop this Mr. Farnsworth stuff, I'm James, and this is my fiancée, Nicole."

Angela said, "Would you two like something to drink?"

Nicole said, "Angela, what do you have on board?"

Angela said, I've got some daiquiri mixes, like strawberry, lemon, lime, banana, and cherry. I also have some margarita mixes. What would you like?"

Nicole said, "I think I'll have a strawberry daiquiri."

I said, "I'll have a margarita made with 1800 if you have it."

Angela replied, "I'll fix you guys right up."

And she walked to the back of the plane. Within a couple of minutes, she was back with our drinks. Nicole and I drank our drinks, had some small talk. It wasn't too long before Bruce was saying over the intercom, "Please fasten your seat belts. We are making our approach into Atlanta."

Nicole said, "I hope the food is better this time around than it was the last time we flew out of Atlanta."

I said, "Let's just eat some snack food just to hold us over until we get to Flagstaff, then we can sit down and have a real meal."

I felt the plane touch down on terra firma, and we were coasting in. The plane finally came to a full stop, and Bruce came back and opened the door and dropped down the steps. I grabbed our bags, and we thanked Bruce and Angela for a great flight. We made our way to the terminal and to the reception desk. I set the bags down and reached inside the side pouch and got our tickets out and handed them to the receptionist.

The receptionist punched in a few numbers in the computer and said, "Mr. Farnsworth, you'll be leaving from gate C35, flight to Flagstaff, Arizona, and it leaves in twenty minutes."

She handed the tickets to me, and I tagged the bags, and we headed down the concourse to gate C35. Lucky for us that this was in the middle of the week and not a weekend; there was not a whole lot of pedestrian traffic.

I asked Nicole, "Do you want to walk or take the moving sidewalk?"

Nicole said, "Let's take the moving sidewalk. These new shoes are killing my feet."

I said, "Why didn't you wear something comfortable?"

She just gave me that look.

I said, "I know, the shoes match your outfit."

As we were riding along on the moving sidewalk, I saw some posters on the wall that were advertising everything from Viagra to the newest vehicles on the market.

I said to Nicole, "Everywhere you look, somebody is trying to sell you something. Why don't they display artwork or something more appealing to the eye? It's almost as bad as billboards on Interstate 75."

She commented, "In the European airports, they do have artwork and advertising mixed in together. Nowhere is safe from advertising."

I said, "Look over there, there goes the police escorting some hookers to the pokey. They were probably exercising the hard sale."

We both laughed. We arrived at gate 35, and I placed our bags on the baggage carrier. I didn't need the hassle associated with carry-on baggage.

I said, "Honey, do you need to go to the can before we go through the security check point because I do."

She said, "I'm okay, you go ahead. I'll wait for you here."

We proceeded through security and according to the flight time, we just made it. I handed the tickets to the flight attendant.

She said, "Hello, it looks like you two will be in the first-class section. I hope you enjoy your flight."

We made our way to the plane and found our seats.

I said, "Do you want my window seat?"

Nicole said, "It don't matter to me."

I said, "If you want to take a nap, you won't be bothered by the flight attendant as they go down the aisle."

She sat by the window and put on her seat belt, and I sat down and did the same.

The pilot's voice came over the intercom system and said, "Please fasten your seat belts. We'll be taking off in about five minutes, and once we get into level flight, you can release your seat belts. Thank you for flying with Delta Airlines."

I got settled in my seat, and I decided to try to take a nap. I didn't sleep too well last night. I turned to Nicole and said, "I think I'm going to take a nap."

Nicole said, "I think I will also, it helps pass the time since it's about a two hour flight."

So once the plane climbed to altitude and leveled out, we took off the seat belts and reclined the seats. A flight attendant came by and asked us if we needed anything. We told her no and that we were going to take a nap. Nicole did request a pillow from the attendant. The attendant brought the pillow back, and we settled down to take a snooze. It took a while before I could go to sleep, but I finally succumbed to the urge to sleep.

I was running through a pine thicket, but I was looking through a different set of eyes. I was hearing sounds of the night so acutely, I can't explain. I was picking up smells, odors carried by the night air. I was driven forward by the scent, a scent that smelled familiar, an animal scent. Before I could get to the target, Nicole and I were awoken by the flight attendant.

She said, "Excuse me, sir, we are about to land. Please return your seat to the upright position and fasten your seat belt."

Boy, what a weird-ass dream! It seemed so real.

Nicole said, "Did you have a good nap?"

I told her that I did, even though it was fucked up.

The captain came over the intercom saying, "We will be landing in Flagstaff in about five minutes. If you haven't already fastened your seat belts, please do so now, and I want to thank for flying with Delta Airlines."

I could feel the plane slowly descend, and I couldn't stop thinking about the dream I had. It was some weird shit. Within a few minutes we were on the ground, and we were unfastening the seat belts then exiting the plane. We went into the terminal and waited at the baggage retrieval carousel for our baggage to show up.

Nicole was standing next to me, and I said, "What do you feel like you want to eat tonight for dinner?"

She said, "I could really go for some seafood. How about you?"

I said, "That's fine by me. I haven't eaten any fish or shrimp in a while."

Our bags showed up, and just as I was about to pick them up, a voice said, "Let me get that for you, Mr. Farnsworth."

I turned around, and it was Tim Jackson, my technical manager.

Tim said, "How was the flight, James?"

I told him it went well, and he told us that there is a limo out front waiting on us.

I said, "Who arranged that?"

Tim replied that it was compliments of Desert Reign's manager.

I said, "That is nice of him to do so, but a taxi would have been fine."

Then we all got into the limo and were on our way to the hotel. On the way to the hotel, I couldn't stop thinking about that dream I had. What does it mean?

I was looking at the nightlife as we made our way into town, and Tim said, "Have you two ever been to Arizona before?"

I said, "We haven't, but I've always wanted to visit Arizona and the Southwest region. Nicole wanted to come to Arizona to get some turquoise to wear."

Tim said, "She won't have any trouble finding it, but be careful! There are some knockoffs floating around. They look like the real thing, but they are synthetic. If you're serious, you might get lucky and find what you're looking for on the reservation in Rough Rock, where we will be filming."

I asked, "How far is Rough Rock from Flagstaff?"

Tim said, "It is 130 miles by helicopter."

I said, "You know how I feel about helicopters. Aren't there any bush pilots in that area?"

Tim said, "Afraid not, James, if we go by car, we'll just have to leave a hell of a lot earlier."

I said, "Well, I'll just have to bite the bullet on this one and ride an eggbeater."

Nicole said, "It's not so bad. I've ridden in helicopters before, and I'm still walking around."

I said, "Well, if it crashes, I won't be leaving here by myself."

We were pulling up to the front of the Courtyard Hotel and coming to a stop. The doorman opened the door, and we got out. We got our baggage, and the doorman placed them on a cart for the bellboy to push to the lobby. Tim approached the reception desk and told the receptionist that Nicole and I were here.

The receptionist said, "Hello, Mr. Farnsworth and Ms. Adams, we have been expecting you, and welcome to Courtyard. We have your room ready, and your room number is 215 on the second floor. You'll have a great view of the hotel's atrium. We have an excellent restaurant here, lounge, a gym, and a house masseuse for those tired muscles if you so desire. And of course, we have room service." She handed us our key card. "Call me if you need anything, or I can direct you to our concierge, and once again I would like to thank you for choosing Courtyard, and if you just follow the attendant to the elevator, he will show you to your room."

We said our thanks and followed the attendant to the elevator.

I asked Tim, "Where's a good place to eat at in this town?"

Tim said, "Me and couple of guys from the film production crew have eaten at this great Mexican restaurant here in Flagstaff for the past couple of days. They have great margaritas and good food too."

The attendant said, "Excuse me for interrupting, but what type of food are you guys in the mood for?"

I said, "Could go for some surf and turf, how about y'all?"

Nicole said, "I told you earlier today I would like to have some shrimp."

The attendant told us, "There's a restaurant on the edge of town called the Grill. They have great food and atmosphere, or you can eat here at the Courtyard International restaurant, which has a wide variety of cuisine."

I said, "Let's try the food here at the Courtyard tonight. I'm tired, and I want to be close to my room."

The elevator stopped, and the door opened.

The attendant said, "Here we are on the second floor. Just follow me to your room."

I asked Tim, "Where is your room, Tim?"

He said, "I'm at the other end of the hall. Lucky for us, our reservations were made a month ago, there's a golf tournament going on here in Flagstaff, and rooms would be hard to come by for the unaware traveler. I'm going to go and take a shower and meet up with the guys at the bar, so you two can get settled in and have some time to yourselves."

Tim made his way down to his room, and we continued on to ours. We came to our room, and I stuck in the entry card, and the attendant brought our bags in. I gave the attendant a ten-dollar tip, and he said that I needed to go ahead and call the restaurant to see if there's a table open because of the golfers in town for the PGA tournament. I told him thanks for the information as he was walking out the door.

Nicole said, "I'm going to the bathroom and freshen up before we go to the restaurant."

I said, "Okay, I'll turn on the tube and see what the weathers going to be like."

Nicole takes her bag and goes to the bathroom, and I go over to the entertainment center and turn on the TV. I flip through the channels to see what is on while on my way to the weather channel. TV in Flagstaff, as I can see, is no different than in Georgia, a bunch of channels and nothing but bullshit. It's pretty bad when the only thing decent to watch is the history channel. As I continued to channel-surf, I saw that they were selling turquoise on the HSN, so I quickly changed it before Nicole came into the room. I called the hotel operator to connect me with Tim's room to find out what time were we leaving for Rough Rock.

The operator rang Tim's room, and Tim answered, "Hello, this is Tim."

I said, "Tim, what time in the morning are we leaving to go to Rough Rock?"

Tim said, "It will be about a forty-minute flight from Flagstaff to Rough Rock, and we are to be at the airport at six o'clock in the morning. Since most of the filming for the video is outside, it would be better if it is done in the mornings due to the intense heat plus less makeup touch-ups due to people sweating."

I told him that we would meet him in the lobby at 5:45 a.m.

Nicole came into the room and overheard me say 5:45, a.m., and she said, "Five forty-five in the morning! I'm staying at the hotel and go looking for some turquoise, remember?"

I told Tim that I would see him in the morning, and I hung up the phone.

Nicole said, "Are you ready to go and get something to eat?"

I said, "Let me call the restaurant first to see if there is a table available."

I called the concierge to find out if there was a table available at the restaurant. The concierge told me that the restaurant had available seating, and he would reserve a table for us. I told him that would be fine, and I told him my name and that we would be there in a few minutes. I hung up the phone and told Nicole that I was going into the bathroom and shave right quick. So I went into the bathroom and removed my shirt, turned on the hot water, got my shaving kit and a washcloth. I leaned down to wet my face with hot water and reached for the shaving cream. I put a mound of shaving cream in my hand. When I looked into the mirror to begin smearing the shaving cream on my face, there in the mirror was my grandfather for just a brief moment, and he was gone. It didn't take long for me to shave. What is he trying to tell me? Why is this happening to me? I dare not tell Nicole about this. She is big into this paranormal shit. She'd have me going to see some medium or psychic person about this. I don't need this shit right now.

I went into the bedroom to where Nicole was and said, "Ready to go, baby?"

She said, "Of course, I'm starving."

So I grabbed the room entry card, put it in my pocket, and we headed for the elevator.

So as we got into the elevator, I asked Nicole, "How much cash do you need for tomorrow?"

She said, "I'm okay, I've got a couple a hundred dollars and my credit cards. I don't plan on going on a spending spree. I might buy a turquoise ring or bracelet for the right price. Mostly I'm going to hang out by the pool and relax tomorrow while you're working."

At that time, the elevator stopped at the first floor, and we made our way to the restaurant. As we entered the restaurant entrance, I looked around, and the décor was what I imagined typical Southwestern, earth tones and desert pastels, soft and inviting. The receptionist asked me if I had a reservation. I told her my name is James Farnsworth.

She said, "Oh yes, Mr. Farnsworth, we have a table for you and Ms. Farnsworth."

Nicole looked at me and smiled. A waiter came up to us and led us to our table.

We sat down, and the waiter said, "Would you two like something to drink while you look over the menu?"

Nicole said, "I think I'll have a strawberry margarita for now and sweetened ice tea with my meal."

The waiter said, "What would you like, sir?

I said, "I'll have a Texas margarita using Cuervo 1800 on the rocks and I'll have sweetened tea with my meal also."

The waiter said, "I'll be right back with your drinks."

I asked Nicole, "How do you like the Southwest experience so far?

She said, "I like the artwork, the plants, the building architecture, and the weather, as long as I have a way of cooling off like a swimming pool or air-conditioning. I know it gets pretty hot in Georgia, but in Georgia we have humidity. In Arizona, there isn't any moisture content in the air, just a dry heat. So tomorrow be sure to drink a lot of water while you're outside."

I told her, "Don't worry about me, it's you that don't drink water. I know you'll be by the pool tomorrow. Just be sure you get you some bottled water to drink by the pool."

Nicole said, "Listen, there's one of your favorite songs playing."

She always does that to get me off her case, but in this instance, it was one of my favorite songs. The song was "Don't Dream It's Over" by Crowded House. I like the song because of the guitar effects used and the organ in the song. I think the song also takes me back to a time when my life was easier, my father was alive, grandfather was alive, and I didn't have the pressures of life weighing heavy on me.

Nicole said, "What's wrong, baby?"

I said, "Nothing really that a good night's sleep can't cure."

Nicole then said, "When I get through with you tonight, you'll be too tired to dream."

I said, "We'll see when we get back to the room after you've had a few drinks."

The waiter came back with our drinks and said, "Have you two decided what you'll have to eat?"

Nicole said, "I'll have the grilled shrimp and blackened mahi mahi with a salad and Italian dressing."

I said, "I'll have a medium-well rib eye and fried shrimp and an order of prairie peppers."

The waiter said, "I'll bring your appetizer out in just a few minutes. Also, happy hour is in effect until seven thirty. All margaritas are half price. You've only got a half hour to go. Would you like me to bring you another round of margaritas before the price goes up?"

Nicole said, "Sure, why not."

The waiter said, "All right then, I'll be right back."

I said, "I'm only drinking two drinks. I can't get too smashed because I don't want to feel like shit tomorrow."

Nicole said, "You can take some aspirins and drink you some water before you go to sleep, and you won't get a headache either."

I said, "Where did you hear that bullshit?"

She said, "I've tried it, and it works. I forgot where I heard the remedy. What time do you think you'll be back from the video shoot?"

I told her, "I should be back to the hotel by at least seven o'clock. There won't be any night shooting going on. If things go well, we might finish things up early tomorrow so we can go home just in time for the weekend to start. You do realize that we aren't too far from the Grand Canyon?"

Nicole said, "Cool, let's go see it."

I said, "Let's come back in the fall when it's not as hot."

She said, "Why did you even mention it then?"

I told her, "I was making conversation by stating where we are geographically. Besides, when we get back, I have to review the video and get with the sound techs so that the music is synchronized with the video and edit things that may require it. I have an idea. Why don't you go with me to Indian reservation day after tomorrow. You might find some authentic Navajo jewelry that you'll like. I'll scout things out for you tomorrow in between shots to see what I can see."

The waiter showed up with our drinks and said, "Your prairie peppers should be done in a few minutes, and I'll bring them out. Would you two like some goblets of water?"

I said to the waiter, "You wouldn't happen to have any aspirin, would you?"

Nicole said, "I have some in my purse back in our room."

The waiter told us that he would go check on the food and would be right back. Just across the restaurant, the wait staff was singing happy birthday to someone over to our immediate right.

Nicole said, "I know someone else that will be having a birthday soon in about one week."

I said, "Don't remind me, I'm slowly creeping up on forty."

Nicole said, "That's two years away. Besides, didn't you have some friends that didn't make it this far."

"I know I'm lucky in a lot of ways, especially to have someone like you by my side."

Nicole said, "You keep talking like that and I might give you some tonight."

The waiter and a waitress walked up with our appetizer and food. They set the plates with food down, and the waitress said, "Is there anything else we can get you?"

I said, "No, thank you, the food looks great."

So Nicole and I ate our meal and finished off our drinks. I left a tip on the table and made my way to the counter.

Nicole said, "Wait for me at the counter. I have to go to the ladies' room."

I said, "Okay, I'll be out in the hotel lobby."

So I paid for the food and drinks, walked out in the hotel lobby. Tim and some fine-looking woman walked up to me.

Tim said, "Hello, boss, I'd like you to meet Katherine. Katherine, this is my boss, James Farnsworth."

I said, "Good to meet you, Katherine."

Tim asked, "Where's Nicole?"

I said, "She should be coming out from the restaurant any minute now. Have you guys already eaten, or are you about to?"

CHAPTER 2

Katherine said, "We've already eaten. We're just heading to the room. How about you and Nicole, coming by for a nightcap?"

I said, "Thanks but we've had a long day, and we're going to go the room and crash. Don't keep my help up all night 'cause I got to get some work out of him tomorrow."

Nicole walks up.

Tim said, "Nicole, this is Katherine. Katherine, this is Nicole."

They both said, "It's nice to meet you."

I said, "I would like to party with you guys tonight, but like I said earlier, tomorrow is going to be a busy day. It was nice to meet you, Katherine. Maybe we can all get together before we go home and have a few drinks."

Katherine replied, "Sure, we can, I am glad I got to meet you and Nicole. Hope you have a good night's rest."

We made our way to the elevator. We stepped inside the elevator. The door closed, and I said, "I could use a hot bath. My neck is killing me."

Nicole said, "I'll fill up the bathtub, and we can get in."

I said, "Why don't I order up a bottle of wine since we don't have any weed to smoke."

Nicole said, "While you're on the reservation tomorrow, see if you can score some peyote."

I said, "I've never tried the stuff. What is it like?"

Nicole said, "I haven't either, but I heard that it's like acid, but your body doesn't ache from the aftereffects like acid does."

I said, "I'll get one of my tech guys that' s tight with one of the band members of Desert Reign to hook us up."

By this time we've gotten off the elevator, and we've made our way to our room. I take out the passkey and open the door. We walk in, and I got a weird feeling in my gut that something isn't right. I walked to the bathroom and opened the door and looked to see if anyone was in there. I didn't see anyone, but as I made my way across the room, I heard a muffled gunshot like from a silencer. The sound came from the bedroom. I ran toward the bedroom, and as I swung open the door, I saw Nicole on the floor and a person with a stocking on his face aiming a pistol at me.

The guy said, "Good-bye, Mr. Farnsworth."

And before I could say anything, he squeezed off a shot. I guess the shooter heard knocking next door and announcing room service.

The shooter was about to put another round in me but, decided to bolt. The shooter left the door open and the room service attendant came in and found us. I heard him dialing the phone, telling the front desk that there has been a shooting in room 215, to call the ambulance and the police. The room service attendant stayed with us until the EMT's arrived. It seemed like it took forever for them to get there. I could see that the glimmer from Nicole's eyes were gone.

The ambulance crew came in and placed me on a stretcher and placed me in the ambulance. They didn't put Nicole in with me, so then I knew for sure that she's gone. I could taste my blood in my mouth. The EMT was busy putting an IV in my arm to replace the blood I lost, I guess.

The EMT kept saying, "Just relax, we'll be at the hospital in a few minutes."

I didn't know if I was going to make it or not. I just kept thinking about my beautiful Nicole lying lifeless in the floor and what would've our children looked like. Within minutes the ambulance was backing up to the emergency room door of the hospital, and the doors of the ambulance swung open, and people were hurrying me into the emergency room.

A nurse came over to the gurney and said, "It's okay, Mr. Farnsworth, we know who you are. The hotel called and told us."

I tried to get someone to tell me about Nicole. Finally, a nurse said, "I'll check on her. You just relax for now, Mr. Farnsworth."

The emergency room doctor came up and said, "Take him to operating room 3 and prep him for surgery now."

The EMTs were pushing the gurney hurriedly to room 3. Next, the nurses were cutting my shirt off of me, and another nurse was unfastening my pants. I grabbed her hand.

Another nurse said, "Okay, Mr. Farnsworth, we'll leave your pants on. Just relax, you'll be fine."

A doctor came over to me and rolled me over on my side. The bullet went straight through. "Get a unit of whole blood in the patient. I need an X-ray of the chest. Get the anesthesiologist in here. We need to put this guy under."

The movement around me was starting to blur. I guess someone had given me a shot of something through the IV. They placed an oxygen mask on my nose. It was hard to keep my eyes open any longer. I had given in to the sedative. The next thing I know, I'm awake and lying on the operating table in a room full of mist or fog.

Am I dead?

Then I heard a voice say, "No, you are not dead, James."

I rose up to see where the voice came from, and out of the mist came my grandfather. He walked up to the end of the operating table and stopped.

I said, "Grandpa, you're gone. I must be dead if I'm able to see you at the foot of the bed."

He said, "You weren't dead when you saw me in the mirror of your home, and you're not dead now."

I said, "Nicole is dead, isn't she?"

My grandfather said, "I'm afraid so, my dear grandson."

I said, "How come I can't talk to her like I'm talking to you right now?"

My grandfather said, "She's having a tough time dealing with death, everyone does at first until they get used to the transition."

I said, "What about Dad, where is he now?"

My grandfather said, "He has been reborn to a new life."

I said, "How come you haven't been reborn?"

My grandfather said, "I cannot yet. There is some unfinished business that I and my partner have to finish."

I said, "Who's your partner?"

My grandfather said, "You are my partner."

I said, "What is it like to be in heaven?"

My grandfather said, "I'm not in heaven yet. I'm in, let's say, the halfway house to heaven."

Before I could ask any more questions, I was being awakened in the recovery room by a nurse. She said, "Wake up, Mr. Farnsworth. The surgery is complete. You're in the recovery room."

I opened my eyes. I was feeling groggy and dizzy. I felt my chest, and it was bandaged. A man walked up to the side of the bed. I'm assuming he's the doctor.

He said, "You're okay! Just relax, the bullet grazed your heart and barely missed your spinal column. You are a lucky man, Mr. Farnsworth."

I struggled to strain the words out, "How's Nicole?"

The doctor said, "Just relax and we'll talk about her tomorrow. The orderly will be taking you to ICU, where we can take care of you. There will be a pain-management system hooked up to you, so if you feel pain, you only press this button, and it will deliver relief so that you'll be able to rest. I'll be in to see you in ICU tomorrow."

It wasn't long after the doctor left that some orderlies came in and slid me on a gurney and wheeled me to ICU. I started thinking about if mom and my grandmother and also Nicole's family, if they have heard about what's happened here in Flagstaff, Arizona. My mom and my grandmother just a few months ago witnessed my grandfather's and my dad's funeral and now this. Nicole's family must be reeling now from the shock of losing their only daughter. The police are going to want to talk to me once I feel strong enough. I heard some talking outside my room door; it sounds like Tim talking to a nurse, pleading with her to see me.

Tim was saying, "But, nurse, I am his friend, and I'm his production manager. His family is a thousand miles away. He needs to see a face he knows."

The nurse replied, "Okay, but don't ask him any questions. He was shot in the chest, and you don't need to get him upset. Just reassure him that everything is okay and do not tell him that his fiancée is dead. Just keep Mr. Farnsworth calm."

I heard Tim say, "Okay, nurse, I won't make him upset, I promise."

He opened the door to my room and walked in and said, "Don't worry about anything, James, I'll make sure that the video gets completed. It will be a cake walk. Look on the bright side, you won't have to ride in the helicopter. I know how you detest the eggbeaters, as what you call them. Just think about getting well."

The nurse said, "You need to leave now, sir, so that he can rest."

Tim said, "I've called your mom and talked to her. She said that she would tell your grandmother and that they are going to fly out here tomorrow."

I said a weak okay and shook Tim's hand, and he left the room. Another set of nurses came in and plugged up an automatic morphine delivery machine.

One of the nurses said, "If you start hurting, press this button, Mr. Farnsworth, and it will take about fifteen minutes or so, and you will get some relief. You've had a tough night."

She came over to the bed a checked the contents of the IV bag, checked my pulse, and stuck a thermometer in my mouth. The electronic thermometer beeped, and she took it out of my mouth.

The nurse said, "You have a low-grade temperature, but that's normal after what you've been through. Just push the buzzer button, and I'll be in here in a flash."

I began to get a splitting headache, and my chest was hurting like fuck. I mashed the button to the automatic morphine delivery machine. There was no immediate relief that I hoped for.

The nurse said, "You should be still feeling the effects of the sedatives that were administered during surgery. Are you still sleepy, Mr. Farnsworth?"

I told her, "No, I'm just hurting like hell in my chest and back."

She then said that she would check the orders left by the doctor to see if he included a sedative for sleep. The nurse found the TV remote and turned on the TV and stopped on the weather channel.

She said, "Here's something boring to watch to give the morphine a chance to work so that you can sleep."

She told me that she would be back to check on me, then she left the room. I watched about three seconds of the weather channel and started channel-surfing. I stopped on the history channel; they were talking about my favorite subject, secret aircraft of the Luftwaffe during WWII. I couldn't get into it because I kept thinking about what my grandfather had told me. My beautiful Nicole is gone. What was grandfather talking about, unfinished business and a partnership? Then I could feel the medication start to kick in; things started to get a little fuzzy from then on. I guess I fell asleep and started dreaming some whacked-out shit. In the dream I was driving my car down town back home and stopped to get a burger, and when I walked back to the car, there was that stray dog that saved me from getting shot in the parking lot and the same dog that I gave the remainder of my burger to that day.

Well, the stray walked up to me and sat down and said, "I know you want to pop that motherfucker, but you will get your chance, and you won't need a gun 'cause you are or, should I say, will be a powerful motherfucker."

I asked the dog, "What do you mean 'powerful'?"

The dog said, "I cannot tell you as of yet, it is not my place."

I said, "Why me? What have I done?"

The dog said, "It is not something that you've done."

Before I could ask the dog any more questions, I was awakened by a nurse. The TV was still on. I guess I fell asleep and left it on.

The nurse said, "I'm going to check your temperature and change out the IV bag."

I pushed the morphine machine button again. My back was hurting like fuck. I was thinking to myself, *The police will be in here tomorrow to question me plus my mother, Nicole's parents, the people from the production company and, with my fucked up luck, probably the local news. I hope the hospital has enough sense not to let the news crew in here. I don't need this type of publicity.*

She walked out of my room, and I began to watch the TV again. I flipped to the weather channel to see what the time was; it was 4:30 a.m. I'm not sleepy; my chest and back are hurting too much to think about sleeping now. I started to flip through the channels to see if anything worth watching was on just to occupy my mind. I started thinking about that fucked-up dream that I had about the dog talking to me. Just what does all of this mean? What is in store for me according to the appearance of my dead grandfather and the talking dog? Now facing me is, what am I going to tell the police, when they question me? Should I mention Serlinni to the police? I don't have any proof to tie him to the shooting. Should I treat this like a failed robbery attempt or stalking? Nicole's parents will want answers to the reason behind their daughter's death. I guess at this point it would be safer to treat this like a failed robbery because if I let anyone know of Serlinni's previous attempts to muscle in on my company, I would be blamed for not saying anything about it. Besides, if I told the police, they would simply say, "What proof do you have? Where's the evidence?" Right now, I'm all alone in this, but what I've got to do now is somehow try to keep anyone else of my family from being harmed or killed. I just hope that my cousin Chris has the good sense not to talk to anyone about that incident back home when my car got shot up. There is no doubt about Vincent Serlinni; he's not going to stop until he kills me or I give up the studio to him. The only way that I can see to get this guy off my back is to get the bureau involved. As far as the authorities know now is that the shooting here in Arizona was an attempted robbery that went bad. I was going to have to play the shooting at the hotel like a robbery gone bad for now because I had no proof otherwise. Come to think about it, Serlinni did call the studio and wished me a good trip to Arizona. Too bad I didn't know beforehand and record him saying such.

I looked at the time on the weather channel, almost 5:00 a.m. People will start coming in here in a little while. I wish I could go to sleep and wake up from this bad dream. I had to let the head of the bed down; leaning upright was making the pain worse. I hit the painkiller button and waited for the relief to come. I could hear the activity of the next batch of nurses coming in for the shift change outside my door.

I hit the nurse call button, then a voice said, "I'll be right there, Mr. Farnsworth."

The nurse came in and said, "What can I do for you, Mr. Farnsworth?"

I told her that the pain was keeping me awake, and I couldn't sleep. She said the doctor did prescribe a sedative for me in case I couldn't sleep, then she left to get the injection then returned and inserted the needle into the IV receptacle.

She said, "It will take a few minutes for it to take effect. Just relax and give it a chance. I'll be going home. My shift is over, but you'll be taken care of by my friends on day shift. I hope you get some rest, Mr. Farnsworth."

I turned off the TV and hoped to catch a little shut-eye before the police and family members started showing up. I finally dozed off to sleep and started to dream. In the dream, I was in a different period judging by the style of clothing people were wearing. It looks like the turn of the century. There were horse and buggies in the street, no paved roads, no traffic lights, just the dust kicked up by someone passing by on a buckboard wagon.

Then I hear a voice say, "Son, you need to back up a bit before someone runs you over."

I turn to see a policeman motioning me to back up out of oncoming traffic.

He said, "You're not from around here, are you, boy?"

I replied, "No, sir, can you tell me how far it is to the next town?"

He said, "Atlanta is about a day's ride from here."

I said, "Where is here?"

He said, "It's Manchester, Georgia, and if you know what's good for you, you need to find somewhere safe before it gets dark. There has been a killing, a person found torn to pieces beyond recognition and no clues to whom or what has been doing it."

I said thanks and kept walking, hoping to see anyone that I could recognize. As I made my to the wooden-planked sidewalk, a lady was walking her poodle toward me. As they drew ever closer to me, the dog began to walk slower, and the minute I got within six or so feet from the woman and her dog, the dog stopped and lay down. The woman jerked on the dog's leash to get the poodle to move, and as I moved away from the dog and its owner, the dog got back up and kept on walking with its owner at the same pace again as if nothing happened. As I walked along the sidewalk, I could see a man making his way to me. The man looked vaguely familiar to me. Once the man got within a few feet of me, he said, "Hello, James, it's me, your grandfather, Gerald Houston Farnsworth."

I answered by saying, "What year is this, Grandfather?"

He replied, "The year is 1915, and I have returned back to States from the war."

I said, "What are you doing in this town instead of our hometown?"

He told me that he was convalescing in Warm Springs, which isn't too far from here.

I said, "What are you convalescing from?"

My grandfather said, "I was injured in Germany and was discharged from army intelligence, and the doctors from Atlanta sent me there. Warm Springs is where I met and married my first wife from Manchester."

I said, "Your first wife, what are you saying?"

He said, "My first wife, her name was Marie Bartlet. We were together for almost a year. She didn't want to have the child, and she couldn't take it anymore and took some poke salad berries and went to sleep and didn't wake up."

Before I could ask him anything else, I was awakened by the nurse coming into my room. She was checking the IV bags and the morphine drip machine.

She said, "I didn't mean to wake you, Mr. Farnsworth. I was trying to be ever so quiet."

I said, "That's okay, I've got a feeling I won't be getting much rest today anyway."

The nurse said, "Is the morphine drip working, Mr. Farnsworth?"

I said, "It only dulls the pain, not stop the pain."

She said, "The doctor will be in a couple hours from now."

I looked at the TV, which somehow was on the weather channel. I guess the nurse had switched it to the weather channel when she came on this side of the bed to check the morphine machine. The time on the weather channel clock had 7:45 a.m. It won't be long now; the hospital staff will be in full swing along with a new day just starting. I know in the back of my mind, this day is going to be tough. I asked the nurse to see if she would tell me anything about Nicole.

The nurse said, "Mr. Farnsworth, you need to relax, and the doctor will fill you in on your fiancée's condition once he comes in this morning."

I hope I was wrong in assuming that Nicole is dead, but according to my dream, my grandfather said that she is having a hard time coping in the afterlife—that is if the dreams are valid and not the result of the high-powered medication that was pumped into me for the surgery and not to mention the morphine machine next to my bed. I must admit that was some pretty weird-ass shit that occurred with the dog in my company parking lot that day. My car got some holes shot into it. The dog talking to me and me being able to understand is something that I can't wrap my head around. I'm going to have to tell the FBI about the attempted assassination, but then again, I have no proof, no positive ID of the perps that squeezed off a few rounds. I definitely need to keep the local authorities at home out of the mix; this is a much larger predicament.

I started thinking about what my grandfather said about his first wife. I wonder if grandmother knew about her and what happened to her and what made her go over the edge like she did. I know one thing: this morphine drip machine ain't getting it. I'm going to have to talk to the doctor, for sure, when he makes his rounds to tell him to put me on something else. The morphine isn't allowing me to relax enough to go to sleep; it only dulls the effects of the pain. My back and chest feel like an elephant has stepped on it. The morphine acts more like a stimulant, like amphetamine. I feel more like I can't be still long enough to rest plus the agonizing pain in my chest and back. I might as well stay awake and just hit the autodrip. I know it will be a matter of hours before some detectives will be in here to ask me questions.

I just hope the doctor comes in before the detectives get in here. My mom and grandmother will probably be in here today also. I'll have some more drama to go through. And if Nicole is gone, which I feel in my heart she is, her parents will undoubtedly blame me for her demise. In a way, I wished she hadn't come with me, but fate dealt a bad card for both us. So I started flipping through the TV channels to see if anything was worth looking at. As I continued channel-surfing, I stopped on the science fiction channel to see if a decent movie was on. It was a movie I had already seen before. There are some good parts in this movie. It shows some scantily clad females lurking about in the night to put the bite in some unsuspecting victims. As I was watching the movie, I started thinking about the weird dreams I had, the experience with dog in the company parking lot, my dead grandfather showing up in my bathroom mirror, not to mention him telling me in my dreams that he had been married before plus actually being involved in World War I. My grandfather was at least 130 year. old when he died accidently from a reaction to a supplement.

Here I am, lying in ICU, shot in the chest almost point-blank range. The bullet grazed my heart, exited by my spine by a fraction of an inch, yet I am alive. Where is the irony in that? Is it coincidence? Is it karma that has aimed the cannon barrel at me and fired a bad juju bullet at me, or is it my whole damn family? My chest was hurting like fuck again so, I just held the morphine drip button down. I watched to see if more medication was coming down the IV tube, and it wasn't, fucking timer was limiting the amount. I'll be glad when the damn doctor decides to get his ass in here so that I can tell him that the morphine drip isn't helping me, it's wiring me out. They might as well have given me some cocaine instead.

I flipped the channel on the TV over to the weather channel just to see what time it was, and the clock had 8:30 a.m., and temperature here in Arizona is gonna be another hot one today, as high as a hundred-plus degrees. In Georgia, a hundred-plus degrees means a lot of sweating going on if you're outside, and the humidity makes you feel like you weigh twenty pounds more. According to my people that work for me, the climate out in the Arizona desert is dry and hot. The sun will draw out your body's water and cause dehydration. I would rather be going on the video shoot and go out with my beautiful Nicole after the video shoot, but instead I'm here, waiting to find out if she's dead or alive, then being interviewed by the police about the shooting.

My cubicle of a room will be busy with activity today. So I kept on channel-surfing and stopped on the local news channel just in time to hear about the shooting that I was involved in. The newscaster said that two people were critically wounded and that no names were being released until the family was notified.

I thought to myself, *Well, they didn't say that anyone was dead just critically wounded.* That could also mean that the authorities had a lockdown on the media and did not allow any more than what they wanted to be reported at this point. So I continued flipping channels out of frustration of being helpless and hurting like fuck through my chest and my back. A nurse came into the room and said that she will be taking care of me today. She stuck a thermometer into my mouth and grasped my wrist to check my pulse rate.

The electronic thermometer beeped, and she removed it and said, "You don't have any fever, Mr. Farnsworth. Your pulse rate is normal."

Then she fastened the blood pressure band around my arm and began pumping away.

She then said, "Your blood pressure is normal, and the doctor will be in here shortly to see you. He is at the nursing station waiting to read your chart when I take it back to him."

I told her to hurry and give him the chart so that the doctor could come in here so that I can talk to him.

She said, "Okay, Mr. Farnsworth, I'll get him in here for you."

She left the room, and I said to myself, finally, I might get some real relief from the pain that I'm feeling and tell the doctor that I didn't sleep worth damn either. It wasn't too long before the doctor came in with a nurse in tow.

He said, "Good morning, Mr. Farnsworth, how are you feeling?"

I said, "Before I explain how I'm feeling, tell me, how is my fiancée?

The doctor said, "Mr. Farnsworth, your fiancée, Nicole Adams, did not make it. She passed away on the way to the hospital. I'm sorry about your loss, Mr. Farnsworth, and right now, you being my patient, you are my main concern, and that is to get you well."

I said, "Thanks, Doctor, but at the moment, the morphine drip isn't helping me at all."

I still had the drip control button in my hand and angrily snatched the chord right out of the machine.

I said, "I'm sorry, Doctor, I've lost my future wife and best friend."

The doctor said, "I would probably react the same way if I were in the same situation. I'm going to have the morphine drip removed and have the nurse to give you something stronger for the pain and a sedative so that you'll be able to rest today. You have been through a lot, Mr. Farnsworth. I left specific orders at the nurses' station that you are not to be disturbed today and that only your immediate family will be allowed to come into your room. I put you on a very light liquid diet since you are recovering from major surgery. Let me look at the wounds to make sure that no infection has set in."

He lowered the bed rail and checked out the stitches in my chest and asked me to roll on my side so that he could look at the exit wound in my back. He retaped the dressing on my back and the nurse retaped the dressing on my chest.

The doctor said, "The wounds have a healthy color, and no infection is present. Mr. Farnsworth, the police will want to ask you some questions. Do you want me to postpone it until tomorrow, or do you want to just get it over with today?"

I said, "I don't have anything concrete to tell them. The person that shot Nicole and I was wearing a mask and didn't say anything.

He just shot us and left us for dead. If he hadn't left the door to our hotel room open when he left, there would have been two bodies in the room. The hotel room service guy found us and reported it."

After telling the doctor this information, he said, "Mr. Farnsworth, I am deeply sorry for your loss, and my job, as I said before, is to get you well. I'm going to make sure that while you are under my care that you will get the best possible care that I can make happen at this hospital."

I said, "Thanks, Dr. Miller," as I glanced at his name tag, "I know you'll do your best to get me back on my feet as soon as possible, but right now, could you do something about the pain right?"

He said, "Of course, Mr. Farnsworth."

And he sent the nurse that was with him to get the injection.

The doctor said, "I'll have the drip mechanism removed, and the injection that I have prescribed can only be administered every four hours as needed and a sedative to keep you calm and relaxed so that you'll be able to rest and sleep if you want to."

It wasn't too long before the nurse had returned with a syringe and said, "This should help you to relax, Mr. Farnsworth, and the pain to subside."

The nurse stuck the syringe into the IV, and Dr. Miller said, "I will come back this afternoon to see how you are doing."

Then he and the nurse left the room.

CHAPTER 3

Well, just like the nurse said, it didn't take long before I fell asleep and was in dreamland. In the dream, I was in some large city like Atlanta, driving down the street. The surroundings seemed familiar except the period looked like in the thirties or forties by the appearance of the cars parked on the street and the clothes that the people were wearing. As I came to a traffic light, I began to slow down because the signal was going to change to red. As I rolled to a stop, a man in a pin-striped suit opened the passenger door and got in the car.

I said, "What do you think you are doing, sir?"

The man replied, "Don't you recognize me? I'm Gerald Farnsworth."

I said, "You're my grandfather, but you look about forty something."

He replied, "Sixty-seven years old, to be exact. It's 1944, when cars were made of steel and not of plastic."

I said, "What am I doing here in your past?"

He said, "What occurred to me during WWI changed everything in my life. It took a serious U-turn on the turnpike of life."

I said, "We aren't going to run into my father here, are we? I would really trip seeing him. Is he about five or six years old in 1944?"

Grandfather said, "He's six now, and the war is almost over."

I said, "How did you miss going to war?"

"I don't think that the military would have any use for a sixty-year-old man besides, warfare and the technology to make war had changed."

I said, "I still don't understand. Why am I back in your past? What does this have to do with me?"

Grandfather said, "Once you have your next birthday, you'll make the connection to me and the year 1915. After Germany surrenders, I wanted to go back to Germany and find out things that tie you and I and possibly your child."

I said, "But, Grandfather, my beautiful Nicole is dead. Are you saying that I will marry again and be a father?"

He said, "Yes."

And before I could ask him anything else, I was awakened by my mother and my grandmother as they both walked up to the side of the bed and touched my hands.

My mom said, "We just found out about Nicole." She had tears in her eyes. "I'm so glad that we didn't lose you."

Both my mother and grandmother were crying and sobbing.

I, being drugged up pretty good, said, "You just missed the doctor. He seems to be a good guy. The morphine drip they had me on wasn't working so good, so he prescribed something better, and I'm hardly hurting at all right now. The way I was feeling, I could have jumped from a ten-story building and not have felt a thing."

My mom told me that she had already talked to the doctor, and he told her that I was out of any immediate medical danger. She said that the doctor told her that I could be out of the intensive care unit by tomorrow as long as I keep showing signs of improvement. I was having a hard time trying to focus, so I just closed my eyes and talked to them.

I said, "Mom, have you talked to Nicole's parents?"

My mom told me that she had talked to Nicole's mother and said that she was pretty torn up about losing her only daughter.

I said, "I can only imagine what her parents are going through right now. They are experiencing some heavy-duty grief like me but in a different way. I can't believe you two beat the police here first."

My mom said, "They are here. The nurse let us come in first."

I was wondering when the cops would get here. Sure enough, it wasn't long before two men walked in. One of the men introduced himself as Detective Greene, and the other guy introduced himself as Detective Toms.

Detective Greene said, "We are aware of your injuries, and we won't stay long so that you can get your rest."

Even though the sedative that the nurse gave me is still kicking ass, it took all I could do to keep my eyes open.

Detective Toms said, "Did you see the shooter's face, Mr. Farnsworth?"

I said, "The shooter was wearing a mask and was wearing gloves also."

Detective Greene said, "How tall was the shooter, and what kind of clothes was he wearing?"

I said, "The shooter was about six feet tall, wearing jeans and a black sports jacket."

Detective Toms said, "What happened after he shot you, Mr. Farnsworth?"

"I told the detectives everything that had transpired in the hotel room that night that Nicole was killed. I didn't divulge the part the killer said, "Goodbye Mr. Farnsworth."

Detective Greene said, "Mr. Farnsworth, did the shooter say anything?"

I said, "No, I think the shooter was there to rob us but was stopped because the hotel waiter interrupted things."

The two detectives said, "Thank you, Mr. Farnsworth, and we are deeply sorry about your fiancée, and we'll do everything we can to catch the shooter. We hope you get well soon."

I waved bye to the two detectives as they exited my room, thinking to myself, it's only a matter of time before I have to confront Nicole's parents.

Grandmother said, "Did you get any rest last night?"

I told them that the morphine kept me jacked up, and I couldn't sleep.

My mother said, "I doubt you'll be eating anything solid for now until they are sure your system is stable."

I said, "The doctor said that I could have very light liquids."

My mom broke down and started to cry and said sobbingly, "I'm so glad that you didn't get killed, you're still my baby."

I said, "I know Nicole's family must be taking it hard because, like me, she's an only child."

My grandmother told me she made arrangements with the florist on a beautiful wreath from all of us. She said that she wasn't positive about the funeral arrangements, but the local undertaker will notify her as soon as things are finalized.

She said, "Don't worry, James, just concentrate on getting well for now. I could use another cup of coffee." And she asked my mom if she would like a cup.

My mom said, "Let's go to the hospital cafeteria and get some coffee there. I don't want to drink coffee in front of James because you know he loves his coffee."

My grandmother said, "While we are gone, try to get a catnap in case, you know, people are going to be in and out of here today." Then she leaned over and kissed me on the cheek.

My mom said, "We'll be back, just rest."

They both left the room.

I said to myself, *Grandmother's right, people will be in and out of here today along with the nurses coming in here also. Besides, that medication is still kicking my ass, and I could use a nap, maybe pick up were my last dream left off.*

I went to sleep, but the dream I was having wasn't even close to the last dream. In this dream I was a kid again. I was playing in the yard with my foam glider, throwing it and watching it just float effortlessly along. It was a hot summer day, and after the glider landed, I went into my friend's house to get something to drink. I thanked Sidney's mom for the iced tea.

I asked, "Where's Sidney at?"

She quickly answered, "You'll see him tomorrow. He's not feeling well."

I went back outside to play with my plane some more. I picked it up and threw it as hard as I could. It sailed over the hedges, and I quickly ran to retrieve it because the neighbors had a Rottweiler, and if he got it, he would tear my shit to pieces. I crawled through the hedges and over the fence, and there he was with my plane in his mouth. I was scared shitless. I froze in my tracks. The dog walked over to me and dropped the plane at my feet.

The dog spoke and said, "Go ahead and get your toy. I'm not going to attack you."

I said, "I thought you hated kids. Sid says you're always barking at kids?"

The dog said, "You knew that you weren't in any danger when you crossed the fence on that day. Your friend has a fear of dogs, and yet you've shut that memory off."

I said, "I don't understand. What is happening to me?"

The dog said, "I am not the one to tell you right now, but when the time comes, things will become crystal clear."

He told me to go back to my friend Sidney's yard before his owner sees me. I threw my plane over the hedges to my friend's yard then climbed the fence and through the hedges. I was awakened as my mom and grandmother came to the side of my bed. I asked them where they were staying.

Grandmother said that she and my mom were staying at the Marriot. Mom said that they did not want me to fight to stay awake to talk to them because they found out from the doctor that I had a tough night last night. Mom said that they would go back to the hotel so that I could rest. I was struggling to keep eye contact on them and kept my eyes closed while I talked to them. The medication was kicking my ass, and it felt good. They both took turns kissing me on the cheek and told me they were leaving and would be back later on today.

I started thinking about what I'm going to do to Serlinni and how I can pull it off. I could pay somebody to whack him, but I couldn't trust that person not to talk after it's over, plus they would try to blackmail me, and they would continue to suck money out of me. Then if I tell the FBI about him, there would be a long-drawn-out investigation, Serlinni would get wind of it, and he would just lay low while the heat was on. I kept on channel-surfing until I stopped on a movie that grabbed my interest, *Scarface*. The scene was where Tony was in a car with a Columbian bomb expert that had just wired a bomb to a diplomat's car. The diplomat's car had stopped and picked up the guy's kid, then Tony said that he wasn't going to blow the car with the kid in it. The Columbian kept arguing with him, then Tony shot him.

By this time, I had fallen off to sleep. In the dream I was walking down a sidewalk somewhere like Miami. There were palm trees and buildings painted up art deco style. As I was walking, I had the feeling I was being followed, I turned around, and there was a car slowly creeping up to me. I began to pick up the pace, and I heard the car engine revving higher. The faster I ran, the closer they got. I looked for an alley to go down; there was none. I kept on running. The car pulled up beside me. The window went down, and shots rang out.

I'm hit, then I tumble on the concrete. I lay there thinking, *Are they coming back to finish me off?* Then out of nowhere, this stray dog comes up to me and began licking my face.

I said to the dog, "You better get out of here before they shoot you too."

The dog said, "You're only wounded. They can't kill you like that. You the baddest there is, you just don't know it yet."

I said, "What are you saying?"

Before the dog could reply, a nurse came in and awakened me to take my temperature.

The nurse said, "I'm sorry to have to awaken you, Mr. Farnsworth. The doctor wants to keep a check on your temperature to make sure that you don't have any infection going on inside your body. So open your mouth please."

She placed the thermometer under my tongue. Within seconds, it beeped.

She said, "You have a low-grade temp, but that's normal."

I said, "Would you get my watch out of the drawer for me?"

She replied, "I think your watch and other belongings are locked up in the hospital safe. They were removed and placed there the night you came in. I'll talk to the head nurse about getting you your watch," as she was leaving the room.

If I want to know what time it is, I'd just look on the weather channel. I thought to myself, *It's just a matter of time before someone from Nicole's family will be in to see me, or they will be bitter because I lived and their daughter didn't.* I wish this nightmare was over. I flipped over to the weather channel, and time said 11:00 a.m., and it's going to be warm today, the guys at the video shoot should have a good day of filming, I hope. My mom and grandmother came back to my room.

Grandmother said, "We talked to your doctor, and he said that he is sending a nurse in with some soup."

I told them that soup sounded appetizing. Grandmother told me that I have to take it slowly because my body had been through some serious trauma. I asked if they had heard any word about the funeral arrangements yet. She said that they plan on having graveside services in two days, and Nicole's aunt told her that Nicole's father flew to Arizona to fly back with her body along with Mr. Stoddard, the mortician.

She said, "I asked the doctor if you would be strong enough to attend the funeral, and he said it would depend upon you and if you're up to it."

I was having a hard time keeping my eyes open for any length of time. Mom and Grandmother sat down in some chairs that were in the small room. It wasn't long afterwards in between my periods of going in and out of consciousness that Nicole's father came into the room, and I reached my hand out to shake his hand. He approached my bed and took my hand. I told him that I wish that it was me that St. Peter is meeting at the gate instead of Nicole. Everyone in the room started crying.

Nicole's father said, "You are very lucky, you almost went with her according to what your mom and grandmother told me. Knowing your mother and grandmother, you'll be on a plane as soon as the doctor releases you."

Mom and Grandmother hugged him and walked with him out of my room. I figured they would talk about the funeral arrangements and make further condolences to the family. I was already dreading the day of the funeral. I know that I don't want people walking up to my casket, peering in, and saying, "He looks really good, doesn't he?" I just want to have a short graveside service, no open casket, no sad music, maybe some upbeat music, like the type of music like "The Dream Is Over" by Crowded House, "Never Tear Us Apart" by INXS, or Whiter Shade of Pale by Procal Harum, the music that I like. If I'm getting a send-off, get me some music that I like. Mom and Grandmother came back into my room; both were wiping their eyes.

Grandmother tried to change the somber subject by saying, "We've got to get you home because you've got a birthday coming up."

I said, "What's so special about my birthday?"

Grandmother said, "Well, the good Lord let you live to see another year, that's what's special."

She said, "I know it hurts to lose someone that you love. Look at what your mother and I have been through. Life is about experiences, and it's up to you to learn from them."

Mom said, "Do you have any bedroom slippers?"

I told her not to worry about it now; there's a cath in now.

Mother said that she and grandmother had packed too light and had to buy some things that they needed. Grandmother said that hopefully the cath, the i.v. and the drainage tube in your side will come out, then they could buy me some pajamas. I told her by then the doctor will probably release me.

I gave them a hug as they exited out of my room. I flipped through the channels to look for the weather channel to see what time it was. The time shown was 12:00 p.m. I was wondering how the video shoot was going, wishing things could've been different. I miss my Nicole, and now I've got to do something about Serlinni before he does something to someone else that's close to me. Right now, I'm in the damn hospital with a gunshot wound through my rib cage and out of my back, and I don't know if I'll have any nerve damage in my back from the exit wound or have a weak spot on my heart.

A nurse came in and said, "I'm changing out your IV and putting in a fresh one. Would you like for me to give you a bath and a shave, Mr. Farnsworth?"

I said, "Maybe a shave for now."

She said, "Okay, Mr. Farnsworth, I'll just give you a shave today and bath maybe tomorrow."

The nurse got the plastic pan and put warm water in it, got a washcloth and razor, and brought them over to the bed stand. She dipped the cloth in the water and wrung it out then wiped my face with it. The warm cloth on my face felt refreshing. She then put some shaving cream on my face. I must say, she's a pretty woman. Nicole would be pissed off if she walked in and saw this. The nurse was meticulously maneuvering the razor across my face. She then took the cloth and removed the shaving cream.

She said, "Would you like to brush your teeth?"

I nodded yes.

She said, "Just don't swallow any of it, okay."

She emptied the shave pan in the sink and got the toothbrush, toothpaste, and a cup of water. She dipped the toothbrush in the water and spread toothpaste on it and gave it to me. I took the brush and brushed my teeth. She gave me a little water to swish around in my mouth, then she held a small pan for me to spit it out.

I told the nurse, "Thank you."

She said, "You're welcome, Mr. Farnsworth."

Then she washed out the pans and my toothbrush.

She said, "Try to get some sleep when you can, Mr. Farnsworth. I imagine there will be some more of your family and friends in and out of here today. Just buzz the desk if you need someone, okay!"

I gave her the okay hand signal, and she left my room. I felt a little better; my mouth doesn't feel like a cat box smells. My right arm started hurting where the IV is; it was throbbing. I picked up the nurse call button and pressed it.

A nurse said over the speaker, "I'll be right there, Mr. Farnsworth."

I said, "There's something wrong with my right arm. It hurts where the IV is."

The nurse came in and said, "What's wrong, Mr. Farnsworth? Let's see what the problem is."

She walked over to the right side of my bed and looked at my arm and at the IV bag.

She said, "It looks like the IV has been infiltrated, and I'll have to relocate it to another spot on your arm."

She began removing the tape and disconnected the IV from the syringe. At that moment, my mom and grandmother came in.

My mother said, "Nurse, what's wrong?"

The nurse told mother that she will have to move the IV to another location because the IV had become infiltrated. She carefully pulled the syringe out and massaged my arm.

She said, "I've got to go back to the nurses' station and get another syringe."

My grandmother said, "Have they even given you a bath yet?"

I said that they just missed the nurse. She had given me a shave, and I told her I'd would get a bath tomorrow. I wasn't up for it now.

Mom said, "Here's some aftershave lotion to put on to keep the stench down."

I snickered and so did Grandmother. I splashed on some Halston.

Grandmother said, "How about the pants?"

I pointed to the catheter attached to the side of the bed.

She said, "I guess we can wait till we move you out of here."

The nurse came back with an IV kit, and she said, "Let me see your other arm."

She rubbed the top of hand, feeling the veins under the skin.

She said, "Here's a good-looking vein." She rubbed the underside of my forearm and asked me to make a fist. "You'll probably feel a little sting. It will only last for a second or two."

I closed my eyes just as she stuck the needle in. Before I knew it, I said, "Shit, that stings."

The nurse said, "I'm sorry, Mr. Farnsworth," as she finished hooking up the IV and made sure that it was flowing in my arm before she gave me the thumbs-up signal.

I gave her the thumbs-up signal back and she left the room. Grandmother walked over to a chair and sat down.

Mom sat on the end of my bed and said, "Have you heard anything from the film crew yet?"

I said that I would probably hear something from Tim later this afternoon after the film shoot is over.

Grandmother said, "You can get some rest. Besides, my feet are killing me."

Mom said, "We're going back to the motel and get some rest. Neither one of us got any rest last night. We'll be back later to check on you."

Both of them came over to me and hugged me then left me alone in my room.

I was getting thirsty as hell. I wondered if I could have something to drink, so I pushed the call button.

A nurse's voice coming from the wall speaker said, "I'll be right there, Mr. Farnsworth."

A nurse came to my room.

"Can I have some water to drink?"

She said, "I think your doctor is still here. Let me ask him."

She walked out of my room and was gone a little. In the meantime, I'll just flip the channels on the idiot box. I need to write myself a reminder note, "Don't forget about the watch and my wallet. Make sure everything is there, meaning credit cards, two k's worth of traveler's checks, driver's license, and my insurance card."

Why is it that time seems to crawl by while you're awake and fly by while you sleep? I'll just flip through the channels to pass the time. Maybe the nurse will come back with something cold to drink.

The nurse came back with a Styrofoam cup in her hand, and she said, "I talked to your doctor, and he said that you could have a cup of water. He wants to make sure you can keep things down."

She handed me the cup. I took the cup and took a sip, and when the nurse reached for the cup, I slammed the contents of water down my throat like a man dying of thirst.

The nurse grabbed the cup and said, "I'm glad I didn't give you a bigger cup. We want to see if you can keep it down without getting sick."

The nurse then threw the cup in the trash and said that she would come back later to check on me. I started to think about those weird-ass dreams that I have been having again. What was the dog in my dreams trying to tell me? What is my dead grandfather trying not to tell me? I've got a gut feeling that my grandmother knows something. I had better play it smart and not draw attention to myself any more than I have to. I've still got the gangster to deal with for killing my Nicole.

I started to flip through the TV channels to see what was on, stopped briefly on the weather channel to get the time of day. The time was 1:00 p.m. The doctor walked in.

He said, "Well, Mr. Farnsworth, from what I'm hearing, you are getting better pretty fast, but you don't need to rush yourself. The nurse told me that you asked for something to drink, and you've had some water. I want to make sure that you can keep it down, and by the looks of your catheter, I don't see any blood in your urine and I may start you on a light diet. Let me look at your wounds."

He peeled away the bandages from my chest and taped it back down then asked me to roll over on my side to look at the exit wound on my back. I told him that I can at least relax now since they removed the morphine drip. He told me that the injected medication will help to ease the pain but will make me sleepy.

The doctor said, "That's remarkable, your wounds looks exceptionally well for the amount of trauma that has been done to it. You've got to be the healthiest person I've ever treated, meaning I've never seen such quick recovery."

I told the doctor that I have been taking vitamins and other supplements plus I work out.

The doctor said, "When you get back home, I want you to send me a list of the supplements that you are taking. I'm going to start taking them myself. How do you feel about trying something soft to eat, like some soup or even a bowl of grits for dinner? I'll be in here in the morning to see about you."

He looked at his watch and told me that I'll get another injection in an hour, and then he walked out of the room. After what the doctor said about fast recovery, it confirms that something is going on with me. I just can't put my finger on what it is. I flipped through the channels, skipping the morning-talk-shows crap. I hate television when you can flip through thirty or more channels and ten of the channels are trying to sell some bullshit merchandise that you can find at a drugstore chain. Daytime television is worse than late-night television, especially when it comes to movies that guys like. The Lifetime Channel needs to be called the Wife Time Channel because it's geared to the homemaker. I guess that's why we guys are supposed to be out in the work world, bringing home the bacon, instead of watching shows about women who poison their husband to get an insurance payout.

I continued to scan the channels, looking for something that will buy me some time before I get my next shot. According to the doctor, it's only an hour away. Maybe I can take a nap and find out in my dreams what is happening to me. I started thinking about the times that I had spent with Nicole, now only cherished memories. I wished I had taken Serlinni's offer now, but it's too late, and I can't reverse time. Things have gone too far. I'll have to find out from Grandmother who Grandfather was friends with inside the bureau. I did finally find a decent channel to watch. It is the cooking channel. A hot-looking chick was cooking Italian food. What really made me stop on the food channel wasn't the food preparation. The babe cooking had a nice rack and wasn't afraid to flaunt it. I would let her cook me anything she wanted.

By the time I got halfway interested in the show, Mom and Grandmother came in carrying shopping bags.

I said, "I hope you guys didn't go overboard and get me matching slippers and a Hugh Hefner smoking jacket."

The doctor came in to see me while ya'll were gone. He looked at my catheter and said it could possibly come out, as long as no blood is present. He also mentioned he'll start me on a light diet. That means a shorter hospital stay.

Grandmother said, "I hope it's soon because we want you at home. You have a birthday coming up."

I said to myself, she knows something. As mom was hanging the robe and putting the slippers in a small closet in an already cramped room, a nurse came in carrying a syringe.

The nurse said, "I have your medication, Mr. Farnsworth."

She walked over to the side of my bed where the IV bag was hanging and inserted it into the line. She checked my blood pressure and my temperature and recorded it on the chart. She emptied my cath bag and reattached it.

Before she left the room, she said, "Page the nurses' station if you need anything, Mr. Farnsworth."

I asked Mom and Grandmother if they had eaten lunch. They told me that they had gotten something to eat while they were shopping. I could feel the effects of the drug moving through my system. It was great timing on the doctor's part because my chest was beginning to start hurting again. It hurts to take a deep breath. I can sympathize with people who have had open-heart surgery. My eyes were becoming heavy again. Before I got to the point where I couldn't carry on a conversation without nodding out. I told them to check on my belongings that the hospital has, and I gave the name of the hotel I was staying at to find out if they have my baggage. I told them after they find out those things, to just go to their hotel and chill out because I'll be sleeping for a couple of hours because of the injection, no need for them to sit in my room and watch me sleep.

Mom said, "The doctor told us that you will get a light meal today, so by the time you wake up, you'll have something to eat."

They both took turns giving me a kiss on the cheek and told me that they would return later today. I told them that I would see them later as they walked out of the room. I was fighting to keep my eyes open to talk to them, and they knew it.

I looked back at the television just to see if that babe was still there. There was some kind of chef competition going on, so I changed the channel and stopped on the weather channel, and I went to sleep. It wasn't long before I was in a dream state. I was sitting poolside underneath an umbrella-shaded table. My nose had caught the scent of something that smelt heavenly.

A voice from my right says, "The shrimp are almost ready. Would you be a dear and get me a plate?"

That voice was coming from the hot babe from the cooking channel. I told her that I would get her a plate and asked her if she would like a Corona with it. She told me yes as I went inside this kitchen to retrieve the plates and two beers from the refrigerator. I came back out, and the hot babe wearing a bikini top and a sarong was waiting anxiously by the grill for me. I held the plate as she picked up the shrimp with tongs, placing the grilled shrimp on the plates. We walk over to the table and sit down. By the time she sticks a fork into a shrimp and puts it to her mouth, I hear a thump sound. The hot cooking-show babe was face down in her plate. I rushed to the other side of the table and raised her head. She had a bullet hole in her pretty head. I looked in the direction to where I heard the noise, and there was a guy with a stocking covering his head walking toward me.

He had a silenced pistol aimed at me and said, "You should've taken the money, and the pretty lady wouldn't have gone bye-bye, so now it's your turn."

He shoots me a couple of times, but I'm not falling. He keeps walking up on me and empties his whole clip. I'm still standing. He throws his gun down and comes at me. I wrestle him to the ground and snapped his neck like a twig with my bare hands. I stepped back, trying to figure out what is going on. I hear footsteps approaching from behind me. I turn around, and it's my grandfather.

I asked him, "Grandfather, tell me what is going on."

He said, "For one thing, this is a drug-induced dream and characters brought forth by your memory. The second thing is you can't be killed by being shot. Have you even wondered why you've never been sick, never missed a day of school, college, or work? You've never had a cavity, though your parents took you to the dentist only to have your teeth cleaned. Your friends around you suffered from accidents, broken bones, and stitches, not to leave out braces and retainers. You, on the other hand, did not have to suffer such maladies."

I said, "I don't recall you ever being sick or going to a doctor either, Grandfather. Why didn't my father inherit this, whatever it is?"

Grandfather said, "I knew your father didn't have the gift when he contracted bronchitis when he was very young. I watched for all of the signs and waited for his thirty-eighth birthday to arrive. I didn't know why until he was diagnosed with cancer. He was born with a cancer gene, something he had gotten from your grandmother's side of the family."

I said, "Yes, I remember grandmother talking about her brother dying from cancer at the age of forty. My dad made it past forty."

Grandfather said, "I was setting a bad example and smoked every day."

I was about to ask him some more questions. I was awakened by a nurse coming into the room. She had sat a food tray on the roll-about hospital bed table.

She said, "Mr. Farnsworth, here's some soup, juice, and Jell-O. I want you to eat this slowly and take your time so as not to put your stomach into shock."

I was still kind of groggy and told her that I would take my time. She walked out of the room, and I took the cover off the tray to reveal the cuisine beneath. The bowl contained some kind of clear broth, a small bowl of orange gelatin, and a small plastic cup with grape juice. I unwrapped the silverware and dipped into the soup first. The taste wasn't appetizing, but it was food. I scooped it up by the spoonful and found it to be too slow of a process. I picked up the bowl and drank the broth down, scarfed down the Jell-O, and drank the grape juice like a starving man rescued from the desert.

The nurse came back in the room to check on me and said sarcastically, "Good thing you took your time." And she shook her head.

She picked up the tray and walked out of the door. I touched my chest and pressed down on it gently. It doesn't hurt as bad as it did earlier. Are the meds or is something happening to me that's causing rapid healing, or is this some kind of a psychosis of the mind? What is going on with me? What does this have to do with my birthday coming up? According to the dream I had, something occurred to my grandfather when he was thirty-eight. I'll be thirty-eight in a couple of days. Grandmother knows something. Even in my dreams, there are hints that my life will change, but into what?

I turned the TV volume back up and started channel-surfing again to see if anything worth a shit was on. Boy, a joint would be nice right now. Me and Nicole loved to get high and take drives in the country during good weather. I sure am going to miss her. She was my friend, my love. My life is going to be different from now on, and it's happening regardless of what controls it. I just hope I'll have a sane thought left after Nicole's funeral and then my birthday—whatever that brings.

I flipped the TV button a couple of times and stopped it on a classic movie with Christopher Lee as Dracula. I thought to myself that vampires possess supernatural abilities. Damn! I'm turning into a vampire but, there's a problem with that theory. All of my family members can walk about in the daylight hours. But the positive side is, Dracula has great-looking babes hanging with him, doesn't he. One thing's for sure, in Dracula and James Bond movies, they got the prime crop of babes, not an ugly one in the bunch. I don't think that vampirism is the verdict. I know, I'll become a highlander, an immortal, like Chris Lambert in that movie of the same name. There's something wrong with that scenario, also highlanders don't age. Grandfather aged, but he aged at a different rate, or was he able to control how he appeared so that he wouldn't draw attention?

I watched a little of the movie but decided to keep channel-surfing, hoping something worth watching would surface. This I do know: it will be a couple of hours before I can get another shot. I started thinking about what my grandfather had said to me in a dream. He told me that in 1944, he was sixty-seven years old. That means he was thirty-eight years old in 1915. This means that thirty-eight years prior to that put him being born the year of 1877. His tombstone marker outs him at ninety-six years, but in actuality, he was a hundred thirty-five years old when he was put in the ground.

Hell, the man didn't look ninety-six or act ninety-six years old. He could pass for someone in their sixties or a little older.

I kept flipping through the channels, looking for something to either pique my interest or bore me to the point I get sleepy enough to fall asleep. I am having a hard time trying to understand what is going on plus the fact of dealing with the grief of losing my Nicole to a killer. I stopped on the weather channel to see what time it was, and it was almost two o'clock. This time yesterday, my Nicole was alive and breathing. Certain events can really humble a person. So many things we take for granted, things that you wouldn't even consider when you are younger. For instance, growing old—that concept didn't enter my mind when I was in my teens and even in my twenties. I was too busy enjoying the moment, the future seemed a millennia away. I wished I could've spent more quality time with my dad and grandfather, likewise with my Nicole. I guess everyone goes through the should-have-, would-have-, and could-have-done things differently if they had only realized that moments in life are limited.

I might as well stop having a pity party for myself and start thinking about the possibility that someone that is working within the production company could be working for Serlinni. Someone within my organization is working for Serlinni; someone had to tell Serlinni. Why else would he call to tell me that he was offended that I didn't take the envelope with the money plus, at the end of the conversation, tell me to have a good trip? It could even be my technical manager, Tim Jackson. The guy has been with the company about five or so years, someone I've been led to trust with the workings of the company. I have to be careful and not let on that I suspect him or anyone in the company. Now is not the time to try and ask pointed questions. I'm in a hospital bed in a very vulnerable position. All I can hope for is that the doctor doesn't find anything medically wrong to keep me in here longer than necessary.

As I continued flipping through the channels, a nurse came into the room. She told me that she needed a blood sample to take to the lab. She took a vial of blood from my right, since the left had an IV in it. She told me thanks and walked out of the room. I imagine I won't find out how the video shoot goes. The hospital won't allow anyone in the room except for immediate family. I could give Mom Tim's cell number for her to call later this afternoon. He may even be resourceful enough to pass himself as a relative in order to come in and brief me on today's video shoot. I will have to see what unfolds.

Time seems to crawl slowly by while lying on your back in a hospital room. I kept flipping through the channels to see if anything was worth taking a look at. I stopped on the syndicated cable news channel to see if there are any good things occurring in other parts of the world. As usual, the United States is playing big brother to some country at the same time the United States is saying that the government is going broke. What happened to the term "Don't spend beyond your means"? I kept on channel-surfing. I stopped on the weather channel to see what the time was; it is was almost four o'clock. So far, I have been able to keep the food down. I hope they remove the catheter; it isn't very comfortable. They'll probably do an MRI on me tomorrow to see if I am healing up correctly. Right now I'm at the mercy of this bed I'm lying in.

It probably won't be too long before Mom and Grandmother come back to check on me. I began to reflect on my life aspirations, you know, the usual stuff: having a good career, getting married, having kids, and trying to be the ideal parent and husband. It seems that just when you think you have things planned out, something happens. Before I could get deep into the depression pool, Mom and Grandmother walk in. They took turns asking me questions like was I able to keep the food down and had the doctor came by again.

Mom informed that they had picked up my and Nicole's belongings from the hotel. Mom took my wallet from her purse and gave it to me. She asked me to check and see what is missing from it. I took a look into the wallet. The traveler's checks were gone, the cash was gone, but the credit cards were still intact, including my driver's license. The shooter must have taken the money and the traveler's checks. I asked mom to call my bank and have the traveler's checks canceled. Mom walked from the foot of my bed to position herself so that she could talk in a lower audible voice.

She started asking me some questions like, "Do you think that Serlinni had this attempt on your life orchestrated?"

I said, "What do you now about Serlinni?"

She said that my father had made mention of his name and that he tried to strong-arm my father into selling the studio.

Grandmother said, "Let's not talk about such things in here, no telling who could walk in us."

My heart dropped to the bottom of my soul; my mom knows about this character and now my grandmother. I dare not tell them about the incident with my vehicle getting shot up. Grandmother commented that if I continue to improve that I would probably get moved to a private room. I asked them if they had heard anything about when Nicole's funeral is planned. Mom told me that her body was flown back to Georgia today. She said that the arrangements have not been finalized as of yet. Grandmother told me not to worry about that now and be concerned with getting well and getting home.

Mom said, "I know you want to be there for her and her family. It could have been a double funeral."

She started crying and sat down in a chair in the room. Grandmother came over to her and began consoling her and told her that they didn't lose me and that I was on the mend.

Grandmother looked over at me and said, "Just rest, baby, and try not to worry about things. I know things may seem screwed up for you, but you have me and your mother in your corner. I know you loved Nicole, we all did. Right now you need to concentrate on getting well and stronger. Dealing with loss never goes away, but you learn to dwell on the happy times that you've had together. Your mother and I have had to deal with losing a partner. A day doesn't go by that I don't think about your father and your grandfather. Their physical body has been taken from us, but their memories can't be erased from our minds and hearts."

While Mom and Grandmother were there, my doctor stepped into the room. He said hello to all of us in the room and asked me if I was able to rest better since the morphine drip was replaced with an injected drug. I told him that I was able to calm down enough to get some sleep. He told me that the lab results from blood samples hadn't shown any elevated levels of infection in my body. He moved down to the foot of my bed. He asked me to pick up my left leg and then my right leg. I picked them up individually as he asked. He asked me if I felt any pain as I lifted them. I told him that there was some pain like a pulling sensation in my chest. He told me to wiggle my toes, and I wiggled them. He asked me if I experienced any tingling. I told him that I could feel the toes moving and feel the touch of the sheet on my toes. He then said that he had scheduled an MRI scan tomorrow morning. He wants to take a look and make sure that the area on my heart that was nicked by the bullet isn't leaking and is healing. He then said if the MRI doesn't show him what he needs to see, an arterial dye procedure will be done.

Grandmother asked the doctor, "If the test shows that his system is working normally, how much longer would he have to stay in the hospital?"

He told us his plan is to remove the urinary cath, and get me back on my feet and make sure that there is no nerve damage at the exit wound in my back. He then said he doesn't want to make any promises he can't keep but told us that so far I am healing very well. Mom thanked the doctor for such good news and for saving her son's life. The doctor told us that he plans to do everything humanly possible to get me back home.

As he was walking out the door, he told me that I would going for testing early in the morning, and he would see me after the testing. I replied by telling him that I would see him tomorrow and thanked him for his deeds. I was glad that Mom and Grandmother were there to hear the doctor's comments. Their level of worrying can be toned down now.

I lowered the head of my bed down to a lesser angle. My back is starting to hurt. Grandmother asked me if I was hurting, and I told her that I was. She then told me to hit the nurse-call button. I hit the call button, and a nurse asked me if she could help. I asked her if I could get an injection for the pain. The nurse replied by saying that she would check the chart and see if it was time and would call me right back. I told her thanks. My mom said that she had gotten a call from Tim Jackson, my production manager. He had asked how I was doing and that he had expressed his sympathy for the loss of Nicole. Mom told him that I was in the intensive care unit and doing as well as can be expected. I guess she was trying to get my mind off the pain by engaging in conversation. It wasn't working.

I hit the remote on my bed to raise my head. I stopped at the position I was in before I moved it; the pain was still agonizing. I grabbed the safety rail and pulled myself up to an upright position. The pain changed its intensity from sharpness to a dull throb. Grandmother told me to lie back and slow down, stop trying to rush things along. I told her that I am trying to find a comfort zone to minimize the pain. A nurse came in, and my mom asked her if she could get in touch with the doctor. The nurse told Mom that I would be able to relax after she gave me the injection. Mom told her that she would still like to talk to my doctor and to tell him that I had sat up in the bed. The nurse agreed that she would get in touch with the doctor and have him come by. Mom thanked her as the nurse inserted the hypodermic into the IV bag hanging on a stand next to the bed.

CHAPTER 4

The nurse increased the speed of the drip for fluid delivery of the IV. I was still sitting up in the bed, and the nurse asked me to lie back down and give the medication time to work. I could feel the medication entering my arm and start to course through my body. The medication was starting to work. Holding on to the rail, I eased back into the bed, resting my head on the pillow. My eyelids were getting heavy, and my vision was becoming blurry. I told Mom and my grandmother that I was having a hard time keeping my eyes open.

Mom said, "Just relax and take a nap. Your grandmother and I will come back later and see about you."

I struggled to keep my eyes open long enough to tell them that I would see them later. Before I was taken over by the drug-induced sleep, I thought about the comment my grandmother said. She told me to slow down and to stop trying to rush things along. Was she making an off-the-cuff statement, or does she know something? Whatever it is that's going on, my mom is oblivious to the situation.

The next thing I know is that I'm in a bar on an alien world. When I say alien, I'm putting it mildly. There's every sort of configuration of creature in this room as I look around my surroundings. As I walk closer to where the bartender is serving the multiracial creatures, a hooded figure walked up to me. The hood concealed the figure's face, and I couldn't recognize the voice as the hooded figure spoke.

The hooded figure said, "Don't worry about these creatures, you are invincible. You have something more powerful than the force. Let me show you."

The hooded figure tells one of the creatures that I said that the creature's mother is a whore. The alien creature takes out his weapon and started squeezing off rounds into me. The rounds pass through me and kill alien bystanders behind me. I ran my hand across my chest and stomach, trying to detect holes left behind by the alien's weapon. There were no entrance holes at all. I turned to ask the hooded figure who he was. Before the hooded figure could answer, up walked my grandfather with two hooded figures dressed in all-white garment.

My grandfather said, "The figure in the dark hood is not the emperor nor the Sith lord of a George Lucas film."

I turned to look where the dark hooded figure was standing, and the figure had disappeared. I said, "Who was that, Grandfather?"

"That was the great corrupter of minds and destroyer of all that is good in the world," replied my grandfather.

I said, "You're telling me that was Satan?"

My grandfather replied, "Yes, that was him. But let's not talk about him. It only glorifies him when we speak of him. So from now on we will only refer to him as the dark one. These two beings with me are the reason he didn't stick around for the introduction."

I said, "Let me guess, you have two angels at your side."

"Actually, they prefer to be called messengers, and they are here for two reasons. The first is that they are here to keep the dark one from corrupting you because you are mentally compromised by the drug and weighed down by the sorrow of losing Nicole. The dark one knows that when people are at a place in their life, when people are at their lowest point, then and there is when he comes to them and corrupts their thinking. The dark one is a master of deception. He's had several centuries to perfect his sales pitch."

I said, "What is the other reason that the messengers are here for?"

Grandfather said, "They are here to make sure that I only tell you things that you are ready for, and now is not the time. The dark one won't try to approach you directly since he found out that the messengers won't be far from the scene."

One of the messengers turned to Grandfather and was telling him something. I couldn't understand what the messenger was saying.

I asked my grandfather, "What did the messenger say?"

The messenger walked up to me and put his index finger on my forehead and stepped back. The messenger then said, "Now you'll be able to understand and hear when we speak. I merely told your grandfather that there are things that you will have to go through, but what you don't need is the dark one distorting things to suit his own agenda."

Before I could ask any more questions, I was awakened by a nurse entering the room, carrying a food tray. The nurse said, "I brought you a light diet meal, Mr. Farnsworth, and if the urine remains clear in in the cath. Bag, the doctor left orders to remove it. The only things left to remove, will be the abdominal drain tube in your side and then your i.v.. Just take your time eating okay. I thanked her and asked what time it was?

She then put the food tray on the serving table. I thanked her and asked her what time it was.

"It's almost five o'clock," she answered.

I've been asleep for almost two hours. The television was off. Mom or Grandmother must have turned it off before they left. I don't remember turning it off. I adjusted the angle of my bed so that I could sit upright and see what kind of meal is under the plastic cover. There is broiled fish, rice, a roll and a pat of butter. And for dessert, there was Tapioca pudding and a can of ginger ale to drink. I wanted to just scarf everything down instead, I savored every bite of food, relishing every nuance of the taste and smell. I only drank half of the ginger ale; I was hungry more than anything. I got the TV remote and turned it back on and surfed the channels to see if there was anything of interest. All the while I thought about the dream I just had.

In the dream, I was in the presence of good and evil at the same time. The dream was so lucid. I asked myself, was it the drugs or did it really happen? I pushed the tray support table to the left of the bed and eased the bed down some because my back started to hurt. I began to think about what occurred in the dream. What makes me so special that Satan—I mean the dark one—himself appeared? He told me that I am invincible and have something stronger than the force. My grandfather and the two messengers show up just in time before the dark one could reveal anything else. I had some scary dreams before but nothing as realistic and lucid as the latest episode. In the dream, my grandfather said that the drug made me vulnerable. I pondered on the notion to stop the pain meds. It's gotten to the point that I'm afraid to go to sleep.

A thought occurred to me. What if the pain is not from the bullet wound but my own body is repairing itself at a different rate than the normal individual? That would be a kick in the head if that's the case of regeneration. I wouldn't have to worry about the mob as much as I would be worrying about the medical community wanting to use me as a lab rat.

I flipped the channel over to the weather channel to see what it was. The time showed it is almost a quarter to six; the sun will be going down soon. The film crew should be finished with their on-location shoot by now. I got a feeling that Tim won't be showing up. I could be wrong. I continued flipping through the channels, looking for something worth stopping for and watching. I did manage to find a classic movie. Even though I had seen it before, I couldn't resist not watching it again. It reminded me of the first time I ever saw it. The movie is *Guess Who Is Watching the Store,* a Jerry Lewis classic. I remember being a young boy at my grandparents' house during a weekend. I recollect watching this movie with my grandfather and my grandmother and laughing so hard that my chest hurt. That time seems a million years away. I'm sure that everyone wishes that they had relished that time in their own way, such as the time that my father had taken me fishing for the first time. At that moment, my father's time belonged to me on that day. You never think that any moment could be that person's last, and that moment is gone.

I watched TV for a little while until I started thinking about the possibility of another attempt on my life while I'm lying here in this hospital bed. It wouldn't be that complicated if Serlinni had hired someone to dress as a hospital orderly and walk in my room and shoot an air bubble into my IV. Though the dark one in my dream said that I'm invincible, how can I believe him when he is the king of lies and deception? I came to realize that I need to stay vigilant, and my faculties need to be sharp. I've got to get the hell out of here. I feel like a sitting duck. Before my mind ran wild with all kinds of scenarios of potential killers coming in to finish the job, my mom and grandmother walked in with Tim Jackson.

I asked Tim, "How did the video shoot turn out?"

Tim replied by saying, "The video shoot went well. The entire crew and myself are very sorrowful for the loss of Nicole and are glad that you are alive. I asked your mom if flowers could be sent to your room, and she told me that it wouldn't be allowed in the intensive care unit. I had to tell them that I'm a relative in order to come in here to see you."

I replied by telling him that I appreciate the visit and told him to tell the crew that I hope to be out of here soon so that I'll be able to commend everyone for their efforts in person.

Mom said, "The doctor told me that if James's test looks good tomorrow, he will be moved from the intensive care unit."

I said that the nurse has orders from the doctor, as long as there isn't any blood in the urine bag, it will come out tomorrow.

Grandmother chimed in and said, "The doctor seems to think that could be a possibility if things go well tomorrow."

Tim commented, "That would be a step in the right direction towards getting out of here sooner. Plus hopefully, the police will catch the person that did this injustice."

I said, "I trust everything went according to as planned for the on-site shoot. I don't want to have to worry about that while I'm in here."

Tim replied by saying, "The location shoot at the Navajo reservation was a success. All we have to do now is the studio shots that we will be doing in Georgia at Red Sand Studio. By then you'll be well enough to go to work and won't be blowing up my cell phone, checking on things."

I told Tim that I appreciate his dedication to the company and thanked him for doing a good job. Tim told me that he would check with my mom on my progress tomorrow before he and the crew fly back to Georgia. He shook my hand and told us good night as he walked out of the room. All the while, Mom and Grandmother were settling down in the chairs that are next to my bed.

My food tray was still on the bed table, and Mom had noticed that I had wiped out everything but the half can of ginger ale. I told her that I would save it later in case I got thirsty. I tried to get their minds off of me and asked them about their hotel digs. Mom told us that she had to go to the bathroom and that it must have been something that she ate. She got up and left the room. This is my opportunity to ask my grandmother a question.

I said, "Grandmother, something weird is going on, and you know something, don't you?"

She said, "Yes, but this is not the place to discuss it. You'll be out of here in a day or so. When you get home, I have something to show you that will clear up a lot of questions. We must keep this between you and me for now."

I told her that I was relieved in a way, sort of, to find out that there is something going on and I'm not losing my mind. Grandmother told me that my grandfather loved me so much and that I would find out later just how much. Luckily, our little conversation had ended when Mom came back into the room. I asked Mom if she was okay. She told me that she will be okay; it's probably something that she had eaten.

Grandmother said, "We'll stop at a CVS and get your mom something for her stomach before we go to the restaurant on the way back to the hotel for the night."

I said, "I don't want to be worried about you two out rambling in the nightlife."

Both of them laughed at my comment. Mom replied by saying not to worry about them and concentrate on getting a passing grade on the medical test tomorrow. Grandmother stated that after she gets something to eat, she will be ready to lie down and rest. I told them both to sleep late in the morning and take their time to relax, and I should be through with the testing at least by ten o'clock, I guess, depending on what time they start.

I said, "When I see you two tomorrow, I'll have some good news for you."

They both took turns hugging me, telling me that they love me. I told them to go have a nice meal and relax at the hotel. They walked out of the room, and I was alone. I started thinking about what Grandmother had told me. She acknowledged that something is going on, and I'm a key piece in the puzzle. It appears that Grandmother has the answers. My dreams are not giving up any clues either. All I know is that a dark figure had said that I am invincible.

I said a prayer asking for answers and even asking for forgiveness for the bad decisions I've made in the past and in the recent days, especially the decision that got my Nicole killed. I asked Jesus to forgive me and help me to make things right with him. Lying in bed with my eyes closed, I had finished my prayer. I opened my eyes, and for a brief millisecond, a figure appeared at the foot of my bed. The encounter only lasted for about the speed of a blinking eye. I sat up in the bed and looked around in the confines of my cubicle-sized room. Did I actually see something? Was that a sign my message was heard or traces of the medication affecting my senses? It wasn't but a minute or two afterwards, an orderly came in and got my food tray, and I thanked them. I have to admit that the experience was kind of eerie. I couldn't make out anything that was recognizable to me. I just saw a shape that was at least normal height—well, normal to the average person—say, five eight or so. It can't be the grim reaper because the dark one said that I am invincible. Besides, the figure didn't seem to have a scythe in its hand.

I chuckled to myself. I suddenly realized that I was sitting straight up in the bed. I guess it was an impulse to react in such a way, like the time a model had fallen off the shelf during the night in my room when I was a kid. I remember sitting straight up and looking around in my dimly lit room. I was too afraid to get up and see what the noise was. I was afraid to even go to sleep. To my amazement, the next day, on the floor was a broken model of the Frankenstein monster. The figurine broke off even with the pedestal. I guess I didn't glue it well enough.

I eased myself back down onto the pillow. Then as I had flipped through the channels and stopped as a movie had just started, I realized what was on the television. The movie *The Omen* was on. I started realizing some similarities between me and Damian Thorne. Damian never got sick, was brought up in a very influential family, and the devil was in contact with him. Oh fuck, I'm the Antichrist. I began to feel my scalp to see if there were any raised areas or depressions that felt like the three sixes as shown on the movie. I felt nothing of any abnormalities, but what if it can't be felt? My mind was awash of scenarios like, guess what, I have a penthouse suite in the tropics of hell. Now that would be some fucked-up news—that Grandmother is going to wait and tell me once I get home that my real dad is the prince of darkness himself. No wonder the dark one told me that I am invincible—because we're related. That is pretty fucked up.

I changed the channels and tried to find something a bit more cheerful to watch. I sped by the news network channels. They are usually talking about some third world on the horizon of becoming a nuclear threat or some ex-lawyers using the media as a way of glamorizing criminals. I hurried and moved off those channels before my IQ started declining. Besides, I've got my own dilemma to worry about. I'll have to ask Grandmother tomorrow in a way so my mom isn't aware. I began to wonder, Was I switched at birth at the hospital like Damian Thorne?

As I was getting into deeper thought of the situation, a nurse came in with a tray of vials.

The nurse walked up to the bed and said, "Hello, Mr. Farnsworth, I need to get a blood sample from you."

She placed a rubber band around my bicep and told me to make a tight fist. She retrieved a syringe and found a vein with the precision of a skilled dart thrower. The nurse filled a couple of the vials with blood. She extracted the needle, put a bandage on the exit wound. The pain was minimal; it was evident she had lots of practice. I asked her if she could find out from the nurses' station if it was time for my injection. I told her that the pain is coming back. I really wasn't hurting, I just wanted to be knocked out. Maybe in my dreams, I'll find out something.

As I lay there, thinking about how Damian also had an effect on canines and the circumstances with dogs just in the past week, a nurse walked in with a sheathed syringe.

She said, "I've brought you some relief, Mr. Farnsworth."

I replied by telling her that she was right on time, that the pain was keeping me from resting. She walked over to the left side of the bed to where the IV tube entered my arm. I watched her as she squeezed the air from the syringe and inserted into the IV injection port. She asked me if I needed anything. I told her that I appreciated her bringing me some relief. She said that she would check in on me in a little while as she walked out of the room. I could feel the cold tingling sensation as the medication moved up into my arm, making its way to my torso and central nervous system. It wasn't too long before my eyelids became heavy. My focus became blurry to the point the television was distorted. I quit fighting the urge to hold my eyes open and surrendered to the narcotic. I don't know how long it took from the time I closed my eyes and the amount of time it took to get to dream state; I couldn't tell you.

The next moment, I was at a familiar location with my grandfather. I'm about ten or eleven years old here, and I rode along with Grandfather to get a hamburger at a local food vendor. We had finished eating and had left the restaurant. As we got closer to Grandfather's car, we heard a noise sounding like dogs growling and yelping. I followed Grandfather as he walked toward to where the noise was coming from. There was a dumpster, and two larger dogs were ganging up on a smaller dog. Grandfather whistled, and the two larger dogs stopped with their attack on the smaller dog and retreated. The smaller dog had been pinned down on his back, but now he had rolled over on his stomach. I saw Grandfather point in the opposite direction that the larger dogs had gone. The small dog got up and went in that direction.

I asked my grandfather, "What did you just do?"

Grandfather said, "I merely aimed the smaller dog into a safer environment."

I suddenly remembered this event actually happened when I was a kid, and now I'm reliving the event in a dream. We got into his car and were riding back to the house.

Grandfather said, "Nature can be cruel sometimes, but when the odds are unbalanced, such as the case of the two dogs beating up on the smaller, weaker dog, something has to be done to tip the scales, sometimes in favor of the one that needs rescuing. There's a lot of bad stuff going on, and you are going to be the one to tip the scale. Don't beat yourself up because of what happened, it was meant to be."

I said, "Tell that to Nicole's parents. She was an only child."

Grandfather then said, "There once was an only child that gave the ultimate sacrifice.

"Yes, I know who you are talking about," I replied.

Grandfather told me that the lamb is responsible for giving him a second chance at redemption, and my prayer was heard. I asked grandfather if I was the Antichrist. Grandfather laughed at my comment and told me that I wasn't the Antichrist but said that I would be a tool in the arsenal of weapons that will be used against the dark one and those that choose the wrong path. Grandfather told me that I won't need any more injections for pain because the pain will be gone, and there won't be a reason to keep me in the hospital after the testing tomorrow.

CHAPTER 5

On the outskirts of Nashville, a meeting took place within hours after the shooting. Information about the failed assassination of James Farnsworth, was made known to Serlinni's underboss. The underboss, Saul Scalia, tells his underling capo, Pete Gespari, that the boss isn't too happy about dropping a lot of cabbage on a hit and the intended target lives. He asked him what he is going to do about it. Gespari says the hit was hired outside his organization, and the hitman has never had a person live through a hit before now.

Saul said, "The boss doesn't want the hitman to make a mistake again, if you get my meaning."

According to the boss, the hitman has got three options. He can complete the mission, return the money, or he gets hit.

Gespari said, "Farnsworth is too hot right now to try again."

Saul said, "Did the boss give you a time limit to fulfill the obligations?"

"Ten days," Gespari replied.

Meanwhile, Vincent Serlinni, in comfort of his home, sits and thinks about his next move without drawing attention to the family. He thinks to himself, *Farnsworth will probably go to the feds about this. I'll see in ten days. If the hitman botches it again, I'll have to wait it out and try again. The circumstance will show itself. When the opportunity presents itself, Farnsworth won't be this lucky again.*

A noise woke me, and I found a nurse had walked in with a pitcher of ice.

The nurse said, "I tried to be quiet as a church mouse, but you woke up just as set the pitcher down on the table."

I said, "You are right on time. I'm a bit thirsty and could use something to drink."

She poured some ice water into my cup and handed it to me. As I was drinking the water down, the nurse told me that she had stepped in to check on me an hour earlier.

She said, "Mr. Farnsworth, you were mumbling and talking to someone in your sleep."

"I wasn't cussing, was I?" I replied.

The nurse laughed and said that she couldn't understand what I was saying but said that I was in a deep conversation with somebody. The nurse told me that a nurse heard a patient saying a series of numbers. The nurse played the numbers and won ten thousand on Cash 3. I told her if she hears me spouting some numbers, she had better split the winnings with me.

"I sure will, Mr. Farnsworth, right after I pay my car off."

We both laughed as she was just finishing taking my blood pressure and temperature reading. The nurse told me that she would be back to check on me as she was walking out of the room. I thought to myself, it was a good thing I was mumbling and not speaking clearly enough for anyone to listen in on the conversation that I was having with someone on the other side of the fence.

I began to reflect on the content of the conversation in my dream. Grandfather told me as long as I keep asking for something to stop the pain, the doctor will keep me here and do a battery of tests on me. Grandfather didn't come right out and tell me to man up. He said that I won't need any injections after the test tomorrow. I understand what grandfather is implying. He didn't have to say it, my body is healing itself and I need to get the fuck out of this hospital.

I grabbed the bed safety rail and pulled myself up, sitting up in the bed. I was testing the range of movement to the level of pain that I had been experiencing. The pain wasn't at a level that it impaired my movement. Here I am, sitting up in the bed, just one day after a bullet passed straight through me. The doctor told me the bullet nicked my heart and passed to the edge of my spinal column. According to him, I was within a fraction of an inch from taking a dirt nap. I grabbed the guardrail and eased myself back down into the bed.

I got the television remote and began to flip through the channels again, hoping that something would be on worth watching. I finally found a good movie to watch. Even though I had seen it before, just one more time won't hurt. I've got nothing else to do. The movie is *Pulp Fiction*, one of Tarantino's best works. After watching the movie, I was thirsty and poured myself some ice water. I flipped over to the weather channel to see what time it was, and it was already around eight o'clock. It won't be long before the sun goes down.

Back in Georgia, it would be eleven o'clock at night. The crickets and cicadas would be in full chorus in a presummer serenade. Nicole and I liked sitting outside on the patio after the heat of the day had surrendered to the cooler, tranquil sounds of a spring night in Georgia. That time we had together is now only a memory to reflect upon. I wonder if Nicole's family is going ahead with her burial before I get out of the hospital. I wouldn't hold it against them if they did. It has to be tough burying your only child.

I flipped through the channels and watched a few old retired TV shows that have found a new life on TV land. Time moves so slowly while you're awake and flies by while you're asleep; at least it seems that way. In another hour, it will be time for an injection. I'll see if they bring it on schedule or if I have to request it in order to get it. I continued to watch television, and an hour went by, and there was no nurse with the injection. So it appears the injection is administered only if the patient needs it, or perhaps my timing could be off.

I suddenly started getting hungry. I wonder if the nurse can bring me some gelatin or something. I can forget about going to sleep once a hunger urge hits me. Television makes things even tougher by showing food-related commercials. They are always showing stuff that you take for granted until you can't have them. I feel like I could eat two double-meat burgers with cheese, an order of fries, and a chocolate milk shake. I hit the call button to the nurses' station.

A nurse replied by saying, "Yes, Mr. Farnsworth, can I help you?"

I said, "Can I have some gelatin or soup? I won't able to go sleep without this hunger pain being satisfied."

The nurse told me that she would round up some gelatin for me, and I thanked her. I kept on watching television and contemplated the possibility that my body is healing itself at a faster-than-normal rate. The hunger is part of the process, like fuel for the engine. About ten minutes or so, an attractive young nurse comes into the room with a tray. On the tray were two small cups of orange gelatin and a syringe.

The nurse said, "I'll wait for you to eat your gelatin because if I give you the injection now, you won't be awake long enough to finish the gelatin."

I told her thanks for the gelatin. I peeled off the top and inhaled them.

The nurse said, "You weren't joking around about being hungry, were you, Mr. Farnsworth?"

I chuckled and told her that these food commercials aren't helping matters at all. She told me that if I continue to improve, it won't be long before I'll be back eating fast food again. She walked over and injected the medication into the IV port.

"Good night, Mr. Farnsworth, now that you've had something to eat and the injection to help you relax."

I again told her thanks for taking care of me as she was on her way out of the room. I flipped the channels on the remote to look for something relaxing and found a program about the ocean. I turned the volume down to a setting that I could still hear it and lowered the angle of the bed a little. I could feel the tingling in my arm as the medication was flowing into my bloodstream. It wasn't long before I was having a hard time focusing on the television.

My eyelids began to get heavier to the point of total submission to the drug. I found myself in a state of relaxation, and it wasn't long before I was now in a café setting in dreamland. It was one of those roadside cafés that had a retro look about it, you know, lots of chrome and bright colors and a jukebox at each table. Something about the scene looked familiar. I couldn't put my finger on it. While I was sitting at a table facing the main entrance, the waitress came up and asked me what I wanted to order. I told her a burger, fries, and a cola. She wrote it down on her order pad and walked away.

To my left, sitting at the bar next to the cash register, an older blind man was eating as his Seeing Eye dog sat patiently at his feet, looking at me. I looked to my right at the window, but there was nothing to see but pitch-blackness. I turned around to survey the scenery behind me, and there were only two empty tables. I looked back to my left; the dog was stilling staring me. I grabbed the menu from the holder attached to the jukebox. I looked at the items on the menu to pass the time until the waitress brought me my order. I looked up from reviewing the menu, and the waitress was standing at the end of the table with my order.

I told the waitress, "That is what I call fast service."

She replied by saying, "It's a slow night, not many customers."

She walked away, and I started eating my burger. I unfurled the silverware from the napkin wrappings and placed the butter knife on the table. As I was biting into a juicy burger, the entrance door opened, and in walked two people. A man and a woman approached the cash register being manned by the manager. I kept eating and watched as the event began to unfold.

The man pulls out a gun and tells the manager to empty the cash register, and at the same time, the woman takes out a gun and tells the cook and the waitress to sit down at the bar by the cash register. The woman points her gun at them as they hand over their valuables. The female robber puts the night's take into her purse. The male robber tells the female robber to watch the people at the bar as he walks toward me. My hand is very close to the only weapon at hand, a damn butter knife.

The male robber kept on walking closer and said, "Who brings a knife to a gunfight?"

I said, "Who's fighting? I'm trying to get something eat."

The male robber gets even closer to me and aimed his gun at me. All the while, I was sizing up the situation. I waited for the guy to move a little bit closer to me. I quickly grabbed his gun hand and forced it down on the table and pinned his arm to the table with the butter knife with my right hand. The female robber was squeezing off rounds at me as I wrangled the gun from the screaming male robber. I put two slugs in her, and she hit the floor. The male robber was reaching into his jacket for something, and I put a round in him. The robbers had expired, and I'm looking around in the restaurant to see if anyone else got shot in the crossfire. The blind man and his Seeing Eye dog were okay. The waitress, cook, and manager were looking at me and pointing. I looked down at the front of my shirt; there was blood leaking out some obvious bullet holes.

The blind man remained sitting, looking straight forward at the wall behind the bar, and asked, "Did the robbers get taken out?"

The Seeing Eye dog replied, "The robbers got taken care of. I knew they were trouble when them punks came in here. Dirty Harry over there took care of business."

The waitress said, "Mister, are you okay? Do you want me to call an ambulance?"

The Seeing Eye dog said, "He's all right. They should've known better than fuck with him anyway. Besides that, he can't be taken out like that."

The blind man said, "You're getting stronger, James. Most people would have succumbed to the fact that they are done for. Not you, you embraced the moment and took the initiative not to give up."

I said, "Who are you, and how do you know my name?"

The blind man said, "My identity is not important, but you probably have an idea. I know you want revenge for the killing of your Nicole."

The dog chimed in by saying, "How did it feel to drop these two fools? It felt good, didn't it?"

The blind man snatched on the dog's leash and told him to be quiet.

I said, "I don't understand what's going on, seems that everyone is in on the deal except for me."

A voice from behind me said, "Why don't you tell him the deal, tell him that you planted the shooting in Serlinni's head, and Nicole got killed because she was there. Go ahead and tell him."

I turned to see a man dressed in a tan tailored suit sitting in the booth behind me.

"I didn't make Serlinni do anything. Serlinni is just a bad seed that was allowed to grow," exclaimed the blind man.

The stranger in the tan suit said to me, "You do realize who the blind man is, don't you?"

I said, "My first guess is that the blind man is Satan by the look of the tortoise shell Wayfarer shades he is wearing. Plus the robbers that came in didn't try to shake him down."

The blind man, the devil in disguise, said, "That's very perceptive of you, James. I have been watching you since you were a child."

After he said that, he removed his glasses and revealed two lava-orange eyes and simply disappeared.

The stranger in the tan suit said, "The dark one was testing two things. He wanted to see how quick the killer instinct in you reacted to a given situation, and he wanted to see if one of us showed up to keep him at bay."

I said, "You are telling me that Satan—I mean, the dark one staged this as an experiment?"

The stranger in the tan suit said, "The dark one knows he has a brief window of opportunity, a matter of a few days before your powers will surface. The dark one knows that when you learn how to harness it, he will lose his ability to try and influence you. Though he may try to put stumbling blocks in front you in your conscious life, you'll be able to see it as it happens and be able to react to it. Let's call it advanced intuition for now. You'll need to steer clear of the powerful drug that they are administering to you that your grandfather had told you about. The drug weakens your mental constitution. Your constitution is akin to a computer firewall. If the constitution is compromised, you become susceptible to outside influence, like a computer virus. The dark one is the first virus, so to speak."

I said, "So in a few days from now, it won't matter because I'll be immortal, right?"

The stranger in the tan suit said, "Yes, and if you are wondering what you saw in your hospital room for just a brief moment, it was one of my field agents letting you know that your message was received. You won't need any more of the drug. Tell the nurse that the pain is gone and that the medication is making you groggy during your waking hours and clouding your ability to think clearly. The doctors won't find anything medically wrong with you once the test results are in tomorrow. They won't have a reason to keep you unless you tell them that you are hurting. You won't have any pain once you wake up in the coming morning."

I then asked the stranger in the tan suit, "Why was I chosen instead of someone else?"

The stranger in the tan suit said, "You were born into this situation, it has been your destiny."

I asked the stranger in the tan suit, "Just what is my destiny?"

The stranger said, "Your destiny can be used for good as long as you don't agree to any terms that the dark one promises. Otherwise, if you are swayed by his lies, neither I nor the upper management will be able to help you."

I said, "Why is the dark one so interested in me?"

The stranger said, "You are an indirect product that the dark one created. I'm not talking about your grandfather but the first of its kind."

As I was asking what the stranger meant by not my grandfather but the first of its kind, a nurse came in and woke me by saying good morning. I awoke looking at a young fresh-out-of-school nurse.

The nurse said, "Mr. Farnsworth, they are about to get ready to take you to MRI for testing. I know it's early, but if everything goes well, you may get to go home soon."

"I sure hope so," I replied.

Two big male orderlies came into the room pushing a gurney. One orderly pushed a button to lower the safety rail, and the other orderly unclipped the catheter and placed the IV bag in a rack. The orderly told me to get ready to slide from my bed to the gurney.

I said, "Before you guys grab the sheet, let me try and move over to the gurney myself."

One orderly said, "Okay, Mr. Farnsworth, but at the first sign of pain, we'll have to take over."

I said, "Okay, here goes."

I sat up in the bed and slid from the bed to the gurney. The orderlies were pleased that they didn't have to manhandle me so early in the morning. The orderlies put the side rails up on the gurney, placed a sheet on me, and proceeded to push down the corridor. There was a lot of activity going on, I guess because people were just starting the day, and I caught the aroma of coffee in the air. I was still kind of groggy from the aftereffects of the drug, watching row upon row of fluorescent lighting passing overhead. I could hear the ding-ing sound of the elevator as it stopped at its destination. The gurney stopped, and an orderly pushed the gurney into the elevator. A guy with a lab coat was standing in the elevator and asked the orderly what floor, and the orderly told him the first floor. The guy in the lab coat pressed a button on the control panel, and the door closed, and the elevator began to descend. I started thinking about what the stranger in the tan suit had told me. He said that I was an indirect product created by the dark one, and my grandfather is not from whence it started from whatever it is that I suppose to become in a matter of days. I guess I'll have to do the same thing that I'm doing on this gurney; that's ride it out.

The elevator would stop at each floor as we made it to the first floor. The guy with the lab coat held the elevator door with his hand until the gurney cleared. The orderly told the lab-coat guy thanks as he pushed the gurney toward its destination. There was a lot of activ-ity, people moving up and down the hallway. I lay back and watched the fluorescent lights as I passed under them. I caught the whiff of coffee and doughnuts as we passed a group of nurses huddled at the intersection of the hallway.

The orderly turns the gurney to the left and tells me that we are almost there. The gurney slows down and stops at the door on the left. The orderly tells me that he will be back to get me when they finish. He goes into a small office; I guess to tell someone that I'm out here to get something done. The odor of the coffee and dough-nuts smelled like an absolute treasure just waiting to be dug up and savored. I'm so hungry that I could eat a whole dozen glazed dough-nuts and a pot of coffee to wash it down. I guess it's the little things we miss the most once when we can't have them at the moment. The orderly tells me that the X-ray technician is going to take care of me and that he would see me later.

I said, "Okay, and don't forget to come back to get me. I don't think I can drive this thing under the influence."

The orderly chuckled and pointed toward the person walking up to the gurney.

An attractive young woman said, "Good morning, Mr. Farnsworth, my name is Jade, and I'll be taking a series of views of you with the MRI. I have to ask you, do you have on any jewelry, a pacemaker, or a plate in your head?"

I said, "I don't have any metal on or in me as far as I know."

Jade said, "That's good. Let's get the show on the road."

She pushed the gurney into the room where the MRI machine was. She locked the brake on the gurney wheels and told me she is going to get an orderly to move me onto the MRI table. She walked out of the room and was gone for a brief moment then arrived with reinforcement. The petite technician came in with a young black man. He was about six five and could probably bench-press a '72 Buick. The petite tech grabbed the catheter and the IV bag as the orderly reached over the MRI table to grab the sheet that I'm lying on. The orderly told me, on the count of three, he is going to pull the sheet and me on it over on to the MRI table.

The orderly said, "Sir, are you ready?"

"Yes," I replied.

He said, "One, two, three," and pulled me right onto the MRI table.

I didn't even hear the guy grunt. Evidently, the guy has per-formed such procedures many times. The technician had gotten the pillow off the gurney and placed it under my head.

The tech. said, "I know the MRI platform isn't as comfortable as your bed, but hopefully I can capture some good images for the doctor so that he'll let you out of here."

"I'm in agreement with finding some good images," I replied.

Jade said that she is going to start up the machine and for me to just need to relax. The machine started whirring as the sound of the magnets began gathering speed like a large-scale centrifuge. The technician told me that the table will gradually move into the magnetic field that is in the center of the rotation. She asked me to lie perfectly still and to take slow, even breaths. I closed my eyes and began to slow down my breathing.

I pondered about the comment made by the messenger in the tan suit. Just what was the messenger talking about? The first of its kind? Was he talking about the first human immortal? The messenger said that I am an indirect product stemmed from the dark one. An indirect product? Is that like a Japanese car made in America but indirectly tied back to Japan?

Before I could ponder any deeper into this subject, the sound of the machine had changed. The sound of the rotating magnets was slowing, and the whirring noise was fading. The technician walked up to the side of the table on which I was lying and told me to rest for a moment while the doctor reviews the images. I simply complied. I am at the mercy of the moment. The technician returned to the control room and waited for the doctor to review the images captured by the MRI scan. I lay there thinking about dreading the inevitable—facing Nicole's parents. I don't know when Nicole's funeral will occur and if I'll be out of here in time to attend it. Whether I get to make it to her funeral or not, I'll still have to confront them. I can't come right out and tell them their daughter got caught in the cross fire of a failed mob hit. I don't have any proof to substantiate it. I can only imagine the pain they must be going through. My heart aches with the loss, but it fails in comparison to a parents' loss of their child—their only child.

As I lay on the MRI table as a barrage of thoughts ran through my mind, one solitary word came to the forefront of the jumbled thoughts—*retribution*. I wasn't thinking of such a word. I'm not even sure what it means. Time ticked away, and the technician finally came from the control room.

She said, "Mr. Farnsworth, I'm going to get an orderly to help get you back on to the gurney so you can get back into your bed."

I asked her if the doctor had found anything of concern. The technician simply told me that she isn't permitted to divulge information, but she leaned in to me and whispered "You're fine." As she walked toward the door, she said that my doctor would be visiting me this morning. I thanked her as she left the room. She returned within a few minutes with an older man, he's probably the guy that reads the scan and writes up. The findings for the doctor. The orderly was certainly big enough to handle the task of pulling me back onto the gurney while the nurse placed the catheter on the gurney along with the IV bag. The orderly placed the sheet back on me and proceeded forward, pushing the gurney back to the elevator, back to the ICU and my bed.

The orderly helped me back into my bed, and I thanked him as he was exiting with the gurney. I grabbed the television remote and turned the TV back on. According to the time, it is 8:45 a.m., I've probably missed the breakfast cart. To make matters worse, just about every channel I stopped on was showing food-related commercials. As I continued to flip through the channels, a hefty-sized nurse came in carrying a tray with her.

The nurse said, "Good morning, Mr. Farnsworth. I'm here to remove your catheter. You will feel some discomfort, but it will pass."

I said, "There goes any remnants of my dignity out of the window."

The nurse chuckled and said, "It's okay, Mr. Farnsworth. I've seen it all. Besides, there is no one in here but us."

She told me that she had to deflate the small balloon that holds the catheter in place, and she would let me know when she is about to remove it. She put on a pair of surgical gloves and had placed a small plastic pan under my penis and said, "All right, Mr. Farnsworth, I'm going to pull the catheter out. You will feel some pain, but it won't last."

89

She had placed one hand on my penis and the other on the plastic and began to pull. As the tube was being extracted, it felt like she was pulling a truck through that small hole with the doors open. I started breathing again after the tube came out. What a relief. The nurse got me cleaned up from the residual urine that had splashed on me. The nurse then took the plastic tube and threw it in the trash can, removed her surgical gloves, and put on another pair. She walked over to the other side of my bed and told me that she was going to remove the IV from my arm and the drainage tube from my side. The nurse cleaned up the area and put a butter fly bandage on it.

I said, "This looks promising. Does this mean I'll be getting some breakfast?"

The nurse told me that she is only aware of the cath and IV removal and would check to see if my diet had been changed. After she removed the IV, wiped the wound with alcohol, and threw the IV bag along with the tube into the trash can, she walked over to my bed and asked me if I felt like sitting up on the side of the bed. I told her that I was so hungry that if I didn't have this backless gown on, I would walk to the nearest hamburger joint for the biggest, greasiest hamburger that they had. The nurse told me to take this one step at a time and I would be able to get the biggest, greasiest hamburger available. She lowered the safety rail on the left of me and told me to pull myself up slowly by grabbing on to the safety rail on the right of me. I had done this before and pulled myself up slowly. I slid my legs over to where they would hang off the bed. She asked me if I felt dizzy. I told her no, only slight pain in my back.

She then asked me, "Do you feel the urge to urinate?"

"I kinda, sorta feel the urge," I replied.

The nurse then asked me if I felt like walking to the bathroom. I told her that I would give it the old college try. I carefully slid down the edge of the bed until my feet touched the cold tiled floor.

The nurse stepped closer to me and said, "Let me know if you start feeling woozy, okay?"

I told her that I felt fine and took some slow steps toward the bathroom. With each step, the pain seemed to decrease from pain to a tingling sensation. I finally made it to the toilet and was able to stand up and urinate normally again. At some point I was feeling weak, but now, I feel the hunger pangs getting stronger. My body was demanding fuel for energy. I walked back to the bed and sat down on the edge of the mattress.

The nurse said, "Are you feeling okay, Mr. Farnsworth?"

I told her that I felt a little dizzy and that I felt kind of weak. She told me that I could still be feeling the effects of the sedative that was still in my system plus the fact that my stomach didn't have any solid food in it to make energy. She told me to lie back down in the bed, and hopefully the doctor will be in to see me and write some orders for solid food. I complied with her suggestion and lay back down. She picked up the pitcher and checked inside to see if there was any ice in it. She said that she would go and get me some ice in the pitcher, and I could at least have that can of ginger ale that I had saved from last night. The nurse took the plastic water pitcher and left the room. It probably won't be long before Mom and Grandmother will be in here to see what's going on.

Within a few minutes, the nurse came in with the pitcher. She put ice in the cup, poured the ginger ale into it, and handed it to me. I looked at her name tag, and it had Sharris Jones on it.

I said, "Thank you, Ms. Jones, for taking care of me."

Nurse Jones replied by saying, "If there were more people like you, Mr. Farnsworth, that say thank you, it would make my job even more tolerable."

"Gratitude goes a long way, doesn't it," I replied.

Nurse Jones said, "Amen to that, Mr. Farnsworth," as she walked out of the room.

I grabbed the cup of ginger ale and slugged it down like a man dying of thirst. I poured the remaining amount of ginger ale from the can into the cup, downing every ounce, and started eating ice. As I was crunching down on the ice, the doctor walked in with a nurse in tow.

The doctor said, "Good morning, Mr. Farnsworth, how are you feeling since you got up and walked to the bathroom this morning?"

"Besides being hungry and a little weak, I'm okay, considering somebody tried to kill me," I replied.

The doctor told me that he reviewed the MRI images and was glad to report that he saw no damage to my central nervous system and that my heart isn't showing any sign of seepage. He said that I was a walking miracle. He asked me if I experienced any pain in my back as I was walking. I told him that I was experiencing some tingling sensations. He told me that the bullet grazed the nerve endings that extend out from my spine and that he'll give me a referral to a doctor in Atlanta if I start experiencing pain in a week or two. He said that he is going to prescribe some anti-inflammatory medication and mild painkillers to take when I get home.

I said, "Let me guess, are you releasing me today?"

The doctor told me that he is releasing me today but told me that he wants me to take it easy, eat light for a couple of days, and gradually go to the cheeseburgers. He also told me to take a week off from work and not rush things.

The doctor said, "Do you have any questions before I go?"

"Can I have some breakfast? I'm starving."

The doctor chuckled and turned to the nurse that was with him and told her to get me a light breakfast. The nurse left the room, leaving the doctor there with me. I asked the doctor if there will be any long-term effects in years to come because of the injury. He told me that nerve damage can occur in different degrees of injury. The injury can produce immediate and visible damage, and in my case, the injury was minimal. Even though the bullet brushed the heart muscle and the edge of my spinal column, he said that the bullet entered and exited at such an angle that had the angle been a half a degree either way, I could've been dead or paralyzed. While he was talking to me, he was writing my prescriptions.

The nurse came back with a covered tray. The aroma of coffee was present. Ah yes, the morning elixir. The nurse set the tray onto the table and pushed the table over to me. Before I dove into the food, I held my hand out to the doctor to shake his hand. The doctor shook my hand, and I told him that I owed him a mountain of gratitude for the work that he did. The doctor told me that he was just doing his job and told me that I would be able to sign myself out at the nurses' station once my folks come to get me. He then told me good luck and that I could get the stitches removed by my family doctor in about seven to ten days as he walked out of the room.

I removed the cover to reveal a bowl of grits, scrambled eggs, toast, jelly, orange juice, and coffee. I put the packets of sugar and cream into the coffee; the coffee was the only thing that was warm. I didn't care. I put salt and pepper on the grits and eggs and devoured it. Mom and Grandmother walked in as I was putting jelly on the toast.

Grandmother said, "Are they moving you out of the ICU?"

"Better than that, the doctor is releasing me today," I replied.

My mom walked over to me and grabbed my hand. She had that look about her, the look that someone has when they have to tell you something but are reluctant.

I asked her, "What's wrong now?"

She said, "Nicole's father called me last night and said that Nicole's funeral is today at 11:00 a.m. He said that Nicole's mother has had to be drugged ever since she found out that she was dead. He didn't know how long you would be in the hospital, and he had to literally drag her away from the funeral home. Nicole's mother is not wanting to give up her daughter to the ground."

I told Mom that I understand, that her parents are going through what could have easily been our family instead of Nicole's. I looked at the time on the television, and it had 8:45 a.m. There is no way that I could get signed out, arrange a flight, and get back to Georgia in time to make it to the funeral. I asked Mom if she would mind getting my clothes from her hotel room so that we all can get back to Georgia. I'll make a call with the air charter in Macon to see if a flight can be arranged from here. If there isn't a possibility of getting a charter back today, we could fly back to Atlanta on a commercial flight tomorrow.

Grandmother said, "James, there is no use in trying to rush back home today. You already know we can't get there in time for Nicole's funeral, and I know it's tearing you up inside because of it. It will be better if you approach Nicole's parents the day after the funeral than the day of the funeral. Believe me, it tore me up losing my only child, your father, to cancer. Though your father was over sixty, he was still my little boy. To lose a child at any age is tough on a parent, but it is extra hard on the heartstrings to lose a child at a young age."

I said, "I guess you are right because their friends and family will be coming and going in out their house all day today, and they won't have much time for themselves with all of that going on. I just feel like I have been robbed twice by fate."

Mom told me that she is going back to the hotel and get my clothes so that I'll be able to check out of the hospital at least, and when she gets back, we can work on the next move. Mom said that she would be back and that Grandmother could stay with me while she was gone. I told her that I didn't like the idea of her traveling alone. She assured me that she would be all right and that she didn't want to wear Grandmother down going back and forth.

She said, "Besides, the hotel is only about six blocks away from the hospital. I won't be gone that long."

She hugged me and walked out of the room. Grandmother had gotten the chair from the corner of the room and dragged it closer to the bed. She walked over to entrance of my room and closed the door. She walked back to the chair and sat down.

She said, "I know you have questions, and it isn't safe to talk about the sensitive information here. I don't want someone to walk in and hear any part of the conversation, so let's save the question-and-answer session until we can be in a secure setting."

I said, "You have to answer one thing, and I won't go any further.

She said, "Okay, just one and that's it."

I then said, "What really killed Grandfather?"

"Ingestion of colloidal silver," she replied.

Before I could reply with a comeback, there was a knock at the door. I said, "Come in."

In walked two guys. I recognized them as the detectives that had visited me a couple of days ago. As the men drew closer, one of the detectives said, "The reason that we are here, Mr. Farnsworth, is that we have a copy of the video footage of a person of interest leaving out the fire escape stairs that opens into the parking garage. My colleague will run the footage on the laptop that he has."

The other detective opened up his laptop and ran the program for me to see the image. The footage showed a guy exiting from the fire escape stairs, but I didn't recognize him. The lead detective asked me if I recognized the man in the video footage. I told them that I had never seen the man before. I asked them if his face had come up in any police records. The detectives told me that they had given the file data to the federal bureau to look in their database to see if anything comes up. I told the detectives that I appreciate all of their effort to bring the criminal to justice that killed my Nicole. I told them that my bullet wound will heal, but the loss of my fiancée will never heal. They assured me that they would stay in touch with me in further developments once I get back home. They had talked to my doctor and found out that I am to be released today. The detectives each gave me their business cards and thanked me for my time and walked out of the room.

Grandmother looked at me and said, "You see what I mean? There's no privacy in here." She leaned closer to me and whispered, "We'll talk more later."

Grandmother sat down in the chair and told me that I didn't have to eat that hospital food. If I could hold on a little longer, we could get something to eat at a restaurant after I get checked out from the hospital. My mind was reeling with the notion that the word *silver* implicated, as my grandmother was conversing with me to steer me off subject. I asked Grandmother how old she was when she met and married my grandfather.

Grandmother said, "I think I was at least twenty-one years old. In those days people married at much younger years, and my parents wanted me to get an education first, then a career, and then settle down. Luckily, your great-grandfather didn't believe in banks, and it was a good thing. If he had put the money that he had been saving in the bank all those years of farming before I was born, the stock market crash of 1929 would have wiped him out. A lot of people weren't so lucky. I remember hearing my mother saying that even though the family wasn't lacking, they still couldn't show extravagance in their lifestyle. It would draw unneeded attention from robbers. Your great-grandfather on your father's side didn't trust the banks either.

He was a witness to what occurred before and after the Civil War. People now do not have any concept of living off the land. The majority wouldn't fare so well simply because things are just too easy, and in their minds, hard work is for migrant workers."

Before Grandmother started really throwing off on the gimme generation, Mom walked in with my luggage retrieved from the motel that Nicole and I were shot in.

She put the luggage at the side of the bed and said, "I checked through your luggage to see if you had another pair of shoes, and there wasn't."

"I'll wear those lounge slippers, and it won't bother me a bit as long as I'm out of here," I replied.

I told them to wait outside the door so that I could get out of this hospital gown and into a proper pair of pants.

"I'll let you two know once I get my pants on, then you can come back in," I explained to them.

Mom and Grandmother walked out of the room and shut the door behind them. I opened the luggage, got some underwear, a pair of jeans, and some socks. I took off the hospital gown and slid on my underwear and jeans. I went to the door and told Mom and Grandmother to come back in. I told them that it takes a pair of underwear and jeans to make a man feel normal again. They came in and waited patiently for me to finish getting dressed, and I packed up the remaining of my belongings back into the luggage. I picked up the prescriptions from the table that the doctor had written and put them in the luggage. I asked Mom if she had my wallet. She took it from her purse and handed it to me. I opened it, and my driver's license and my debit card were the only things left.

Mom said, "Remember, I called the bank and had the traveler's checks canceled."

I told her thanks for taking care of that for me. Mom handed me the pair of lounge slippers.

I said, "I'm taking off the socks. That would be a fashion faux pas."

Grandmother said, "I know what you mean. I've seen people wear socks and flip-flops. How hideous is that?"

We combed over the room for anything that I'm forgetting. Everything seemed to be in order. I grabbed the luggage and was scolded by Mom.

She said, "Don't do that. You could bust a stitch."

She took the luggage, and we walked to the nurses' station. I approached the nurses' counter and told the attending nurse who I was.

She said, "Oh yes, Mr. Farnsworth, let me get the release form for you."

She walked over to the other end of the counter and came back with a clipboard and an ink pen.

"Here you go, Mr. Farnsworth. Sign on the bottom line and today's date, May 16," said the nurse.

I signed and dated the document. The nurse told me because of hospital policy that I'll need to be transported by wheelchair to the hospital exit. She went to the phone and paged an orderly to the nurses' station. Within a couple of minutes, an orderly showed up, and the nurse instructed him to retrieve a wheelchair and to take me downstairs to the main hospital exit. I asked Mom about our means of transportation. She said that she only has to call the hotel concierge, and the hotel will send over a vehicle to pick us up. Mom took out her cell phone and called the hotel and made arrangements for us to be picked up. Mom told us the hotel van will be here in ten minutes at the main entrance. The orderly went down the hallway and came back with a wheelchair.

The orderly said, "Have a seat, Mr. Farnsworth, and I'll get you to your next destination."

I sat down into the wheelchair and told Mom to put the luggage in my lap so that she wouldn't have to carry it.

Mom said, "It's not that heavy, I can manage."

We proceeded to the elevators and waited for the elevator to stop at our floor.

CHAPTER 6

Finally, the bell dinged, signaling that the elevator has arrived on our floor, and the doors opened. We had to wait until an orderly pushing an elderly gentleman on a gurney had exited the elevator. We boarded the elevator, and the orderly reached over and punched the button for the first floor. As the elevator descended, I began to think about what actually killed my grandfather. Grandmother told me that it was colloidal silver. According to Hollywood, silver is the only thing that can kill a werewolf. That's it, I'm going to change into a werewolf on my birthday. If my grandfather was a werewolf, how come there weren't any gruesome murders occurring in our small town? I didn't get to delve too deep in thought when we had reached the first floor. The orderly pushed me past the main information desk and toward the main entrance.

I said, "I hope the van will be out there. It's too hot to be sitting on the sidewalk."

The orderly told me that there is a staging area for patient departures, and it is air-conditioned. We went through a set of automatic doors that opened into another room with a panoramic array of windows that gives a view of the pickup area. Luck would be on our side; by the time we had arrived into the center of the staging area, a burgundy van that had the Hampton Inn logo on it pulled up.

I looked at Mom, and she said, "Our chariot awaits us."

The orderly pushed me through another set of automatic doors and down the ramp toward the courtesy van. Grandmother said that once we get back to the hotel, we have something from room service sent up.

Something had occurred to me, and I asked Mother, "Does anyone from the studio know where you and Grandmother are staying?"

Mother said, "Tim Jackson knows where we are staying. Why?"

I said that I would explain to her once we get back to the hotel. Luckily, the ride back to the Hampton Inn wasn't far. The van stopped at the front entrance, and we got my luggage and headed inside. We walked into the hotel lobby, and I pulled Mom and Grandmother to the side and explained to them that we all could be in danger.

I said, "I'm not sure, but there could be someone inside the operations of the studio that could be dirty. By dirty, I mean someone could be being paid by Serlinni about our whereabouts. So for everyone's safety, let's check out of this hotel, let's rent a car just for today, and turn it in tomorrow at the airport. That is providing we can get a flight out tomorrow."

I told them that I don't know if Tim is an informant or not, but at this point no one is above suspicion.

Mom asked me, "What makes you think someone at the studio is dirty?"

"I got a call from Serlinni himself telling me to have a good time in Arizona," I replied.

I followed Mom and Grandmother as they led me to their room. I told Mom to give me the passkey and let me check the room out. I pushed the passkey card into the electronic door lock, and it released the lock. I opened the door and walked through each room, checked the bathroom, the closets, and under the bed. The room was clear of any bad guys. I told Mom and Grandmother to get their things packed up, and I would call the concierge to see about arranging for a rental car. I got on the room phone and dialed the concierge desk.

A guy answered and said, "This is the concierge desk. Can I help you?"

I asked him if it was possible to rent a car at the hotel. He told me that there is a car rental service in the lobby, and he gave me the number so that I could call them to see if they had a car available. I thanked the concierge, hung up the phone, and dialed the car rental number while it was fresh in my memory. When I first dialed the number, I got a recording saying, "All of our salespeople are busy. Please hold." I listened to some real elevator-type music while waiting for a real person to pick up.

Finally, a voice from a real person came over the receiver, "Hertz Rental, can I help you?"

I said, "I hope you can. Do you have a vehicle available for rental for at least two days?"

The lady at the car rental place asked me if I wanted an economy model or premium. I told her that I needed a vehicle that a senior citizen can get in and out of easily. She told me that she had a Chrysler 300 available. I told her that I would be right down to do the necessary paperwork, and I thanked her as I hung up the phone.

I said, "Okay, ladies, I have us a car reserved. Are you two packed and ready to relocate?"

In the back of my mind, I wasn't afraid for myself but for their safety. Mom and Grandmother produced two pieces of luggage each, and they were ready to go.

I called downstairs at the desk and requested a luggage cart to come to our room. The lady at the desk told me that someone would be right up. I thanked her and hung up the phone. We didn't have to wait too long before there was a knock at the door. I went to the door, and it was a guy with the luggage cart. I thanked the guy for coming on up, and I looked to Mom, and she handed the guy a five-dollar tip. The luggage was loaded onto the cart, and the man asked the women if they had everything. Mom made one last sweep from room to room and checked the cabinets and dressers. Mom told me that the room is clear.

The bellhop pushed the cart toward the elevator, and we got aboard. I could feel the anger build inside me just thinking about someone that works for me had sold out. Tim Jackson would be the one, if it is him, to reap the benefits. He knows the technical side of the business. I've got to get my mom and grandmother to a safer place so that I can think and get a flight back home.

The elevator reached the first floor, and I went to the concierge desk to see if the hotel could arrange for a van to drop us off at a car rental. The concierge told me that there is a van out front, and he asked me the name of the rental place. He called the van driver and gave him instructions. We got loaded into the van and were off to the car rental location just a few blocks from the hotel. We unloaded the van and walked inside the rental place. I could feel the heat of the day coming, and I needed to get these women out this heat. I walked up to the counter and was met by an attractive young lady. I introduced myself and told her that it was me that called a few moments ago about an available vehicle. She asked me how long I would need the vehicle and where I was going. I told her that at the most I would need it for today and probably turn it in tomorrow, depending on what time our flight out will be. The car rental desk clerk said that they have a four-door Chrysler 300 that is a lot easier to get in and out of for my grandmother.

I asked her, "Would I be able to turn the car in at the airport?"

And she told me, "That isn't a problem because there is a Hertz rental service there also."

I said, "That is perfect. I guess you need my driver's license and proof of insurance."

The desk clerk said, "It sounds like you've done this before, sir."

I told her that I've had ample experience at this. I gave her my license and insurance card, and she entered it into the computer.

She asked me, "Will this be a cash or credit card purchase?"

I handed the lady my card. The desk clerk entered in the information and asked us what color we wanted. They had a black 300 and a red 300.

I looked at Grandmother, and she said, "Let's get the red one."

The clerk said, "Here's your paperwork. You have unlimited mileage, and just fill the car with fuel before you turn it in, and here are the keys."

I asked her where the car was parked, and she told me that she would get the hotel courtesy van to take us to the lot on the backside of the hotel property. She said to hold on for just a moment so that she could find out the availability of the courtesy van. As she was dialing the phone, I turned and saw Mom and the baggage handler walking this way. The desk clerk put the phone down and said that the courtesy will be pulling up to main entrance in a matter of minutes. She thanked us for our business and told us to have a nice time in Flagstaff. I thanked her, and we met up with Mom and the baggage handler and headed for the main exit.

We made it through the last set of automatic doors, and to my surprise, the courtesy van was sitting there waiting for us. The baggage handler loaded up the van, and Mom paid him a tip.

As we settled down in our seats, the driver of the van said, "Is this the first time you've been to Arizona?"

I said, "That is correct, sir, and could you tell us where a good restaurant is?"

The driver said, "It really depends on what you want to eat, whether it's Chinese, Italian, Mexican, or the usual American fare. Once I get you to the rental lot, I'll point you guys in the general direction to where the restaurants are."

"That sounds good to me," I replied.

The van driver put the van into drive, and we were off. We went down about a block from the rental frontage and made a right. I could see the Hertz rental parking lot as we were approaching it. The van slowed down and turned into the car rental property.

The van driver said, "Here we are, folks, and as I promised, I would point you in the direction of a choice of restaurants to choose from. The main road that I just turned off of, if you follow it straight out, the road will carry you straight to your pick of restaurants on both sides of the road."

I thanked the van driver, and he helped unload the baggage. An attendant from the car rental walked up and asked if we were there to pick up the red 300 and asked for the paperwork. I gave him the paperwork to confirm the transaction. The attendant gave the papers back to me and pointed out the location of the car. I told Mom and Grandmother to stay put, and I would get the car and pick them up. I followed the attendant to where the car was, unlocked it with the key, got in, and fired it up. The first thing to do was to crank up the air-conditioning; the heat of summer is on its way. I pulled the car up next to where Mom and Grandmother were and told them to get in while I loaded up the luggage into the trunk of the car. I closed the trunk and got into the driver's seat. Mom was giving me hell for picking up the luggage. Then she tells me to get on the passenger side of the car. I didn't argue, I knew I would hear you just got out of the hospital and you don't need to bust a stitch.

Mom then said, "Put on your seat belts. The last thing I need now is a ticket for not wearing a seat belt."

Mom pulled out of the rental parking lot and out onto the main drag. As she was driving, I looked at the digital clock in the dash, and it had 12:00 p.m. We passed by a couple of fast-food joints, a steak house, a Tex-Mex restaurant. I asked the women did they have a preference of what they wanted to eat. I should've known what was coming. They both said it didn't matter to them, and they wanted me to decide. Up ahead I could see a Red Lobster sign, and I asked them if they were up for some seafood for lunch They agreed on some seafood. I was glad because I was feeling some powerful hunger pangs. Mom pulled in front of the restaurant, I told mom that she and grandmother can get on out, go inside and out of the heat. She wanted to balk, but agreed with my suggestion. I found a parking space, got out, hit the auto lock on the key fob. I noticed at the entrance in front of me, there was a group of young women talking and smoking. One of the ladies was so busy talking, didn't notice the curb as she stepped backward. I was quick enough to catch her before she hit the pavement. The lady I rescued was quite attractive and didn't seem to mind my appearance either. I helped her to stable ground and asked her if she was okay.

"I'm fine, sir, and I'm glad you came along to rescue me. These high-heeled shoes will be the death of me."

She asked if I had lunch yet. I told her that I just dropped my grandmother and my mom off, and they are waiting for me inside.

I said, "You are welcome to eat with us if you like. By the way, my name is James Farnsworth from Byron, Georgia."

The lady said that her name is Jessica Carnes, and she recognized my name.

She said, "I am truly sorry about what happened to your fiancée."

I said, "Can we go inside out of this heat to talk? I was just released from the hospital."

Jessica told the other ladies that she was with that she was going to buy my lunch. I told her that wasn't necessary, but she was more than welcome to break bread with us. As we walked in, I saw Mom and Grandmother sitting on benches in the waiting room.

Mom said, "I was getting worried about you."

I introduced Jessica Carnes to Mom and Grandmother and told them how I met her as I was walking in. The waitress at the sign-in desk asked if we will be adding one more to the party. I replied by saying yes. The waitress led us back to our seating area. I pulled the chair out for Jessica to sit. Grandmother and Mom sat directly across from us. Another waitress came to the table and gave everyone a menu and asked us what we wanted to drink.

I said, "I know what I would like to have, but since I'm fresh out of the hospital, I'll have water."

Everyone else followed suit and got water. The waitress asked if we would like an appetizer, and I told her to bring some cheese sticks. The waitress told us that she would be back with our drinks and place the order of cheese sticks. Before I could get a question in edgewise, my mom asked Jessica what kind of work does she do.

Jessica said, "I'm with the ABI, Arizona Bureau of Investigation. That's how I recognized your name, Mr. Farnsworth."

By the expressions on my mom's and grandmother's face, they were floored.

Grandmother said, "This isn't just a chance meeting James here. You need to tell her about your speculations."

"I don't know if this is a safe place to discuss such sensitive information," I replied.

Jessica said, "That group of people that I was standing with before you saved me from hitting the asphalt are bureau people. They are sitting somewhere in here, and they're all packing plus so am I. So whatever you have to say, don't feel like you have to hold back."

The waitress returned with our water and asked if we had chosen from the menu yet. I asked her if she could give us a few minutes, and she agreed and walked away.

I said, "Before I divulge anything, is your bureau investigating the shooting of me and Nicole?"

She told me that her group is investigating a significant smuggling operation going on. It suddenly became clear to me what the state of Arizona borders close to.

I said, "I get it, the neighbors from south of the border."

I told her about the mob trying to muscle in on my company, various scare tactics, and before Nicole and I left for Flagstaff, the message that the mob boss told me. I then expressed my theory that someone inside my organization is feeding the mobster information on my whereabouts.

"I just got my mom and grandmother out of a hotel that, to my knowledge, only my studio technical manager is aware of. At this point, I cannot trust anyone within my organization that could put any more of my loved ones at risk. I was just released from the hospital about an hour ago, and this will be the first taste of real food since I was shot."

Jessica was simply awestruck from the information. She asked me if I divulged any of this to the police when they asked questions about the shooting.

I said, "I didn't because I don't have any proof that the mob is linked to this, and you know as well as I do, without evidence, it won't hold up in court."

Mom suggested that we decide what to order and then finish the discussion.

Jessica said, "She's right, and it will give me time to put a couple of thoughts together while I look at the menu."

I looked at my menu and already knew what I wanted—the seafood platter. I could eat the menu itself with cocktail sauce on it. I didn't want to turn my head and get caught looking at the ABI agent instead of the menu. Let's say she was real easy on the eyes. Looking out of the corner of my eye at her, I got busted. She was looking up from her menu and saw me. She just smiled.

Jessica said, "James, I bet I know what you are going to order, and it's the seafood platter, isn't it?"

I said, "We have a winner, seafood platter dinner. I'm going to guess that you'll order the shrimp scampi."

Jessica replied by saying, "Winner, winner shrimp scampi dinner."

Mom and Grandmother opted for the shrimp scampi as well. The waitress came back and took down everyone's order and told us that the cheese sticks are almost ready as she walked away.

Jessica said, "Because that you are from out of state and the actual crime occurred here, there will more than likely be a joint-effort involvement, especially concerning organized crime. Could you tell me the name of the crime boss that's involved?"

"His name is Vincent Serlinni," I replied.

She said that she would have to talk to her superiors about this matter, and she advised me not to call anyone back in Georgia to let them know when and how I am coming home.

Jessica said, "I agree with James that it is quite possible that someone inside the studio's organization is an informant to the bad guys. It was good thinking on James's part to get you out of the hotel."

I asked Jessica, "What do I tell my technical manager when he starts asking questions like, where are we staying and when are we flying back? At the same time, I don't want him to think that I'm on to him."

Jessica, without a blink, said, "You call him first and tell him to fly back, look after the operation until you get back. Tell him that the doctor doesn't want you fly just yet because of the three-hour flight, and you're going to stay out here to recuperate."

I told Jessica that Nicole's parents are having her funeral right now. They didn't know how long I was to be hospitalized, plus Nicole's mother wasn't dealing with it too well. Nicole was their only child. I plan on seeing her parents after things calm down. Hopefully we can get a flight out of here tomorrow."

The waitress brought our cheese sticks over to the table and said our orders will be out in a little while.

Jessica said, "Since time is of essence here, I'm going to call my superior now and get his take on this situation. If you'll excuse me, I'll walk outside to make the call on my cell phone."

Jessica got up from the table and walked outside. I looked at my mom and grandmother and said, "Can you two believe what is happening? I am completely astounded by the plausibility that a higher power is in control here."

Mom said, "God works in mysterious ways, and he directed you to the Red Lobster."

Grandmother just smiled and nodded and said that she agreed with what Mom said. She gave me that look that she wanted to say more but not now. The waitress came back with a big tray full of food and began to issue the individual plated orders out. I commented that I hope Jessica doesn't take too long or her food will get cold. No sooner than I said that, Jessica came back to the table.

Jessica sat down, looked at me, and said, "I talked to my boss, and he said that he feels that the Federal Bureau needs to get involved because of the interstate implications involved with organized crime. He feels that you and your family are in danger and that he will contact a field office in Atlanta. In the meantime, let's enjoy our meal, and per my boss, I'm to be your protection while you're in Arizona."

I said, "Before we start eating, I would like to thank the Lord for this food, my family, and sending me an angel in disguise, amen."

Jessica smiled at me and said, "That's nice of you calling me an angel. Some criminals I've put behind bars probably don't think so."

We all chuckled at her comment and began eating. As I was shoveling in the food, I felt a big weight being lifted from my shoulders. I was able to tell someone outside my immediate family about what is going on concerning the mob. And as luck would have it, that someone is an Arizona Bureau of Investigation agent, an attractive one at that. Jessica asked me what hotel we will be staying in. I told her that we had not decided yet. For sure, we won't be staying in the Courtyard, where I was shot, and the Hampton Inn, where Mom and Grandmother were registered. I would much rather get them home, but it appears we'll have to stay tonight somewhere and try to get a commercial flight out. I don't want to run the risk of the assassin trying to find us and make another attempt.

Jessica said, "Let me make a call to see if I can arrange something."

She got up from the table and walked away so she could have some privacy. I continued eating and had almost wiped out the contents of my plate and the last of the cheese sticks.

Jessica came back to the table, sat down, and said, "I talked to my boss, and he said to put you guys up at the Springhill Suites but under a cover name."

I said, "What if the person assigned to the hit pays off the desk clerk to find out whose name was on the charge card that paid for the room?"

Jessica said, "I will pay for the room and get reimbursed for it by the bureau. My boss feels that since the assumed homicide occurred in Arizona, it would give the department a chance to work with the FBI to bring this mobster to justice. He also said that James has an appointment with a federal agent in Atlanta tomorrow at the airport."

I asked Jessica, "Will you be assigned to my case?"

She said, "Probably not, since you are from Georgia and severity of this case, I have already contacted the FBI field office in Atlanta."

She also said because of the nature of the crime and the safety of my family and me that a government-class aircraft will be flying us to Atlanta.

Jessica said, "If Serlinni has some of his people watching the commercial traffic, you and your family won't be walking through the terminal to get on a plane. A vehicle will drive directly up to the plane. You get on and fly to Atlanta and will meet up with an agent in Atlanta. So don't worry, I've got your back."

I gave Jessica my cell phone number, and she gave me hers. She told me that she will call the number into her boss, and then I'm in the network. Everyone had just about finished off their meals, and I remembered about the rental car.

I asked Jessica, "What about the rental car? Where do I leave it since we won't be riding in it to the airport?"

Jessica said, "Don't worry about it. That issue will be taken care of in the morning. Just don't forget to put your phone on charge tonight. You'll need it tomorrow."

The waitress came back to the table and gave me the bill for the meal, and Mom gave her the credit card. She took the credit card and the bill and said that she would be right back. I asked Mom did she have a twenty for a tip, and she told me that she did.

I said, "Normally, I would've taken care of the tip also, but the guy that killed Nicole and shot me took my money, traveler's checks, and left me the credit card. I told her that Mom called to and reported the traveler's checks stolen"

Jessica said, "The traveler's checks will be of no use to any store that tries to get reimbursed. Some liquor store owner will be pissed."

The waitress came back with my card and asked me to sign the ticket. I signed the ticket and thanked her for such good service. We all filed out of the restaurant, and I asked Jessica where she was parked so that we could follow her to the hotel. She told me that she is parked on the west side of the building and will be driving a black Dodge Charger. I told her that we would be in a red Chrysler 300 following behind her. She looked at me, and without saying a word, I knew in her my mind that she was thinking that today was more than just coincidental.

Our rental car was parked on the other side of the building, and as we were walking to the car, Grandmother said, "James, that lady was placed here for you today."

I said, "What are you talking about?"

She said, "It's not just fate at work here, that's what I'm saying."

Mom chimed in and said that she was glad that someone was looking out for us. I unlocked the car and gave the keys to mom and everyone got in. Because of the heat outside, I told mom to let down the windows to get rid of the stored- up heat in the car as we rolled toward the exit. I had the air conditioner on full blast, trying to cool the car down to a tolerable level. Mom turned the corner and saw the black Charger waiting for us. Mom pulled up behind Jessica, and she pulled out onto the main highway. Traffic wasn't too bad, and my mom was able to stay up with Jessica. Jessica was moving with a purpose. I was thinking to myself that Nicole would've been mad if she had seen the way that Jessica looked at me. I really miss her, and there's an empty place in my heart that she used to fill.

We go through a series of traffic lights, make a couple of turns, until we are at the entrance of a Springhill Suites. I followed Jessica into the parking lot and parked next to her car. I told mom to keep the car running and lock the doors until I get back and followed Jessica to the hotel office.

I caught up to her and said, "Do you find any of this kind of odd, or do you do this kind of stuff all of the time?"

She said, "This is the first time an assignment of this magnitude just fell into my lap. Generally speaking, all of my assignments are handed to me from my boss. You're my first out-of-the-blue case. I'm going to be frank with you. This type of case is a heavy hitter in comparison to what I'm working on now."

As we drew closer to the hotel office admission desk, the conversation stopped, and Jessica approached the desk and told the attending desk clerk that she would like two rooms with two king-sized beds for four adults for one night. She gave the clerk her charge card and driver's license. The clerk printed up a receipt and gave Jessica two room entry cards. The clerk said that the two rooms, 305 and 306, are on the third floor on the right-hand side of the property.

As we walked back out to the parking lot, I said to Jessica, "One room with two king-sized beds would have been okay. I could have shared a room with Mom and Grandmother."

Jessica said, "I was told by my boss to stay with you guys as long as you are in Arizona. Plus after I get you guys settled in to your rooms, my boss wants you to come with me to the field office. My boss has some questions for you."

I told her, "I don't have a problem with that as long as I know that my mom and grandmother will be safe while I'm gone."

Jessica said, "As long as they stay in the room for a couple of hours until we get back, they will be fine. They have had something to eat, and they can rest a lot easier now knowing that you are in capable hands. If it will make you feel any better, once I drop you off and get you introduced to my boss, I'll be going to my house to get

110

my overnight bag, head to the hotel where your relatives are, and stay with them until you call me on my cell phone to come and pick you up. Does that ease your mind?"

I told her that I really appreciate it because they are the only two immediate family members I have left. I told her just this past nine months I've lost my father, my grandfather, and recently my fiancée. Jessica asked me if the deaths of my father and grandfather were attributed to Serlinni. By this time we had gotten to the cars, and I told her that I would explain the deaths of my father and grandfather on the way to the field office. I got into the car with Mom and Grandmother and briefed them about me having to go with Jessica to the Arizona Bureau of Investigation field office for a briefing. I also told them that Jessica will be coming back to stay with them while I'm being interviewed and that Jessica's boss had told her that she has to stay with us tonight until we fly out tomorrow. I told them that I shouldn't be gone no longer than a couple of hours and for them to stay in the room. I was explaining all of this as Mom was following Jessica's car around to the side of the hotel property that our rooms are. I knew what was going to be asked next, Whose room is Jessica staying in?

And right on cue, Mom said, "Where is Jessica staying tonight?"

I told her that she will be staying in the room with you guys, I suppose. I glanced at my grandmother in the back seat, and she just winked at me. Jessica pulled into a parking spot facing the building that our room is located, and mom parked next to Jessica. Jessica had gotten out of her car and pointed to the location of the rooms and said there is an elevator on the corner of the building. I grabbed the bags from the trunk, and Mom scolded me about picking them up.

Jessica said, "She's right, James. You don't need to do that. You could bust a stitch loose and would have to go back to the hospital."

I put the bags down, and Jessica grabbed two bags, and Grandmother and Mom grabbed the rest. I shut the trunk and locked the car and walked toward the building, followed the sign that had an arrow and the word Elevator on it. I looked around me to survey my surroundings as I was walking to the elevator location. I didn't see that many cars parked on this side of the property, and the location was not in a busy section of town, kind of quiet from what I'm accustomed to. We all got aboard the elevator, and I hit the button for the third floor. As the elevator moved upward, Jessica asked me if I briefed my mom and grandmother about where I was going for a couple of hours. I told her that I did and that I also told them to stay in their room and that she would be coming back to the hotel to stay with them until I call her on her cell phone to pick me up.

I was about to tell Jessica that I had told them about her staying the night when Grandmother chimed in and said, "I'm glad that Jessica is staying the night with us. I feel a lot better knowing that my grandson will be safe."

Jessica opened the room with the key card and placed the luggage inside. Jessica then placed the key card in her pocket and told Mom and Grandmother not to leave the room because she has the key.

Jessica said, "If you are ready, James, we can head on down to the field office. And don't worry, ladies, I'll take care of him. I graduated top of my class in marksmanship."

She then opened her dress jacket, revealing a shoulder-holstered pistol. I told Mom and Grandmother that I will be back soon and for them to stay in the room and lock the door behind me. I followed Jessica out and into the hallway, walking toward the elevator. As we arrived at the elevator, I pressed the button for the elevator to retrieve us at the third floor.

While we were waiting, Jessica said, "Those two women back there love you a lot."

I told her that is wasn't but a few months ago that they lost their husbands and a son. The elevator stopped, and we boarded, and I told her about the circumstances with my dad's bout with cancer, my grandmother's son, and my grandfather died because of a reaction to a vitamin supplement, that it caused a massive heart attack.

Jessica said, "No wonder they are so protective of you, and I don't blame them, especially if had gone through those awful experiences. And how long were you and Nicole together?"

I told Jessica that Nicole and I had known each other since high school, but we didn't start dating until I started college. I then said that Nicole had been with me at different video filming locations that are used as backdrops in the music-production industry. I said that there were times that she didn't go because the glamour of the experience had worn off, I guess. The only reason she wanted to come out to Arizona was the chance to get some Southwest-style turquoise jewelry.

Jessica said, "It wasn't your fault. Both of you could've been killed, and there wouldn't have been anyone to come forward with such a strong case against the mob. Speaking of turquoise jewelry, my mom has a significant collection of the stuff. I'm not that crazy about jewelry except for earrings."

The elevator had reached the bottom floor, and we walked to her car. She unlocked the doors, and I got in. I put on my seat belt as she got in and fired up the car with the air conditioner on full blast. I had already checked her hands, and I didn't see a wedding ring.

Before I could say anything, Jessica said, "It looks like we have something in common, Mr. Farnsworth."

I said, "What, we both have over protective parents?"

She chuckled and said, "No, we both have lost someone very close to us. We are damaged goods."

I said, "You don't have to talk about it. It is painful, I know."

To change the subject, I turned on her radio to see what type of music she listened to. A crossover country song was on the radio, and I hit the search button.

Jessica said, "Let me guess, you are not a country fan?"

I said, "I have coproduced and, when I was working for my dad, I even codirected a couple of country music videos. As far as my choice of music, it is rock based. The only pet peeve I have is when, I hear a classic rock song turned into a country song. To me, it's like Merle Haggard doing Highway to Hell by AC/DC. Some songs weren't supposed to be changed into country songs. Don't get me wrong, I'm not hating on country. It's just not my choice of personal listening pleasure."

Jessica said, "You are right, some songs shouldn't be attempted, but it happens."

She takes a right and pulls into the parking lot. The sign on the building read Arizona Bureau of Investigations.

Jessica said, "Here we are, James. I'm going in here with you and introduce you to my boss. Tell him everything concerning Serlinni, when the harassment started all the way up to the shooting. Don't hold back."

I said, "Let me guess, I'll probably be recorded, so whatever I tell your boss had better match up to what I tell the agents in Atlanta?"

Jessica said, "Remember, this is an information-transfer mission. The agency needs the necessary information to tighten the noose around Serlinni. You won't be able to fight this battle solo. The criminal network is large and so is the agency to counter the bad guys. I know that revenge is a powerful emotion that can cause people to make the wrong judgment call."

She turned off the car, unbuckled her seat belt, and got out of the car, and I followed her through the security checkpoint and into a staging room, I guess. She told me to have a seat and said she'll be right back. She left the room and wasn't gone very long until she returned with a man in his midfifties wearing the usual attire: pleated slacks, white dress shirt, and a shoulder holster. I stood up as they approached.

Jessica said, "James Farnsworth, this is ABI's executive special agent, Ronald Reese."

I shook hands with the guy, and he told me to follow him.

Jessica said, "I'm going to come back and pick you up, I promise," as she headed in the opposite direction.

I followed this guy to his office and sat down in a chair in front of his desk.

The agency exec said, "Mr. Farnsworth, Agent Carnes has briefed me about your situation. I want you to tell me from the beginning, when did this guy Serlinni come into the picture."

I said, "According to my father, who is now deceased, he was approached by Serlinni and was offered an amount of money to sell him the business. At that time my dad was within a month or so from dying from terminal lung cancer. My dad told Serlinni that the amount of money he offered wouldn't cover the cost of the equipment investment, plus he told him that he is leaving the business to me after he's gone. According to my dad, Serlinni didn't like that answer but decided to lay low until after my dad passed. I guess Serlinni thought that after my father's funeral, he could approach me with an offer. I wished I had taken it, and I wouldn't be having this conversation, and Nicole wouldn't be dead. I told Agent Reese that a couple of days before I left to come to Arizona for a video shoot, I was followed to the local Burger King and was offered an envelope by these two men, and I didn't take it. One of the men told me his boss would take it as an insult, and I left. I was going to my vehicle at the end of the day to go home. I walked to the dumpster to throw away an empty burger bag. A car pulls up and shoots up the driver's side of the car and leaves. If I had gotten into the car, I would've been shot. I don't know, it may have been a scare tactic.

"I reported the incident to the police, but I didn't say anything about Serlinni. I had no proof. I couldn't even tell you what type of car it was because I was on the passenger side adjacent to the dumpster. Then the day I was getting ready to leave the studio to go to the airport for a flight to Arizona, the receptionist tells me I have a call on line 2. I pick up the phone, and it's Serlinni. He asked me if I had reconsidered his offer. I told him that I would think about it. He then told me to have a good time in Arizona. Hindsight on the last conversation with Serlinni leads me to think that someone inside my production company is on Serlinni's payroll."

Agent Reese said, "Mr. Serlinni's name has come up on the bureau's radar that he is indirectly connected with the illegal drug trade and is suspected of using a couple of his music production studios in the upper East Coast as fronts for distribution. It is very apparent that someone in your company is on the take. Because of logistics and the involvement of organized crime, I'm going to get you in touch with the Federal Bureau's field office in Atlanta. Though the killing of your fiancée did occur here in Arizona, we don't have enough of concrete evidence to take Serlinni to trial. What I am going to do is, if the Federal Bureau will allow it, I am going to propose an interstate task force to find and infiltrate Serlinni's network at the same time to possibly trap whoever that is on Serlinni's payroll that's working on the inside. There's no need for me to tell you that this is very dangerous territory that you are in."

I said, "I have no intentions of caving now. I just need for the rest of my family to be safe."

Agent Reese told me that he has a couple of scenarios that he would like to discuss with the bureau, but he can only do what they allow him to do. I told Agent Reese that anything that he could do to help put that bastard behind bars would be greatly appreciated.

Agent Reese then said, "Because of the probability of an informant inside your company, you must not discuss any of this with your fiancée's family. For now let them think it was a robbery that had gone terribly wrong. This also goes for your mom, grandmother, or anyone because the informant could get wind of this in such a close-knit community, disappear, and so does the chance of getting the necessary evidence on Serlinni."

I said, "I realize the importance of secrecy. I also think that because Serlinni's failed assassination attempt on me, he will no doubt try something."

Agent Reese said, "I'm sure that the Atlanta branch will have something prepared for you once they brief you tomorrow. Do you have anything you want to ask me, Mr. Farnsworth?"

I said, "Can your organization guarantee the safety of my family?"

Agent Reese said, "I cannot give you an absolute guarantee. What I can give you is, there will be people putting their lives at risk to protect you and your family. There is one last thing that I must ask you, and you have to be completely honest with me."

I said, "Sure, go ahead and ask, Agent Reese."

He asked me if I ever did take any money. I told him that it was only in the Burger King parking lot where I refused to take it.

"Thank you, Mr. Farnsworth, for coming in and talking with me. I'll call Agent Carnes to come and get you, and I will be talking to the FBI field office in Atlanta." He got up and shook my hand and said, "Most would have taken the money and gotten themselves deeper into the inner workings of organized crime, and I am glad to have met such a citizen like yourself that didn't cave."

I said, "It probably cost me my fiancée."

Agent Reese then said, "It would've cost you more if you took it. It would've cost you your soul."

I thanked him for his help and he took me back to the staging/waiting area. As he walked away, he told me that Agent Carnes will be on her way here shortly. I sat there, reflecting on that last statement that he made about accepting money from the mob costing me my soul. There's no doubt in my mind that the guy isn't in the job just for the money; he has been enlightened about true evil. Agent Reese would've had me put under psychiatric observation had I told him that I had seen the instigator of evil himself. I sat there and waited maybe ten minutes or so when up walked Agent Carnes.

She walked up and said, "I hope you haven't been waiting long, Mr. Farnsworth."

I said, "I'm hoping that your boss can deliver on what he proposes."

Agent Carnes said, "Whatever he told you, you can take it to the bank. Let's get out of here so I can get you back to your family."

I followed her out of the building and back to her car.

CHAPTER 7

She unlocked the car, and I got in, buckled my seat belt. On the way out of the parking lot, I said, "I could use a whiskey and Coke about now."

Jessica said, "I don't think that would be too wise with the medication that you just came off of."

I chuckled and said, "That means I wouldn't have to drink as much."

Jessica said, "I'm like your doctor now. You are under my care, and I'm responsible for your welfare."

I said, "Yes, ma'am, Agent Carnes, I'll be good."

As she pulled out on to the main road, she turned on the radio and a classic Yes song was playing. It was the song called "Roundabout." Jessica glanced over at me and smiled.

I said, "Yes!"

Jessica replied by saying, "Of course it's Yes, I'm not a total country fan."

"I'm glad," I replied.

I leaned my head back and closed my eyes for a minute or two. A voice in my head said, *She's the one.*

I said, "Well, Agent Carnes, what does your boyfriend think about you spending the night in a hotel with strangers?"

Jessica replied by saying, "For now I'm just like you, I'm unattached. My intended was gunned down in a drug sting gone bad. He was in the DEA."

I told her that I was sorry for her loss and can relate to her feelings. "I'm sorry that I brought it up," I replied.

Jessica said, "That's all right, you are just making conversation."

The voice I heard in my head wasn't mine. Evidently, someone is telling me that Agent Carnes is connected to something.

Jessica said, "Once we get back to the hotel, we'll be ordering pizza for delivery. I don't want to run the risk of unnecessary exposure to danger. Serlinni could have some of his people looking for you."

I replied by saying, "I don't have a problem with pizza."

It wasn't only a short time of driving that we arrived at the hotel. Jessica parked the car, grabbed her overnight bag from the backseat, and locked the doors with her remote. We walked to the elevator. I mashed the button to return the elevator to the ground floor.

Jessica said, "You can stop speculating where I'm sleeping tonight. I'll be bunking in the room with you. My job is to protect you. This arrangement is just for tonight. Tomorrow you'll be on a government jet going to Atlanta in the morning."

The elevator had stopped, and its doors opened, and we got in. I hit the button for the third floor.

I said, "I don't have a problem with you staying in the same room with me. There may be some objections from the other women in my life."

Jessica chuckled and said, "Unless they have more guns on them than I do, there won't be a problem."

"Sounds like you have thought this out," I replied.

Jessica took out the two key entry cards and said, "That's why I told your mom and grandmother to stay in the room because I have both entry cards."

She stuck the card into release the lock, but the door was chained from the inside. I told Mom that it was me and Jessica, that it's okay to unchain the door. Mom came to the door, unchained it, and we walked in.

She said, "Did you realize you took both room keys with you?"

Jessica said, "I did it intentionally so that you two wouldn't leave the room knowing you couldn't get back in. I know how headstrong women can be. My mom is at the top of her class at being hardheaded."

Grandmother chimed in and said, "Since we can't go anywhere, anybody got any playing cards or some alcohol?"

I told them to chill out, that we would be flying back to Atlanta in the morning compliments of the US government. Jessica began explaining the reason why we wouldn't be going through the normal process of boarding a commercial plane—because Serlinni could have his people canvassing the airport terminal, looking for me and my relatives.

Mom sat down on the bed and said, "She's right, there's no telling how many people Serlinni has in his back pocket. Some of them may even be employed by the studio, and we don't know who it could be."

Jessica said, "Did either of you ladies call anyone back home while we were gone?"

Mom said that she called her housekeeper and told her that she would be coming home hopefully tomorrow. My grandmother did so likewise. I took out my cell phone and checked for stored messages.

Jessica asked me, "Anything important that you need to take care of by phone?"

I told her that one of the messages was from my recording technician, David Theus. The message was for me to call him on his cell phone when I got the chance.

Jessica asked me, "Do you trust David?"

I said, "Up until now, I've had no reason to distrust him or anyone in the company."

Jessica told me to call him once he's left work, ask him how things are going. She said to keep the conversation work related so that things will appear to be normal.

Jessica then said, "Let David tell you if something is amiss. Otherwise, treat him as a possible informant. If he asks you when you are coming home, tell him that you'll give him a call as soon as you land tomorrow. Remember, you're the boss. You'll be there when you get there."

I looked at my watch, and it had 3:00 p.m.; that means in Georgia it's about 5:00 p.m. David should be leaving work about now, but I'll give him an hour or so to home. I'll call then.

Jessica asked me, "Who are the other messages from?"

I said, "One message is from Nicole, that she had called me a day before we left to go to Arizona. She had called to tell me to pick up a bottle of wine for dinner that night. At the time she made the call, I was probably in the mixing room, listening to the music tracks that will be used for the video shoot in Rough Rock."

Jessica told me that it's going to be hard to let her go as it is, but I shouldn't punish myself by replaying it just to hear her voice.

"I went through the same thing with the loss of my intended husband. It will get easier to deal with as the weeks and months go by."

Mom commented by saying, "She's right, as much as we try to hold on to things, like the sound of the person's voice, the smell of their clothes, and even the lines of their face, eventually, it does get easier to deal with."

Jessica then said, "Yes, I definitely agree. I'm going next door and put my things away, and would any of you like a soda, bottled water, something to snack on?"

Mom got out her purse and tried to give Jessica money. Jessica refused the offer and told her that Uncle Sam has the tab. Jessica said that she would bring back a variety of drinks and some snack food to hold us over until dinner as she headed for the door. She held up the room entry cards and told us to stay in the room until she gets back. I knew what was coming after she left.

I looked for the remote, turned on the television, and sat in a chair near the bed.

I was flipping through the channels, and Mom said, "Which one of us is staying next door with Jessica?"

Before I could say anything, Grandmother spoke up and said, "The person that the feds want to protect the most would be James. Besides, it's just for tonight, and I bet she's armed to the teeth."

I interjected by saying, "Yep, she has three guns on her, one in her purse, one in her shoulder holster, and a gun in her ankle holster. I wouldn't doubt that she could kill someone without a gun due to her training."

I told them that the room has two beds in it just like this one, so nothing but sleep is going to happen. I continued to watch television, and Grandmother came over and lay down on the bed that is next to my chair. I said to myself, *Here goes another lecture in the making.*

Grandmother said, "We don't mean to be prudish about this. Your mother and I love you very much. We just want you to be safe, that's all. In a way we are being kind of selfish by not wanting to let go of you because you are the only thing that ties a connection to your father and grandfather."

I said, "Can you two stop with the lecturing and let me sit here and just think about some things? Look, I'm sorry. I didn't mean to snap at you two. We'll be going home tomorrow, and you both will have to be mindful of what you can talk about to your friends, your housekeepers, your car drivers, anyone else you come in contact with. You cannot talk about this case involving the mob, and as far as Nicole's parents, for now, her death was the result of a robbery that went bad, and that's all that can be said until all of this is over. If any of this got back to whoever is informing Serlinni from inside the production company now that the bureau is involved, this whole thing could go south real quick. More people could wind up dead because of it. I want to hear you two promise me that."

I looked at both of them, and they promised me that they wouldn't. Within about a half hour or so, there was a knock on the door.

I got up and went to the door and asked, "Who is it?"

It was Jessica, and she told me to unchain the door and open it because her hands were full with bags of drinks and snacks. I opened the door and let her in, taking the bags from her. I took the drinks and placed them in the small refrigerator that is in the room. I asked Mom and Grandmother if they wanted something to drink. Mom said that she would like a bottle of water or Coke; it didn't matter which. Grandmother said she would like to have something to mix with a Coke but would settle for just a Coke for now.

Jessica said, "I got some snack food if anyone is interested?"

Jessica looked at me like she could feel the tension in the room.

I said, "It's okay, Jessica, I had a talk with them about keeping this situation with the mob an absolute secret. They are not to talk to their friends, housekeepers, or Nicole's parents about this. The shooting was a robbery gone bad, and that will be the story until this is finished."

Jessica said, "This is some dangerous territory. We don't want the mob to find out that we are in on this at all. It would be best if the cover story is a robbery that went bad. News travels fast in a small town, and we don't need the wrong people getting wind of certain information. More people could die because of it."

While Jessica was talking, I gave Mom and Grandmother their drinks and got myself a Sprite. Jessica told me to hand her a Sprite as well. Jessica sat down at the table, sliding off her shoes in the process.

She said, "It will be a couple of hours before dinner, so I brought this with me."

And she took out a deck of cards from her purse. Grandmother came right over and sat down at the table. It took some coaxing to get my mother to come over to the table, but she finally gave in and sat down at the table. Jessica asked us which card game we wanted to play, a choice between rummy or poker.

Grandmother said, "Poker would be nice if we had some chips to play with."

Evidently, Jessica was prepared. She took out from her purse a stack of red and white poker chips. She divvied out the chips equally until everyone had the same amount of red and white chips.

Grandmother said, "Let's make the white chips one-dollar and the reds five-dollar chips."

Before we knew it, we had been playing a few hours. Occasionally someone would have to excuse themselves to the bathroom. I took out my cell phone and told Jessica that I'm calling David. I dialed the number; it rang twice before David answered.

"Hello, James, I'm sorry to hear about Nicole. How are you doing, and when are you coming back to Georgia?" inquired David.

I told David that I would be flying back to Georgia tomorrow and told him that I'm recovering. I made small talk, asking, "How is the editing of the video and sound overlay going?" David told me that in a day or so, he would be finished, and he was waiting for me to review. I ended the conversation by telling him thanks for his hard work and that he would get a raise if Atlantic Records was pleased with the work. David told me that Tim sent flowers compliments of the studio to Nicole's funeral. I told him to tell Tim thanks for me. I ended the call. Jessica asked me if he implied that anything was unusual. I told her that it was business as usual. I picked up my cards and began playing cards again.

Over the course of card playing and talking, Jessica had my mom and grandmother virtually won over. I too was also taken in by her charm. As I said, time had been clicking on by, and I looked at my watch, and it had 6:00 p.m. on it.

I said, "Is anyone up for something to eat?"

Jessica replied by saying that she could order a large pizza or two, depending on how hungry everyone is. I wanted to tell her that I feel like I could eat a pizza by myself, but I refrained from doing so. I told Jessica that one large deep-dish supreme with everything, but anchovies will suffice. Jessica commented that she wasn't crazy about anchovies either. She walked over to the table where the phone is located and took out the phone book.

She looked up at me and asked, "Domino's or Pizza Hut?"

I told her to surprise us. She chuckled at the comment and began dialing the number. She got through after being put on hold. Jessica orders, hangs up the phone, and tells us that the pizza will be here in thirty minutes. She walks back over to the table and sits down.

Jessica said, "Okay, James, it's your turn to deal and call the game."

I put a dollar chip in the middle of the table, and everyone else followed suit.

I said, "The game is seven-card stud, and if you have an ace, you can get four fresh cards, but you have to show the dealer that you have an ace before you can get four more."

I dealt out the cards, and by the looks on the table, the one with the most chips is Grandmother. I made the comment that I may have to take out a loan from Grandmother to stay in the game.

Grandmother said, "From the looks of this hand that you dealt me, I'll loan ya two red chips."

Mom said, "It looks like I might as well get ready to fold after that comment."

Grandmother said, "I could be bluffing."

Jessica showed me that she had an ace, threw away four cards, and got four fresh ones. I threw away three cards and got three fresh ones. Mom did the same thing and got three fresh cards. Grandmother told us that she's playing what she's dealt and anted up a dollar chip on the table. Mom folded and so did I.

Jessica said, "Here's your dollar and another one with it."

Grandmother anted up and called her out to show. Jessica had a pair of aces and three fives, then Grandmother threw down four kings and a pair of twos.

She said, "Next time I go to Vegas, Mrs. Farnsworth, I'm taking you and putting you at the card table."

We laughed and talked and finally came a knock at the door. Jessica drew her gun and walked to the door and asked who was at the door.

The voice said, "It's Domino's pizza delivery."

Jessica has her handgun behind her back and money in her left hand. She unlatches the door and opens it. There stood a thirty-or-so-year-old black guy.

Jessica asked, "How much for the pizza?"

The pizza guy said "Twenty-two bucks."

Jessica gave him 25 dollars for the tip.

The black guy said, "You call this a tip?"

Jessica said, "The Domino's attendant said it was eighteen dollars over the phone." As she was saying that, she had retrieved her badge from her pocket with her left hand. She shows him the badge, places it back in her pocket without taking her eyes off of him. She held out her left hand and the guy hands Jessica the pizza. The guy really started back peddling, when Jessica steadied the pizza box underneath, with her right hand that held the gun. The guy apologized for his behavior and walked away.

Mom said, "Wow, this is better than watching television. I thought that guy was about to be a statistic."

Jessica said, "I didn't expect the pizza guy to be that old and a shakedown artist."

I said, "The old pizza guy didn't expect to be running into no lady law dog neither."

Everyone laughed as Jessica brought the pizza over to the table, opened it up, and looked it over.

Grandmother said, "What is it, Jessica?"

Jessica said, "I'm checking to see if the guy brought the correct order."

I knew what she was doing; she was checking for food tampering, like someone spitting on your food. I didn't let on that I knew what she was doing because no one would eat the pizza. I walked to the bathroom and washed my hands and dried them off. Jessica had opened her purse and had a pack of hand wipes. She gave Mom and Grandmother a hand wipe. I looked around for some napkins for us to lay our pizza slices on. An idea came to me. I asked Jessica if she had a knife in her bag of tricks. She took out a lock-blade knife with a serrated edge. She handed it to me, and I cut off the lid from the pizza box, folded it twice, unfolded it, and cut on the folded lines. I had cut four equal-sized plates for everyone.

As everyone grabbed their piece of pizza and placed it on their improvised plate, I said, "Before we start eating, I'd like to say a prayer. Thank you, Lord, for giving us a safe place to lay our head, food on the table, and guiding us to the help when we needed it the most. In Jesus's name we pray, amen."

We dug into the pizza and talked about what had happened to us all in a matter of a few minutes leaving the hospital.

Mother said, "Divine intervention sent us to Jessica."

Jessica replied by saying, "I'm chalking it up to pure luck."

We finished eating, and I helped Mom clean off the table and put the remnants of tonight's meal in the trash can.

Jessica said, "Anybody up for some card playing, or do you guys want to take a shower and relax?"

Grandmother said, "With this heat out here in Arizona, I could use a shower and put on my nightgown. At least I'll be able to rest easier tonight knowing that my grandson, his mother, and I are in a safer situation. I am kind of beat. I'm not as young as I used to be."

Mom chimed in and said, "You two don't have to babysit us. We'll be fine. I am ready to lie down and relax myself."

Jessica said, "We all have had a full day, and James needs to get some rest, especially being fresh out of the hospital. Tomorrow morning will be here before we know it."

Mom told me not to get my bandages wet. I told her that I would be careful. I grabbed my bag and followed Jessica toward the door.

Jessica said, "We'll be right next door, so just relax and have a good night's sleep."

I told Mom and Grandmother as I was going out the door, "Good night and I'll see you in the morning."

We walked a brief distance, and Jessica opened the door with the card key. The room was hot, and I immediately found the air conditioner controls and turned it on full blast.

Jessica said, "Do you mind if I take a quick shower?"

I said, "Go ahead, I'm going to sit by the air conditioner and cool off. I feel a little feverish."

She said that I was probably still weakened from the blood loss, and today was the first day my body had solid food in it. I told her to go ahead and shower, that I'll be sitting right here when she gets out. She kicks off her shoes, unstraps her shoulder holster, sits down in a chair, unstraps her ankle-holstered gun, grabs her bag, and walks into the bathroom. I must admit, she is very easy on the eyes. I hope she doesn't torture me by coming out of the bathroom wearing something right out of a Victoria Secret catalogue. Maybe she'll come out with something less revealing.

I found the television remote and turned the TV on. I was surf-ing the channels, trying to occupy my mind and off of what could happen. I finally stopped on something that did pique my interest. It was a documentary about the First World War, what a coincidence. My grandfather was there before America got involved. I watched for a while, looking to see if by chance my grandfather could be in some of the footage. I had taken off my shoes, and I could tell that the room was cooling down finally. I didn't get to watch much of the footage because I tuned in at the last fifteen minutes of the film. I heard the bathroom door open. I leaned my head against my left hand, shielding my vision on my left, the direction in which she will be walking from. I kept on facing forward, watching the television.

Jessica walked into the room, saying, "Don't let me scare you since I'm not wearing any makeup."

I said, "You don't really need it."

She was wearing pajama pants and a powder blue silk top. I noticed her nipples were jutting out, but I diverted my eyes. Mind you, she would look good wearing a pair of overalls. I'm glad she was dressed less sexy. It would be easy to cave in my weakened condition.

Jessica said, "Okay, it's your turn, and don't get your bandages wet."

I grabbed my bag and went into the bathroom. I turned on the water and closed the drain, grabbed a washcloth, and sat it on the edge of the tub. I took off my clothes and sat on the edge of the tub, being careful not to get the bandages wet. I wished I could take a shower, but at least I'm not in the hospital. I wanted to wash my hair, but the possibility of the water running down my back, getting the bandages wet, wasn't worth the risk. I finished washing what I could, dried off, and put on clean underwear and pajama bottoms and a T-shirt. I let the water out of the tub and cleaned up after myself and walked out.

Jessica said, "Do you feel a little fresher now?"

I told her I wished I could wash my hair.

She said, "Take off your T-shirt, and I'll wash your hair in the sink for you. That way your bandages won't get wet."

I said, "If you do that for me, I'll give you the best foot massage you've ever had."

Jessica said, "It's a deal because my feet are killing me."

Jessica took from her bag a bottle of shampoo as I got the water temperature ready at the sink. As Jessica walked closer to me, I could smell her. She smelled like a field of sweet citrus fruit, fresh and clean. I leaned over the sink and got my hair wet. Jessica walked to the side of me, put the shampoo in my hair, and began scrubbing.

She said, "Let me know if I'm scrubbing too hard."

I told her that she was doing just fine. This is making me miss my Nicole so much. I hope she isn't watching this. After a few minutes, Jessica was telling me that it was time to rinse. I rinsed off the shampoo, and Jessica rinsed the areas that I missed.

She said, "Stay just like that until I can get you a towel so the water doesn't run down to your bandages."

She grabbed a towel and began to dry my hair and prevented the water from going down my back and down my chest. I took over and partially dried my hair with the towel and told Jessica that just as soon as I finish brushing my teeth, I would become the foot doctor. I thanked Jessica for washing my hair for me as she walked toward to the bed and began watching television. I opened up my bag and took out my toothbrush, toothpaste and commenced to brushing. I finished brushing my teeth. I walked in the bedroom to where Jessica was propped up on a pile of pillows and watching television.

I said, "I don't want to interrupt your television watching by massaging your feet."

She said, "Oh hell no, I can watch television at the same time as the foot doctor works on my feet."

I laughed and told her to lie on her stomach facing the television. I got on the bed and began massaging the ball of her left foot.

Jessica asked me, "Where did you learn that technique?"

I told her that I flew with my father to Hong Kong a couple of years ago. An executive at Sony wanted my father to collaborate on a recording session there at the Sony studio. At the end of each business day, the Sony executive would tell one of his subordinates to take my father and me to a spa to wind down every day while we were there. At the spa, the masseuse would always begin at the feet first. The subordinate told me that the feet work harder than any part of the body and that certain pressure points in the feet can be manipulated to relieve pain in other parts of the body. As I was talking to her, she had stopped watching television and had turned her head to the side and was in a relaxed position. Jessica told me that she had read somewhere about that but had never experienced it.

She then said, "My right foot is getting jealous."

I went from the left foot to the right foot, and I detected a scent that was familiar to me but usually detected at a much closer range. Something was going on not only with her but also with my senses. My senses were telling me that Jessica was being turned on. She was sighing while I kneaded the muscles in her foot, and I detected her whole body trembled. After about a couple of minutes, I stopped because I was, let's say, getting aroused myself.

Jessica said, "That was great! Did you get a happy ending while you were in the spa in Hong Kong?"

I told her that it wasn't that kind of spa. Before I could say "Don't do it," she was on top of me like a lioness on an injured gazelle.

I whispered, "Jessica, slow down."

Between her kissing me and groping me, she whispered, "I wanted you the moment you saved me from falling at the restaurant. Do you not find me attractive?"

As she was asking me this, she was sitting on top of me, grinding against my now throbbing manhood.

I replied by saying, "You are more than attractive, you are beautiful."

She said, "James, after tonight we may never cross paths again. If I didn't want this to happen, things would not have gotten this far. By the way, do you have a condom?"

I said, "I think I may have some in my shaving kit."

She said, "Stay right there, and I'll get it."

She sprang off of me, hurried to the bathroom, and I heard her rummaging through the shaving kit. She scurried back to the bed, holding the foil packet in hand, tearing it open in preparation.

I said, "Can we take our time so in case, like you said, we may never cross paths again. I want to remember this night when I'm an old man sitting on the front porch, listening to the sounds of the night, and reflecting back to this moment."

Jessica said, "That was absolutely beautiful. Now take your clothes off before I rip them off."

She took off her pajama top, slid off her pajama bottoms and panties, and was now helping me remove my T-shirt so that my bandages wouldn't get ripped away. She undoubtedly was wet with anticipation and began stroking me, then she put the condom on me. She straddled me, gliding me inside her with her hand. She began to grind and bounce on top of me in a fury. I grabbed her and pulled her closer to me to slow her down, pushing into her at the same time, thrusting upward.

She whispered, "Baby, that feels so good. I wish that we could have more time together."

I replied by saying, "We'd better enjoy this tonight. Serlinni may try again, and I might not be as lucky next time."

"He won't be able to get to you if I had my way. Besides, tonight, you belong to me. So stop that crazy talk."

We continued the lovemaking until we both climaxed at the same time. I got up and went to the sink to get myself cleaned up and removed the torn condom. Jessica had jumped into the shower and got herself freshened up. I dried myself off and put my underwear on and my T-shirt. I felt pretty spent after that episode, but I didn't do too bad for someone who had just gotten out of the hospital the same day. I lay back down on the bed, and it wasn't too long before Jessica came from the bathroom. She was drying herself off and walked over to the bed, and I handed her clothes to her.

She said, "Do you mind if I sleep next to you tonight, Mr. Farnsworth?"

I said, "I don't mind."

She put on her panties and her pajama top and got in bed with me. I looked at the clock on the table by the bed, and it had 10:30 p.m., and I asked Jessica, "What time is the wake-up call for tomorrow?"

She said that she'll call Mom and Grandmother's room at 7:00 a.m., and her cell phone will go off at six.

I said, "You need that extra hour to get dressed, your hair and makeup, right?"

She said, "You are partially right. I'll have time for another piece of you before you head back to Georgia."

She kissed me, turned off the small lamp that was on a table on her side of the bed. The television was still on; nothing was really interesting to watch. I asked Jessica if she wanted to watch any television, and she said that she was tired and ready to go to sleep. I too admitted that I needed the rest.

I turned off the television and laid down on my aching back, Jessica placed my arm around her neck so that I could hold her. She whispered, "Good night, James Farnsworth, I'll be seeing you in the morning."

I gave her a quick kiss on the lips and said, "Good night, Jessica Carnes, I'm glad that I met you."

As I was calming down from tonight's total surprise, I listened to Jessica's breathing, as each breath became slower, as she drifted off to sleep. As I lay there before closing my eyes, I reflected upon todays events. Was the meeting with Jessica a planned moment? I finally closed my eyes and succumbed to the sleep cycle. The next instance I find myself sitting by the pool at the patio table in my grandparents' backyard. I had my back facing the house, and I could hear footfalls coming from behind me. I turned around, and it was my grandfather. He walks up, puts his hand on my shoulder, then sits down across from me.

He looks out at the pool and says, "I really miss swimming in that pool on summer days."

I said, "Let me guess, you're here to tell me in two days, I'm going to change into something."

Grandfather said, "You are partly right on your assumption about the change part. You are going to change into something, all right. You've already figured out what that something is since your grandmother told you that it was colloidal silver that killed me."

I said, "So the villagers will be hunting for a killer that only kills people during a full moon?"

Grandfather said, "Yes, I've killed, and afterwards I was contained, but I'm not here just to talk about what's going to happen to you but to tell you about that voice that you heard in your head. That voice was a messenger sending you a message while you had closed your eyes and was in a brief state of trance, so to speak. You were directed to Jessica only because of her ties to the justice department. She may or may not be your intended bride. I know Jessica is beautiful and smart, but she won't give up her job for you because she craves dangerous situations."

"And having a boyfriend that is a werewolf isn't a dangerous situation!" I exclaimed.

Grandfather said, "I am glad that she insisted on you wearing a condom because she would be carrying your child. If she were to have such a child, the child would have a double dosage of killer instinct."

I said, "What do you mean by 'a double dosage of killer instinct'? I understand the werewolf part, the other part I'm in the dark about."

Grandfather said, "Jessica had been taken off an assignment because she got reckless. She shot the bad guys and shot some innocent people, who got killed in the crossfire. It would be different if she felt remorse from the incident, but the messengers can see into the human heart. What they saw is dangerous. Remember, she said that your paths may never cross again. Then again, events can change."

Before I could ask any more questions, I was awakened by Jessica getting up to go to the bathroom. I looked at the clock on the table; it had 3:00 a.m. I guess she had to get up and pee. I didn't let on that she had awakened me. She got back into bed and slid up next to me. I managed to fall back asleep. This time in my dream, I was sitting in a room. In front of me was a long table and a group of men dressed in linens like they did at the time of Jesus.

A messenger was standing beside me and said, "Do you know where you are?"

I said, "Let me guess, this is the scene of the Last Supper, and Leonardo Da Vinci's painting is wrong."

The messenger said, "The man that betrayed the lamb is sitting across the table from him."

I asked, "Why are you showing me this?"

The messenger said, "The lamb knew the traitor was going to be the dark one's property before any money changed hands."

And as usual, before I could ask any questions, Jessica's cell phone alarm went off. I got up as Jessica turned off the alarm on her cell phone. I walked into the bathroom and took a leak and went to the sink to brush my teeth. I put toothpaste on my brush and began brushing my teeth. Jessica walked up behind me and put her arms around me, hugging me. I spit the remnants of the toothpaste from my mouth and splashed away the rest from my face.

I turned around to return the hug, and she said, "Don't get dressed just yet. I'll be right with you after I brush my teeth."

I went back and sat down on the edge of the bed. Jessica knew I was watching her, so she stuck the toothbrush into her mouth and slid off her panties. She'd brush her teeth a little while, then she unbuttoned her pajama top to show me her breasts in the mirror. She is such a temptress. She bent down to spit out the toothpaste and was jutting out her ass to me. She knew exactly what she was doing. She rinsed away the toothpaste from her face, reached into my shaving kit, and got a condom. As she was walking over to the bed, she ripped the package open. I took off my underwear and lay back on the bed.

Jessica said, "James Farnsworth, are you ready for your morning workout?"

She pounced on me like a bobcat pinning a rabbit to the ground just before devouring it. We made love for at least forty minutes. She had completely drained me of energy and love fluid. After the last thrust and the orgasmic finale, she smiled, a look of satiated drunkenness of desire. No doubt there is a big difference the way Nicole and Jessica approached sex. Nicole's was demure versus Jessica's full-on attack of sexual conquest. I got up, headed to the bathroom to get cleaned up.

Jessica said, "Too bad we can't take a shower together, can't get your bandages wet."

I told her that my energy level has hit rock bottom as it is. She just laughed and got into the shower. I bathed off in the sink, shaved, put on some deodorant and fresh clothes. I've got to look rested and act like I got a good night's sleep in front of Mom and Grandmother. I already feel guilty enough without having to look at their faces and wonder if they knew or speculated what happened next door to them. Jessica had gotten out of the shower and was drying off the deadly curves that she possessed.

I got the television remote and turned the TV on. I scanned the channels and found the weather channel. It appears that the central part of Georgia will be getting some rain today. Looks like I'll be driving into the rain from Atlanta while here in Arizona. It's going to be another hot day in the sun. Jessica was putting on her clothes, strapping on her artillery, and went back to the mirror to fix her hair, apply makeup, get ready to face another day as a crime fighter. I thought to myself, I bet she could be hell on wheels if someone got on her bad side. Right now, I'm feeling the need to eat. My body is telling me that it needs fuel. I asked Jessica if she was hungry.

She told me, "After we get your mom and grandmother out of their room, we'll go down to the hotel lobby. You'll have time to eat the continental breakfast, slam down some coffee before your escort to the fed plane gets here. Call next door and make sure that they are ready to go for me while I make a cell call to headquarters to make sure that things are on schedule."

I complied by saying, "Right on it, Agent Carnes."

As she was dialing on her cell phone, she gave me a look as if to peer right through me. I picked up the receiver to the phone and dialed Mom's room. It rang a few times before someone answered. Mom answered the phone, and I asked her if she and Grandmother are ready to go. Mom told me that she is ready and that Grandmother is packing away some of her things. I told her that Jessica and I will be there to get them very shortly. I packed away the remainder of my things, making sure that I'm not leaving anything of importance behind. Jessica finished up her makeup job, packed away her things, and sat them by the door.

Before she opened the door, she turned to me and said, "James Farnsworth, I'm going to have a tough time putting last night and this morning behind me. I messed up by allowing myself to get that close to you."

I said, "We were both vulnerable. You needed me, and I needed you. Perhaps if we had met under different circumstances, we could've made a go of it."

She pulled me into her and gave me a long kiss good-bye. She lovingly wiped the lipstick from my face and rushed back to the mirror to reapply. Jessica said, "Remember this James, when you call me, use a land line and be business like when you are talking to me. Your phone will be bugged and don't use a cell either because the bad guys have found a way to monitor cell traffic. Okay?" I nodded in compliance.

She shoved her lipstick back into her purse and said, "Let's go, James." In a millisecond she changed into agent Carnes, armed to the teeth, crime fighter.

I picked up my bags and walked next door and knocked on the door. I could hear the unlatching of the door, and Grandmother opened it.

Grandmother said, "We have our bags ready to go when you are."

Jessica said, "Let's go, gang, we have just enough time to grab a cup of coffee and some Danish before your ride gets here."

Mom and Grandmother came out with their bags and followed us to the elevator. Jessica pushed the button for the elevator. As we were waiting on the elevator to arrive at our floor, there was total silence. I was waiting for someone to start a conversation, someone just say something.

Mom broke the silence and said, "Jessica, maybe when this whole mess is over, you can visit us in Georgia. We'll treat you with some good home-cooked food."

Jessica replied by saying, "Southern cuisine sounds mighty good. I'll have to check it out one day."

The elevator doors open, and we get on the elevator.

Grandmother chimes in by saying, "I just thought that it gets hot in Georgia, but Arizona appears to have the market cornered."

Jessica said, "Yes, ma'am, it can get unbearable sometimes at the peak of summer."

The elevator reaches the bottom floor, and we follow Jessica to the hotel lobby. I caught the odor of coffee in the air. We walked into the lobby, and Jessica told us to go get some coffee and something to eat while she checks out. There were a couple of elderly people there already eating and drinking coffee, looking at the big-screen TV that was in the dining area. I claimed a table for us to sit down and placed our bags close-by. After I set my bags down, I headed right for the coffee machine. Mom and Grandmother weren't too far behind me; they have the need for the java like myself. I fixed me a cup of coffee with one shot of creamer, grabbed a bear claw and a banana. I headed back to the table and sat down. I watched as Jessica walked over to the table as I was drinking my coffee. She set her bags down and went to the coffee machine, fixed her a cup, and grabbed a doughnut. I wasted no time on getting rid of the bear claw, and I decided to save the banana for on the way to the airport. I didn't want Mom and Grandmother see me scarfing food down. It would be a dead give-away of what went on last night. Jessica sat down at the table with her coffee and doughnut.

I said, "I thought law enforcement only eat doughnuts in the movies?"

Jessica said, "That's just a Hollywood stereotype like the same way that Southerners are portrayed as toothless moonshiners."

We all laughed, and Grandmother commented her father was a moonshiner, but he had all of his teeth. The ice had been broken. I didn't feel like I had done something wrong, and Mom and Grandmother knew about it. The tension was gone. Jessica took a pen and paper from her purse and wrote something on it.

Jessica held out the piece of paper to me and said, "It's my cell number and my e-mail address to my laptop. E-mail me to let me know you guys are doing okay."

By the time she finished telling me that, her cell phone rang. She answered it and told us that the car was outside, waiting. She told the driver on the phone that we were on our way out.

Jessica said, "This is it, guys, don't worry."

We all took turns hugging her and thanking her. Jessica grabbed her bags and walked out with us and talked to the driver of the black Escalade as we loaded ourselves into the vehicle. I heard the driver tell Jessica that her boss wanted to see her in his office for her next assignment. The driver turned around and asked us if everyone was settled in because he was on a strict schedule. And just like that, the driver pulls away. The windows are tinted out, so it would be useless to wave good-bye to Jessica. I did see her wave at us. Grandmother is sitting next to me, and she laid her hand on top of mine.

She said, "I know things seem to be happening faster than our minds can keep up with. In a matter of hours, we'll be back to our homes and hopefully get some normalcy back into our lives."

I said, "Right now, I would relish a nice long shower, but I can't get the stitches wet. More important than my miniscule needs comes your and Mom's safety because of Serlinni. We'll find out what the feds have planned for us when we get to Atlanta."

We had about a fifteen-minute ride to the airport location. As we approached the airport, the driver had called on his cell notifying security that the vehicle was at the gate. The automated gate opened, and the driver took us out to the tarmac were the government jet was parked. The driver parked next to the jet and opened the door for us to get out.

The driver said, "Mr. Farnsworth, you and your party will be meeting up with federal Agent Eric Harrington in Atlanta. Have a good flight."

We got our baggage and headed for the plane. There was no stewardess waiting at the door of the plane. Instead there was a plain-clothes agent waiting at the bottom of the steps of the plane.

CHAPTER 8

He helped Mom and Grandmother with their luggage as they got aboard. He introduced himself as Special Agent Phillips and that he would be flying with us to Atlanta and is a liaison between the Arizona Bureau of Investigation and the FBI. He instructed us to stow our baggage in the overhead bins, get seated, and get buckled in. He told us once we get in the air, he could get us some coffee or soda if we wanted it.

Special Agent Phillips then looked at his watch and said, "If any of you need to go to the bathroom, I suggest you do it know. We have about ten minutes before we can taxi out onto the runway."

He pointed to the rear of the plane where the bathroom is.

Grandmother said, "I might as well take advantage of this moment."

She got up from her seat and went to the bathroom.

Mom looked at me and said, "I didn't have to go until he mentioned it, must be the power of suggestion."

So Mom got up and walked to the rear of the plane and waited for Grandmother to come out. As Mom and Grandmother went to the bathroom, I just sat and stared out the window as the baggage handling carts were moving people's luggage from the terminal to planes and from the planes to the terminal. There was a good bit of movement going on at the other end of the airport from where we were sitting. I also thought about what Grandfather had told me in the dream about how Jessica likes working in dangerous situations. I think he was withholding information. He all but told me that she would probably get killed in her line of work. Instead he told me that she wouldn't quit her job for me and wouldn't like the idea of being tied down to small-town life. It wasn't long before Grandmother had returned to her seat and buckled up. I heard the engines fire up, and Mom made it back to her seat, buckled in, and got ready.

Special Agent Phillips had walked to the cockpit while the women had gone to the bathroom. He now had returned and told us that the pilot is getting ready to taxi out for takeoff, and he sat down just behind the entrance door of the cockpit. I could hear the engines throttling up, and the plane began to move forward. The plane made a right-hand turn, and the engines throttled back down, and we were stopped. I guess the pilot was waiting for clearance to take off from the tower. The engines began throttling up again, and this time we were increasing speed forward. I watched from the window as the plane rose into the air, and the objects on the ground began shrinking in size. Within a few minutes, the plane had climbed to altitude and was in level flight.

Special Agent Phillips said, "Okay, folks, you can unbuckle your seat belts now. Does anyone want some coffee or soda?"

I told him that I would like a cup. I needed to stand up and move around. For some reason, just about every muscle in my body started aching. Was it because of the antics of last night and this morning, or is there something going on? My birthday is only two days away and so is the first full moon of the month. My wounds were also itching at the same time. I walked to the bathroom and closed the door behind me. I unbuttoned my shirt, peeled back the bandage on my chest to look at it. The wound looked a little pink around where the stitches are but nothing unusual. I guess because of my unique metabolism; I could be healing from the inside out. I closed the bandage back up, took a leak while I was in there, washed up, and went back to my seat. Special Agent Phillips brought me a cup of coffee, a couple packs of creamer, and sugar with a coffee stirrer. I thanked him. I could see that he had already taken care of the womenfolk's drinks. The coffee is good and while the women were preoccupied, I scarfed down the banana. I am still hungry. As I was sipping my coffee, I reflected back on what the messenger said to me about the scene of the Last Supper. He said that the lamb knew that the traitor was the dark one's property before any money changed hands. I know the traitor is Judas Iscariot, but what does he have to do with this? Or is he telling me that there is a Judas in my organization? I guess Jesus knew that he had to die and give up his human body in order to ascend into heaven. I guess it would be a matter of time. If it wasn't Judas who betrayed Jesus, the devil would continue to plague Jesus in one way or another.

I finished drinking my coffee and decided to recline my seat and relax. I tried to clear my mind and not think about anything, but that's hard to do when you've found out that you're about to turn into a werewolf in a matter of days. How did Grandmother control Grandfather during the full moon cycles? He would have to be locked away somewhere so that he couldn't get loose and be out of control, killing. I guess once Grandmother and I can have some privacy, she'll be able to enlighten me on the particulars. Besides all of this, I've got to worry about my remaining family members' safety concerning this Serlinni situation.

Despite my mind being bombarded with all of these issues, somehow I managed to drift off to sleep. I found myself sitting on a pier out on the water. I looked behind me, and up walked this figure. As the figure drew closer to me, I recognized that the figure was the messenger that appeared in many of my dreams.

I was leaning against the railing of the pier, and the messenger said, "You are right, James, if it hadn't been Judas that betrayed the lamb, the dark one would've tasked someone else to have the lamb slaughtered. But since it was Judas, by his free will chose to give in to the dark one's lies, he gave up more than his soul. But I'm not here to talk about Judas's downfall. I'm here to prepare you for what is to come."

I said, "From what little information that I have been able to piece together, I'm about to turn into a creature of the night in two days from now."

The messenger said, "That part is true, but unlike your grandfather, you will be more evolved than he."

The messenger touched me on the shoulder, and I woke up. I looked over at my mom, who was sitting across from me.

She said, "Go back to sleep. We just hit a little bit of turbulence."

I told her, "I had better get some more coffee. I won't be able to sleep tonight if I sleep now."

I asked Special Agent Phillips if I could have another cup of coffee.

He replied by saying, "Does anyone else need anything I could get for them?"

Mom and Grandmother said that they were fine, and he went to get me a cup of coffee. I looked at my watch, and it appears that I had been asleep for an hour, per my recollection of the last time I looked at my watch. Grandmother was sitting in the seat in front of me.

Grandmother said, "You must have been deep asleep. You were snoring so loud, I thought the jet engine was tearing up."

We all laughed at her comment as Special Agent Phillips was bringing me my coffee. He overheard the conversation and chuckled himself. He handed me the coffee and the packets of creamer and sugar. I put in the creamer and stirred it up. Special Agent Phillips told us that we'll be in Atlanta in about thirty minutes as he headed back to his seat. I hadn't noticed it before now, but Special Agent Phillips had an earpiece in his ear. It wasn't a Bluetooth; it was much smaller. As he sat down, I could hear what he was saying into a micro mike hidden into his clothing.

He said, We'll be arriving in Atlanta in a half hour. Have someone at gate 7 to pick up the protected witnesses."

I realized now why the sensations were happening a while ago. I looked at my forearm. It looked more muscular. The veins in my arm are now more visible. I felt my calves and my legs; they too were larger. My jeans were loose in the waist but tight on my thighs. I felt of my biceps, ran my hand across my stomach, and it felt like a washboard. I got Grandmother's attention to look at me. I showed her my biceps. She leaned forward to look into the pouch in the back of the seat in front of her. She found a magazine, took a pen from her purse, and wrote a message on a piece paper she tore from the magazine. She waited before she handed me the piece of paper. I unfolded it, and it said, "Your muscles are preparing for what is to come. You'll be all right." I looked back at her after reading the note, and she mouthed the words, "It's okay."

It was too long before Special Agent Phillips told us the usual airline lingo, "Please return your seats and trays to the upright positions and buckle your seat belts. We are in approach to Atlanta."

I brought my seat back up to the upright position and buckled my seat belt. The plane made a slow banking turn left, getting lined for final approach and clearance from the tower to land. As the plane was turning, we were descending at the same time. Looking out my window, I saw that we popped through a cloud, and I could see a series of subdivisions and roadways below as we were gliding down. I could hear the sound of the engines change as the speed of the turbines slowed. We touched down. We're back in Georgia. We sat in our seats until the plane came to a stop. Special Agent Phillips told us to hang tight and that the vehicle will be here to pick us up. Special Agent Phillips took out his cell phone and walked to the front of the plane to have the conversation. Within a few minutes, he came back and said that the vehicle is en route, and the driver said he is only minutes away.

I asked Special Agent Phillips, "Where will the driver take us?"

Special Agent Phillips said, "The driver is going to take you to the FBI field office for a briefing, and there you'll meet the agent or agents that will be assigned to your case. Don't worry, you and your family will be safe. The agents are specially trained for this."

I told Special Agent Phillips that it's not me that I'm worried about. I found out one thing for sure: when the main engines are off on a jet, the air-conditioning sucks, especially on a tarmac in Georgia with eighty-five-degree temp, and it's not even summer yet. Luckily, we didn't have to sit there very long. Special Agent Phillips's cell phone went off; the driver was sitting outside the plane, waiting for us.

Agent Phillips said, "Okay, everyone, the driver is outside. Get your bags, and it's been a pleasure flying with you."

He opened the door and lowered the exit stairs. I got my bags and stepped out first so I could help Grandmother and Mom exit the plane safely. I helped them out and carried their baggage and mine to the awaiting vehicle. The driver got out and helped the women inside the tinted-out Tahoe. I loaded the baggage in the back, and I got in.

The driver said, "It's getting hot out there, isn't it?" And he turned up the AC once he got in. He told us that we'll get something to eat and drink once he gets us to the FBI field office. The driver got on his cell phone and alerted security that he was exiting the airport grounds. We passed through an entrance labeled Maintenance Only Entry. As we went through, the gate closed behind us, and we got on the expressway into downtown Atlanta. By Georgia time it is four o'clock in the afternoon, almost peak hours for the herd of traffic that will funnel in and out of Atlanta. The traffic is why I don't want to live anywhere near Atlanta. I guess if I had grown up around this environment, I would probably be used to it. Within about a ten-minute drive, we were downtown, tall buildings and traffic lights. It seems everyone was on their way somewhere in every direction.

The vehicle slows down and makes a left. The driver stops and shows his ID card to the attendant at a gated entrance. The remote barrier arm rises as the driver pulls forward. We are in a parking garage; the driver pulls the vehicle over to the main entrance. He tells us to get out and to wait for him at the entrance. We get out of the vehicle, walk to the entrance as he parked. The driver walked up to us and told us not to worry about the baggage. He told us that the baggage will be put into another vehicle for the trip back home. The driver walked ahead of us, took his ID card, and swiped at the entrance kiosk. The doors opened, and we followed him in. He walked us over to what appeared to be another security checkpoint. We all had to sign in, and we were issued temporary passes. The driver asked the security attendant to call Agent Harrington and tell him that the Farnsworths are in the lobby.

The driver then pointed to a waiting area and said, "Please have a seat. Go ahead and relax. Would any of you like some bottled water or a soda?"

We all agreed on a bottle of water. The driver disappeared down a corridor. Looking around at the décor, you'd never know that this is the field office of the bureau except for the huge emblem of the FBI, emblazed in the floor that we walked across of as we entered the main lobby. Just to the right of the security desk, a set of elevators were located. I watched the indicator lights moving from the higher floors downward. I'm guessing that the agent that will be assigned to me is on his way down. By the time the elevator reached the first floor, the driver appeared from the corridor holding three bottles of water.

The elevator doors open, and two men are walking towards where we are sitting. The driver walked over to us and handed us the bottles of water. The driver then introduced the two other men to us.

He said, "Deputy Director of Field Operations Perry Wall, this is Mr. James Farnsworth, his mother and grandmother."

I stood and shook his hand.

The driver then said, "The other gentleman is Agent Eric Harrington."

I turned and shook his hand also.

Agent Harrington said, "Ladies, we have to borrow Mr. Farnsworth for a moment, and while he is with us, Agent Haynes, the driver that brought you here, will take care of you. We promise we won't keep him very long."

I followed the deputy director and Agent Harrington to the elevator. Here goes the asking of questions concerning the mob.

As the doors closed on the elevator, the deputy director said, "Mr. Farnsworth, first let me express my condolences for the loss of your fiancée and to tell you that we are going to do whatever it takes to get these people that are involved with her killing plus the attempt to kill you."

I told them, "I'm not worried about me. I'm more concerned with the safety of my mom and grandmother. They are the only remaining members of my immediate family, and I don't want to lose either one them to the mob because he's after me or, I should say, my business."

Agent Harrington spoke up and said, "Mr. Farnsworth, from here on out I'm going to be your guardian angel, and a team of agents will be responsible for your mom and grandmother's protection."

The elevator came to a stop, and I followed them out and down a corridor until we reached the deputy director's office. I followed them in.

The deputy director said, "Have a seat, Mr. Farnsworth."

I sat down in front of the deputy director's desk, and Agent Harrington sat beside me.

The deputy director said, "Don't take an offense about what I'm about to ask you."

Before he could say another word, I said, "I never took any money, though Serlinni did offer it, if that's the question you're asking."

The deputy director said, "Well, it was one of the questions, but have you been trafficking drugs for Serlinni?"

I said, "Let me guess, you're asking that question because marijuana was found in my blood as well as in Nicole's. The reason that it showed up is because we used it as a recreational drug, and I wasn't trafficking it. I make a good living at what I'm doing. I don't have to traffic drugs to supplement my income, and I don't allow it on premises of my business either."

Agent Harrington said, "The reason for these questions is that Serlinni is under suspicion of using one or possibly all of the so-called acquired studios as a front to traffic drugs, launder money, and the sex trade. We believe that because your location is within a mile of Interstate 75, that's why Serlinni wants it so badly."

I said, "Looking at it in that perspective, the location is in Central Georgia with I-75 going right through it, I-16 to the east, and Highway 80 to the west. It would be a central hub to the network."

Director Wall said, "Here's the next question for you. Mr. Farnsworth, are you willing to cooperate with us by helping us shut down Serlinni and his operation?"

I said, "You are asking me, do I mind being the bait so you guys can spring the trap, right?"

Agent Harrington chuckled and said, "Well, since you put it like that, yes. But we also realize that this is a very dangerous coordinated effort. Per your statement that you made to the field director in Arizona, you feel that someone within your organization may be on the take. Is that correct?"

I said, "I received a call at my office from Serlinni telling me that he was disappointed that I didn't take his peace offering the same day I was just leaving the office to prepare to go to Arizona. That same day, I was on my way to my vehicle, leaving the business for the day. A car pulls up, and if I had gotten into my vehicle, I would've been riddled with bullets. Instead, I go over to the dumpster to throw away a Burger King bag. I reported the incident to the local police, but I didn't have a description of the vehicle, didn't see who fired the shots. I told the police officer that some hoodlums shot up my car as I was throwing away some trash. I had no proof to tie the incident to anyone, but I had my suspicion. The officer told me that there had been some gang activity in the area, and that's how he wrote it up. I took my vehicle out to a local body shop and left it to be fixed. Was I supposed to tell the policeman that I think that the mob just tried to snuff me out? A couple of days prior to that, Serlinni called me and offered me two million for my business. I told him that two million wouldn't cover the cost of the equipment that is in the studio. I should have taken it, and Nicole would be alive today."

Director Wall said, "You would have wound up dead even if you had taken the money. The moment that you accepted that briefcase full of money, you probably wouldn't have made it out of the room alive. If you did walk out, someone would be waiting down the road to pull up behind you, blow the back of your head out, retrieve the money, and get a bonus from the boss."

I said, "Okay, I get the picture. Now once I go back to my hometown, make a showing at Nicole's parents' house—"

Agent Harrington stopped me before I went any further by saying, "You will need to take your mother and grandmother with you when you go. The reason being is, first, it has to look like you all arrived back to town at the same time. Two, tell them that you all came straight from the airport to Nicole's parents' house. If they say something to the nature of that they called the hospital that you were in and you had been dismissed and why didn't you come home the day you were dismissed, simply tell them that you weren't able to get a flight out until today. And if either of her parents mention if the detectives had any leads on the case, tell them the names of the detectives that talked to you, and as far as you know, it was a robbery that went wrong. You can't at this time tell anyone that the feds are involved."

Director Wall then said, "Once you leave Nicole's parents' home, this is what I want you to do. After Agent Harrington has checked out your house and made sure that no one is hiding in there, waiting for you, plus made sure your vehicles aren't rigged, I want you to spend the night in your home just for one night. The reason being, it will appear normal to someone that is possibly watching your house. After tonight, I want you to move in with your grandmother because we're going to put your mom in a safe house in Atlanta two days from now. The cover story for her will be that a close friend of hers in Atlanta has fallen ill and that her friend is close to dying. That will be the reason your mother will tell her friends at home, her housekeeper, and whoever she has contact with. Then you will move in with your grandmother so that there will be only two locations under surveillance, your grandmother's house and your place of business. Now on the subject of your business, you will carry on day-to-day business as usual. We will place listening devices in your business during after-hours so the employees won't get suspicious. According to what you've told us, Mr. Farnsworth, it shouldn't take too long before the informant is flushed out in the open. Then we can put the squeeze on them."

I said, "How are you going to flush Serlinni out in the open?"

Agent Harrington said, "Once the people at your business find out you are back in town, Serlinni or one of his underlings will contact you. That's when you finish talking to them, you get on a land line or a cell phone, if a land line isn't possible, and tell me what was said, like if the underling asked you to meet them somewhere and so on. Like Deputy Director Wall said, I won't be the only agent in Byron, Georgia, that's on the case."

Deputy Director Wall asked me, "Are you ready to do this, Mr. Farnsworth? If you say no, then good luck taking on the mob by yourself, and if you tell me yes, then it's game on."

I said, "It's game on."

Deputy Director Wall stood up and shook my hand and said, "It's game on then." He turned to Agent Harrington. "Mr. Farnsworth will need a rental car to drive home. Get Agent Haynes to take him to a rental business and come back to get the women. It will give me time to brief them on what's about to happen and prepare them while Mr. Farnsworth is car shopping."

Then the deputy director turns to Agent Harrington and tells him to bring the two ladies to his office please. I thanked the deputy director, shook his hand, and followed Agent Harrington to the elevator. As we got on the elevator, I asked Agent Harrington if he had ever been involved with something of this magnitude.

Agent Harrington said, "Yes, I have, Mr. Farnsworth. I can't discuss the cases, but I can tell you that Serlinni is a big fish that my boss wants to hang on his wall. He has assembled the best field agents for this case, and above all, he has you and your family's safety at the top of the list."

The elevator stops, and we get off the elevator.

Agent Harrington takes out his cell phone and calls Agent Haynes to meet us in the lobby. Agent Harrington walks with me over to the waiting area where Mom and Grandmother are sitting. I tell them that everything is okay, that Agent Harrington wants to take them upstairs to talk to his boss, Deputy Director Wall.

Agent Harrington chimed in and said, "It shouldn't take long, ladies, and you'll be on the road home before you know it."

As they started for the elevator, Agent Haynes walks up and asked Agent Harrington what he needed to happen. Agent Harrington told Agent Haynes to take me to a car rental business so that I could rent a car for my trip back home.

Agent Haynes said, "Let's go get you a ride, Mr. Farnsworth."

I followed Agent Haynes to the vehicle that our baggage was in. He unlocked the vehicle, and I got in. He pulled out of the underground parking garage and into the downtown traffic. On the way, I had time to think of how this arrangement is going to impact our everyday lives.

Agent Haynes started up a conversation by saying, "How far are you guys having to drive to get back home?"

I told him that I had to drive to Byron, just fourteen miles south of Macon. Agent Haynes told me he knows where it is because he has relatives in Macon. I thought to myself, Haynes isn't just a driver. He's a plant to extract information if he can, so I played along.

Haynes said, "You must be in some heavy-duty stuff for the boss to send out the A team."

I said, "My business is legit. It's the mob and gangstas that give the business a bad name."

Haynes said, "So your studio doesn't record rappers?"

I said, "I would if the so-called rappers were musicians. Bands like the Commodores are musicians."

Evidently, I had struck a nerve with Haynes, and he stopped trying to pick me for information. The ride wasn't much longer before we had arrived at a Hertz car rental center.

Haynes pulls in and parks and says, "Here it is, let's go and get you a vehicle."

Agent Haynes procured a midsized car so at least Mom and Grandmother can ride back home in comfort. The lady at the car rental gave him the keys after he had signed the necessary paperwork and paid with credit card. I walked out to the vehicle, and Haynes popped the trunk so I could get the baggage out. I got the bags out and loaded them into Chrysler 300. Haynes let his window down and told me to follow him back to the field office. I told him to lead the way. I followed him back through the twist and turns of the city streets until I arrived back at the federal building parking garage.

I parked the car and walked to the entrance, waiting on Haynes to use his ID card to open the main doors. We walk in, and Agent Harrington was sitting with Mom and Grandmother in the waiting area. I walked over to them and tell them that I have a car and asked

Agent Harrington if he was going with us. Agent Harrington then told me that he had contacted some agents in Macon, and they are to link up with him as he goes through Macon. He told us that he wants to have our vehicles and our homes checked before we enter them.

He said, "The agents that are to link up with me are trained professionals. They are skilled in explosive detection, covert surveillance, and electronic espionage. I'll be tailing you all the way home."

I said, "Is everyone ready?"

Grandmother said, "I'll be glad to sleep in my own bed for change."

She and Mom stood up, and we all walked toward the main exit of the federal building.

Mom said, "I'm going to be in a safe house here in Atlanta per the feds. I don't like the idea of them using you for bait to catch Serlinni."

On the way to the car, I told Mom that Serlinni isn't the only one that they will be after. Someone or a group of individuals inside the studio could be on Serlinni's payroll. They are just as guilty as the person that pulled the trigger that killed Nicole and tried to kill me. I'm going to do whatever it takes to flush out whomever is involved and get them put away.

I unlocked the doors on the 300, and we all got in, buckled up, and pulled out of the underground parking lot of the federal building. I used the voice command on the GPS to get the closest route to I-75 south. The machine told me to take a right, go through two traffic lights, and turn left, and that will put me on I-75 south. I took the directions given to me and found I-75 south. I turned onto an entrance ramp, and by the looks of the traffic, I can forget about putting the cruise control on until I can get out of this mess. To say that the traffic was busy would be an understatement. I had to floor it just to get out there to be in pace with the oncoming traffic. No one was moving over to allow merging. It was balls to wall.

I looked at the car's digital clock, and it had 4:45 p.m., traffic jam time. I was able to get in amongst the herd of cars and trucks, trying to get into a lane that is moving the fastest. Traffic was moving at least seventy-five or better until we got to a choke point down the road. Traffic was merging to the right because of construction, and the pace slowed down to about fifty miles an hour. I told Mom and Grandmother that I am dreading going to Nicole's parents' house.

Mom said, "We all are, but they would do the same out respect for you if events had been reversed."

Grandmother said, "They will probably offer us to eat dinner with them, but we can tell them that we haven't been home ourselves, driving straight in from the airport in Atlanta. Before we get into Macon, you'll need to stop and let your mother drive into Byron and to Nicole's house. Remember, you just got out of the hospital yesterday and still wearing stitches. They don't need to see you drive up in their yard like nothing happened."

I said, "You're right, perceived appearance is everything. Did the feds suggest that?"

Grandmother said, "No, I put myself in their place looking out the window at whoever has driven up into my driveway. And the scene of you getting out from behind the driver's seat coming from Atlanta doesn't fit right. It may be a good idea to change up in Forsyth so that the feds see you changing drivers as well, if you get my meaning. Like you said, perceived appearance is everything."

Mom said, "Sounds like somebody has been doing some thinking about this. Grandmother Farnsworth must have been a secret agent in her past life."

We all chuckled about that comment. I thought to myself, I am dreading to face these people and not be able to tell them who is responsible for killing their only child. I stopped thinking about the inevitable and focused on the traffic. It looks like the cars are starting to bunch up and slow down. We are approaching a construction area. The lanes are being funneled from four lanes down to two lanes. Mom could tell that I was getting irritated about the situation.

Mom said, "Find some nice soothing music on the radio. It probably has a satellite link."

I turned on the radio and searched for some easy-listening music. I found a station that was playing Vegas-type show tunes music. I think it was Bobby Darrin singing "Mack the Knife" song. I asked the women if they were hungry. They said that they could use something to eat since our last meal was a continental breakfast in Arizona. I told them once we can get clear of this traffic jam and see an exit sign that displays any type of fast food, I'm turning off. I picked up my cell phone and gave it to Mom and told her to scroll through my stored numbers. When she finds Eric Harrington's number, I told her to hit the dial button and hand the phone to me.

The phone rang a couple of times, and Agent Harrington answered.

He said, "Yes, Mr. Farnsworth, what's up?"

I asked him how far he was behind me, and he told me only two or three cars back from me. I told him that we want to stop and get a quick bite and get back on the road. We haven't had anything since a continental breakfast in Arizona.

Agent Harrington said, "Just let me know which exit you're getting off on ahead of time."

I told him that I would and told him that I would call him back. I closed the phone and put it back on the seat. Grandmother asked me where my hands-free set was. I told her that it was in my other vehicle, the one that got shot up. I told them to help me be on the lookout for an exit for something to eat after we get out of this crowd of cars. One thing for sure was weighing heavy on my mind. Tomorrow night is when I change. Somebody better get ready to chain me up somewhere before some people in Byron get slaughtered. I hope that Grandmother and I can have a one-on-one conversation about this. Plus all of this will be happening under the noses of federal agents.

We had gotten a few miles down the road, and traffic had speeded up to a good even seventy miles an hour. There's still too much traffic to even think about using cruise control. I looked in the distance, and there appears to be an exit. Could there be food in the next possible exit? As the distance began to close, the sign was about fuel only—damn. I continued to drive southward on I-75. Up ahead, I think I saw a billboard with a couple of fast-food venues on it. I gave Mom my phone and told her to scroll down to Eric Harrington's number and hit dial. She hit dial and handed me the phone.

Eric answered and said, "You want to get something to eat at the next exit, right?"

I replied by saying, "Absolutely, dinner's on me."

I pulled into the right-hand lane, getting ready to exit. My body is telling me that it is time to eat. Under normal circumstances, Mom detests fast-food joints. Today, I think she will put aside her differences for a hamburger and some fries. I look into the rearview mirror. I see a couple of cars behind me preparing to exit also. I didn't get to see what Agent Harrington was driving or the color of the vehicle. I have to wait and see when we pull into a fast-food joint. The sign on the off-ramp had four venues to choose from: KFC, Chick-fil-A, McDonald's, and Wendy's.

As I was within a quarter of a mile from the exit I said, "Okay, which one do you guys want me to stop at?"

Grandmother said that it didn't matter to her.

Mom said, "Stop in at Chick-fil-A since they don't have one in Byron."

"Chick-fil-A it is," I exclaimed.

I turned onto the off-ramp and stopped at the traffic light. I looked to my right, and I saw where the restaurant is located. I waited for the light to turn green, and I made a right. I looked in the rearview to see how many other cars followed me. There was a string of cars going in the same direction. I went about two blocks and turned into the chicken empire. I pulled over to the side of the parking lot, stopped, and got my phone. By the time I could flip my phone open, a car pulled up beside me. The tinted window on the passenger side goes down, and it's Agent Harrington. I hit the switch to lower my window, and I asked him if he was hungry. He told me that I needed to get the food to go because we have to rendezvous with a group of agents in Macon. He told me that he would also pull in behind me to order his food also. I told him that I'm getting my mom to drive the rest of the way in. I'm feeling kind of winded. He told me that I didn't need to push myself since I had just recently gotten out of the hospital and was still wearing stitches.

I pulled up just enough to clear his vehicle so that Mom and I could trade places. I got on the passenger side as Mom took the driver's seat and buckled up. Mom told me that she had hoped that we would be going in, but she can do this. I told her that I would get her food and drink laid out for her once we get on the road. She pulled up to the drive-through window, and we placed our orders with the window attendant. Amazingly, we didn't have to wait too long before we had our orders filled, and I told Mom to pull over to the side. This will buy us some time for Agent Harrington to order plus get our food situated before we hit the interstate again. I looked at the dash to see where the pop-out beverage holders were. I found it and got the drinks placed. I looked back, and Agent Harrington had just pulled away from the drive-through window.

I told Mom, "Go ahead and get us on the interstate, and I'll get your sandwich ready."

Mom pulled out onto the road and stopped at the red light.

As I was handing Grandmother her sandwich and some napkins, I asked her, "Why does life have to be so complicated?"

She answered by saying that life isn't complicated, it is the people that make life complicated.

Mom said, "Just because we live in a technologically advanced society, the technology doesn't necessarily make life any easier. For instance, it costs more to have a cell phone than a house phone. The cell phone is just a phone without the wires and has probably cost more people's lives than alcohol. I can remember when we could watch television for free with an antenna until there was a push for everyone to get hooked up to cable or satellite and then the push to go to high definition. With each advancement, the cost went up, and the cost of living didn't move."

Light changed to green, and Mom got on the off-ramp that merges with I-75.

I said, "The FBI told me even if I had accepted Serlinni's offer, I would have been killed shortly after receiving the suitcase full of money. I wouldn't have made it to the bank with it."

Grandmother said, "Money is the root of all evil, yet we have to have it to live. Serlinni will get what's coming to him eventually. There is always someone higher up on the food chain than the one below it."

I fixed Mom's sandwich so that she could eat it and drive. Luckily, the traffic isn't as bad as it was in downtown Atlanta. If we don't have to make any more stops, we'll hit Macon around six thirty or so. I guess Agent Harrington will call me to let us know where to stop off in Macon for the linkup with the other field agents.

Mom said, "Tomorrow's your birthday, and the FBI will be taking me to a safe house on the same day."

I said, "They'll be doing it so you'll be safe. Besides, I'll just be one more year older and wiser."

I had finished off my chicken sandwich, my crosscut fries and was now draining the last of my drink, leaving the ice to melt down for a later drink. I looked into my rearview mirror. I could see Agent Harrington tailing us about two cars behind us. I sat there thinking about tomorrow and what was to happen me. My thoughts flashed to the first werewolf movie I'd ever saw, the movie starring Lon Chaney Jr. as the Wolfman, the scenes showing him walking on his toes through the mist, looking for his next victim. That film made the Wolfman more man than appearing like a long-eared canine depicted on the films that followed. I'll find out tomorrow night which of the films came the closest to the real deal. We passed a billboard advertising someone's discount liquor store. I could use a big drink about now. Grandmother asked me to hand her the bag that the sandwiches came in with so that she could put her trash into it. Mom was about finished with her sandwich and asked me if I wanted her crosscut fries.

I said, "Is a two-pound robin fat?"

I felt a wetness on the back of my head because Grandmother had a mouthful of Coke and sprayed me from laughing at the comeback I told Mom. Grandmother took her napkin and wiped the drink off of me, telling me that she didn't mean it. Mom was laughing and asked me where I heard that from anyway.

I said, "You saw how fast I got rid of my food, and of course, I wanted your fries. Now, where did I get that phrase from, I don't know. It just came to me. The miles clicked away; no one was saying too much. I guess we all are dreading having to see Nicole's parents. Each one of us was rifling through our thoughts on what to say to someone who has lost their only child. I saw a sign that had Macon 20 Miles on it; we'll be reaching the rendezvous point. That is, once I get the call from Agent Harrington telling me where to go once we get into Macon. As I watch the billboards go as cars speedily passed us, my cell phone rings. I pick it up and look at the incoming number, it's Agent Harrington. I answered the phone, and he tells me that we are to exit onto Hartley Bridge Road and to follow him to Kroger's parking lot. Agent Harrington drove around us and was now in front.

Agent Harrington said, "Just follow right behind me, and I'll see you at the parking lot."

The phone conversation ended, and I told Mom to just follow behind Agent Harrington, who was in front of us. Mom followed Agent Harrington right into the Kroger parking lot. Agent Harrington parked his car next to a gray-colored Mercedes. Mom pulled our car along beside Agent Harrington and parked. We were not alone. As I watched Agent Harrington get out to approach our rental, so did others. Agent Harrington motioned to get out of the car, and we complied. I opened the door and got out.

Agent Harrington said, "I know these vehicles that you see parked out here don't look like your run-of-the-mill, traditional government-issued vehicles. They aren't supposed to. They look like high-profile society-type vehicles."

As he was talking to me, a group of people were converging upon us.

I said, "I hope they are friends of yours, Agent Harrington."

There were three men and a woman, an attractive black woman at that.

Once the individuals got closer to us, Agent Harrington said, "Agents, this is Mr. James Farnsworth. Go ahead and introduce yourselves to him."

Each agent stepped forward and introduced themselves to me, and I shook each of their hands.

Agent Harrington said, "These agents and myself will be the protective shield for you and your family. Each of these agents will be assigned different tasks all geared toward taking down Mr. Serlinni and his operation."

He told two of the agents to go ahead and get themselves motel rooms in Byron and that he will be in contact with them shortly. The two agents got into their vehicles and sped towards the interstate. Agent Harrington went on to explain that the two remaining agents, Agent Williams and Agent Le Claire, would be checking out our houses and vehicles for explosives. Mom and Grandmother had gotten out of the car. They were saying that they needed to stand up from sitting for such a duration. Agent Harrington continued to explain that Agent Le Claire is a weapons expert and is trained in martial arts. He then told me that Agent Williams is a munitions detection and electronic countermeasures specialist.

Agent Harrington said, "I'm going to send these two ahead to check out your houses to make sure that no one has wired it up to explode. I understand that you will be taking your mother and grandmother to Nicole Adams's parents' house to pay your respect to her parents. One of the two agents that left before Williams and Le Claire are trained in close and electronic surveillance. That is Agent Franks, and the other agent is Agent Stevens. He will be linking up with the FBI's eye-in-the-sky satellite system. He'll be able to give real-time locations of potential threats and relay it back to the team of agents. Before you go put this on your key chain…"

He handed me this bullet-shaped trinket that looked like an ordinary key chain fob.

I said, "Let me guess, this is a tracking device."

He told me that it is exactly what it is. Agent Harrington then said, "I don't want to detain you any longer because I imagine that your mother and grandmother want to get back home and rest. For tonight, after the agents have made sure that your houses are safe, Agent Le Claire will be staying at your mother's house, and you will be staying with your grandmother because for the moment, we can only watch over two locations at a time right now. I know that's not what my boss said. He called me and made a last-minute change."

I told him that I needed to get some clothes out of house because I'm limited on my wardrobe right now.

Agent Harrington said, "That won't be a problem once the agents have made sure the house is safe. Just call me before you take your mom home and go to your house. I want to hear from my field agents first that everything is clear."

I told him that I would call him, and we got back to our vehicles. As I got back into the car, I told Mom to head back to Nicole's parents' house so we can get this over with. Mom pulled back onto the street, waited for the light change, and headed for the off-ramp to get back on I-75 south towards Byron.

Mom said, "After I'm sent to a safe house, is my house being closed down and I'm to lay off my housekeeper until further notice?"

I said, "My guess is that once you're safe in Atlanta, the agents will use the house as a base of operations. Some agents will be staying in motels in Byron. It will be a waiting game to see what Serlinni does next. The agents will probably wire the phones in the houses and at the business to anticipate Serlinni placing a call."

Grandmother said, "This has turned into a real cloak-and-dagger situation. This is the kind of stuff I've only seen in movies. I would've never even dreamed of anything like this happening to my family."

Mom chimed in and said, "Only if your father had sold the studio to that animal, we wouldn't be going through this."

I said, "Don't you remember what the agent said? Even if Dad had accepted the money, he wouldn't have made it to the bank with it."

Mom said, "I'm sorry, it's not your father's fault or yours. I guess for now I can lay all the blame on Satan for corrupting people's minds and leading them to damnation."

I thought to myself, she would trip if I told her that the dark one had appeared to me more than once in my dreams. Within about fifteen minutes, we were turning off onto Exit 149 going into Byron. My stomach began to knot up with anxiety, knowing that I am going to Nicole's parents' house. I don't know what kind of reception I'm about to walk into. Mom made a couple of turns, and we were going down the street—the same street I went down on many times to pick up Nicole and drop her off before she had moved out into her apartment. I looked into the rearview mirror, and Agent Harrington was hanging back a couple of car lengths from us.

As Mom approached Nicole's parents' house, there were a few vehicles already parked in the yard. Mom pulled into the drive. I looked at the car tags of the parked cars, and they were local. It won't be too long before the sun will be going down, and heat of the day will be gone. I am dreading this. Mom parks the car, and I looked back at the highway. Agent Harrington drove right on by. I got out and opened the door for Grandmother. She stood up and held on to my arm.

She said, "I've been sitting for a while. Let me get my legs to working."

I told her to take her time. I gingerly guided Grandmother toward the house. As we were drawing closer to the house, some people that Mom knew were coming out. Mom spoke to them briefly and walked up the entry with us. I knocked on the door, and Nicole's cousin Angela came to the door.

She said, "Come in, we're glad to see you."

We walked into the front room, and Nicole's mom and dad were sitting and talking with Reverend Parker. Nicole's father stands up and walks over to us. Nicole's mother reaches out toward my mom. Mom goes and sits by Nicole's mother. Nicole's father, Mr. Adams, asked my grandmother to please have a seat.

Grandmother said, "Thank you, Mr. Adams, but I need to stand for a little while, all of that time sitting in the car from Atlanta. I've got to get the blood circulating again. I'm not as young as you."

Mr. Adams said, "Well, can I get you something to drink, Mrs. Farnsworth? And how about you, James?"

I told him no thanks, that we're fine. Grandmother asked Mr. Adams if he could tell her where the nearest bathroom was. Mr. Adams told Grandmother where the bathroom is, and she headed off. Mr. Adams asked me to follow him to the kitchen. I thought to myself, either he's going to lash out at me or ask questions about what led up to the shooting. I hoped it was the latter. I followed him into the kitchen, and he told me to have a seat at the table. I told him that I wasn't able to get back in time for Nicole's funeral.

Mr. Adams said, "James, I couldn't bear to see Nicole's mother spend another night at the funeral home with her child. The family doctor has got my wife on some strong medications right now to keep her calm."

By this time, I was overcome with emotion.

Mr. Adams then said, "I know you and your folks are tired from your journey. It means a lot to me that you came here straight from the Atlanta airport to see us before you went home. That shows me that you carry with you the same integrity and decency from your father and your grandfather, God rest their souls. I only ask that you tell me the events that led up to the shooting. Forgive me, James, are you hungry?"

I told him that Mom had stopped at a drive-through restaurant between Atlanta and Macon, and I appreciated the offer. I began to tell him what happened before the shooting took place, a detailed event right up to when I walked in on the shooter. I left out the part about Nicole's lifeless body as I crawled to her before passing out.

Nicole's father said, "Was anything taken from the room?"

I said, "I had a thousand dollars in travelers checks and the cash was taken from my wallet. The robber could unload the traveler's checks in a liquor store. They weren't signed."

I mentioned that I got Mom to call the bank and report stolen the traveler's checks. I told him that I didn't know if the robber came in through the door or if he was already in the room, hiding. I told Nicole's father that I had an appointment with a private investigator tomorrow. Nicole's father asked me how much this investigator is costing me. I told him that he didn't have to worry about that because I am footing the bill. He simply asked me to keep him informed about what transpires with the case. My emotions were just spilling out. I had to gather myself before I got up to see Nicole's mom before I left. The tears were falling as Nicole's father walked with me into the room where Nicole's mother was. I made my way through the crowd of people and gave them a quick greeting as I entered the room. Nicole's mother was sitting on a couch with Mom and other women that I did not know. As I made myself closer to her, she made eye contact with me and held her arms out to me. The lady sitting next to her got up and let me sit next to her.

Nicole's mom said, "Your mother told me that you didn't get released in time and get a flight until today. It was a beautiful service, and thank you and your family for the beautiful floral display that was draped on her casket. She loved you a lot, James Farnsworth. You brought a lot of joy into her life and experiences that her father and I couldn't have imagined giving her. I know you are hurting just as much as we are, and you will be wearing the scar from that night the rest of your life. I wasn't prepared to give up my baby that way. You could have been taken also."

We both started weeping and holding each other.

After we hugged each other and wiped tears from our faces, I said "Know this, I will use all the resources available to me to find out who is responsible, and they will pay.

Nicole's mom grasped my hand and said, "You would have made Nicole a good husband."

I only nodded and exited the room to find Mom and Grandmother. I had to get out of there. I found Grandmother; she and Mom were talking to Nicole's aunt.

Grandmother said, "James, we should get you home. You look like you need to lie down."

I said, "Yes, let's go home."

I needed an excuse to get away from here, and Grandmother came up with a perfect solution. I also had to call Agent Harrington to find out if the houses were safe. I opened the door for Grandmother and helped her in. Mom got in the driver's seat. I took out my cell phone and called the Agent Harrington.

He answered, "Mr. Farnsworth, your mother's house is clear. Agents are working at your house and your grandmother's. Why don't you all to wait at your mother's home until I can call you back."

I told him that would be okay, and I told him that I would wait for his call. Mom backed out of the Adams driveway, and I told her to head to her house and filled them in on the information that Agent Harrington had told me. On the way to Mom's house, I looked in the rearview mirror. There was a set of car lights following us. I hope that it is Agent Harrington. Mom drove through town toward her house on the outskirts of the city. I was able to see the color of the car that was following us due to the streetlights; it was Agent Harrington.

A few more miles and we were at Mom's house. Mom parks the car, and Agent Harrington pulls in behind us. I opened the trunk and asked Mom which was her luggage.

Agent Harrington walked up and said, "Mr. Farnsworth, you shouldn't pick that up. You could bust a stitch loose."

Agent Harrington grabbed the bags and took them to the front door. Mom approached the front door to unlock it. The door opens, and Agent Le Claire was standing there.

Mom said, "Let me guess, the FBI has resourceful ways of entering and disabling alarms."

Agent Le Claire said, "The house is safe and so are you and your family, Mrs. Farnsworth."

We all walked into Mom's house, and Agent Harrington asked me what kind of car do I have parked at the Macon airport and said that he needed the keys to it. He told me that once Agent Williams checks back in with him, he wants me to ride with him to the airport to get the car. Mom asked if anyone was hungry.

Grandmother replied by saying, "What do you have in the refrigerator?"

I asked Agent Le Claire if she was hungry because it may be a little while before Agent Harrington and I get back. She said that she could eat something light. Mom told us that she had eggs and bacon, and it wouldn't take too long to build a meal.

Mom said, "Besides, I got to burn off some of this nervous energy I got."

Agent Harrington asked Agent Le Claire where her vehicle is, and she told him that it's in the garage, out of sight. Agent Harrington's phone was ringing, and he took the call. I heard Agent Harrington say to stay there, and he would be on the way.

He put away his phone and said, "Take a ride with me, Mr. Farnsworth."

I followed Agent Harrington out to his car and got in.

I said, "Something up, Agent Harrington?"

"Agent Williams said that he is in need of my assistance at your house, Mr. Farnsworth," replied Agent Harrington.

Agent Harrington then programmed his dashboard GPS with my home address and pulled out of the driveway. He told me that Agent Williams had parked his car off-site, meaning that he parked somewhere away from the house and walked into the property. He said that Agent Williams walked up to the side of the house and did an electrical current reading of the house. Agent Williams said that the current had been turned off.

"That could mean two things. One reason would be to disable the power to disarm the alarm and wire the fuse box with a bomb, then when the power switch is turned on, you know. The second reason would be that the power has been turned off to disarm the alarm system, and someone is in the house, waiting on you to come in and investigate the fuse box then, you know. Where is the fuse box located?"

I told him that it is in the laundry room located in a rear room of the house. He asked me if I had a basement. I told him that I don't have a basement, but there is a large attic in the house.

He said, "That's good to know when you're walking into unknown territory."

Agent Harrington asked me about the adjacent property next to mine. He told me that if someone is in the house, he doesn't want to tip them off by parking in the driveway. I told him that there is a field road next to my property and that he could pull into the field road, and we could walk in.

Agent Harrington said, "There is no *we* to this. You will sit in this car until I get back."

I told Agent Harrington to slow down and turn off his headlights but leave the running lights on. The field road is coming up on the right. He slowed down and turned onto the dirt path that runs parallel to my property. There is an open field on the right of us, a patch of woods to the left and through the woods about forty yards or so is my house. Agent Harrington took out his cell phone and began texting a message. He finished the message, opened his glove box, and took out a flashlight. He turned to me and told me not to leave the car until he gets back or he calls me on my cell. He gets out and closes the door in such a way so as not to make any noise. I watched the flickering of his flashlight as he disappeared into the darkness. I sat there feeling helpless as the two agents were heading into the unknown.

As I sat waiting in the agent's car, agents Williams and Harrington met up at the back of the house. Agent Harrington told Williams that the fuse box is in a laundry room just to the right of the back door. He told Williams to make sure that the backdoor isn't wired also with explosives. The two agents approach the rear entrance, and the agent took out an explosive-detection device and scanned the door. He gave Agent Harrington a hand signal signifying that there were no explosives detected. He then took out an infrared detection gun to make sure that there is no one waiting on the other side of the door.

CHAPTER 9

The infrared showed no heat signature. Agent Williams picked the lock and carefully opened the door. Agent Harrington motioned for Williams to go to the laundry room and check the fuse box. Agent Harrington watched the doorway as Williams checked out the fuse box and turned on the lights. After the lights were turned on, the two agents went farther into the house as Williams was holding the infrared sensor, aiming it ahead of them and over them also because of the attic. As they got closer to the front room, Agent Williams had picked up a heat signature above him. Williams gave Harrington a signal, pointing above him. Harrington gave Williams a hand signal to stay put as he looked around. Harrington checked out the rest of the rooms, came back to the front door, and saw that it was wired to go off. Harrington went back to Williams and traded places with him. Harrington had the infrared sensor still on a heat signature up above. Williams went to the front door and disarmed the bomb. Williams signaled to Harrington that the bomb has been diffused. Agent Harrington took out his cell phone and texted Williams this message, "Go out front door slam door hard. I will watch attic door will advise."

Agent Williams went out the front door and shut it hard while Agent Harrington watched to see if the attic door opened. Agent Harrington waited and listened for any movement. There was no sound and no movement. Agent Harrington opened the bathroom door that is in the hallway where the attic door is. He reached in and turned on the vent fan, took out his cell phone, and called me. Agent Harrington asked me where the hot water heater was located. I told him the water heater is in the attic. He then told me to drive the car over to the house and sit and hung up. Agent Harrington turned off the vent fan and listened. With his gun drawn and on the ready, he peeped through the crack of the door hinge toward the attic location, and nothing had changed.

I drove Agent Harrington's car over to my house and parked the car in the drive. Both agents walked up to the car, and I let the window down.

Agent Harrington said, "Mr. Farnsworth, you are probably wondering why I asked where the hot water heater is located, the reason being that the infrared scanner had picked up a heat signature in the attic. After doing a couple of tactics to entice the would-be perpetrator to move, that's when I called you. Also the front door was wired to go off after you close the door. Agent Williams disabled the bomb, and we'll go back inside with you so you can get your things. Agent Williams will also remove the bomb from the house while we are in there."

He told me to look around to see if anything is out of sorts. I walked behind Agent Williams as we entered my house. I asked Agent Williams if he checked the refrigerator to see if it is rigged. He said that he didn't but will look at it. I told him to check the refrigerator because I hope the perp didn't drink up my beers I had in there. The agents laughed about my comment. I looked around in the front room to see if anything was gone or out of place. Things seemed okay other than the door being rigged. Agent Williams walked into the kitchen and looked over the refrigerator before he opened.

Agent Williams said, "I see four beers and a half gallon of milk that's out of date, some eggs that probably need to go along with what used to be lettuce."

I got a trash bag and cleaned out the out-of-date stuff because it may be a few more days before I get to come back since I'll be staying with Grandmother. I told them that I had to go in my bedroom and get some clothes to take with me to Grandmother's. Agent Harrington walked ahead and checked my bedroom, under the bed, and the closet before I went in. I told them that it shouldn't take me too long. I grabbed a couple pairs of jeans, a pair of dress slacks, some casual short-sleeved shirts and a dress shirt, several pairs of socks, underwear, my dress shoes, and my sneakers. I put it all in a suitcase that I had put on my bed. I went into my bathroom, got a couple of razors, my toothpaste, mouthwash, and shampoo. I then thought about my stash; it was with my pistol. I started talking to the agents to distract them as I went to my closet to get the stash and slid it in my pocket. They were standing in the hallway as I asked them how can I secure the doors or at least what can I do that will alert me that someone has broken in even if the doors are locked. Agent Williams walked to the doorway as I was taking down my holstered pistol that I had hidden. He asked me what kind of pistol I had. I told him that it is a Dan Wesson .44 Magnum. I asked them if they had a problem me taking it with me to my grandmother's. Agent Harrington said that he didn't mind as long as I don't shoot any of his field agents by mistake.

Agent Williams said, "The question you asked about detecting a break-in. First, Agent Harrington and I don't want you to go anywhere unless you call one of us on your house phone or on your cell phone. Is that understood?"

I said, "Sure, I understand perfectly. I don't plan on taking on the mob single-handedly."

Agent Williams told me he has a special compound that once they close up the house, he can put the compound down to make contact with two surfaces. The contact surfaces can be a door and doorjamb, a window and windowsill. The compound hardens and is not noticeable to the untrained eye. If the window or door is opened, the compound will crack or fall off. Then you'll know that your house or car has been compromised. He told me that he will show me when they close up the house. Agent Harrington told me to get everything that I need at least for a week. I put more underwear, socks, and two more pairs of jeans in the suitcase along with the pistol and some extra bullets. I asked them if my grandmother's house had been cleared.

Agent Harrington said, "That's where we are going to next. We're to meet up with Agent Franks there. Agent Williams and I will assist in scoping out the property. While we are doing that, you will be sitting in my car until I call to tell you that the coast is clear."

I said, "I've got to get one last thing, my laptop."

I walked into the den and got the laptop out of the roll top desk, picked up my luggage, and followed the agents to the door. I reset the alarm system and locked the door. I walked out to Agent Harrington's car and got in. Agent Williams got into the backseat, and as Agent Harrington got into the driver's seat, he asked Agent Williams where he parked his car. Agent Williams said that he had pulled into a pecan orchard about a block away and walked in through the hedgerow to the back of the house. Agent Harrington fired up his vehicle, pulled out of my driveway, and stopped, where Agent Williams had his car parked to let him out. Agent Williams got out, and Agent Harrington waited to see if Williams made it to his car, watching to see his headlights come before pulling away. I looked in the rearview mirror as Williams pulled onto the highway and caught up to us.

On the way, Agent Harrington asked me how far off the road my grandmother's house is. I told him that the house is about a half mile straight down Farnsworth Lane. I also told him that there is an electronic eye located halfway down the driveway. It was put there to alert the occupants of the house that there is company coming and also sends a signal to the house alarm that puts it on standby.

I said, "My father had that installed because my grandparents live in a secluded area."

Agent Harrington then said, "According to the GPS, we're almost there. You need to show me where to stop so that we don't trigger the alert."

I told him to slow down, that we are approaching it on the left.

Agent Harrington asked me, "How will I know where the sensor is?"

I told him that I count the pecan trees as I enter the driveway. I told him during my high school days, I would bring girls out here and park.

As we drove by the pecan trees, I counted them off and told him, "Stop here, the sensor is between the next set of trees."

I told Agent Harrington to kill the lights. Agent Williams pulled behind us and stopped. Agent Harrington asked me which way would be the best way to approach the house. I told him that he and Agent Williams should stay close to the hedgerow on the right and approach the house on the side. The front yard and the backyard have sensors to turn on floodlights when an object crosses its path. He told me to stay in the car and not get out until he calls me on the cell phone.

Agent Harrington gets out of the car and eases the door closed. I watched the two agents' silhouettes as their shadows were being cast against the hedgerow by the light of a semifull moon. I thought to myself that it's a good thing that it isn't tomorrow night or those two agents could've been dinner. I sat and waited in the car, pondering about the crazy stuff that has been going on the past few days and nights, especially the really screwed-up dreams that I had. I remembered what the dark one told me. He said that I'm an immortal, and tonight will be my last night living as a normal mortal man. I guess tonight when I go to sleep, I'll get my last-minute instructions from the messengers. As I looked out the window, the detail of the landscape seemed to be different somehow. I looked down at my watch to see the time. Under normal circumstances, I would have to hit the light on my watch to see it in the dark. Tonight, the dial was legible even if the light of the moon wasn't on it. I realized that now I can see in the dark. I looked at my hands to make sure that my fingernails hadn't grown exceptionally long and felt of my canine teeth to make sure that they haven't grown. This effect must be some residual beginnings of what's to come. This was exciting stuff and at the same time kind of frightening. In the movies, when the person changed, the beast was an out-of-control killing machine.

I sat out there in the agent's car for about thirty minutes, then my cell phone rings. I looked at the incoming number; it is Agent

Harrington. I answered the phone, and Agent Harrington told me to go ahead and drive the car up to the house. I told him okay, closed the phone, got behind the wheel, and drove the car up to the house. I hope everything is okay. I didn't hear any gunshots. I don't know what I'm about to find out. I drove toward the house. As I passed the object detection sensor, the security lights came on in front of the house. I parked the car at the entrance of the garage. Agent Harrington walked up to the car and motioned for me to let the window down.

Agent Harrington said, "The house is okay. Agent Williams is checking the building in the back."

I said, "That's the guest house."

Agent Harrington said, "Would your grandmother mind if Agent Williams stayed in the guest house tonight and each of us will be rotating for guard duty?"

I told him that Grandmother wouldn't have a problem with it; the guest house is set up just like a motel room. I then asked him about my car at the Macon airport. He told me that it would be safer for his agents to check it out tomorrow in full daylight. Agent Williams walked out to where we are standing. He said that the guest house checks out. Agent Harrington told Williams and me to stay here. He's going to pick up Grandmother at my mother's house. I told him that I might as well get my stuff out of his car, and he told me to go ahead and get it. I got the luggage and my shaving kit from the backseat and walked toward the house. I heard Agent Harrington tell Williams that he would be back shortly. Agent Williams walked into the house behind me and closed the door.

I said, "Are you thirsty, Agent Williams?"

He told me that he could go for a glass of tea. I put my luggage down in the hallway, went into the kitchen, and washed my hands. I got two glasses out of the cabinet, filled the glasses with ice, and took out the pitcher of tea and filled the glasses. I gave Agent Williams one of the glasses.

Agent Williams said, "Damn, that's some great tea. It beats the hell out of any restaurant tea I've ever tasted."

I told him that for one thing, the water comes from a deep well and is better than any bottled water you can buy.

Williams said, "That would definitely make a difference, and without the chlorine, that is a real plus."

I told him that once Agent Harrington brings Grandmother back, we can get something to eat. She's kind of weird about her kitchen.

Williams said, "My mom is the same way. She says the only man she'll let in her kitchen is Emeril."

I told him that Grandmother doesn't mind if I'm in her kitchen as long as she is in here. We both laughed at quirks attributed to the eccentric people in our lives. I told Agent Williams that he'll like staying in the guest house better than any hotel room tonight. He told me once Agent Harrington gets back, he'll set up some motion sensors around the perimeters of the house. He told me that he had noticed the security cameras set up on the corners of the house. He told me since my house didn't have the security cameras, they wouldn't waste their time to break in to get the recording tape.

I said, "I guess they figured with me out of the way, my mom would sell the business. Then whoever is working for Serlinni on the inside of the business would be Serlinni's puppet."

Agent Williams said, "Sounds like someone has been doing some thinking."

"I don't think that Serlinni had in mind that I was to survive the shooting and killed Nicole because she was just there," I replied. "Will you guys have to break into everyone's house that works for the studio to bug their house?"

He told me that with the current technology, all they would have to do is drill a hole somewhere in the wall of the home or office, place a signal booster in the hole, and the electronics will be able to send a signal to the receiver, allowing us to hear a cell phone or land-line conversation between anyone. I told him that is some bad-assed technology. He said the days of someone wearing a wire like in the movies are over.

"We can put a device in your wristwatch, sewn into your sneakers. The possibilities are endless."

I said, "I guess with the invention of microtechnology, the field is wide open to opportunities."

Before the conversation could go any further, Agent Williams took out his phone and answered a call. I assumed that the caller was Agent Harrington because I overheard Williams say that everything is still okay here, that all there's left to do is put up motion-detection sensors around the house, and he closed his cell phone and put it away. Agent Williams told me that Agent Harrington is returning with my grandmother. I told him that is good, then we can get something to eat. I went into the den and turned on the television and started channel-surfing. It seems that the television programming hadn't changed from Arizona to Georgia. There are just as many channels on trying to sell you something from jewelry, knives, computers, and hordes of fitness crap than there are actual movies or documentaries. The sad thing about it is that more than half the crap they are pushing on the American public isn't made in America, thanks to Bill Clinton and the passing of the North American Free Trade Agreement.

It wasn't too long before Agent Harrington walks in with my grandmother. Agent Harrington tells Agent Williams to get his car and start setting up the equipment. I see that Grandmother has some kind of cookware in her hands.

She said, "I've brought some bacon and eggs if anyone is hungry."

Agent Williams says on his way out, "I'll be right back, save some food for me."

Grandmother walks to her kitchen and places the food dish on the counter.

Agent Harrington said, "Mr. Farnsworth, I've talked it over with your grandmother about Agent Williams staying in the guest house tonight. I'll be going to the motel in town as soon as Williams gets finished setting up the perimeters around the house. You have my cell number, and I want you to call me before you leave to go to work in the morning. By the way, what is your normal time showing up to work?"

I told him that I'm there around seven forty-five in the mornings after I stop off at a fast-food eatery to pick up something to eat for breakfast.

Agent Harrington tells me, "Tomorrow, I want you to call in to your subordinate and tell them that you'll be in around nine o'clock or so and that you don't plan on staying all day until you can build up your strength. I want you to call me before you call the office, okay?"

I said, "Sure thing, Agent Harrington. I see where you are going with this. This will give the traitor information on when I'm coming in to work so that the traitor can alert the bad guys of my whereabouts."

Agent Harrington said, "That's true, plus it gives me the time to put my other field agents on stand-by to be on the ready."

I asked if the motion-detection sensors are triggered, will it alert the house or Agent Williams. Agent Harrington told me that it will alert Agent Williams and be able to show the object that broke the beam with a wireless infrared camera without alerting the perpetrator also.

Agent Harrington then said, "Agent Williams will have a monitor in the guest house much like the monitor you have in here except that it's a wireless setup."

Within fifteen minutes or so, Agent Williams was walking into the house. He tells Agent Harrington the system is set up and working, and he asked Agent Harrington to be the test interloper.

Agent Harrington said, "Go ahead to your command station, and I'll give you a few minutes before I give your setup a checkout."

Agent Williams went out the rear door of the house and to the guest house. Agent Harrington told me to cut off the floodlights around the house. I went to the main security board and turned off the floodlights that illuminated the grounds around the house. Agent Harrington went out the front door. I watched him on our own night-vision camera system. Off he went into the hedgerow that is on the left side of the house. I switched to the next camera, looking to see if the camera could pick him up. Nothing was showing up. It was the same thing as I kept switching cameras and moving them with the joystick. Finally, I saw a red beam of light on an object, then a flashlight beam had Agent Harrington painted. Agent Harrington walked out, and I turned the floodlights back on. I continued to watch on the monitor as Williams goes back into the guest house, I guess to turn off the system alarm. The two agents walk in the back door and into the kitchen. Agent Harrington told Grandmother and me that he is leaving us in very capable hands.

Agent Harrington asked me, "What are you going to do before you call your job to tell them that you'll be in later?"

"I'm to call you first," I replied.

Agent Harrington told me, "That's right, and you'll have an agent tailing you wherever you. Get some rest tonight. I'll relieve Agent Williams tomorrow night."

Agent Harrington walks to the front door and locks it as he closes it. I asked Agent Williams if he was hungry, and he said that a sandwich and a glass of tea would be all that he needed.

Agent Williams said, "If it's not too much trouble, could you make me a sandwich and a cup of tea to go to the guest house. It's not good if the fort gets overrun while the guard is in the kitchen, eating."

My grandmother said, "I'll be glad to fix you something to take to the guest house. How do you like your bacon sandwich fixed?"

Agent Williams told Grandmother what to put on his bacon sandwich. She fixed him a large plastic cup with iced tea and wrapped his sandwich in cellophane. Agent Williams grabbed his tea and sandwich and told me to lock the door as he exits plus give him a few minutes to get in the guest house before I arm the house security system. I went to the monitor room and watched as Agent Williams walked to the guest house. I armed the system when I saw him close the door of the guest house. I walked back to the kitchen, and Grandmother was building me a bacon sandwich. Grandmother asked me what I wanted to drink. I told her that I want something stronger than iced tea. I asked her if she was going to eat anything. She told me that she had eaten at my mom's house.

She then said, "I'm going to fix me a vodka and pineapple drink. Do you want one?"

"Make mine a double vodka and a splash of pineapple juice," I replied.

As I was devouring the bacon and mayo sandwich, Grandmother was mixing up the drinks. I probably could eat another one, but for now, a strong mixed drink is in need for what's coming up. It will be question-and-answer time about what tomorrow night brings. I had finished the sandwich and was wiping my mouth with a napkin when Grandmother walked over with my drink. She handed me the drink and told me to follow her to the den. We go into the den, and she goes over to the desk in the corner of the room, grabs a pen and pad. As she was writing on the pad, she was saying that Nicole's mother looked like she had aged five years since she last saw her. She handed me the pad to look at, and on the pad it said our conversations are probably being monitored. She made a motion with her hands to continue with the conversation.

I said, "I could tell that her mom was still being sedated. She's usually a bubbly person. I guess with losing her only child, her will to go has been stomped on."

Grandmother took the pad from me and was telling me that she knows exactly how Nicole's mother feels. I had totally forgotten the fact that my dad was her only child. I told her that I was sorry for the unthought-of statement.

She handed me the pad and said, "I know that you have been through a lot and, like myself, could use a good night's sleep. I have been missing my own bed in my own house. Though you won't be in your own bed at home, your mother and I can sleep better now that you are under protection."

I said, "Luckily, I don't have a housekeeper like you or Mom. If I did, they would've been killed by the bomb rigged to the front door of my house."

As Grandmother was agreeing that it was a blessing that no one went through the front door, I was reading what she put on the pad.

She had written, "Do you have any earplugs to plug into the VCR?"

I nodded my head for yes as she walked across the room to the large collection of books that Grandfather had amassed over the years. She was talking and making conversation as she was reaching for the bookcase. She took a VHS tape from between books the book and walked over to me.

She handed me the tape, and she said, "I'm going to take me a bath and get ready for bed. I'm going to finish my drink in my room."

I took the tape and placed it on top of the television.

I said, "Speaking of rooms, which room do you want me to stay in, since I may be here for a while until we can get Serlinni and his friends put away?"

Grandmother told me to take the first one down the hall since it has a full bathroom, amenities, plus a television. I told her good night and that I am fortunate to still have her and Mom around.

Grandmother said, "I love you, James, and don't you ever forget it."

I replied back, telling her that I love her also, as she disappeared down the hall. I picked up my luggage and put them in my new room, went back to the den, turned off the lights, walked back into the kitchen, and left the small over-the-counter light on, in case Grandmother gets up during the night, wanting to get her something to drink during the night. As I walked back to my new room, the answers I seek are probably on the tape. I wished I could take a shower, but I can't get the stitches wet. I went into the bathroom and got a washcloth out of the cabinet. I took off my clothes, turned on the water, and waited for it to warm up. I pondered at the possibilities of what is on the tape. At the same time, I'm reluctant to really find out the answers to the questions that have been spinning around in my head. I bathed off and put on fresh underwear and a clean T-shirt. I took a few more gulps of my drink, and I remembered bringing back something from my house. I reached inside my left pants pocket and took out the happy sack and rolled a joint. Whatever is on the tape, there isn't a better time than this to get my mind prepared for the unknown.

I went back into the bathroom and turned on the vent fan so Grandmother wouldn't catch a whiff of the greenery burning. Then I began to panic. What am I going to use to light this candle? I looked in my shaving kit, looked in my luggage—nothing. I realized that Grandfather was a serious cigarette smoker. There has to be a lighter in one these drawers in my new room. I began checking nightstands by the bed, and I checked the drawers in the small desk. I found one. Let me see if I can get this party started. I hit the thumbwheel a couple of times and then the flame, the harnessing of fire in the palm of my hand. Ain't technology great? I walked back into the bathroom, turned on the vent fan, and closed the door. I took one long toke to start with and held it in. I released the smoke slowly and watched it rise and dissipate into the fan. My Nicole certainly liked smoking almost as much as I do. I really miss her now. Nicole would freak out if she was here now, especially that the FBI is camping out in the guest house and I'm in my grandmother's bathroom, smoking dope. I've got the feeling that if I were to smoke the whole bag, it's not going to prepare me for what's on the tape and what's destined to happen to me tomorrow night.

I continued smoking and nursing the drink that Grandmother made for me. The more I thought about things, the more anxious I became concerning the contents of the tape. I took a couple more long tokes and snuffed out the flame. Curiosity was taking control. I looked in the cabinet under the sink; there is a can of air freshener. I gave the spray button a couple of quick spurts around the room. I picked up the joint and flushed the ashes that I had dumped in the toilet. These are almost the same motions I went through as a teen-ager except now I'm older and changing into a monster tomorrow night, the night of my thirty-eighth birthday. I turned off the vent fan and closed the bathroom door. I rummaged through my bags, took the earplugs from my CD player, and walked back to the den. I looked around to see if the curtains were drawn closed, and they were. I turned on the television, hit the power button on the VCR, and switched channels on the TV set in order to view the tape. I inserted the tape, plugged the earphones into the jack. I sat down on the floor in front of the set; the earphone cord only forded me only so much distance. I placed in my earphones, pushed the tape in. My heart was pounding with anxiety. I hit the play button, and the program began.

What I saw was my grandfather sitting on a wooden barstool inside a steel jail cell, the kind of cell that was used to hold the hardened criminals of Alcatraz or to surround the gold bars at Fort Knox. Grandfather began by talking to Grandmother, telling her to make sure that she's far enough back to get the full view of the cage and out of reach.

I can hear Grandmother saying in the background, "Okay the view is good, and the tape is rolling."

Grandfather says, "My dearest grandson, I have been dreading the coming of this day. I've written a lot of stuff for you in my journal for you to read. It would've been easier for your grandmother to hand you the journal for you to read about what's going to happen to you. I'm creating this recording for two reasons. One reason would be that you'll be able to see what happens to me in a little while, and you'll see for yourself that this is real. The second reason is in the event that something happens to me, you'll have this recording as a reminder to pass on to your siblings in the future when they turn thirty-eight years old. I'm sure by now that you've had some pretty screwed-up dreams and experienced weird stuff happening to you lately. That's how it started with me after I was attacked in Europe during the First World War in 1914. I was a thirty-seven-year-old Lieutenant Gerald Houston Farnsworth over a detachment of what would be considered in today's terms as special ops. Then it was called an army intelligence unit. I could tell you what happened from the beginning, but there isn't time. You'll be able to read my accounts in the journal. I want you to know that you are about to become an apex predator. Human beings are not the top of the food chain. This apex predator considers human beings as food, and it doesn't discriminate between friends or foes. It only has an insatiable appetite for killing and consuming flesh, whether it's animal or man. I cannot control the beast which I am about to become. The messengers have probably made themselves known to you as well as the dark one. The messengers told me that you would be different. I don't know in what ways you'll be different. They did tell me that your will is stronger than mine. Perhaps you will be able to force your will upon this beast to control it. I pray that your will keeps you from being swayed by the dark one. The dark one is the prince of lies, and don't even entertain the thought of trying to beat him at a game that he invented. He knows our weaknesses and knows when to prey upon us. The messengers told me that if you follow their instructions, they will keep the dark one at bay. I'm starting to ache all over my body. It won't be long now. I love you, James, and your grandmother will be there for you in the event that I'm not. I have witnessed many things over these many years. Some are wonderful memories, and others are things I wished that I could simply erase from my mind."

My grandfather stopped talking and started twitching on the stool.

My grandfather said, "I know this is hard to believe, but now is the time for me to show you what's going to happen to you, dear James, once you turn thirty-eight years old and experience the effects of the full moon."

He fell from the stool and was convulsing on the floor as his body started changing. I could see the muscles outgrowing the shirt he was wearing as he continued to writhe about on the floor of the cell, moaning in pain. He even asked my grandmother at one point, "Are you still filming this?" And she replied, "Yes, I am." Then my grandfather rolled over on his hands and knees as his body had completed the formation into a new creature. He looked up and into the camera then lunged forward only to be stopped by the steel bars of the cage. Then I heard my grandmother's voice say, "He doesn't look like the Hollywood werewolves, does he, James?"

Then the unexpected happened. My grandfather, in a hoarse, gravelly voice, said, "They look like dogs, and I am not a dog. Now let me out of here."

My grandmother's voice on the tape says, "I am not and you know why. You cannot control yourself."

Then my grandfather takes the stool and splinters it against the cage. The next scene is grandmother throwing a ham at the edge of the cage and saying, "Are you hungry?" My grandfather goes to the edge of the cage where the ham is and grabs it. Because it is too big to be pulled through the bars, he just starts shredding the flesh from the bone until it is narrowed down to fit between the bars, then he goes to the far corner of the cage to eat it. I hear my grandmother's voice say, "He doesn't like to be watched while he's eating."

She moves the camera's all-seeing lens to another area within the room. She walks in front of the camera, and I see my grandmother as a younger, youthful woman. She says, "We kept a watchful eye on your father and realized he didn't have the curse that your grandfather has. We watched him as he grew up. He was an ordinary child. We knew that he didn't have the curse he got bronchitis as a baby, then chicken pox later. Since I've known your grandfather, he has never been sick, never been to a doctor from any kind of ailment."

I heard a guttural voice from my grandfather, saying, "I'm still fucking hungry."

Grandmother said, "Okay, I'll get you something to eat. I'll be right back."

As the camera was still focused on the cage, my altered grandfather walked to the edge of the cage, grabbing the bars with his clawed hands, and said in his gravelly sounding voice, "There will be two more nights of the full moon and two more nights in this fucking cage."

The recording stops. I took off my earphones. There was a knock at the door, and I almost shit in my underwear.

My grandmother asked me from the other side of my door, "Are you dressed, James?"

I told her, "Let me slide on my jeans, and I'll be right with you."

I put on my jeans and opened the door.

She winked, and she said, "I have something to show you that belonged to your grandfather."

I followed her back down the hall, and she walked back to the den. She turned on a small table lamp and walked over to antique painting hanging on the wall. She tilted the painting just enough to reveal a hidden button recessed into the wall. She made a motion for me to step back. A four-foot-by-four-foot section of the floor dropped down and slid out of the way, revealing a stairway that led downward. At the opening, Grandmother reached down with her hand and flipped a switch. The lights came on, illuminating the stairs. She motioned for me to go first, and she followed behind me, holding on to me until she could get a hold of the stair railing. As I walked down the stairs, it occurred to me now I know why that the other end of the basement section only goes half the length of the house. The hidden section was walled off for a reason. We reached the floor of the basement, and Grandmother hit a switch on the wall, and I heard the secret entrance close. Over in the corner of the room was the same cage that I saw in the recording.

Grandmother said, "I brought you down here because it's the safest place we can talk. There's no telling what kind of listening devices the FBI has at their disposal. I know you have a lot of questions. Before I answer your questions, did you watch the recording?"

I said, "Yes, and I'm still in shock. I'm having a hard time believing that tomorrow night I'm to be locked up in the cage."

Grandmother said, "It is very important that you get back here to the house several hours before sunset simply because it will be your first transformation, and it could occur sooner than expected. We don't need to take any careless risk about it."

I asked Grandmother, "Why did he drink the colloidal silver?"

She said, "Your grandfather did it because he loved you more than life itself, and there was nowhere that we could put you and keep this a closely guarded secret. I was so hoping that you would've been married to Nicole, and she could take over for me. I'm not as young as I was in that recording you saw. That recording was made about the time you were ten or eleven years old."

I said, "How did you know that I had the curse? You explained how you knew that my father didn't when he got bronchitis."

She said, "Your grandfather kept close tabs on you during your first two years of your life. You started walking and talking sooner than the average child. Plus once you began talking, you started telling your grandfather about the messengers. Are they still making themselves known to you?"

I was really floored when she said that. I said, "Not only have they made themselves known to me in my dreams but so has Satan or, should I say, the dark one, as the messengers make mention of him."

Grandmother said, "Your grandfather told me that he too had been visited by the dark one. That encounter is mentioned in your grandfather's journal, which I'll give to you once we go upstairs. One of the main indications that you had the curse is that you never got sick. Though your mother took you to get your required vaccinations for school entry, she never had to take you to a doctor for any illness. You always got perfect attendance at school. You excelled in sports until you fell in love with the music world that your father was so deeply entrenched with. Most of any question you may have will be answered in your grandfather's journal he created for you. Your grandfather told me that you will be different. Now let's go back upstairs. I'm pretty tired, and you need your rest for tomorrow."

I said, "Before we go up, what happened to Grandfather's first wife?"

Grandmother then said, "Your grandfather told me that she died because she had poisoned herself, but her poisoning was not reported as a suicide. A doctor had examined her and determined her death was attributed to her pregnancy going wrong. I guess she didn't want to risk her child being born with the same affliction as your grandfather and decided to take the lives of both her and the child."

I said, "Grandmother, how have you been able to keep your sanity through all of this?"

Grandmother said, "If it wasn't for the shot of whiskey and a Zanax, I would've been put in the loony bin. I don't think your mother could handle this. I saw how it has affected her. With the death of your father, your shooting, and Nicole's murder, this would probably push her right over the edge."

Grandmother hit the switch on the wall, and the floor panel retracted.

Before we walked up, Grandmother turned to me and said, "Know this, with your knowledge that you acquired tonight about what is going to happen to you, you can't be killed the way that us ordinary human beings are subjected to. You will be able to use that to your advantage. Who knows, you may even have powers that your grandfather didn't have."

I said, "What are you talking about?"

She said, "In humans, the newest generation is learning things at a faster rate at a younger age than the previous generation in the teen years, so you being a different generation than your grandfather, your grandfather told me that you would be different. The transformation would be the same, but you may be bigger in size. Your senses could be greatly enhanced. We won't know until after your transformation, a very painful one as you saw in the video of your grandfather. Immortality is a gift no matter what comes attached to it. Your grandfather was able to witness events in history from the invention of the airplane to the landing on the moon. Who knows what you will witness in the decades to come."

She grabbed the handrail and ascended up the stairs.

On the way up the stairs, I said, "Grandmother, I'm going to need another drink before I go to bed."

She said, "Go get your glass from your room, and I'll show you where my private stock is."

We reached the top of the stairs. I hit the switch and turned off the light, and Grandmother walked over to the painting and hit the button to close the hidden stairs. I walked to my bedroom and got my glass. By now, the ice had all but melted, and I drank what was left. Grandmother met me in the kitchen. I pressed my glass against the ice dispenser, and ice cubes tumbled into the glass. I watched grandmother open the cabinet door under the sink and retrieve a bottle of Absolute. I sat the glass on the counter, and she poured me about five shots worth of vodka and took the pineapple juice from the refrigerator. She poured just enough pineapple juice to give it some color.

She said, "This should help you sleep. You'll have a busy day tomorrow. I'm on my way to bed. Turn off the lights in the den for me."

I said, "What about Grandfather's journal?"

She told me that she would give it to me later. She didn't want me sitting up half the night reading it. I waited for her to walk her way to her bedroom before I turned off the lights in the den. With my drink in my hand, I walked back to my room and closed the door. The first thing I did was to remove the tape from the vcr and put it in the plastic case. I'll give the tape to grandmother to put away, it would not be good to be seen by the wrong people.

I turned the television on with the remote, turned the volume down, and surfed a little bit until I found something of interest. I stopped on the history channel, and it was a program about the Roman Empire. I decided to go ahead and finish of the rest of the joint, so I went into the bathroom and turned on the vent fan. I managed to coax out the remaining remnants of butane from one of Grandfather's old lighters that I found to be able to light the half of a joint. I leaned against the counter, taking a long, slow toke and holding it in for a little while. I exhaled, aiming the smoke toward the vent fan. I took a gulp of my vodka and pineapple drink and continued to smoke the rest of the joint until it was too short to hold with my fingers. I threw the dead roach in the toilet and flushed it down with the ashes that I had been flicking into it. I sprayed some air freshener, put the canister back into the cabinet, and grabbed my drink. I opened the door, turned off the bathroom light, took off my jeans, and got on the bed. I adjusted my pillows so I could sit up in bed and drink plus watch television.

The effects of the chronic were kicking in with the alcohol. I don't feel as tense even though I just watched my grandfather transform into a monster. It's probably a good thing that Grandmother didn't give me the journal. I would have stayed up most of the night reading it, trying to get a grip on what's ahead of me. I guess there is nothing I can do about it at this point. A friend of mine told me that some bad things happen in good people's lives, things that they cannot avoid because of circumstance, like having to go bankrupt. Some people can't handle it and commit suicide. Those that choose to swallow their pride and keep going forward wind up a lot wiser for it. In my case, it's not bankruptcy that I'm facing, but the lesson my friend had conveyed is to persevere no matter what life throws at you.

I suppose I can finish off this drink, watch a little bit of television, and go to sleep. I almost forgot to set my alarm on my cell phone to wake me up in the morning. I set my drink down and set the alarm for six thirty in the morning. I then placed the phone on charge so it will be ready for tomorrow. I flipped through the channels on the TV, looking for something to either interest me or bore to the point where I can't keep my eyes open. I can only imagine that the messengers will have something to tell me once I fall asleep. I slugged my drink down and put the empty glass on the dresser by the bed. I channel-surfed some more until I stopped on the military channel, and it had a segment about the air war over Europe during the First World War. I watched half of it before the mixture of cannabis and alcohol took hold of me.

I turned off the television and the small table lamp next to the bed. I glanced at my watch; it was 11:30 p.m. I adjusted my pillows and settled down, trying not to think about anything but to sleep. I know it's hard for the average person to shut off the activities that plague their thoughts, like having to go to work and deal with a spoiled brat for a boss or trying to think of ways to make extra money just to get by. In my case, normalcy or average has been thrown out of the window. I just tried to think of a time in my life when things weren't as complicated. I thought of the summer when I was about ten or so years old when I went to the beach with my mom and dad. Dad had rented a house for a week on St. George Island in Florida. I spent time with my parents, walking the beach early in the mornings to see what had washed up onto the beach, seeing the sand crabs scurry along just ahead of us. I really miss those times with my father. Nicole loved the beach also. She thought that there was something wrong with me because I didn't get a sunburn. I only tanned. I finally drifted off to sleep, and I found myself walking down the water's edge of a deserted beach.

Then I hear a voice from behind me saying, "It's a soothing sound of the ocean lapping against the shoreline, isn't it?"

I turned around, and it's my grandfather walking toward me. I stopped walking and waited for him.

He said, "James, later today you will experience that which you saw me go through on the video recording. I've got to tell you that it will be the most intense pain that you can even imagine. After the pain subsides, you will feel like you can do anything but fly. Unlike me, except in appearances, you will be an evolved creature."

I said, "In what way will I be evolved and different from you?"

He said, "Do you remember the show *The Six Million Dollar Man*, the part where you hear the guy saying that Steve Austin will be better, faster, and stronger? Well, that will be you except that you won't need bionics. Your evolution will be of such a change that I don't know the powers that you will have until after the transformation. I'm here to tell you that your enemy will come for you very soon. That's all that I can tell you because this event has already been put into motion."

I said, "You can't tell me because the messengers told you that it is forbidden, right?"

CHAPTER 10

Grandfather said, "I can't interfere with, let's say, your first test. Do you remember when you were studying for a test and hoping that the parts you focused on are going to be on the test? Then out of nowhere, the teacher puts a question in from a chapter ahead of the section that you've been studying. The teacher is merely testing to see if there are any students looking ahead, eager to see what's up ahead. I can't tell you how to pass the test, but I can prepare you for it."

As we were walking on the beach, I noticed in the distance that there is a condo or a high-rise motel about two or three hundred yards from us on my right.

I said, "They are coming for me, and I'm guessing that I'm supposed to let them take me without a struggle."

Grandfather stopped walking and turned to me, smiled, and said, "I told the messengers that my grandson is smart and won't put innocent people at risk. You will pass the test as long as your rational mind can keep the primal mind of the creature in check."

I stopped walking and said, "To my knowledge, I saw you locked up because you couldn't control the creature."

Grandfather said, "You're are right. I couldn't control the urge to kill. The primal mind of the beast wouldn't let me intervene at all. My rational mind was forced to take a backseat while the primal mind was driving. You on the other hand will be able to have control to a point you won't be able to control the beast while it is hungry. It's like giving a bulldog a nice juicy steak, and as he's eating it, try telling the dog to stop eating it and watch television with you. You know as well as I do the dog won't stop until he is full.

"Look on the balcony on the top floor of the condo on the right."

I look, and as I focus on the face of the person on the balcony that's waving to me, it's Nicole. Just as I was about to bolt and run to her, Grandfather grabs my arm.

I try to pull away from him, and he tells me, "James, you cannot go to her. Just wave to her and tell her that you love her. She's leaving."

I tried to pull away. Grandfather wouldn't let go. All the while I was waving and telling Nicole that I love her as she faded away.

I said, "Is this some kind of cruel trick?"

Grandfather said, "I had to plea with the messengers to make this happen. It wasn't meant to be a cruel trick. I wanted you to be able to see her as she was before the assassin's bullet found her."

My heart felt like it had been torn from my chest. It was like losing her all over again.

Grandfather said, "Soon, you'll understand what I have told you."

Just as I was about to ask him how do I control the creature or, as he put it, the primal mind, the alarm on my cell phone goes off. It's 6:30 a.m. and time to get up and face a different day. I turn off the alarm, sit up on the edge of the bed. I reflected on seeing Nicole wave to me before she faded into particles of the universe. I go into the bathroom, take a leak, turn on the hot water at the sink, and get ready to shave. I hear a knock on the bedroom door. Grandmother was asking me if I had gotten up yet, and I leaned out of the bathroom doorway and told her that I would be right out as soon as I finished shaving. I gathered up the weed and papers and put it in a safe place. I won't need it today. I went back into the bathroom, shaved, and bathed the best I could without getting my bandages wet. The whole time I was thinking about what Grandfather had told me in my dream. He said that they will be coming after me soon. Soon could be today, and I'm supposed to give up without a fight. I guess I'll have to wing it and find out as it happens. I finish shaving, put on some deodorant, clean underwear, and got dressed. I opened my bedroom door, and the odor of coffee filled my nostrils, and it smelled good. Grandmothers says, "Happy Birthday James Farnsworth Jr., you're thirty eight years old today. Have a seat while I pop some waffles in the toaster. She asked me how I slept last night as I watched her writing something on a pad. I told her that I probably would have slept better if I hadn't watched an old horror movie before I went to sleep. She chuckled as she was walking over with a coffee cup in her hand and handed me the note to read.

The note said, "I'll give you your grandfather's journal in three days."

As I was reading, she asked which horror movie I watched. I told her it was a remake of *Dracula*.

She said if Christopher Lee wasn't playing Dracula, it wasn't worth watching. I tore up the note and walked over to drop the paper in the trash.

I said, "I'm the same way with *James Bond* movies. Sean Connery is the best actor for Bond. The rest are just knockoffs."

The waffles pop up from the toaster, and she places them on a dish.

She walks over to the counter where I'm standing and says, "Be careful out there today."

I told her that I'll be okay because I trust Agent Harrington and his team of agents to have my back on this.

Grandmother said, "It's too bad that you couldn't run the business from here."

I told her, "If I did that, it would automatically send a message that something isn't right. We want the bad guys to get comfortable, and when they get comfortable, they'll start making mistakes."

In my mind, what I just told my grandmother was something to help ease her mind and also the agent who was listening in, a total line of bullshit. Whatever is going down today is going to happen almost right in front of the agents. Like my grandfather told me in my dream, I shouldn't fight against the predicament, just give in to it. I ate my waffles and drank my coffee.

I said, "I wonder if Mom has gotten up yet."

"She probably didn't sleep much last night knowing that she's going to be staying in a safe house in Atlanta, and her son is going to be used as a target to flush out the mob," replied Grandmother as she winked at me.

She asked if I wanted some more coffee or waffles. I told her that I definitely wanted some more coffee. Grandmother is not afraid for me; she knows that she'll be seeing me again. The laws of nature don't apply to me. The natural order of things has turned supernatural. While Grandmother was pouring me another cup of coffee, I got on the house phone and called mom.. Mom answered her phone.

She said, "I figured you'd be calling me this morning."

"I wasn't about to let you get out of town without me talking to you."

Mom started crying, and I told her to not worry about me. She said, "It's not fair, I'm leaving you behind on your birthday to be used for bait." I told her once this mob situation is over, I can sell the business to someone that's legit and not in the mob. I can do freelance work with any studio in the world. She told me that I need to think about staying alive and making her a grandmother before she gets too old to hold a baby. I told her that I would think about that while she's on vacation in Atlanta. Mom told me that she loves me and to be careful then asked me to hand my phone to my grandmother. I was drinking my coffee and heard Grandmother telling Mom that she would take care of me and for her not to worry. Grandmother made some more small talk with Mom and handed me the phone back. Mom told me that she would call me when she gets settled in Atlanta. I told her that I would be waiting for her call and hung up the phone.

I looked at my watch; it's 6:55 a.m. I called Agent Harrington.

He answered, "Good morning, Mr. Farnsworth, I trust that you got a better night's sleep at your grandmother's than in the hospital."

I answered back by telling him at least at my grandmother's, I didn't have a nurse coming in every hour or so, waking me up to take my temperature.

I then said, "Agent Harrington, please just call me James since we'll be dealing with this together."

Agent Harrington then said, "Okay, James, from now on, call me Eric instead of Agent Harrington. If you are in mixed company and you need to address any of the agents, it would be best to say their first names or say Mr. Williams or Ms. Le Claire until you get familiar with them and they with you. Now what time are you planning to call the studio?"

I said, "I thought about calling in around eight fifteen or so and telling them that I will be in around ten o'clock and that I would be there for only a few hours."

Agent Harrington said, "That sounds perfect. That will give me and my people time to put some things into action. In the event that one of your subordinates calls your cell phone before you call in, just follow suit with the same story."

I asked him about my car that's parked at the Macon airport. He told me that he would need my keys and have his field agents check the car for explosives.

He said, "Just give the keys to Agent Williams when he comes into the house for the changing of the guard. Agent Franks will be moving into the guest house tonight while Agent Williams gets some sleep in a motel. I'll be tailing you in, and Agent Stevens will be surveilling the business."

I said, "I feel like I'm in an Allstate commercial. You know, in good hands."

Agent Harrington said, "I cannot guarantee anything, but you are better protected with us than without us."

I told him that I don't doubt that fact, and I will call him just before I make the call to the studio then ended the call. I asked Grandmother if she had taken a look at the local news this morning to see what the weather was going to be like.

She said, "I watched some of the local news this morning, and the weather is going to be as expected for this time of the year, warm, muggy, and a chance for some showers, typical weather for this time of year in Georgia."

I could tell that she wanted to tell me more just by looking at her facial expressions. She said, "Agent Harrington asked me to tell Annette that you will be staying with me, while you recover. He said that Annette could be used unknowingly to gain entrance on to the property by the bad guys.. I called Annette and told her to take some time off, since you'll be staying with me until you get better because your mother is going to be staying with her gravely ill cousin in Atlanta."

I said, "That sounds like a good cover story. Just need to remember what her cousin is dying from and keep the story the same."

Grandmother said, "I can pretend that I'm saying my lines like when I was in drama class in college."

I said, "I didn't know you took drama class in college."

She laughed and said, "I didn't, I just made it up."

I said, "You had me fooled. If you hadn't told me any different, I would have swallowed that story hook, line, and the boat."

We both laughed and drank coffee as time grew closer for me to call Agent Harrington I looked at my watch and it is already eight o'clock. I called Eric and gave him a heads-up that I will call the studio exactly at eight fifteen. He told me that things are in place and that I was to act just like it's a normal day at work, let the situation play out as it happens, and observe the people around me. He ended the call, and I thought about what Grandfather said in my dream. Agent Harrington (Eric) had told me almost verbatim the same thing that Grandfather had said, to let it happen or play out and not fight it. I poured myself another cup of coffee and sat back down at the table with Grandmother.

Grandmother put her cup down and laid her hand on top of mine and said, "No matter what happens, you'll be fine." She then slid the notepad in front of me. "You're immortal." I looked at my watch, and it had eight fifteen. I told Grandmother that I've got to call the studio. I picked up my cell phone from the table and called the studio as I watched Grandmother scribble through the words she had written with a pen. I dialed the studio and the receptionist, Trina, answered the phone.

I said, "Good morning, Trina, is Tim Jackson in yet?"

The receptionist told me that it was good to hear from me and that she would put me through to Tim.

Tim picks up the phone and answers, "Good morning, James, are you coming by to see us today?"

I told him that I would be in around ten o'clock and won't be staying all day because I'm still under doctor's orders to take things slow until I build my strength back up.

Tim said, "That's perfect, James, David has edited the videotaping in Arizona and mixed in the sound track, waiting for you to give it the okay before sending it to Atlantic Records."

I told him that it sounds good, and if Atlantic likes the end product, everyone will get a bonus. I then told him that I would see him at ten and ended the conversation.

I looked at Grandmother and said, "Things are now set into motion. Whoever is telling Serlinni information will convey my whereabouts to him."

Grandmother asked me if I wanted some waffles. Before I could answer, there was a knock on the back door. I went to look at the monitor to check to see who was actually doing the knocking. It was Agent Williams. I hit the intercom button and said to Agent Williams that I would be right there. I walked to the back door and opened it for Agent Williams to come in. I asked him if he wanted a cup of coffee. He told me that Agent Harrington had asked him to retrieve my car keys on his way out. He said that he was going to crash at the motel after he hands the keys to Agent Harrington.

Agent Williams said, "Agent Franks has pulled up into your driveway, and he will be taking my place here tonight."

The doorbell rings.

Grandmother is by the monitor and says, "I think it's Agent Franks."

Agent Williams walked over to the monitor and said, "It is Agent Franks. If you don't mind, I have to show him the setup in the guest house before I leave."

I told him that it's all right and for him to do whatever he needs to do and go get some sleep. I go and open the door for Agent Franks and invited him in.

Agent Franks said, "Good morning, Mr. Farnsworth, I'm Agent Franks. I'll be taking Agent Williams's place tonight."

Grandmother walked up and asked Agent Franks if he wanted a cup of coffee. He told Grandmother that he had his fill of coffee.

Agent Williams said, "If you'll excuse us, I'll show Agent Franks where he'll be staying tonight and put him to work."

Grandmother asked, "How about Agent Franks's food and something to drink?"

Agent Franks told her that he has everything that he'll need in his car and will get it after he is briefed by Agent Williams. As the two agents were going out the back door, Agent Williams told Agent Franks that he'd have to park his car in the garage once he removes his car. I told Grandmother that I was ready for two more waffles. I kept a watch on the time as it was ticking away. Grandmother put two waffles in the toaster and motioned for me to follow her.

As she walks toward the front door, she says, "I think I left a bag in the rental car, and I want to get out in case you turn the car in today."

I said, "Let me get the key so I can open the trunk."

I went to my room and got the keys to the rental and walked outside with Grandmother. We walked out to the car, and I disarmed the alarm and unlocked the car. Grandmother opened the back door, pretending to look for something.

She said, "It must be in the trunk."

I opened the trunk, and she walked to the rear of the rental and said, "Before you change, you'll start feeling pain in your teeth first, and then the body aches. If you start experiencing those symptoms, you need to get back here ASAP."

I retrieved my briefcase from the trunk and closed it. Before I could respond, up walks the two agents.

I asked Grandmother, "Are you sure you didn't take the bag out last night?"

She said, "I guess I did, but at least you know where the brief-case is now."

With the briefcase in my hand, we walked back into the house as the agents traded places with each other. I told Grandmother that I'll have just enough time to gobble down the waffles and wash it down with some coffee.

She said, "I'll have to reheat your waffles, and you'll be really buzzing if you drink any more coffee."

I told her that I'm going to need that boost today. Under normal circumstances, I would have smoked one with my coffee on my way to work. I felt of my canine incisors to make sure that they felt like they are of normal length. And for now they don't seem longer or sharper than normal.

Grandmother saw what I did and said, "It's okay, relax, maybe you shouldn't drink any more coffee. I have some orange juice if you want it."

I told her, "I'm okay, just a case of butterflies in my stomach."

She had reheated my waffles and set them in front of me. I finished them off with a wash-down of coffee. I looked at my watch, and it's almost nine forty-five. I thanked Grandmother for the breakfast as I took my dish and cup to the sink in the kitchen. I told Grandmother that I'm going to brush my teeth and get ready to go to the studio. I went to my room and walked into the bathroom. The first thing I did was to look at myself in the mirror to see if my ears started looking pointy like a Vulcan. I looked to see if I had extra hair coming out on me and to see if my teeth were okay. My appearance is normal. I brushed my teeth and splashed on some cologne.

I walked back out to where Grandmother is and told her, "I'm on my way to work. I'm planning on being back here by lunch for the day."

She walked up to me and kissed me on my cheek and said, "I'll see you at lunch then."

I told her, "Don't worry," as I walked out the door.

I took out my cell phone and dialed Agent Harrington. I told him that I was getting into the rental car and was on my way to the studio. He told me that he would be tailing me on my way in. I then told him that I plan on leaving the studio at lunch.

He said, "Just remain calm and do as we talked about, and everything will be fine."

I said, "Okay, Eric, I'm placing my faith in you and your team. I'm not so much worried about me but my next of kin."

He said, "James, we have you and your family members back. Don't worry, and I'll talk to you once you leave at lunch."

I then told him that I'm going to have to turn the car in soon or call the rental place for an extension. He told me to call and make an extension for one more day, use it as a right-off. I told him that I would talk to him later and closed the phone. I got into the rental car, buckled up, and made my way down Farnsworth Lane and turned onto the main highway going into town. I looked in my rearview mirror, and about three or four car lengths behind me was a car. I'm assuming that it's Agent Harrington.[I'll find out once I get to the traffic light. I arrive at the intersection, and the light is red. I watch in the rearview mirror as the car behind me gets closer; it's Agent Harrington. The light changes to green, and I proceed on my way to the studio. I've got another set of lights to go through, and I'll be within a mile or so from the studio. I went through the next set of lights with ease and then to the studio parking lot. I parked the car and looked at my surroundings before I got out. I watched in my rearview mirror as Agent Harrington drove by. I got out and walked into the main entrance. As I walked in, Trina, the receptionist, got up from her desk and walked toward me with outstretched arms to hug me. I told her to be careful, hug gently because of the stitches.

She said, "I'm glad to see you, and my deepest sympathy for Nicole. We will miss her."

I thanked her and asked her if I had any messages from anyone at Atlantic Records. She told me that she forwarded the calls to my answering machine. I thanked her and walked down the hall to my office. I saw that the Recording in Session light was on, so I sat down at my desk and hit the call light button. The call light will alert someone at the board that they are being paged without disturbing the session. Tim saw that the call indication light was from my office, so he left David at the controls and came to my office.

Tim walked into my office and said, "It's good to see you up and around again. You must've gotten in late last night. I called your house and didn't get an answer."

I told him, "After we left Nicole's parents' house last night, Grandmother insisted that we stay with her since it was so late."

Tim said, "I am glad to see you, but don't you think you're pushing yourself too fast to come back to work this quick?"

I said, "I came in to make sure that things are on track with Atlantic Records. There is a lot of money at stake here, and Red Sand Studio is under contract to deliver a marketable product. Is the video and the sound track spliced in and ready for me to review before we send it off to Atlantic?"

He said, "David and I were just doing some finishing touches on the sound track. We layered in some effects sequencing that we want you to hear."

I told him that I am anxious to hear the work.

I then said to Tim, "I saw that the recording light was on. Who do you have in the session room?"

Tim said, "It's the all-chick group, Trailer Dolls from Atlanta. They are a blend of Lita Ford meets Alice in Chains. They are excellent musicians that need someone with an ear to refine them into superstars."

I said, "Are they under contract with anyone yet?"

Tim told me that they are linked up through a talent agency called Black Swan in Atlanta.

I asked him, "Who's paying for the studio time?"

Tim told me that the group and their manager are paying for the studio time.

I said, "Before I delve any deeper into another project, I want to hear and see the material we're sending to Atlantic. Since Atlantic is footing the bill and Red Sand is under contract, we need to finalize it."

Tim agreed with me and told me he is going to get the disc with the last upgrades and let me see it. He walked out of my office and was back with a DVD disc.

Tim said, "Take a look at this while I see how David is doing with the session."

I was turning on my computer and was waiting for it to boot up. My cell phone was vibrating in my pocket. I took out my cell phone and looked at the incoming call. It's my cousin Chris.

I answered the call, "Hello, Chris, what's up?"

Chris asked me if I could meet him in the parking lot. I told him that I would be right there, and I put my phone in my pocket. I thought to myself, *Is this how it happens?* As I walked past the receptionist, I told her that I'll be right back. I walk to the parking lot, and there's Chris's car parked next to the rental. I walk up to Chris's car, and I automatically see the look of terror in his face.

A voice from the backseat of Chris's car says, "Get in, Mr. Farnsworth, or your cousin gets one in the back of the head."

I walk over to the passenger side and get in.

The guy with the gun in the backseat then says to Chris, "If you want to live, get this car moving."

As Chris cranks the vintage Road Runner, he turns to me and says, "I got shanghaied into doing this. Please don't let my kids grow up without a father."

The guy in the back told Chris to shut the fuck up and drive. I told Chris that I know that it's not his fault. I looked in the rearview mirror, and I see an agent's car coming up onto us.

The guy in the backseat said, "Hey, Farnsworth, if you're expecting the cavalry to save you, it ain't happening today. Now step on it before I lose my temper."

Chris eased into the Chrysler big block, and the car was winding up, ready to do what it was built to do. I watched in the rearview as the agent's car was attempting to stay up. As things couldn't get any more fucked up, I saw a car up ahead waiting to pull out. As we passed the waiting car, it pulled out into the highway. Two men jump out and start firing on the lone agent, disabling the car, and I don't know about the condition of the agent. I continued to watch in the rearview mirror as the accomplice car moves up on us. The guy in the backseat tells Chris to pull over at the next road on the right. I tell the guy with the gun to let Chris go, that he has me, and I'm what Serlinni wants. The turnoff road was coming up, and Chris turned onto the road only to be followed by the accomplice car. The guy with the gun tells Chris to slow down and stop. Chris slows the car down and pulls onto the shoulder of the road.

The guy with the gun said, "Okay, Farnsworth, get out of the car."

I open the door and get out. I see that the men in the accomplice car have gotten out, guns pointed at me. As the guy in the backseat was getting out of the car, I yelled at Chris to get the fuck out of here. Chris floored the Road Runner, slinging gravel and dirt as the men behind men squeezed off a few rounds. The guy from the backseat told the men, "Stop shooting, we have Farnsworth." I watched Chris's car fade in the distance. The guy with the gun pointed at me told me to get in the backseat of the accomplice's car.

The driver of the accomplice's car said, "We need to get to the rendezvous point and change cars before the government boys are on us."

The guy sitting in the backseat with the gun pointed on me said, "We know, Farnsworth, that you've recruited the feds into this."

I said, "So are you taking me to your boss?"

The guy with the gun said, "Just enjoy the scenery, and you'll find out."

The thug sitting in the front passenger side was on his cell phone, telling someone that they would be at the 96 Bypass in fifteen minutes and to be ready with a change of clothes. I guess that would be code for a different car in case someone was listening in. The guy that's driving asked the guy with the gun if he had frisked me or checked me for a wire. The guy with the gun gave the guy in the front his gun and told him to point it at me while he frisked me. The guy patted me down and told me to open my shirt.

I unbuttoned my shirt, and the guy said, "What you got hiding under the bandage?"

He peeled back the bandage and saw that there were stitches and did the same to the bandage on my back. He felt the cell phone in my pocket and told me to take the phone out and give it to him. I gave him my cell phone, and he threw it out the window.

I said, "It's time for me to get a new phone anyway."

Then he told me to take out my wallet. He took the money and looked through it and handed it back to me. It wasn't too long before we were on the bypass on 96 on the way to Reynolds. We were about a mile or so down the bypass when a car pulled out from the intersection and got behind us.

The driver said, "Our new ride is behind us."

The driver pulled over to the shoulder and parked. We got out and walked to the Crown Victoria as the driver of the Vic was walking toward us.

The driver of the Vic said, "She's all gassed up and ready."

The guy with gun told the driver of the dropped-off Victoria to take the car we just got out of and get rid of it.

The drop-off guy said, "I know what to do, I'll throw them off your trail."

The guy with the gun pushed the gun barrel into my back and told me to get in the backseat. The other thugs got in the front, and we were heading west again. I looked at my watch, and it was just 10:45 a.m. I kept thinking about the dream and what Grandfather told me and that I'm not to resist. I think now I understand why I shouldn't resist.

As the car passed through the small towns of Reynolds then Butler, traveling westward toward Columbus, the guy in the front seat gets on his cell phone, and I heard him say a few things, like we are on schedule and about an hour away, and ends the call. I just sit there, thinking about Chris and the agent. I hope they are okay. I don't need another innocent death on my conscience like my Nicole. I sat quietly, listening only to the conversations between the thugs talking about the women that they had been with and the debauchery.

"Are you a sports fan?"

A thug from the front seat says, "I bet he's a golfer, one of those country club types."

I answered, "I play golf when I get a chance to, but I don't play enough to join a country club."

Then I heard the guy sitting next to me say, "If you don't go along with Mr. Serlinni, you might be playing golf in the afterlife."

The thugs laugh at the comment. The thug in front seat turned on the radio and was searching through stations and stopped on an oldies goldies station that play tunes from the fifties and early sixties. I thought to myself, at least he didn't stop on a country station. That would be worse than torture. I would insist on them just clipping me now. I just hope that the dreams and the things that have happened to me prove after all that I am an immortal. Otherwise, this could be my last day. Within an hour of driving and listening to the thugs talk about where they're going after today and how they're spending the money that they're getting paid for delivering me to Serlinni, we had arrived on the outskirts of Columbus. The car pulled into a Super 8 motel. The driver tells the guy in the front seat to get a room on the back side. The thug gets out and goes into the motel office. The driver pulls the car over to the side and waits for their fellow thug.

A few minutes passes, and the thug gets back into the car. He tells the driver to pull around to the back of the next row of rooms on the right. The driver pulls around to the rear of the structure and parks. The thug gets out and unlocks the door, looks around for any bystanders, and motions to get me inside. One of Serlinni's goons told another goon to tie me up before Serlinni gets here. I asked if I could go to the bathroom first. I went into the bathroom and took a leak and came back into the room. The goon with the gun tells me to sit down in the chair, and he tied my hands behind me as I was sitting in a chair. One of the thugs uses the motel phone and calls Serlinni to tell him where we are located, and I hear him say that they will be waiting in room 218. The thug sets the phone down and tells his fellow goons that Serlinni's flight is running a little late. I sat there listening to the Neanderthals talk about meaningless bullshit for an hour or so. It wasn't too long before Serlinni shows up with some more goons in tow.

Serlinni entered the room and said, "So good of you to meet with us, Mr. Farnsworth, on such a short notice."

I said, "Forget about the small talk. Let's get down to business. I know you were responsible for killing Nicole and for trying to knock me off as well. The last offer you sent me is now going to be double for the shit you have put me through."

Serlinni said, "Why, Mr. Farnsworth, I don't think you are in a position to bargain with me. The offer I sent you was my last offer. The only reason you're here now is, you are going to tell me who your beneficiary of the studio will be."

I said, "Why don't you show up at the reading of the will, then you'll know, you piece of shit."

One of his goons backhands me across the head.

Serlinni then says, "Okay, Mr. Farnsworth, this meeting is over, and my associates are going to take you on a vacation. It will be a one-way trip."

Before I could say anything else, a goon had stuck me with a hypodermic needle, and I was out.

Serlinni then said, "Take him somewhere secluded and leave the car."

A goon opened the door to make sure no one was around so that they could put me in a trunk for my last ride. The goon motioned to the other goons to go ahead while he popped the trunk lid open. They threw me in like I was a bag of dirty laundry. I didn't feel a thing. While I was in a drug-induced state of unconsciousness, I was back with Nicole at a restaurant that we had gone to on our first date together.

We were sitting across from each other at a table, and I said "Do you think we will still love each other as much as we do now when we have become an old married couple?"

Nicole replied, "I will never stop loving you, James, even if I am dead."

At that moment, the dream was interrupted because two goons had woken me up while they were lifting me out of the trunk. I was still groggy and was trying to focus on what was happening. I was standing at the edge of a dirt road, near some type of run-down old industrial site. I don't know what time of day it is. My hands are tied behind me, and I can't see my watch, and I looked around to try and get my bearings. There was a pine-laden forest to the right of me and a row of buildings behind rusted hurricane fencing. A car had just pulled up, and I heard a goon say, "Hurry up, get his ass over here."

The goon with the gun pushed the gun in my back and told me to walk. I got to the back of the car, and the last thing I remember hearing was a gunshot and nothing. Everything went black, then I was standing in the middle of the highway with deserted buildings all around me. There were no cars, no people, no birds singing, no angelic choir, no sounds whatsoever. I started walking around and looking at the storefronts as I walked by them. The surroundings did not look familiar to me, and as I got closer to the end of the street, I could see that someone is standing on the corner. I was thinking to myself, *Is that Jesus or Satan standing there waiting for me?*

Then a voice said, "It's neither one of those guys just yet."

As I got closer to the figure on the corner, I could see who it was. It's my grandfather.

I said, "Grandfather, is this heaven or hell?"

He replied "It is neither, welcome to limbo land. My dear grandson, you're not dead, and you're not alive either."

I said, "What do you mean?"

Grandfather then said, "You are in a type of stasis. Though your body is in a car trunk, and your breathing has stopped. Clinically, you're dead, but supernaturally, your body is waiting for the change to occur within a few hours, the full moon begins its rise on the eastern horizon. You are thirty- eight today and as fate or an upper management plan would have it, the full moon will be taking charge.

I replied by saying, "I got a bullet in the head for my birthday, in a few hours I'll become a monster plus, I'm in a place called limbo land talking to my dead grandfather. Now if you are truly dead, how is it that you are in limbo land?

He then said, "Normally, when someone commits suicide, they go to hell, but since I made the sacrifice for you, I have been given a reprieve by the lamb of God."

"Have you met Jesus?"

Grandfather said, "No, but was told so by a messenger."

I said, "So an angel or messenger is your parole officer?"

He said, "You've been programmed by society about how angels are perceived. In this realm, there are two ranks. For instance, it was a messenger that delivered Lot and his family out of harm's way, but it was a legion of angels that destroyed Sodom and Gomorrah. The dark one was a warrior angel. Here no one speaks his name and uses the term *dark one*." Grandfather points his finger. "Just to the west of here is the gateway to hell, and to the east of here are the gates of heaven. The Catholics would call this halfway place purgatory. I just know that this place is better than the other place, and I don't mean heaven."

I said, "What is going to happen to me, Grandfather?"

He said, "Well, in about three hours, you are going to change into a werewolf while you're in the trunk of that car."

I said, "How is that possible, Grandfather? They shot me in the back of the head."

Grandfather said, "Once the change starts, the bullet that is lodged in your brain will be pushed back out of the same hole that it entered. The wound will seal itself over like it never occurred. Remember, you cannot be killed in just any ordinary fashion. Silver in any form or any blessed object that pierces your body will be your demise. I am bound to this plane of existence, and I can only advise you on certain things. I can't tell you to go on a killing spree of people, but I can tell you where the men are that wronged you."

I then said, "Grandfather, is there a way to control the beast once the change happens?"

He said, "Because you are a new-generation werewolf, you will evolve in such a way that even I don't know the powers that you may possess. The normal five senses, hearing, seeing, smelling, tasting, and touching, will be super enhanced, but that is not the powers I'm talking about. I'm talking about the possibility of a sixth sense, clairvoyance, precognition, telekinesis, or any combination of the type of supernatural powers that you may evolve.

"As far as being able to control the beast, I can only say from experience that I wasn't able to control the will of the beast. My human consciousness was only along for the ride inside the same brain as the monster, a silent witness to only remember what happened while I was changed. Like I said, I don't know what powers you'll have until you've made the change."

I said, "In my dreams, you've told me that I will marry again. How can you know this and not know what my new powers will be?"

He then said, "I told you that you would marry again, but I didn't tell you her name because I don't know her name yet! Besides, I told you a lot of stuff while you were dreaming, but you don't remember all of it simply because until now the link between us has been semiattached. Once you've made the change, the link between us will be stronger, and I'll be able to advise you while you sleep."

I said, "Will you be able to communicate with me as the beast?"

He said, "No, not while the beast is conscious, no one will be able to control the beast. At least I could not. That is why my father, your great-grandfather, had the cage built in the basement. The cage is the only thing that controls the beast or, should I say, contain the beast."

I said, "Grandfather, are there others here in limbo land with you?"

He said, "Yes, there are a good many souls here. The messengers cleared the streets for you and I could talk. Let's just say there are some" used to be famous celebrities" that would love to talk to you, but let's not waste our time speaking about them. I want to use this moment to try to steer you in the best direction because what I tell you could determine my fate here."

I said, "You mean there is a possibility of you getting out of here to go to heaven?"

He then said, "Yes, or even the other place that is just over the horizon. I have to be careful about divulging certain types of information to you like certain aspects of future events. For instance, I could tell you that a major geological event is going to occur in Alaska in December 2017, but I cannot tell you the day."

I said, "Why not the day since you've given me the month and year?"

He said, "If you tell someone else about the event and the word gets out that you foretold this event before it happened, this would put your life in more of a spotlight, and you being a werewolf every time a full moon occurs would not be good for your image, now would it?"

I said, "I suppose you're right, but if something like that occurred, wouldn't it be better if people were made aware of it to reduce the amount of casualties?"

He said, "Many would die anyway because they wouldn't believe it until after it occurs and many lives are lost. Then once they found out you foretold of such an event, you would be pressured to produce more upcoming predictions about other cataclysmic occurrences to see if your predictions were a fluke or not. Then people would start coming out of the woodwork, seeking you out by any means possible, just to get that next prediction. Speaking of predicting the future, you need to stay away from psychics. There are some real psychics and a lot of phonies, a real psychic will know what you are and could possibly blackmail you for money. Trust the messengers to give you direction. That is enough about that. I want to tell you where you will find the men that wronged you, and it is going to be important to remember every detail because once you've changed, the beast will be only looking for something to kill and eat. The strength of your will will be put to the test. You may be able to put thoughts into the beast's mind, tell it where the men are, but you won't be able to tell the beast what to do. If some innocent person happens to be at the wrong place and time, you may not be able to force your will upon him. The beast knows that he is on top of the food chain."

I said "Okay, where are these men, and which direction should I go when the beast breaks free of the car trunk?"

Grandfather then said, "Once you, I mean, the beast breaks free, you'll be presented with an opportunity. You'll be able to use your voice. Remember me in the video. A cell phone will be on the scene. Use it. They are still in that room where they took you to the back side of the hotel in room 218. You get those guys to come back, destroy the bodies, and burn the vehicles but one. You'll need it."

I said, "Then I'll have to come up with some story about how I survived the kidnapping to the FBI agent."

Grandfather said, "Tell him that they left you in a car trunk, and when you woke up, you managed to break out and escape, but you will need to distance yourself from the area where the beast slaughtered the hoodlums. You'll need to make it to the next town in order to place the call to Agent Harrington."

I said, "Okay, Grandfather, by some chance that Agent Harrington buys my story, Serlinni will no doubt send another batch of hoodlums to try and finish me off again. My question to you is, will I be able to get close enough to Serlinni to take him out?"

He replied, "Serlinni will be furious over the fact that his people got butchered and somehow you managed to be alive. You will need to make your move on him on his turf and without the FBI."

I said, "How am I going to pull this off because after this episode, the FBI will be in my back pocket from here on out."

Grandfather said, "I will come to you when the time comes, but for now, you need to focus on what I've told you about what to do on your first change, and there is something else I want to tell you. It won't be easy to try and enforce your will upon the beast. His powers are very strong. The reason that he will be so powerful is because his powers were conceived by the dark one himself and placed on the very first werewolf, the werewolf that attacked me in Germany."

I said, "Let me guess, you didn't write about this in your journal."

He said, "No, it isn't in my journal because I didn't find out about it until I got to limbo land."

I said, "Who told you this?"

He then replied, "They call themselves "The Elite Guards", but actually, they are God's warrior angels. A type of upper level security control force that polices over the middle ground between heaven and hell. They make sure that there are no gate-crashers from down the road where the entrance to hell is."

I said, "I always thought that hell was in the center of the earth, where the core keeps things hot."

Grandfather said, "It has been a misconception intentionally because early humanity didn't understand a separate dimension other than the known natural world. The Holy Bible states that God holds dominion over the seen and the unseen, so scholars placed heaven above and hell below.

"What is important now is that you know the type of power that you will be dealing with. As I stated, the werewolf that attacked me is the first of its kind."

I said, "Do you know the werewolf's true name?"

Grandfather, with some hesitation, said, "I may get in trouble for telling you this, but here goes. Jesus was betrayed by a disciple for a handful of silver."

Before Grandfather could say another word, I said, "You mean Judas Iscariot is the first werewolf? I thought he hung himself."

Grandfather said, "He did hang himself but was resurrected by the dark one. This was told to me by an elite guardian, that the dark one told Judas that he brought him back to life. He told Judas he was saving him from being heaven's whipping post for that fact he gave up Christ to be crucified. The dark one told Judas that he would be immortal, and he would have to pledge allegiance to him. He told Judas that he must leave and never come back until an appointed time. He was not to try and see anyone that knew him, family, friends, that could identify him because he is supposed to be dead. Well, according to the messengers, the dark one didn't exactly explain to Judas who he was. So Judas didn't exactly leave town that night and tried to get in contact with a Roman centurion. Judas thought he was face-to-face with the centurion that arrested Jesus. It was the dark one. He told Judas, since he defied his warning, that Judas was to bear a double curse. The first would be immortality and that Judas would be ruled by the full moon. Judas was thirty-eight years old when he sold Jesus out. I was thirty-seven years old when I was attacked by Judas. I was not supposed to have survived the attack and I changed on the 1st full moon after I turned thirty-eight years old."

Then Grandfather said, "The beast gets his power from the source of evil, and when I changed into the beast, the voice in my head was always plotting and scheming to sway me, and it took every ounce of my mortal soul to fight it. I would hate to think of what would have become of the people around me if I wasn't locked up to keep the beast in check. It won't be long before you will leave limbo land and wake up a new creature, but you must remember that you have free will, and that free will can keep you from falling completely into the hands of the dark one."

I said, "If he approached you in your dreams, what did he look like?"

Grandfather said, "It doesn't matter what he looks like. It is what he represents, and it is pure evil. And don't think that you can outsmart him either. He is older than mankind itself and knows our weaknesses."

I said, "Because Judas was paid in silver, that is why silver is the werewolf's Achilles's heel."

I said, "Grandfather, why don't I find this Judas and kill him myself?"

Grandfather said, "According to the messengers here in limbo land, your path isn't destined to cross with Judas, but an heir will. Time is growing short for you here in limbo land, and it's almost time for a new James Farnsworth to awaken."

As we continued to walk down this deserted road, he turned to me and said, "I want you to remember everything that I told you, especially about free will—that's one of the greatest gifts that God had built into us."

The next thing I know, I'm opening up my eyes, and my body feels like every inch of it is being pulled apart. Despite the pain and my body temperature having shot up, my ability to see in the dark has dramatically improved. Writhing with pain, I can feel my skeletal structure stretch. I can't help but to yell as the change runs its course. Within a few moments, the pain of the change has stopped, and I lay there kind of exhausted. As I lay there, getting my wind back, my acute hearing had detected a car was coming this way. I lay still and listened as the car got closer, the then engine cut off. I look at what used to be my hands, which are now slashing tools for ripping anything that gets in my way. I heard two doors close and two sets of footsteps walking to the car in which I'm locked in the trunk of. The footsteps split up. One set goes to the driver side, and the other goes to the passenger side.

The one on the passenger side speaks, sounds like a young male, and he said, "Do we want to take this back to the shop or strip off what we can sell now?"

The voice on the driver's side said, "Let me check out the inside first. There might be a decent stereo system inside because this is an older Cadillac. It would be a waste of time to strip."

The next thing I heard was the window being smashed out and the door being opened, then the electric door lock released so that the passenger door could be opened. As the beast lay there, listening, I tried to force my will upon the beast to wait for an opportunity to escape the trunk. I told the beast to save his strength and let the thieves open the trunk for him. I told him to bang on the trunk lid a couple of times to get their attention, and once they walked around to the back of the vehicle, then it's on. Just like that, the beast hit the trunk lid a couple of times, and I could read its mind. It was thinking about what it was going to do next. In its mind, it is thinking as soon as the trunk lid opens, it will pounce on the closest person first. One of the thieves told the other to hit the trunk-release switch in the glove box as he walked around to the back of the car. The trunk-release latch clicked, and the thief that was standing at the trunk opened the trunk, and the beast pounced on the thief. The thief had a gun in his hand and put a round into the beast's stomach. The bullet did nothing to slow the onslaught of carnage. The beast took a bite out of the thief's neck and, with a quick side motion, ripped flesh and muscle like someone tearing newsprint. The other thief tried to make a run for their vehicle; he didn't make it. The beast caught the other thief and tore his throat out with one blow from his talon-tipped fingers. The beast began to feast on the second thief with the voracity of a starving animal. I tried once again to invoke my will upon the beast. I sent the thought to hurry up and put the bodies into the trunk and leave before anyone else drove up. A couple of minutes go by before the message was received. I guess it would be like trying to tell the family dog to stop eating that steak because there will be more later. The beast ate enough to slake his appetite for now. Now that I have the beast's attention, an idea popped into my head. As I thought the idea, the beast complied. The idea is to check the two bodies for a cell phone. If they didn't have a cell phone on them, the phone must be in the car they came in.

The beast put the dead bodies in the trunk of the car and closed it. Again as the thought process was synchronizing, the beast's clawed hand felt to see if my wallet was in my back pocket, and it was still there. The beast then went to the car that was once owned by one of the deceased. It opened the door, and on the seat was a cell phone. The beast picked up the phone, and as I thought, he went through the application searching for the nearest Super 8 motel. The number came up, and a map grid indicated our location from the motel. I remembered that my grandfather could speak when he changed, according to the film made by my grandmother. So before we place a call, let's do a test. Again as I thought it, the beast began to test his vocal chords.

With a gravelly voice, the beast said, "Connect me to room 218."

The beast tried the same phrase again and with better results. He then dialed the motel, and I heard an Indian accent say, "Super 8 Motel, can I help you?"

The beast replied by saying, "Connect me to room 218."

I motel desk clerk told the beast to hold one minute while he rings the room.

A guy answers the phone and says, "This is room 218. Who do you need to speak to?"

The beast replied, "Hey, moron, are you sure that Farnsworth is dead?"

Before the guy on the other end of the line could say anything, the beast ended the call. As I was sending my thoughts, the beast was setting up the scene. He cranked the would-be car thieves' car and moved it behind the abandoned building on the left so that Serlinni's boys wouldn't get spooked by seeing a different car at the scene. There is a deep drainage ditch that runs parallel to the road. That's where to hide and wait for the dinner party to begin. The beast was anxious for another kill. I had to assure him that the prey is on its way. About eight to ten minutes go by, and then he hears a car slow down at the end of the street to turn. Sure enough, the headlights of the approaching car reflect off the rusted security fence behind me.

The beast is anxious. I tell him to wait until the car stops and move in from behind Serlinni's boys' car. He eases down the drainage ditch towards the thugs' car. He hears two car doors open as the driver turns off the headlights. The beast stealthily goes up the side of the ditch, keeping his profile low. One of the men has a flashlight, and the other has his gun drawn as they walk toward the car that they left with James Farnsworth dead in the trunk.

The beast is super anxious. I tell him to let the men open the trunk and, at the same time, hit the trunk lid of Serlinni's boys' car to see how the driver reacts. As the guy takes the keys from the ignition to open the trunk, the beast hits the trunk lid with his mighty hand and ducks down behind the car. The driver turns on the car lights and walks around to the back of the car. The beast grabs the guy, throws him on the ground, rips out his throat before the guy could squeeze the trigger of the gun that he had in his hand. The two guys are oblivious to what had happened to their partner. The beast then reaches into the car and turns out the lights. He then rushes the two men at once. They fire a couple of rounds into him—the bullets are useless. The beast executed an all-out slaughter and fed until he got full. Then I thought, *Stuff Serlinni's boys in the trunk of their car and check the men for their cell phones. One of them may have Serlinni's number on it.*

The beast searched the men's pockets and found two cell phones. He searched the phone address on the first phone, and it didn't have Serlinni's number, and he just threw it in with the bodies. Now he checked the second phone and found Serlinni's phone number and stuck that phone in his pocket. I then sent the message to get the men into the car they arrived in. Now there was a need to destroy the evidence of the killings. It would be better if the cars were parked in the inside of the abandoned buildings because if we set fire to the cars here, someone would see it and possibly put it out before the fire consumes everything. The beast sees that the road dead ends and understands what needs to happen. The building where he parked the would-be thieves' car behind has a large door that is partly opened. He drives the first car through the gate, opens the door, and drives the first car in. I express the urgency to the beast that we need to hurry and get this done and leave the scene. The beast drives the Serlinni boys' car in with the boys in the back, of course. Now we'll use the car thieves car as a way to get out of here. The beast found a lighter in the mobster's car, ripped part of the car seat cover, and stuck it into the opening of the gas tank. He took a section from the cloth seat cover from the Cadillac and stuck it in the tank. He made a check outside the big door before lighting the candles. He closed the big door, leaving a gap just big enough to escape. He lit the cloth on the first vehicle and then to the second. He moved to the door and waited for a moment to make sure the fires were going. The flames were going, and I told him to close the door and get to the other vehicle quickly. He hurried to the car thieves' vehicle, and by the time he opened the door of the car, the first explosion happened.

The beast cranked the car and left from the industrial site and could hear the second explosion going off. I told him not to speed and to go back towards home. We must distance ourselves from the scene. Luckily, we were able to catch the green lights on the way out of town and not be seen by onlookers. The beast looks at the digital clock in the dash; it's almost 4:00 a.m. The sun will be up in two hours. The scent of blood is heavy since it has soaked my shredded shirt. We need to get rid of the car somewhere and wash off the blood. I was trying to think of where there is a pond or creek that I passed by while riding with the Serlinni boys to Columbus. Then it occurred to me that I remember seeing a lake beside the road in a small community called Howard. The beast looked at the gas hand, and we have enough fuel to get us close to there plus torch it. We drove another ten miles or so when we came up on a dirt road on the right.

He drove the car down the dirt road about a mile or so in, stopped, turned off the engine and the lights. He glanced to the left. There is an endless row of pine trees. He gets out of the car, and to the right is an open field edged with a thick forest of darkness except for the occasional glimpse of the full moon as clouds pass in front of it. The beast sniffs the air and tells me that the rain is coming. I sent a message of urgency that the car has to be destroyed. I sent the message to the beast that the trunk lid must be damaged from the inside before he lights up the car. The beast complies by opening the trunk and kicking the underside of the trunk lid, leaving a huge dent. The beast ripped away a section of the stained seat cover, opened the lid of the gas tank, and stuffed the rag into the opening. He took the lighter off the seat, lit the rag, and threw the lighter back into the car. He backed away far enough to make sure that the car had caught on fire. Within seconds, the gas tank had exploded, and the car was a roaring inferno. I then thought about the footprints around the car, and the beast reminded me again. The rain is coming, and all traces of tracks will be gone. So again as I thought, the beast reacted to my thoughts. My thought is that we have to travel east, stay out of sight, and stay away from the main highway. The beast looked at the pine thicket, and I agreed. Pine straw won't show footprints like an open field. So let's test the equipment. The beast sprang into the pine thicket, sprinting at first, testing muscle and reflexes, as he moved from row to row of pines. I could hear cars on the main highway in the distance. Before I realized just how much ground was covered in a short amount of time, he had come out of the pine thicket, and the main highway was about sixty feet in front of me—us.

Remember to stay out of sight and to head east.

The beast crossed over the dirt road and into a tangled maze of virgin forest. The beast was right. The cloud cover was getting denser. Rain was on its way. The moon was entirely hidden by the clouds, but with the enhanced nocturnal vision, I—we—were moving through the forest, dodging fallen trees and undergrowth like a white-tail deer. The beast's ever so sensitive nose was testing the air, catching scents of animal trails that have been used. I have to keep him focused on getting some distance closer to home and to water. My new instinct tells me that sunrise is only about an hour or so away. It is imperative that we pick up the pace. I was amazed at the speed and the agility of my new body. I wasn't even beginning to get winded or tired. Then the beast got a scent trail of an animal that's close-by. He stopped and listened. He could hear movement, and the scent was stronger just ahead. It was a group of wild pigs, the other white meat. I guess using this newfound energy requires a fuel source.

The beast changed modes and went into predator— a hungry predator. He was able to catch the pigs off guard and tackled one, biting into the pig's flesh until the animal expired. The beast gorged himself until the hunger was satisfied. I've got a mixture of animal blood and human blood on my tattered clothes now. The beast tells me the rain is coming. We must keep moving eastward closer to home and find water.

The beast began to sprint through the forest, constantly sniffing the air, listening to the surroundings, as he moved swiftly, effortlessly through the darkness. As he moves through the undergrowth, he hears with acute precision off in the distance to the right of him the sound of a diesel engine carrying off a truck driver eastward. We are not too far from the highway, maybe a mile or so deep in the woods. The beast tells me that he can smell water, an element that even he needs, I guess to wash down the swine he had for breakfast. As he continued to move forward, the scent and sound of running water was just ahead. I reminded him to take the cellphone from his pocket before he plunges into the water.

The beast slows down as the forest opens up to the edge of a creek. He reaches into his pocket, places the phone on the creek bank, and kneels down to drink in the cool water from the creek. After satisfying his thirst, he wades in, washing off blood from the night of carnage, first kill. He scooped up sand and mud and smeared across the face, arms, and what was left of the shirt and pants. Then while rinsing in the creek, his vision started to get blurry. He got back onto the creek bank, and I realized what was happening—the morning sun was coming.

CHAPTER 11

The pain returns as I change from beast to man again. It is hard to explain the intensity of pain, especially when you can't compare it to any experience that one has ever had. As the transformation completes, I lay on the creek bank exhausted, I look at my hands and they are no longer the tools of a killing machine. I look at my tattered clothes, my shirt still has blood stains on it. I thought about what the beast had eaten. Repulsed by the beast actions of the night I vomited up, that which the beast had swallowed down. I washed off in the creek, put the cellphone in my pocket and walked toward the sounds of the highway in the distance. Just as the beast told me earlier the rain comes and it did. I already had the shivers from bath in the creek and now the rain has set in. I'm barefoot, soaked to the bone and looking like Bill Bixby after he changed from the incredible hulk. Now I've got to come up with a good story about what had happened to me. A story good enough for the FBI to believe. I followed what looked like a well-used deer trail along the creek bank. The forest opened up to a clearing and a bridge that crossed the creek. I have no Idea how far I am from the nearest community. As I make my way toward the embankment that leads up to the highway, I see something that catches my eye. It looks like someone had lost their plastic tarp, the remnants of the blue plastic tarp would help shield me from the pouring rain. I pulled the tarp free of the brush and other debris that had collected on it. I then draped it over as much of my body that it could cover and crossed the highway, heading eastward, maybe someone will take a chance, stop and pick me up. With my back to the oncoming traffic, several truckers had passed by without slowing down. I guess I had traveled a couple of miles and I came upon a sign that had the words Geneva Unincorporated, there has to be a store just up ahead. As I continued walking, I think that I have an explanation that I can give to Agent Harrington, but first I have to get in contact with him plus record Serlinni's number on a piece of paper before I get rid of the phone. I'm tempted to call Serlinni myself to tell him that his boys won't be coming home, but the feds could be monitoring cell phone traffic and could zero in on me. I would have to account on how I got the cellphone. It's already going to be tough enough to explain how I escaped without getting killed. I kept walking and finally reached a small store. There was only one vehicle parked out front, so I laid my covering next to the ice machine outside and walked inside.

There was a lone man behind the counter, and I said, "Sir, please excuse my appearance. I was abducted and left for dead. If you would do me a favor and call this number for me, I will reimburse your call."

In an Indian accent, he asked me, "Sir, who is this person that I am calling?"

I told him the number that I'm going to give him is the number to a Federal Bureau of Investigation agent, and I called out the number to him. As I watched him dial the number, I could smell the aroma of coffee floating in the store.

I heard the store manager say, "This man walked into my store and asked to call you," and then the store manager asked me my name and I told him. The manager said, "His name is James Farnsworth, he looks in pretty bad shape." The manager told Agent Harrington where his store is and Agent Harrington told him that he is dispatching a Georgia State Patrol to pick Mr. Farnsworth up and to help Mr. Farnsworth until the state trooper gets there. The store manager told me to walk to the end of the counter. I could tell that the man was unnerved about the sight of me. I walked to the end of the counter and he told me to sit down in the chair at the end of the counter. He told me that the state police is coming according to the FBI man that he talked to. So I sat down to make the manager comfortable. He was watching my every move.

I said, "I going to check to see if the kidnappers had taken everything from my wallet. I slowly reached in my back pocket and grabbed a soaked through leather wallet. I looked through it and all I had was my driver's license. I told the manager to take a look at my license to confirm my identity and I asked him could I have a cup of coffee and I would get the state patrolman to pay you for it. The store clerk took a look at my license and told me, "As long as you just get a cup of coffee. I am taking a great risk by trusting you. How do I know that the man I called, is an actual FBI agent? He could be showing up to rob me and you are only acting this out." As the man was talking, he had taken a pistol and laid it on the counter. I assured him that he has nothing to fear and I asked him, could I wash my hands in the rest room before I get my coffee? He told me to go through the door marked employees only and there's a bathroom in there. I walked through the door and to the bathroom. I opened my shirt and my bandages were gone, stitches still intact. I looked at my face and I looked at my teeth, I appear normal. I washed my hands and tried with some soap to scrub off some of the blood stains. The stains were coming out. I don't need Agent Harrington wondering where the blood came from. I finished getting myself somewhat presentable. I took out the cellphone and brought up the address page and recited the number in my head and dropped the phone in the trash. I walked back out into the main part of the store. I thanked the manager for letting me use his bathroom. He gave me my license back to me. I asked him for a piece of paper and a pen, I wrote the number down and stuffed it behind my license. The store clerk was acting really nervous, so I told him that I would get the cup of coffee and wait outside for the state trooper. I got a large cup, filled it almost full and four packets of sugar. I was needing a sugar rush, I was feeling tired. I took a stir stick and swirled the hot liquid around. I walked toward the door and told the clerk, thanks for his hospitality. The rain was really coming down, but I didn't care.

I took the tattered tarp and shielded myself from the rain. I squatted down, leaning against the ice machine, sipping the hot coffee, savoring every drop. My thoughts reflected back to the night before, I think of the power that dwells inside. I fully understand what my grandfather had told me. I know firsthand, how it would be easy to just let the beast have control. The beast has no fear of anything, not even death itself. A shift in the wind direction, was blowing the rain right on me. I pulled the tarp overhead, trying to keep the rain from my hot cup of coffee. I continued nursing the Styrofoam cup in my hands, sipping from it. My body began to shiver, from being soaked through to the bone. I realized the frailty of this human form in comparison to the apex predator that I was just an hour or so ago. My ears caught the sounding of fast-moving vehicle coming from the east. I waited to hear, the indicating sound of the vehicle slowing down as it got closer. I opened up the tarp, just enough to peer through. I saw a gray charger with orange letters spelling out Georgia State Patrol. I wasn't about to spring up, if it wasn't. I sat there and waited as the trooper pulled up and parked. The trooper saw me and said, "Sir, are you James Farnsworth?" I slowly stood up and answered, "Yes, officer. I am James Farnsworth." I then asked the officer if he didn't mind? Would he pay for this cup of coffee, since I had no money. The patrolman asked me why am I out here instead of being inside? I explained to him that, the clerk was nervous. I said, "He thought I was a vagrant begging for food or possible robber, so I sat out here waiting for you." The trooper opened up the rear door of the Charger and told me to get in. I placed the tarp on his seat so as not to soak up the water from my drenched clothes. He walked into the store, paid the clerk and back to the driver's seat of the Charger. Before he even hit the ignition he asked, "Mr. Farnsworth do you need to go to the hospital to get checked out?" I told him that I'm just tired and cold and want to go home. He told me that if I didn't need medical attention, that he is to take me to meet Agent Harrington in Butler. The trooper fired up the Charger and he was laying into the accelerator, heading eastward toward Butler.

The trooper called in on his radio, stating that he is en route with the person in question to the Taylor County Sheriff's Office and gave his unit number. A voice, I suppose a dispatcher, acknowledge him.

The trooper said, "Mr. Farnsworth, a lot of people have been looking for you and some, including myself had figured that you had bit the dust." I told him, "I almost did, if I hadn't gotten away when the opportunity presented itself. I stayed in the woods and headed east. If I wasn't so desperate to get access to a phone, I wouldn't have risked going into the store in fear that the bad guys, would pick me back up and finish the job." The trooper said, "I liked to see them try it, I got an itching to draw down on somebody like that." I told him that I hoped that my cousin is okay along with that agent that got their cars shot up. He told me that he's not aware of those things. He did hear that there was a chase in Peach County, and that's all he knew.

He said, "You must have somebody upstairs that likes you, it's a wonder that you didn't get snake bit trapesing these woods this time of year, bare footed at that…. it's a miracle." I asked him did he minded if I closed my eyes and took a power nap before we get where we're going? He said, "Sure thing Mr. Farnsworth, you've had a rough night from the looks of you." I leaned my head to rest it on the seat and the side interior panel. I could feel and hear the resonance of the engine as it roared down the wet road until, the continuous hum had lulled me asleep. The next thing I knew was, that I felt as if I were floating. I hear a familiar voice and I turn around and it is a messenger.

He said, "Make no mentioning that you were taken to a motel but you were taken to a secluded area, met with Serlinni and his men. Tell them that Serlinni asked you, who your beneficiary was and that you told him that he needs to attend the reading of the will to find out. The next thing you know, someone had injected you with needle and you wake up in the trunk of a burning car. You were able to escape just before the car blew up. Remember and trust your instincts." Before I could ask him anything, the trooper wakes me up and said, "Mr. Farnsworth we're at the sheriff's office." I crawled from the backseat of the cruiser and was being snapped to reality by the rain hitting me in the face. Agent Harrington had come out and walked with me to the building.

Agent Harrington said, "It's good to see you, Mr. Farnsworth. Let's get you in here. Are you hurt, do you want me to get a doctor in here to check you out?" I told him that I'm extremely tired and soaked to the bone. Let me see if I can get you some clothes and some shoes." They lead me to an interrogation room and told me to sit down while someone finds some dry clothes for me. Agent Harrington sat down in a chair across from me. I said, "Before I tell you how I came to look as I appear to you now, tell me how's my cousin and the agent doing after they got their cars shot up?"

Agent Harrington said, "Agent Franks got hit in the shoulder and he's okay. Your cousin is fine just his car will need some cosmetic surgery. Now tell me, what happened last night." I said, "As you know one of Serlinni's underlings had Chris at gun point from the backseat of his car. The underling told me to get in the car or Chris was going to get it in the head. I got in and as Chris sped away, Agent Franks had witnessed what had happened and was in pursuit. Another car with Serlinni's people had pulled in front of Agent Franks car and shot up his car. As Chris's car got closer to Fort Valley, the underling with the gun told Chris to pull over to a side road. Chris pulled into the side road and as the gunman followed behind from Chris's car, I told Chris to go and not slow down. He did just that, the group of men fired several rounds at him. I didn't want Chris to get killed because of me. He has a wife and kids to live for. The guys roughed me a little bit and put me in their vehicle and went a couple of miles until they changed vehicles again. Agent Harrington said, "What kind of vehicle was it." I told him that it was a black either a dark blue crown vic or impala type of vehicle. On the way toward Columbus they were telling me that I should have taken Serlinni's offer. I heard one of the underlings call Serlinni on his cell phone and tell him that they have a present for him. He said that they would meet him at the location. The underlings were saying that the boss is going to give them a bonus for capturing me. I was watching to see where they were taking me and on the outskirts of Columbus, they turned off into a subdivision that led into a tennis court. Serlinni and his entourage were parked there in a Lincoln town car. Serlinni and his boys get out and walk over to the vehicle that I'm in. The driver uses the window remote switch and lets down my window so that, Serlinni can see me because the windows were tinted out. Serlinni asked me, who is the beneficiary of the studio once I'm gone? Since I figured that I'm going to get killed anyway. I told him to show up for the reading of the will if he wanted to find out. The guy with the gun in the backseat with me cracked me in the head. It didn't knock me out completely, I could still hear what was going on. Serlinni told the men to take me to the country. The next thing I felt was a needle stick into me. The next thing I remember was waking up in the trunk of a burning car. I kept kicking the trunk lid until it opened. I got clear of the car just before it blew up, bailed off into the woods and that's where I stayed.. I stayed just inside the tree line from the main highway, traveled eastward until I found a bridge to get under, out of the rain until daylight. I began walking eastward, walking the tree line until I saw the blue tarp in a ditch. I put the tarp around me to shield myself from the rain and found the convenience store and took a chance. That's when the store clerk called you after I gave him the number." Agent Harrington said, "You are one lucky man Mr. Farnsworth Are you sure you don't need some medical attention?" I told him that I'm just tired and want to lay down, the only time I've slept was in the backseat of the troopers car on the way here." Agent Harrington said, "You were right Mr. Farnsworth, one of your people had contacted Serlinni yesterday before you were abducted. He shot himself in his car before we could get him. I guess guilt had taken him over or he didn't want to go to prison."

I said, "Let me guess, it was Tim Jackson? Did your guys get his cell phone? Serlinni's number could be on it."

Agent Harrington said, "Yes, it was the same guy that was down the hall from you when you and Nicole were shot. There could be one more in your company. It's either the receptionist Trina or David."

I said, "I'm not sure, but I think Tim was banging Trina even though he has a girlfriend. She could possibly be a link, but without proof, how can you catch whoever is left."

Agent Harrington said, "Now with your survival of last night's second failed attempt to kill you. I'm issuing a nationwide manhunt and a reward for the capture of Vincent Serlinni and any of his henchmen that were involved with the attempted murder of James Farnsworth and the murder of Nicole Adams. Also I'm thinking of planting a seed with the other mob families that if Serlinni isn't found or ratted out, the FBI will start leaning on organized crime families and make their way of life a lot more difficult to make money."

I said, "I thought of this idea while sitting under that bridge. What if the local media runs a story that James Farnsworth, owner of Red Sands Studio is missing and presumed dead. Anyone with information to the whereabouts of this man will be paid a reward. Of course, we would have to tell the convenience store manager to stay quiet, and by doing so, I could pay him out pocket to stay quiet or run the risk of going to jail for obstruction of justice. I stay out of the public eye for a day or so. This would give Serlinni and his colleagues a chance to come out of hiding. Then in a day or so I'm found alive."

All the while I look through the bureaus photo album of bad boys and pick out the guys that were involved in my abduction."

Agent Harrington said, "It sounds like providence gave you an inspiration. Let me call my superior and get his input on this. In the event he tells me to run with this ruse, you'll need to talk to your mother and tell her to appoint David as head of the operation until further notice. David would have to e-mail your mom the payroll statements and any other important workings, that would need to be monitored until you miraculously reappear on the scene." He told me that he's going to make a call to his boss and would see if, the sheriff's department was able to round me up some dry clothes and shoes. Agent Harrington opened up the door to find, the sheriff standing there with an orange jump suit and slip on shoes.

The sheriff said, "Mr. Farnsworth, here's something dry that you can put on. I hope the shoes fit, they are a size 10?"

I told the sheriff thanks and asked where the fitting room was? He told me to follow him. I got up from the chair and followed him. He pointed to a men's restroom and also said he would be back with a bag for my wet clothes. I went into the bathroom and took off my wet clothes. Under normal conditions, the inside of my thighs should be raw from the wet garments, chaffing my skin. I looked and I couldn't see any signs of irritation, nor did I feel any soreness. Only the discomfort of the wet clothes, was bothering me and plus, I'm hungry again. I took some paper towels and dried off the best I could, before slipping on the convict attire. The shoes fit perfectly and the jumpsuit, felt a whole lot better than the drenched clothes. I looked at myself in the mirror, ran my fingers through my hair, rolled up my wet jeans, the tattered shirt, and walked out into the hallway. The sheriff gave me a plastic bag for my wet garments.

He said, "You look like you could use another cup of coffee. Are you hungry?"

I told him that I could use a cup of coffee for now and maybe a pack of crackers, to tide me over until I can get home. The sheriff told me to follow him back to the interrogation room and he would get one of his deputies, to bring me a coffee and a pack of crackers. I sat down in the chair, as he closed the door of the interrogation room. I could feel the presence of the nonblinking eye of a surveillance camera pointed right at me. I sat there and waited a few moments, until the door opened and a female deputy entered the room. She placed a cup, two packets of sugar with creamer and a pack of peanut butter crackers on the table. She said, "Here you go, Mr. Farnsworth." as she sat down in the chair across from me." I bet you'll be glad when this is all over, you've been through a lot." I told her, "That's an understatement, you are already aware of what happened to me last night. That is if you have been observing what the camera sees."

She said, "Mr. Farnsworth, I'm not in here to extract any information from you. I am merely here to bring you something to eat, drink and lend a friendly face to you in this isolation room." I looked at her name tag, it read Deputy Jones. I said, "deputy Jones, I appreciate the hospitality and I didn't mean to be cross with. I am so tired right now, I could lay down on broken liquor bottles and worry about the bleeding, once I wake up. I wished, I could just turn off for a couple of days, no thinking, no dreaming, just put my body in neutral." She got the message and left me to be alone, in the isolation room. I drank the coffee despite that it tasted horrible, I ate the pack of crackers and laid my head on the cold table top. By the time I closed my eyes, I heard the door open. Agent Harrington came into the room and I sat back up in the chair. Agent Harrington said, "Let's go, Mr. Farnsworth. I'll fill you in on the information that, my boss had just relayed to me while on the way to Byron." I asked him about the orange jumpsuit and shoes? He told me that, he would send them by via UPS. I followed him outside and the trooper that picked me up, was getting ready to leave as well. I thanked the trooper for picking me up and the cup of coffee. The trooper said, "Mr. Farnsworth, so far this has been the most intriguing moment in my career. Just knowing that you survived, I'll have a story I can tell my grandchildren. From here on out, just keep a very low profile." I gave the trooper a thumbs-up and got into the car. Agent Harrington hit the ignition and fired up his car, we were on our way. We were rolling as I buckled my seat belt, as Agent Harrington had turned on the air conditioner. The climate was thick with humidity after the rain, a balmy 78 degrees, the cool air felt good. Agent Harrington said, "I know you're hungry, I'll stop and get us something in Fort Valley." I was really starving, but I told him that I was more exhausted than hungry. I was lying, of course. My body had repaired itself, I wasn't tired, but I had to play the role of someone, that had been put through the ringer.

Agent Harrington said, "My boss said that we'll have to observe the usual missing person protocol, then the following day or so, you show up at the convenience store. You won't have to physically show up there. That will be the story. The convenience store clerk will be approached to comply or else. A makeup artist will work on you and we'll stage a taping of you being filmed at the sheriff's office in Taylor County."

Then something occurred to me and I said, "What if my cousin Chris comes over to my mom's house to console her, thinking that I'm dead." Agent Harrington said, "That's where Agent Le Claire will run interception, she will assure him that she'll get the message and that now we are treating this like a kidnapping and not a homicide."

I said, "On the subject of family members, have you contacted my mom and my grandmother?" He told me that my mother and grandmother have been notified of your survival.

Agent Harrington said, "I would feel much better, if I got your family doctor to examine you. You don't need the risk of any infection setting up at the injury sites." I told him, that my grandmother is a retired veterinarian, and she would know how to treat me. Besides, we don't need anyone else knowing that I'm alive. Agent Harrington said, "Okay, I want her to check you out while I'm there. You are my sole responsibility, and I got my ass handed to me on a platter by my boss because there was a gap in the system that no one saw coming. It is evident that Tim Jackson had fed more information to Serlinni than just your whereabouts. Serlinni used your cousin as a decoy and knew that you would walk out to his car It was a carefully executed plan, but they didn't plan on you surviving."

Before I could say anything in response, Agent Harrington's cell phone began to ring. He told me to hold that thought because he has to take the call. I leaned my head against the window and I could hear with my keen sense of hearing.

The voice coming through his earpiece was saying, "I found the burned out shell of a car, on a dirt road just eight miles west of the convenience store."

Agent Harrington replied by saying, "Thank you, Officer, for that information. I will notify you, if I need any more assistance. Good-bye. The trooper found the burned-out shell of car due west of the convenience store. It was parked down a dirt road, off the beaten path from the main highway. For the life of me, I am having a problem coming to terms with your very existence. James Farnsworth, by all accounts from my experience, you shouldn't be sitting in the car next to me."

I said, "Look at me Agent Harrington. I'm right here." At that moment, Agent Harrington looked at me and almost ran off the road. I grabbed the steering wheel and Agent Harrington asked me what just happened? I said, "It looks like someone besides myself needs some sleep."

Agent Harrington said, "You are right James. I probably got about two hours sleep last night. Now, what was I talking about before I zoned out?"

I told him that we were talking about staging a fake news report.

"That's right!" replied Agent Harrington.

He then repeated to me about the makeup artist and whole scenario. I knew then what evolved power I had unknowingly released. Without even thinking about it, I had induced a type of hypnosis. I forced my will upon Agent Harrington, without his knowledge of me doing it. I must be careful especially now, with the full moon in phase for the next 2 nights. I listened to Agent Harrington's plans of executing staged event, as we were entering the city limits of Ft. Valley. I said, "Agent Harrington, if you pull into the drive-through at McDonald's? I will reimburse you when we get back to Grandmother's."

Agent Harrington said, "That's nonsense! I'll use Uncle Sam's credit card for this. Besides, I need a large coffee and something to eat myself." I looked at the clock in the dash and it showed 10:45. I told Agent Harrington that we may be a little late for breakfast but we could still get some coffee and a burger. I was starving, my body was screaming for some protein. I remember throwing up all that the beast had consumed, and all I had in my stomach was coffee and crackers.

Agent Harrington pulled into the drive-through at McDonald's, and a voice said, "Welcome to McDonald's, you can place your order when you're ready."

Agent Harrington asked if they had stopped serving breakfast.

The voice from the box replied, "Yes, sir, we are now serving from our main menu."

Agent Harrington turned to me and asked what did I want to eat? I told him, "Two Big Macs and a large Coke." Agent Harrington placed an order of three Big Macs, a small order of fries and two large Cokes. The voice asked Agent Harrington is the order correct as displayed on the scene? Agent Harrington replied by saying, "Yes, ma'am." He then pulled forward and gave the attendant the credit card. The attendant ran the card, gave him the receipt and asked him to pull up to next window. We sat at the second window for a minute or two, until received the goods that were ordered. Agent Harrington gave me the bag of food and one large drink. He thanked the lady at the window and drove back onto the main highway. Agent Harrington placed his drink in the drink holder, told me to hand him his hamburger and his fries. I said, "You could pull over and you could eat, without having to drive and eat at the same time." He told me, that he is used to having to eat on the move. He explained that now, he must get me to a safe place and beef up the security. I told him, "Go ahead eat your food before it gets cold, we'll talk after we finish. Besides, I was dreaming of this hamburger while I slept out in the wilderness." There wasn't any talking going on, only chewing and slurping from a straw, until the food had been consumed. I went through two burgers before Agent Harrington could finish one. Agent Harrington said, "Damn! You wasn't joking about starving, were you?" I told Agent Harrington that I had spent all my energy and now I feel revitalized. I thanked him for the food and he said, "You ate through those burgers so fast, I don't think you took the time to taste them." I jokingly said, "What was that I just ate?" Agent Harrington chuckled at my comment and told me that I was going into lockdown until my premier. I said, "Would you call the safe house, so that I can talk to my mom? I bet she is being a hand full, to the people that are watching over her." He agreed that it would ease her mind to hear my voice." Agent Harrington took out his cell phone and placed a call to the safe house. Once he got an answer, he told them to put my mom on the phone, so that he could talk to her. He said, "Mrs. Farnsworth, this is Agent Harrington. I have someone sitting next to me that would like to talk to you." He handed me his phone and I said, "Before you start crying and raving about wanting to come home. You have to listen to what I'm going to say. First I'm okay; just extremely tired from the ordeal, just so you know when you see any news footage about my disappearance. It is a ploy to draw out the mobsters into thinking that I'm dead and that their plan worked. They are going to try and make contact with next person who would be in charge of the operation in the event of my death… that person is you. You won't have to see these people, phone contact will be first and when they call your home Agent Le Claire will be ready. I want you to call David at the studio and tell him that he is in charge and if the material is finished according to the company's best quality, it is to be sent out to Atlantic Records and that the transaction is to be carbon copied to your e-mail. After you receive the e-mail, send it to my laptop e-mail. I'll be staying with Grandmother and not leaving the house for the next couple of days to see how this ploy works out."

By this time, she was already crying and I tried to console her and tell her that this thing can't go much longer, I told her that I loved her and through her sorrowful voice told me that she loved me. I told her that I would be e-mailing her and would be in contact with her. I gave the phone back to Agent Harrington. I told Agent Harrington thanks for that. He told me no problem. I just sat there going through my mind about what occurred last night and if the two cars that were put into the building blew up, destroying any evidence of a massacre. It's good that I came up with the idea of laying low for a couple of days because there will be a full moon tonight and tomorrow night. At least I'll be locked up and not causing any mayhem. Agent Harrington asked me does the garage at my grandmother's linked with the main house? I told him that it is. He told me that he wants to park in the garage, close the door and enter the main house. He said, "Someone could drive up as you get out and the cat is let out of the bag. As soon as I deliver you to your grandmother's house and touch base with Agent Williams, I'll be going to the Peach county sheriff's department and get them to release information to the local media. Then it will be a matter of waiting to see what happens next. Of course we'll be monitoring the phone traffic in and out of the studio. With Tim Jackson out of the picture, Serlinni is going to reach out to his next connection. Travelling eastward on Highway 96 and onto the cutoff to Highway 49, we were on about twenty minutes from Grandmother's. I remembered that my cell phone is beside the road, somewhere between Byron and Fort Valley. The keys with the tracking device is still on my desk at the office. I told Agent Harrington about it. He said that he would get an agent dressed in a Peach county sheriff's uniform to go in and get it and ask questions while he's in there. Per his comment, "Whomever is involved with

Serlinni will begin to squirm." I told him that the rental car needs to be turned in before I get fined. Agent Harrington said, "Don't worry I'll have it taken care of, it will add to the mystery of your disappearance. I'll have your grandmother to call the rental place and act upset because her grandson is missing and she wants to find out what the charges are so that the vehicle can be returned. An agent posing as your cousin will drop off the vehicle and pay what is due from her account, you simply reimburse her later." I said, "That just about ties up the loose ends. All we need is for Serlinni to make a mistake and try to contact someone on the inside." I had gotten to the point that I had a hard time keeping my eyes open. My body is tired and the ability to keep a conversation with Agent Harrington is very trying. Luckily, I don't have that much more travel time left before we'll be at my grandmother's house. As we neared the city limits, Agent Harrington told me to lean the seat back, so that no one will see me through the windshield from oncoming traffic; the side windows are tinted. I reclined the seat, I really had to fight the urge to close my eyes. Agent Harrington placed a call into Agent Williams to let him know that we are in the way in and to make sure that the garage door is open. Agent Harrington put his phone down and asked me, "Mr. Farnsworth are you sure that you don't need to see a doctor? I could bring your family doctor here to see you." I said, "I'll be fine after I get cleaned up and maybe a nap." Agent Harrington told me that he had just turned into the drive that leads to my grandmother's house and to stay reclined until the car is in the garage and the door is closed. I waited as the car slowed down and came to a stop. The garage door came down and Agent Harrington told me that I can sit up now. As I opened the door to get out, Agent Harrington told me that he would call me later to fill me in on what's going on. "Go on in and get some rest, "he said. I told him thanks as I opened the door to the house. I hit the garage door button to open as Agent Harrington backed out, then pressed the button to close it. I made my way to the kitchen and Grandmother met me and almost squeezed the remaining energy I had from me.

Agent Williams walked up and said, "Welcome back, Mr. Farnsworth, Agent Harrington has informed me under no circumstance are you to leave the house and make any phone calls for a few days."

I said, "As tired as I am now, I don't want to talk to or see anyone the rest of the week."

Agent Williams said, "From what I've heard from Agent Harrington, you have ran the gauntlet and survived. You deserve a much needed rest."

I said, "If you two excuse me, I'm going to get these jailhouse clothes off and get cleaned up."

Grandmother said, "What about your stitches?"

I said, "I've been in the rain most of the night after I escaped the burning car. When I changed clothes at the sheriff's station in Butler, both of my bandages are gone. When I get cleaned up and if you don't mind, would you put some peroxide on the wound on my back. You can rekindled your veterinary skills on me."

Grandmother chuckled at my comment as Agent Williams told her that he is going back out to the guest house. I walked into my room and got a pair of underwear, a T-shirt, and jogging pants then made my way into the bathroom. I slipped out of the convict orange coveralls, the convict slippers, turned on the shower to let the water get right. I looked at myself in the mirror and I was shocked at the site before me. My abdomen muscles were rippling with new muscle, so was my chest, neck, forearms, and biceps. And my legs weren't bigger; they were defined. The word *extratoned* doesn't describe it. I checked the water temperature and got into the shower. The mediocre hot water felt really good as compared to the rain and the creek I was in this morning after the change. As I lathered myself up with soap, I thought how I was able to have some what control over the beast or should I say, a more evolved James Farnsworth. I was more amazed at how agile and fast that I was able to move during the change. The power was intoxicating to a point, that while running through the forest in the rain, felt like I was a part of the scenery. That is what real freedom felt like. I finished my shower, dried off, put on my fresh clothes, brushed my teeth. I didn't bother to shave since I won't be facing the general public for a few days. I retrieved a pair of socks from the dresser, put them on, and walked back into the kitchen. I looked at the digital clock on the stove, and it had 11:30 a.m. Grandmother asked me if I was hungry. I asked her if she had any milk and cereal. She told me to go into the dining room, and she would bring me something to eat. I walked into the dining room and sat down. It feels good to be in a safe place. Let me rephrase that: I thought I was in a safe place at work until I walked outside. My safety zone had been compromised. The bad guy's used my cousin as a decoy to get me outside. Grandmother walked in with a big bowl of cereal, she had a cup of coffee in her hand and a notepad stuffed under arm. She sat the bowl in front of me and sat down across from me. As she was writing on the notepad, she asked me, "How did the men manage to abduct you?"

Then she slid the note over to me. I looked at the note, and it said, "How many men did you kill, and were you able to control the monster?"

I swallowed down a couple of scoops of cereal and said, "The bad guys used Chris as a way to get me to walk out of the office. There was a gunman in the backseat of Chris's car, and he told me to get in the car or Chris was going to get a bullet to the head."

As I was telling her this, I wrote, "Five people and yes," and gave the notepad back to her.

I said, "I didn't have a choice and didn't want Chris to take a bullet because of me. I feel bad enough that an agent got shot in the process. There was an accomplice car that pulled out in front of the agent and shot up his car to keep him from following Chris's car. Chris drove almost to Fort Valley and turned onto the bypass to 96. The gunman told Chris to turn off onto a side road. There the gunman told me to get out of the car. As the gunman followed behind me out of Chris's car, I told Chris to get the hell out of there, and he did. The gunman fired shots as well as the men in the accomplice car. Another vehicle showed up and I was told to get into that vehicle as the driver that brought the change out vehicle drove off in the accomplice car." Grandmother had written another note and slid over to me. She said, "Eat your cereal before it gets too soggy." I read her note and it said- "We'll talk later, down stairs" I took a couple more scoops of cereal in, finishing off the cereal and drank the milk from the bowl. She asked me did I want any more cereal? I told her that I was good for now, Agent Harrington had bought two hamburgers, that I scarfed down, on the way here.

She said, "What happened next?"

I told grandmother a play by play of what happened from the time I was abducted, from meeting Serlinni, to walking barefoot in the rain, until I walked into the convenience store. I kept the story the same in the event the house is bugged. Grandmother was crying as she listened to my ordeal. I then said, "I didn't have any money, just my driver's license and I was able to talk the clerk into letting me have a cup of coffee. I probably scared the shit out of the Indian convenience store owner because I was covered in mud, no shoes, looking like something from the swamp crawled out. I told him to call Agent Harrington, and he did. Agent Harrington arranged for a Georgia state patrol to pick me up."

Grandmother asked me, "Where was the convenience store at?" I told her that it was in a small community called Geneva. She said, "That is an amazing event that you survived through, my prayers have been heard because you are here with me, thank you- Jesus."

I said, "Amen to that, someone up there is looking out for me." I then asked her to take a look at my wounds before I lay down. I took the cereal bowl into the kitchen, rinsed it out and put it in the dishwasher. Grandmother went to get something to clean the wounds as I sat on a bar stool in the kitchen. I raised up my shirt so she could look at my wounds.

She looked at the entrance wound first and said, "Looks like your skin is trying grow over the stitches. I'll take them out tomorrow."

With a bottle of Betadine and a cotton swab, she cleaned the entrance wound and told me that the exit wound was the same way, just a healthy pink color and no sign of infection.

She swabbed the exit wound and said, "Now go take a nap, and I'll wake you in a couple of hours for some lunch." She hugged me as I got up. "This is probably driving your mother crazy because she's not here to see you."

I told Grandmother that I had already talked to her this morning. Agent Harrington called the safe house. I told Grandmother I had to calm her down and tell her that I am okay and would keep in touch with her.

Grandmother said, "I bet it didn't go as smooth as you said it did. I can understand your mom's feelings when it comes to an only child. I didn't plan on outliving my only son, your father."

"I know, Grandmother," I replied.

Grandmother told me that I needed to lie down and get some rest. I motioned for the pen and I wrote down, I have a newly acquired ability. She took the notes, tore them up and threw it in the trash. I told her that I would see her later and walked into my room, shut the door and laid down. As I tried to relax, my mind was replaying all the events of yesterday, last night and this morning. Finally, I was able to unwind and fall asleep. I drifted off into a dream state and this time, I'm driving my car and I look into my rearview mirror. Sitting in my backseat was a messenger.

He said, "From this time forward, you'll have our full support since you proved that you were able to control the beast instead of the beast controlling you. I have come to tell you that your potential to enhance your known senses even while you're in human form has and will continue to evolve exponentially."

I told him, "I know what you mean. The power of suggestion or hypnosis made an impression on the agent. I scared myself."

The messenger said, "Because the moon is in full phase for the next two days, your extra sensory powers are in over drive. In time, you'll be able to refine the process. When you told the agent to look at you, the power to force your will upon him or persuade him, was directed at full force. If you hadn't grabbed the steering wheel and put your eyes on the road, the agent would have crashed the car. The power of eye contact and the spoken words used the right way can turn a tense situation into a calm situation. You'll be so comfortable doing it, that you won't even realize it at first until it occurs to you later." I said, "I needed that power to pick up girls in high school."

I asked him, "Why didn't my grandfather come to tell me this stuff?"

The messenger said, "Because now you're in a crucial phase and you are no longer a being of just the physical world anymore. The dark one is aware of this and that's why I'm here to protect you from him. The dark one would tell you to exploit your newfound talents, he would be using you for his own entertainment and gaining control over you. Me and my brothers are tasked to keep the dark one out of the equation. He then said, "You have two more nights as the beast, tell your grandmother to leave the television on in the cage room." Before I could ask him anymore questions, I was awakened by the smell of food. I got up and walked to the kitchen.

Grandmother said, "Are you hungry?" I yawned a big jaw stretching yawn. I yawned so hard that it actually hurt. Grandmother said, "I saw you rubbing your jaw, do you have a toothache?" I told her that I yawned, so hard that it felt like I pulled a muscle in my face. She motioned for me to follow her as she hurriedly moved toward the den. Now, I realize what's happening. The pain in my jaw is an indication of what is to come. I asked Grandmother what time it was as she was opening the hidden stairwell to the cage room. She said, "It's almost 3 o'clock, no wonder you're hungry." I followed her down to the cage room and I got into the cage. She locked the cage with the key and put it in her pocket.

I said, "I don't understand why this is happening this early in the day."

Grandmother said, "It's a good thing that the smell of food woke you, I had let time get away from me. The jaw pain is a trigger mechanism that means that the full moon is beginning to crest at the eastern horizon."

I told her that my body has started feeling achy.

She said, "I've got to get you something to eat and I'll be right back."

I told her before she left me, to turn on the television to keep me company. Grandmother grabs the remote and turns on the television that is anchored to the wall outside the cage, well out of reach of course. She hurries upstairs and closes the door to the stairwell. If the agent is monitoring the sounds in the house, he definitely doesn't need to hear the moans and groans of a man changing into a werewolf. Grandmother did turn the volume up on the television to help mask any unusual noises. While she was gone, I lay in the floor with my body racked with severe pains as the transformation takes its course. My very being as man was fading away and at the same time, a different James Farnsworth was taking over. The pain from the transformation was over. I got up from the floor and stood up. I am now looking through a different pair of eyes, which see the surroundings in a perspective not as James Farnsworth. The beast remembers killing, eating, and running through the forest the night before and doesn't like being captive. I tried to quell the feelings of rage in the beast, telling him that food is on the way. The beast grips the cage bars and stops to listen as he hears the stairwell door open. The smell of food, has the beast under a spell. Hunger now controls the beast. My grandmother gets to the bottom of the stairs carrying a plate on which, a nice juicy hunk of pork was resting. The beast says in a gravelly voice, "Give me the food." My grandmother while holding on to the edges of the plate, lobs the chunk of meat towards the cage. The beast reaches out from the cage and catches the big chunk of pork before it hit the cement floor. The beast tries to pull it in through the bars but the large ham is too wide. The beast began to shred off the pork flesh, whittling it down to size to be able to pull through bars and into the cage. By this time, Grandmother had gone up the stairwell and closed the door behind her. The beast took the shredded ham to one corner of the cage, eating the meat off the bone and biting through the bone to get at the marrow. Pretty soon there was only shards of bone fragments lying about on the concrete floor. I knew the beast wasn't full but his hunger had been satisfied. Just as the beast stood up to walk to the other side of the cage to yell for more food, something was wrong. The beast could no longer stand, the meat had been laced with some type of tranquilizer. The beast was able to prop himself up with his back against the cold steel bars of the cage. It was a struggle now to keep his eyes open until the effects of the drug had taken hold until the beast was unconscious. I'm somewhere else. I look at my hands and my arms, I'm still in werewolf form but where am I. I walk around to try and figure out what is going on, there is a fog hugging the ground. I catch the scent of a fresh kill and walk toward it. I hear something approaching from behind me. I hear a voice say, "James it's one of his tricks." I turn to see where the voice is coming from and up walks my grandfather.

I said, "Where am I?"

Grandfather said, "You are dreaming, your grandmother drugged the ham, so that you wouldn't be making a lot of noise, cause she knew that you would want more. I know because I always wanted more than that was given to me.

I said, "What did you mean 'one of his tricks'?"

Grandfather said, "The dark one is who I'm talking about. He knows you killed those five people and he's going to try and sway you. That scent of a fresh kill is only a smell used to tempt you. If I hadn't showed up, he would send one his minions or even show up himself. He knows in this state that you're in now, he could appeal to your animal instinct. He knows that the strongest primal urge is to eat and in your state you would need to kill in order to do it. As I told you while in limbo land, I had to use all my human strength and will to keep from giving in to him."

I said, "What does he want from me?"

Grandfather said, "Two things and the first of them is to pay homage to him by dedicating those you killed to him. The next thing is, he wants absolute control over you and by giving yourself to him of your own free will with your very soul.

Then I heard another voice say, "That's not entirely true, James," as a man walks up closer to where I'm standing.

I said "Who are you?"

The man answered, "You know who I am."

I looked at my grandfather and said, "Is this the guy you warned me about?"

Grandfather replied, "Yes, it's him, all right, the first party crasher."

The dark one is dressed in what looked like the most expensive Italian suit ever designed, blond hair, chiseled build, and a face that came off an Armani advertisement.

I said, "I wondered what you looked like."

Then dark one says, "How do you like my handiwork, James?"

He then says, "I can really make things work to your advantage because of my special abilities."

I said, "You've done enough of damage already, you're the reason my grandfather took his life. If he hadn't been attacked by your lap dog Judas, he would have led a normal life and I wouldn't be changing into a werewolf during every full moon."

Grandfather said, "Don't listen to him. Remember, he's the prince of lies."

Satan said, "It's all about free will, Judas had the choice to die and be ridiculed in heaven for giving up Jesus or to be immortal, never to get sick and even accumulate unimaginable wealth."

Grandfather said, "What is wealth when you've lost your self-respect and your soul in the end."

Satan replied, "In the end, well, the end is when I say it's the end."

I say, "The Bible says that you will lose in the end."

Then Satan says, "Well, until whenever, I still can bring about certain influences that you won't be able to control, especially as you evolve with every change. Remember I created the first and I have a hand in your evolution."

I turned to look at Grandfather and behind him I saw two figures, but I couldn't make out any facial features. And just as mysteriously as Satan showed up, he vanished in the mist.

I said, "Grandfather who are the figures behind you?

He said, "The two figures are warrior angels, they showed up to keep things in check."

Grandfather said, "Don't worry about him. Like I said before, he's the prince of deception and the king of lies. He tells you things that you'll think about later like, when he said that Judas was able to accumulate vast amounts of wealth. The dark one knows that humans have a weakness for wealth and envy. It was envy that caused Cain to kill Abel. He was envious of Abel's relationship with God. Envy was probably the reason that Satan got kicked out of heaven. He was or is envious of us humans because God put us above all his creations, and the dark one couldn't deal with it. That's why he has been trying to undermine everything he can that is directly connected to humanity.

By the way, tell your grandmother that she won't have to drug you anymore after tonight."

Just as the conversation was getting interesting, I was awakened by the sound of the television. I was still a werewolf and groggy from the effects of the drug. It won't be long before the sun comes up. On the television, there was a kung fu movie on, and I watched some of the moves that the characters were performing. I stood up and mimicked the same moves. I was amazed that the beast was able to duplicate the same moves with dead on accuracy. Just as the beast was getting into his newfound talent, the pains returned. The sun was coming up and it was time for the human James Farnsworth to show up. My body was hurting intensely. I know that it only lasted for a little while, but that couple of minutes seemed like forever. When it is finally over, I lay there on the cold concrete floor. I open my eyes seeing through the human eyes that belong to me… James Farnsworth. I look at my hands instead of the hands of a killing machine. I sat up from the floor and retraced through my mind about the occurrence of last night. I was trying to figure out what my grandfather meant by telling my grandmother, that she doesn't need to drug the meat before she gives it to me. I do know this: I need a cup of coffee to get this awful taste out of my mouth. I hear the door to the stairwell open and footsteps coming down.

Grandmother unlocked the cage and said, "Let's get some breakfast and have some time for ourselves before Agent Harrington comes in." I said "I've got to take a shower first and by the way great plan for drugging me." She said, "I had to, we didn't need you raising hell making a bunch of noise because you were caged up. Don't need the feds hearing something that they can't explain. Your Grandfather said that he didn't like being cage up at first either but after a while he found that it was useless to rant and rave. Grandmother told me to get the bottle of bleach and clean up the cage floor with the mop and a bucket, that is next to the water faucet. Grandmother said, "Pour the liquid from the bucket into the drain that is in the floor." I quickly finished cleaning up the mess and as we were walking back upstairs, I told her that she won't have to drug me tonight according to a messenger. I didn't tell her that I've been talking to my grandfather in my dreams. It would only cause her to miss him more and cause her grief. It's bad enough that she has to lock up her only grandson during the full moon cycles. By the time we've gotten to the top of the stairs, we had changed our conversation. Because we don't know if the phones are the only things that are bugged in the house. Grandmother had closed the hidden passage and as each of us headed for a different part of the house. Grandmother went into the kitchen to get some breakfast going and I went to bathroom to take a shower. I started thinking about what occurred in the dream I had last night. Especially what the dark one had to say about immortality and accumulated wealth. Grandfather was right about what he had said about the dark one, about how he can provoke a certain way of thinking. I think by using the power of suggestion, he's using our weakness for wealth, greed, lust for power and envy as a way of getting inside our heads. And those not strong enough to really see what is going on, is going to get consumed. I guess because of the human condition, everyone is subject to fall prey to lusting over the shiny new car in their neighbors yard. I need to get finished in the shower and get some food in me, that raw ham I ate in the cage didn't go that far. Then as I was showering off last night's events, it occurred to me what the messenger had told me. I can get Grandmother to invite Agent Williams in for breakfast and I can use my power of suggestion to get some answers from Agent Williams. I think there may be another reason, that Grandfather told me, that I wouldn't need to be drugged other than opening up a chance for the dark one to intervene. I'll be able to focus on honing my skills to find out if the whole house is bugged or just the phones. I finished with my bath, dried off and put on some fresh undies and jeans. I looked at my chest in the mirror, where the bullet entrance hole is located. I could see that my skin was over taking the stitches. Grandmother will get to practice on her earned veterinarian skills on me. No since in going to the family doctor and him, seeing how fast the wound has healed, then start wondering what the hell is going on with me. I slipped on a T-shirt and walked into the kitchen. Grandmother gave me a hot cup of coffee just the way I like it…a shot of milk in the coffee. I smelled some waffles getting ready to pop out of the toaster.

I'm not in the mood for some bacon this morning. I don't think I'll ever look at pork the same again after the past couple of nights. I asked Grandmother had she already eaten breakfast? She told me that she had been up since six this morning. She said that she didn't sleep to well last night. I asked her what was bothering her? She told me that she thinks that she's getting a kidney infection because she kept getting up and going to the bathroom. I told her to lay off the coffee and the soda pops and drink water instead. She chuckled and said, "Okay, Dr. Farnsworth."

I asked Grandmother does the intercom connected to the guest house? I asked her to invite Agent Williams for some coffee before they do a changing of the guard. She walked over to the house intercom and asked Agent Williams did he want any coffee or breakfast? Agent Williams answered back by saying that he is okay and thanked her for the suggestion. I figured that he might would do that, so I got a cup from the cupboard, poured in the coffee, spoonful of sugar and cream. I put the two waffles that were to be mine on a plate put syrup on it and headed out the back door to the guest house. Before I could get to the guest house, Agent Williams met me halfway. He said, Mr. Farnsworth you should be inside. Are you trying to get me in trouble?" I told him, "This is a mere token of appreciation for what you guys are doing." I handed him the coffee and the plate with waffles. I said, "Damn, I forgot to get you a fork." He said, "I'll follow you back into the house, before my replacement gets here." So as I walked back to the house, I asked Agent Williams had anything developed yet, as far as anymore traitors from my company blowing their cover?

Agent Williams said, "Let's get you in the house and we'll talk." As we got into the kitchen, I sat the plate and coffee cup down then went to the eating utensils drawer and retrieved a fork. I gave the fork to Agent Williams and he had already started drinking the coffee down. I sat down across from him and said, "Has any other agents picked up any phone traffic from the business?" He said according to another agent that is monitoring the phone and internet traffic in and out of the business. It appears that the receptionist is planning to leave town and has booked a flight out of Atlanta to Buenos Aires. I said, "Wow! She must have been saving up a while for that trip."

Agent Williams chuckled and said, "Right, and my mom is the queen of England."

I leaned forward and made eye contact and said, "My grandmother thinks you guys can even hear when we flush the toilets. Is that true, Agent Williams?"

Agent Williams said, "No, we are only monitoring phone and internet traffic in case Serlinni tries to contact your grandmother." I broke eye contact and said, "Grandmother, you can relax now. According to Agent Williams he didn't know how many times you got up last night to go to the bathroom." The agent continued to finish off the waffles and coffee because he knows he has to hurry back to his post. The replacement will be showing up soon. I was able to find out what I needed to know. Agent Williams thanked us for the breakfast, and as he was getting up from the table, I asked him how Agent Franks was doing. Agent Williams told us that Agent Franks will be off the case until he recovers.

"The bullet had broken his collar bone," replied the agent.

He told us that Agent Stevens will be staying in the guest house tonight. No sooner than the words left his mouth, his cell phone rings; it's Agent Stevens. Agent Williams answers the call by telling Agent Stevens that he'll meet him out front and hangs up.

Before Agent Williams walked out, he said, "It is imperative that you don't leave the house Mr. Farnsworth, it could jeopardize the whole scam. Are we clear on this?" I told him that I won't leave the house until it's time according to when Agent Harrington deems this so.

Agent Williams said, "That's right, we want the bad guys to think that you are taking a dirt nap. We want them to make a slipup so we can pounce on them. Also, don't call anyone but us, okay?"

"I promise," I exclaimed.

Agent Williams walked out the door.

Grandmother said, "It looks like we're stuck with each other for a while, doesn't it?"

I said, "Well, it will give us some time to reconnect and I'll be able to read Grandfather's journal. "Grandmother told me that his time during the war, were times of uncertainty. She said that things that are happening now, parallel the events that were happening then. Grandmother said, "There were German sympathizers here blowing up stuff then except, they weren't called terrorist. They were against the United States aiding any country that was fighting against the German war machine."

I said, "Don't tell me any more. I want to read about it."

She said, "That isn't in there. I remember doing term papers in college."

I said, "Let's have some more coffee, and we'll go and watch some television. I can read the journal later. I better enjoy this little vacation while I can. I said, "Before we jump on the coffee, are you steady enough to remove my stitches, Dr. Farnsworth?" Grandmother said that she had to get her operating tools and some anesthetic. I got a bar stool from the kitchen and pulled off my T-shirt. As I was waiting for Grandmother to return, I thought about how the beast was able to mimic the kung fu moves that he saw on the television last night.

Grandmother walked up and said, "You looked like you were deep in thought about something."

I told her that I saw something on television last night that really got my attention. As she was taking her hemostats and the mini scissors to snip the stitches. She asked me, "What was so intriguing on television that grabbed your attention, it wasn't porn was it? I said, "Of course not, I was watching a martial arts movie. It sparked an interest." She said, "Sit still and I'll get these stitches out. It looks like the skin is trying to grow over the stitches." I heard her snip the stitches and felt the small sutures being pulled from my skin on my back, then the cold anesthetic being applied. She told me that she had finished with the back and now to remove the sutures from my chest. She snipped the sutures and pulled them out with the hemostats. With a cotton swab she cleaned the area with anesthetic. She asked me did I learn anything from the movie last night? I told her that some of the moves I saw were Hollywood camera tricks but yet, other moves are achievable.

Grandmother said, "Absolute recall? Could you give me a demonstration?" I looked at the partition that separated the hallway from the den and ran straight up the wall, did a midair flip and landed on my feet facing my grandmother. She was astounded and told me that, it's one of the perks that was foretold by your grandfather.

I said, "I guess because no one told me that I couldn't do it, my subconscious didn't try to override the thought process and question, could I achieve such a feat."

Grandmother said, "The human mind is capable of setting up barriers to limit oneself from doing things. I don't know if it is the thought of doubt that is built in or it could be that an unseen force is at work that keeps us from doing the possible, by telling us in our minds that it is impossible?" I said, "Wow! That is some heavy philosophy to be throwing out on me this morning." She told me that she and my grandfather had talked about such things before that related to corrupted thinking. I put my shirt back on and went into the kitchen to get a refill of coffee. I was pouring coffee in my cup when the doorbell rings. I walk over to the security wall monitor to see who is at the front. It is Agent Harrington, I hit the call button on the intercom and told Agent Harrington that I would be right there. I went and opened the door and invited Agent Harrington in. I asked him if he would like a cup of coffee? He told me that he had already had his fill of coffee for the day and that he had some news for me. I asked him if he wanted to go into the den to have a seat.

He said, "Your receptionist, Trina Collins was apprehended at the Atlanta airport getting ready to leave the country. After my agents had been monitoring internet traffic in this area. Trina had gone on line and booked a one-way ticket to Buenos Aires. A team of agents was sent to tail her to Atlanta and observe to see if anyone was travelling with her. She was travelling alone and she was placed under arrest, is now being held at the FBI field office for questioning. Tomorrow Serlinni will find out that Trina Collins didn't make it to Buenos Aires. ." I said, "Too bad, I didn't keep the clothes that I had on when the state trooper picked me up." Then a thought came to me. I asked Agent Harrington if it was possible to drug Trina, implant her with a tracking device, like they do animals. Agent Harrington told me that won't be necessary. He said that it's likely that the trip to Buenos Aires would be the last trip that Trina takes.

He said, "Serlinni will have someone eliminate her thus sever any connection to Serlinni. The plan going forward is, a media release will come from the sheriff's department in Taylor County stating that they had found you. This in turn will get leaked to a national news service thus, alerting Serlinni that James Farnsworth is alive."

I asked, "What will be the FBI's next move?" He said that the FBI will issue a million dollar reward for the information that, leads to the capture of Vincent Serlinni. In the event that he gets out of the United States, our European counterpart, Interpol will be issuing alerts throughout Europe. In the big picture if Serlinni survives and makes it to court, there will be two witnesses to testify against him in a court of law." I said, "I know who the two witnesses are, it is Trina and myself, but what do you mean if Serlinni survives?"

Agent Harrington told me that other mob bosses that have had dealings with Serlinni, they don't want the possibility of Serlinni telling anything to link them at all. They would simply have Serlinni taken care of, and Serlinni's capos and underlings would just join up with another mob family.

I said, "It would be cheaper on the tax payers if a rival mob takes care of Serlinni. My only concerns are now is that, I have only one person left at Red Sand Studio and that is David."

Agent Harrington said, "Why don't you write down some instructions for your mom to call into the studio for the time being. After the event tomorrow you'll be able to call David yourself and make recommendations yourself. I imagine that David is feeling isolated about now. I asked Agent Harrington could I call the safe house or will he have to do it? He told me that only recognized incoming calls can get through. I said, "If you can spare a few moments while I gather my thoughts, would you place the call through so that, I can tell her the information to give to David?" Agent Harrington said that would do it and sat down at the table while I got a pad and pen to write down a few things. After I came up with a list of task that has to be taken care of at the studio, I asked Agent Harrington should I mention anything about the whereabouts of Trina Collins?

Agent Harrington said, "When you talk to your mother, get her to ask David how are things at the studio. That way, David can give an indication about Trina's whereabouts. If David says something like, Trina hasn't called in or anything. Convey to your mom that David is to start interviewing for a new receptionist immediately and promote him to Tim Jackson's position and an increase in salary. That way if, David had any loyalty to the studio at all, the loyalty percentile will increase exponentially.

He then said, "If David asks your mom about your whereabouts, tell her that as of now, James Farnsworth is considered missing until a body can be produced."

As I was listening to the things that Agent Harrington was telling me, I was writing down some things that are contractual and has to be taken care of because of the big account with Atlantic Records. Thinking to myself, I have only tonight to complete the cycle as a werewolf until next month. I wrote down a few things and told Agent Harrington to dial the number and I would tell my mom what to do. Agent Harrington called the safe house and asked for my mom.

He handed me his cell phone, and I said, "Hello, Mom, I'm calling you to let you know that I'm okay, and I need for you to call the studio for me. You'll need to get a pad and write these things down, okay!"

She said, "I'll do it but please tell me that this thing is coming to an end. I don't like feeling like a prisoner and shut off from my family."

CHAPTER 12

I told her to calm down and that things are about to change for the better. I went through the list of things that she is to tell David and I told her about the receptionist being held for questioning. She asked me if I was sure that David wasn't one of Serlinni's inside people. I told her that I wasn't 100 percent sure, but giving the guy a new position in the company plus a significant raise would tip the scale in my favor. Plus if David was involved, he too would be leaving town like the receptionist. I told her that Agent Harrington's people are still monitoring the communication traffic from the business as well as the employees home location. I told her to just sit tight and this thing will be over so that our lives can get back to normal again. She told me to be careful and that she misses me and Grandmother. I told her that we will be okay once this is over and I told her that I would call her later to find out what David said and ended the call by telling that I loved her. I gave the phone back to Agent Harrington and told him thanks.

Agent Harrington said, "I heard from Agent Williams that you left the house. You took an unnecessary risk."

I promised him that I wouldn't leave the house until it's time for me to be found. Agent Harrington told me that I would be found tomorrow afternoon and to give him an old pair of jeans and a shirt. He told me that he would get the clothes ready for authenticity for the cameras. He then said that he would have a makeup artist to work on me for the debut. "Don't shave in the morning." He replied as he made his way to the door. He said that he would call me ahead of time to let me know when the ball gets rolling, and he walked out of the front door. Grandmother said, "I've lived a long time but have never experienced anything like this. I would expect this if, I were watching this on a television show. It seems surreal doesn't it?"

I told her that the past couple of weeks have been surreal to me. There has been a lot going on. I won't know how to act once things get back to normal after all of this is finally done. Grandmother said, "Now is a good time to read your grandfather's journal and see life from his point of view." I told her that it would help pass time and help me to connect to him. She went into the study and brought me the journal. She told me to go and read it in my room while she puts a load clothes on to wash. I told her to let me help her but she insisted on doing it herself. I guess in her own way, it keeps her mind and body active despite she's pushing eighty. I took the journal with me to my room and sat at the small desk table. To look at the journal itself with its own appearance of an aged relic that through the years, has shown evidence of being handled. I could even smell the traces of cigarette residue from my grandfather's fingers, still evident on the now yellowed pages. Before I started reading it, I just thumbed through it and looking at the entry dates on the corner of the pages. I noticed that my grandfather wasn't making daily entries. Judging by the time frame between the dates entered, there were some lapses of time. So I started at the beginning to see if there was a reason why there were time gaps or was it just random instances that he put his thoughts on paper. In the right hand corner of the first page was the date, April 21,1914. He writes, "Since I've been back to the States, the nightmares have become more realistic. The men that found me all torn up told me that it was a bear that ravaged my body and consumed some of my flesh. In the dreams that I'm having. I am seeing through the eyes of whatever attacked me. It's not the eyes or the mind of a bear. Whatever it is, it stands upright and only crouches down when stalking. The bears that I'm accustom to, only stand on their hind legs when being attacked and walk on all fours in normal locomotion. Whatever it is that I have been dreaming about, has the ability to think and strategize. To my recollection about animal behavior, bears attack only when threatened or going through extreme stress like starvation or a mother bear protecting her young. In the mind of whatever attacked me, I know what his thought process is. In its mind, it has a single objective. That objective is to seek out, kill and eat anything whether it's a farm animal or a man. It doesn't matter because it is an opportunistic killer and has an insatiable hunger for flesh, and the urge to kill compels it forward—a constant force to kill without mercy or remorse. In my dreams, I'm helpless to warn the poor man that is being stalked, as the man steps outside just to relieve himself. I want to warn the man and tell him to go back inside to the safety of the building. This thing of the night won't allow it. I am only along for the ride, a silent witness to slaughter. While during the day in the Army hospital here in Warm Springs. The only thing that takes my mind off the horrors in my sleep, is this angel of mercy that I've met here. Her name is Marie Bartlett, she's a nurse here. I've met my share of beautiful women in my life, but Marie was so beautiful, she didn't need to wear makeup like other women. Her skin was flawless, she had that wholesome grown in the country look about her with a personality to match. She was the whole package, I had to have her as my own. She would come and see me every day until I was released from the hospital. I asked her to be wife while we were on a picnic overlooking the valley from Pine Mountain. She accepted and we got married, went on a honeymoon, stayed at a ritzy hotel in Atlanta. Her father had given us a house in Manchester to stay in until I start my job with the state in Atlanta. Marie is already a few months pregnant and I had to make the house livable. The house needed some repair work to do and I didn't want to stay at the house for free, I felt like I was obligated to do the right thing. That was the way that I was raised so while I was doing repairs on the house, Marie left with her cousin Katherine to go to Atlanta to look for a house to move into. Marie was reluctant to go without me because of my birthday. I'll be thirty-eight today. I was replacing some loose shingles on the roof, it is a couple hours before dark, my whole body was racked with excruciating pain. It took all of my strength to get down the ladder until the pain was so unbearable that I had fallen on the ground and managed to crawl into the house. The pain was nothing like I had ever experienced in my life, I had no control over my body anymore. I was no longer seeing through the eyes of a man but a creature more than animal and more than human. Everything about me was enhanced, muscles, sight, hearing and smell. I looked down at what used to be my hands were now ten fingers tipped with sharp claws with fur on the back of my hands, arms and all over my body. The mind of a man had disappeared and had been taken over by a monster that I couldn't control. As the beast, I was seeking something to eat. I ransacked the kitchen looking for something to stop the hunger craving and found nothing. Then the predatory instinct took over and went outside to listen for sounds or smells of potential prey. I got the scent of an animal, so I walked stealthily through a patch of woods behind my house until it opened up to an open field. Instead of walking across the field straight to the hog pen across the field, I stayed against the tree line ;the moon was so bright that the element of surprise would be out of the question. I followed the tree line into a hedgerow an crept to the edge of the hog pen. The animals started squealing an alarm before I could pen an animal to the ground, I snagged the slower animal while the others were squealing in a panic. I ripped the animals throat open with my claws and began eating its flesh, the blood was gushing in my mouth while the hogs heart continued to pump blood through its dying body. The squealing of the hogs had alerted the farmer, I heard him as he closed the door of his home. I stopped feeding on the hog and hid behind the clump of trees inside the fence, waiting until the farmer got close enough for me to attack. I crouched down waiting, listening as I heard the farmer approach then I lunged. I knocked the shotgun from his hand, pinned him down and bit into the soft tissue of his neck, tearing through muscle and arteries. Human flesh had a more appealing taste than animal, so I gorged myself on the lifeless farmer until my hunger was gone. The next thing I remember was waking up in the woods behind my house and remembering the horrific actions that the beast I became had committed. Realizing that I had to erase any trace of tracks back to my house and I retraced my steps back to the edge of the forest. I went back to see if the beast had left a trail and there was no trail. Luckily there is a pine tree forest and the pine straw had masked any evidence of any type of footprints. I went back to the house and got cleaned up and thought, what if my wife had been here? She would have been slaughtered like the hog and the man. The beast doesn't differentiate between prey, whether it's human or animal. I don't know what triggers the change except that it occurred before dark. I have to figure out a way to limit the beast ability to get loose and go on a killing spree, spilling blood …. innocent blood. Luckily, the house that my father in law is letting us live in, there isn't any neighbors close by to have heard what happened in the house that night. I had to clean up the house after the beast had looked for something to eat and ransacked the kitchen. I had taken off my bloody clothes and cleaned myself up. As I was dressing, I noticed that my muscles were more defined, my sense of smell, hearing and sight are also different. Whatever this change is, has altered me completely. I had to get to an area away from people before night falls. I knew I had to get back to my father's farm. I don't know that many people in this area except for my wife's family, but I wasn't about to let them in on my terrible secret. I packed a few clothes and wrote a note to my wife, stating that my mother is ill and I've gone to Byron. I put my bloody clothes in a burlap bag with brick inside. I would throw it in a creek on my way to Byron. As luck would have it, my wife would be away for a few days anyhow in Atlanta. I wrote down my parents' phone number; only a few people could afford such a luxury then. As I was getting things in order and about to walk out my door, I heard a car pull up outside. I go to the window to look out and it's a police car. I wait to hear them walk up on the porch and knock at the door. I went and answered the door. The sheriff and a deputy were standing on the porch. I invited them in and they told me that they are here to let me know that there was a murder about two miles to the rear of my place and they told me to keep the place locked up tonight. They told me that that it appeared that a wild animal had killed a black man named Thomas Hill last night as well as one of his hogs. They asked me did I hear anything unusual last night? I told them that that I had been so busy renovating the house, that when I went to sleep I was out of it. The sheriff knows my wife's family and asked where she was and I told him that she is in Atlanta staying with her cousin Anna shopping for a new house to move into, when I start my new job in a couple of weeks with the state. I told him would he mind driving by here for next two days to check on the while I'm gone because my father had called me and said that my mother had taken ill. The sheriff said that he didn't mind checking on the place for me since he only lives 3 or 4 miles down the road. The sheriff told me that he hoped my mother gets well and would check in with me once I got back into town. I told them thanks for dropping by as they were heading back to their car. Though I was nervous on the inside about their visit, I remained calm and didn't crack under pressure. I locked the back door and grabbed my bag of clothes with burlap bag, locked the front door and got into my model A. I turned over the motor and looked at my fuel gage, I'll need to stop and get some fuel before I leave town. I drove into town and stopped in front of the gas pump at the general mercantile store. I walked in to pay the cashier for the gas, and I overheard some men talking about the black man that had gotten killed last night. I told the clerk to get me a pack of Camel cigarettes, and I paid him for the gas and the cigarettes. As I headed for the door, my keen sense of hearing picked part of the conversation that the men were having. One of the men said, "It had to be a big panther that did it because there aren't any bears around here." I walked on out to the pump and put in four gallons of gas. As I was putting gas into the car, the thought of what the beast did to that poor guy, the guy didn't have a chance. The same way the beast had taken out the men in my squad and almost finished me. I had pumped the gas in, replaced the gas cap and headed for Byron. I took out my pocket watch and checked the time it was already 11:00 a.m., I should be in Byron by 1 o'clock. How does one go about explaining to their father that their son turns into some kind of monster at night. That their son has already killed someone because he can't control what he becomes. I'll have to convince him to chain me up so that I don't get loose. The beast that I become has no conscience about what it does. I remember that day very well, I almost ran the poor automobile hot; pushing it to get back home. I pull up into my father's yard and I ran into the house looking for him. My mother wanted to know if my wife is okay. I told her yes, but I need to talk to my father. My mother told me that he is in the barn working on the tractor. I ran out the back door and as I got closer to the barn, I slowed down because I could hear my father talking to someone else in the barn. I walked into the barn and with my father was his trusted field hand Jake. I said, "Father I have to talk you in private about something very urgent." My father told Jake to take the farm truck and go to town and order the tractor part. Jake told me that he would see me when he got back. As soon as Jake got out of hearing distance. I proceeded to tell my father about what had happened. My father asked me, "Are you sure that you didn't dream this?" I went through all of the details and he was struggling to believe me. I said, "Do you remember seeing the scars on my body, when you and mother visited me in the hospital in Warm Springs?" I took off my shirt and to his amazement the scars were gone. I told him whatever attacked me and caused those scars, had passed this affliction or whatever you want to call it over to me. I told him that I began to change before it got dark and I don't know what triggers it. I just know that when the beast takes over my body, it is in control and I have to be chained up before it even gets close to dark. Father told me to get the chain that was hanging on the rafter and he got a lock that he uses to lock the barn door. He told me to put the chain in the back of his truck and to get my car and to follow him. I followed him down a field road that runs the length of my father's property until we had gotten to the end that opens up to a huge open field surrounded by old growth oak trees. I stopped my car behind him and took the chain out of his truck. I told him that the beast is very strong and needs to be bound in a way so that escaping wouldn't be possible. My father told me, "Son, this causes me great pain to have to chain my son to a tree because of what my son has told me."

I told him that if he doesn't, the creature will cause more than just pain. My teeth started hurting and I begged my father to hurry and finish because the pain has started. My father had chained me in a standing position and placed the lock in the chain on the back side of the oak tree that I was bound to. I told my father to get his gun out in case I escape. As I was changing from man to beast, my father was in shock from what he was witnessing. After the change was complete, the beast became angry because he couldn't move.

I remember my father asking the beast, "Where is my son Gerald? Where did my son go?"

The creature answered him back in a guttural voice saying, "Let me out of these chains old man." My father had walked to his truck and got his rifle as the creature tried to wiggle loose from the chains. The creatures arms were bound behind the tree and it just angered him more because he was bound. My father walking toward the creature asking again, "Where is my son?"

The creature, being very irritated, said, "Get these fucking chains off of me old man!"

My father said, "My son doesn't talk like that. Now what have you done with my son, you devil?"

As he was pointing the rifle at the creature, the creature said, "I told you to get these fucking chains off of me, I'm hungry you weak old man."

My father said, "That's what you want me to do don't you is shoot you, don't you?"

The creature said, "Go ahead and shoot and see what happens old man." The next instance I heard the gun go off and intense pain going through my head. I was out for a couple of seconds and I opened my eyes. I could see the horror on my father's face as I opened my eyes and said, "I'm still here old man, now let me out of these chains." My father realizing that shooting me again is useless so he said, "If my son is back in the morning I'll set you free if not, I'm going to purge the demon from my son with fire tomorrow. I watched my father walk back to his truck with the gun. He gets in and sits there and watches to see if the beast would continue to struggle to get loose. The creature spent all of his energy trying everything to get free and just roared a loud growl of defiance. I guess my father was satisfied to the point that he could leave. I heard the truck crank up and I yelled at my father again to let me out of these chains. I watched my father drive away, leaving me chained to a massive oak.

The creature was furious and realized that it was useless to struggle anymore. As time crawled along and the sun had been overtaken by the night, my ears were picking up the sounds of the forest. My vision had adjusted to the darkness as well as my keen sense of smell. My nose was sampling the air and had picked up the scent of someone's cooking, that was carried by the wind. My stomach yearned for something to eat. Then as the night went on and the full moon rose higher in the sky. I realized what had triggered the change. The night that I was attacked in Germany was during a full moon. Last night when I changed and killed a man and his livestock, the moon was full; just as it is now. Hopefully there will only be the last change tomorrow night until next month when the phase starts again. I hope I'm right and I can convince father to contain the beast in a different way than being chained to a tree. Several hours pass, and I hear an automobile engine, and I see a pair of headlights coming down the field road. Soon it was apparent that it was my father's truck, he had driven back here to see if I was still attached to the tree. It was very brave of him to take this chance. He had to satisfy his curiosity I guess. He stopped briefly to shine the light on me and turned toward the house. I remember it being a long night, and waiting for the sun to come up. I couldn't feel my clawed hands anymore because the way I was shackled with my arms stretched back behind me. All I could do, was move head left to right and scan the surroundings laid out in front of me. I was awake the whole time right up to when I changed back to my human form. I then feel asleep due to exhaustion. I had a dream of being visited by these beings, they were telling me that one day an heir would be born. This heir would be used as a weapon against the dark one. I had asked them were they messengers of God. They said that they were here to protect me from the dark one because I'm in such a weakened state of vulnerability. Before I could ask them anymore questions, I was awakened by the sound of my father's truck driving up. My father had stopped the truck and hurriedly made his way over and removed the lock. I collapsed on the ground and he finished removing the chain.

He said, "I'm glad to see my son again. I was afraid that if you hadn't changed back, I was going to have to put you down by fire. I didn't any sleep last night thinking about shooting my own son in the head to free him. I didn't tell your mother about this. I don't think she can handle it. I can barely handle it myself. Because you are my son and I have a responsibility to keep this beast from just running rampant and killing at will. I wouldn't be able to live with myself if that happened." Because I was so exhausted, he helped me to get to the truck. I told my father that I think that I had figured out what triggered the change and I explained it to him on the way to the house. Before I could read any more from the journal, Grandmother walked into my room. She asked me if I was ready for some lunch? I looked over at the digital clock by the bed and it said 12:45. I told her that a sandwich would do. My appetite was quelled by what I had read. I could only imagine the mental anguish that my great-grand-father had to muster, after finding out his son turns into a monster. Then having to chain him up so tightly that he can't move and even thinking about killing his only child. I walked into the kitchen and Grandmother said that she had taken a nap while I was reading. She said, "How far in the journal did you get?" I told her that I had stopped at the point where Grandfather was unchained and being taken to the house.

She said, "Your grandfather had experienced a lot of things while he was alive. Somethings he probably wished he didn't have to experience. I'm not going to spoil your reading and tell you what happens next, I want you to read his words and his thoughts as he laid it out on paper. Just think after tonight, you won't have to be locked up until next month." According to the timeline yesterday, my teeth and jaw started hurting around 3 o'clock. I have but a few hours before I'm locked up. Grandmother and I had a sandwich and some potato chips and briefly talked about things like. How did she and Grandfather keep my father in the dark about it all of those years? Grandmother said, "On up until your father was six years old it was easy to get your grandfather locked up in the cell and be back upstairs before your father knew I had disappeared into the secret cellar. As he got older it became more difficult. If the full moon occurred during a weekend, I would ask my sister to keep him. Luckily, during the day your father would be at school when the change occurred. Your grandfather would just stay locked up for three to four days depending on the phases of the moon during certain times of the season. When your father left for school I would go downstairs and check on your grandfather, take him some food and water, letting him out to relieve himself in the bathroom downstairs and lock him back up. We couldn't run the risk of letting your father know what was going on. Because children are curious and the beast that your grandfather became couldn't be trusted. Just prior to your father' teenage years. Your grandfather had gotten 'Houston', your father interested in music. At the same time, he planted the notion that girls like musicians better than athletes. Your grandfather had a way to convey an idea, so thought provoking. He could force his will upon a person, and they wouldn't even realize that it was happening. I remember once, your father came home from school. He was either in the first or second grade and told your grandfather there was another kid in his class named James like himself. Your grandfather asked him what name would he wished to be called? Your father said he liked his middle name "Houston" the best. Your grandfather looked him straight in the eyes and said, "okay, Houston Farnsworth from this day forward you are Houston Farnsworth and you are your own man from here on out. He broke eye contact and told Houston to go play and he turned to me and smiled and said, "There goes Houston Farnsworth." I began calling my son Houston Farnsworth after that. I did have to talk to the teacher about using his name.

I said," Was it grandfather's influence that my dad playing the guitar?"

Grandmother said," Your grandfather introduced your father to the blues guitar legends, by way of the phonograph. Houston was exposed to the greats like Muddy waters, Robert Johnson and John Lee Hooker. It was there style of playing that got him hooked. Your father took guitar lessons and struggled with it until, your grandfather sat him down, made eye contact and told him, he has the ability to master the instrument instead of instrument mastering him and that playing music will fun instead of a chore. From then on, your father dove head first into the instrument. When the electric guitar hit the mainstream your father started his fascination with electronics and music. Your grandfather did get your father a part time job in a studio in Macon, while he was a senior in high school. There during his college tenure, your grandfather was working behind the scenes to get your dad the funding for the beginnings of Red Sand Studio. Your grandfather had instilled a drive mechanism in your father that, your father had been willed to push the envelope of technology of the time and not to except just the status quo. So now you don't need someone to will you forward. The program is already installed. Because of your unique situation, you could perhaps slowly remove yourself from the limelight and be the man behind the scenes, that is grooming a protégé."

I asked Grandmother, "How did she get so wise?" She told me by listening and observing the world around her plus the fact that my grandfather had been telling her about certain events told to him by the messengers. We talked some more for a couple of hours until my grandmother noticed that my eye color was changing. She said, "We had better get down stairs." I asked her, "Why my jaws haven't started hurting yet!" She told me that my eyes have changed color as she hurried me to the hidden stairwell. As we were going down stairs, I notice that my eyes had become light sensitive. I walked into the cage and Grandmother locked it. I asked her, "What do you think is going on?" She told me that the trigger mechanism could be changing, meaning that I am evolving in a different way. It wasn't long before the pains started. Grandmother had preplanned for today, she placed two pounds of ground beef in an ice chest. While I was writhing in the floor in pain, she was unwrapping the ground beef and waiting for me. After I had completed the change, I walked over to the edge of the cage and watched my grandmother push the package of ground beef over within my reach, using a broom. I grabbed the Styrofoam container of ground beef and began stuffing the ground up meat it in my mouth. I finished the one pack off and asked for more. Grandmother said, "This pack is still half frozen but I'm sure you'll be able to eat it. She pushed the package across the floor with the broom within my reach and grabbed it. I bit into the semi frozen meat. I wasn't able to consume it as fast. Grandmother said, "That'll slow you down from eating it so fast." She turns on the television and told me that she would see me in the morning as she walked up the stairs. I didn't give a reply, my mouth was frozen form trying to chew the frozen hamburger meat she had given me. I stopped eating it and wound up breaking it up into smaller chunks with my claws. Frozen meat is a real chore to eat. After I had broken it up, I let it set and thaw out as I watched the television. It was a good idea of my grandfather to put a television in here, it keeps the beast's mind calm and off the fact that he is in a cage. I sat on the floor and watched a couple of movies to pass the time as the meat thawed out so that I could eat it. I finished off the last chunks of ground beef, I had a lot of pent up energy I had to burn up. I started doing pull ups by holding on to the bars overhead. I had become bored with watching television, my body needed to burn off some anxious energy. I did a hundred pull-ups easy, a hundred push-ups, a hundred squats, a hundred crunches. Normally I couldn't be able to do this amount of routines back to back. The beast wasn't even winded so he did another circuit of routines and doubled the reps. After that the beast was tired enough to just lay down on the floor and fell asleep. I then found myself in a dream state of consciousness. I'm not a creature controlled by the moon but myself, the normal human, James Farnsworth. I look around and nothing looks familiar to me. There's a clump of trees and an open pasture and the horizon seems endless in every direction. I walk to the clump trees and on my way, I hear a voice from behind me say, "Hold on James, I'll walk with you." I turn around and it is a messenger. I asked the messenger, "What is the name of this place?" He told me that this place represents sanctuary, a place of tranquility. I said, "Let me guess, you are here to relay a message of importance?" The messenger said, "There are things that are happening and though it is foretold in the Holy book, myself and those in my realm are not ready for this war. Since the dark one has tried a few times to corrupt you to his way and found out that you are under our protection. He has stepped up the pace to create his army. Through our agents, we have uncovered the probability of the dark one's agents posing as human, possible Nephilim.

I said, "I thought the great flood destroyed the Nephilim?"

The messenger said, "The scenario has changed. Just as I was to ask the messenger, "What scenario?" I was awakened by the pains of transformation back into the human Farnsworth. The sun was coming over the eastern horizon, time to face another day, a busy day at that. I was waiting at the door of the cage, as I heard the door of the hidden stairwell open. Then the sound of slow steady footsteps of my grandmother as she walked down the stairs. Good morning, she says. She walks over with the key and unlocks the door. I asked her did she have some coffee brewing? She answered back by saying, "Is a two pound sparrow fat?" I chuckled and said, "I'll take that as a yes." She told me that we had better get a move on because Agent Harrington will be here soon. I can clean the mess when I get back later today. As we got to the top of the stairs the doorbell was ringing. I hurried off to my room to change clothes as Grandmother checked the security monitor. Agent Harrington was at the front door. Grandmother pushed the button on the intercom and told Agent Harrington that she would be right there. I went into my room and slid on a clean pair of jeans and a T-shirt, brushed my teeth. I didn't need agent Harrington to see raw hamburger stuck in my teeth. I walked into the kitchen and agent Harrington was talking to my grandmother.

I said, "Good morning, Agent Harrington."

Agent Harrington replied back by saying, "Good morning to you, Mr. Farnsworth. I see you didn't shave this morning which, is good. The makeup job will look more believable. I've got everything lined up, the convenience store manager has been briefed and now, we must be on our way to get you ready for your debut. We have to rendezvous with our field makeup specialist first.

I said, "Let me get my shoes on, and I'll be ready."

I asked Grandmother does she have a to go cup I can take with me with coffee inside? She brought me a Styrofoam cup with coffee and said, "How about this?" I told Grandmother thanks and that I'm so lucky to have her. She gave me a hug and told Agent Harrington to take care me. Agent Harrington assured her that I would be back and he said, "Your grandson should be back home in time, so that you both can watch him on the local news today. Now, let's get going Mr. Farnsworth." I had put my sneakers on without socks and followed Agent Harrington out to his vehicle. I got in, buckled my seat belt and reclined the seat.

Agent Harrington got in the driver's side and said, "Keep it reclined until we can get out of town. We don't want to run the risk of someone recognizing you." I told him that it's going to be tough trying to drink this coffee laying down. He told me that it would be a good idea to chug some of the coffee down so that, I don't spill it. I think he's more worried that I may spill it in his vehicle than on myself. I leaned up and slugged a good bit of the coffee down. The coffee was good going down, though it was on the warm side. It didn't matter, I was getting my morning fix. As the vehicle headed out of the drive, Agent Harrington made a call on his cell phone. I heard him tell someone that he is on the way and would meet with them at the Flint River boat ramp on 96 and ended the call. I said, "Once this goes public, you know Serlinni will be trying extra hard to get rid of me." Agent Harrington said, "Serlinni will be too worried about his own people turning him in for the reward money. He'll more than likely go into hiding after the videotape goes to the local news, and then it will go viral. The airports nationwide will be alerted of his identity. Serlinni will be like a roach when the lights come on—he'll hide. Money changes people, people have turned in relatives for the reward. "I said, "Especially now with the way things are now economically, people are desperate. The chance of becoming an instant millionaire, would be very appealing." Agent Harrington said, "The reward has gone up to two million per the conversation with my boss. The government has decided to kick it up a notch because it will be high profile case once this goes public. Once this is over, your business value will increase simply by association alone."

I said, "I hope to sell the business so that I won't be a target for another mobster to move in on."

Agent Harrington then told me that if Serlinni is captured and this goes to court. The businesses in the music industry that has any ties to organized crime will be under the microscope from the federal government.

I said, "It could create an organization like the gaming commission that put the squeeze on organized crime out in Vegas."

Agent Harrington said, "It would be possible that some type of regulatory mandate could come out this, who knows? One thing for sure is that, the other crime families will be looking at this situation and reevaluating on how they are currently doing business." Agent Harrington told me that we had left the city limits and it is safe to let my seat up. I pull the seat lever and now I'll be able to finish off the coffee. I put the cup to my lips, it was mediocre warm, I drank it anyway. It will probably be a while before I get some breakfast. It's a good thing I had a high protein diet last night. I drank the last of the coffee and held the cup in my hand. Agent Harrington told me to reach behind my seat and there's trash bag to place the cup in. I had to unbuckle the seat belt and placed the cup in the trash bag. By this time, we weren't too far from the rendezvous point at the Flint River boat landing. Agent Harrington wasn't much of a conversationalist, so I asked him if they found out who the car belong to that I was supposed to have been cremated in. He told me that the VIN had revealed that the car had been stolen from its owner in Phoenix City, Alabama, a year ago.

Agent Harrington said that a state trooper had confirmed this while I was be interviewed at the Taylor county sheriff's dept..

I asked Agent Harrington, "What am I to say about the two day lapse in time if someone interviews me?" He said, "It would be best if you have a lawyer do all of the talking for you. He would tell the press the same account that you told me.." I asked him, "Will we have to wait for the news crew to get there?" He said, "no, our field crew will tape the interview with you, the state patrolman that picked you up and the sheriff of Taylor county. The tape will be copied and sent to a TV station in Columbus and in Macon, then another copy will be sent to a syndicated news station in Atlanta. After that happens, your grandmother's phone and the phone at Red Sand Studio will be ringing off the wall. The calls will be from these television stations wanting interviews. The calls can be directed to your lawyer to limit the questioning by the media with you and instead of having separate interviews with different stations, a single interview will take place with a few local networks to keep the the paparazzi down." Agent Harrington had pulled into the road that led to the

263

boat ramp at the Flint river bridge, there were two vehicles parked there, a van and a black SUV. If this was on a Friday or Saturday there would be fisherman here, unloading the crafts into the river to go fishing. Since it is on a Wednesday, the boat ramp area is empty except for the three vehicles parked here now. Agent Harrington lets his window down so that the people in the van can see him because of the dark tint on the windows. People started pouring out of the vehicles and Agent Harrington told me to get out and go to the van while he talked to the other field agents. I opened the door and made my way over to the white van. A woman had walked from the other side of the van and said, "come over to this side of the van and get in Mr. Farnsworth." I walked over to the passenger side of the van where, a side door was opened and I climbed in. To my amazement, it was like what you would see in the movies. A makeup chair, mirror, and plenty of lights. The woman I assumed being the makeup artist; closed the door behind me and told me to have a seat in the makeup chair. I sat down in the chair and she started to work right away on me. She began by applying some type of adhesive on my face and she was explaining to me what she was doing as she went along. She said, "It is good that didn't shave this morning, the beard growth helps to hold your new scruffy look on. I'm going to give you an appearance of three days of beard growth, make your hair not so neat and make it look like you slept on the ground." I replied by saying, I did sleep on the ground two nights ago." She told me that when she finishes with me, I'll look like a vagrant that has been living in the woods with the addition of the proper attire to achieve the look. She all but groped me and I could smell that she was turned on. In about thirty minutes or so, She had completed my makeup and turned me around to let me see myself in the mirror. I looked like a bona fide hobo.

The makeup lady said, "Now Mr. Farnsworth, take these clothes and put these on. I'll turn around to give you some privacy as you remove your pants. Let me know once you've put on your altered pants." I removed my jogging pants and placed them on the makeup chair, slid on the dirtied up pants and told the makeup lady that I had pants on now. She told me to go ahead and put the shirt and sit back down in the makeup chair. I sat back down as she took an air brush and painted simulated mud stains, grass stains and mottled colors of grunginess. She folded part of my shirt collar inward and did some touch up on my neck. She then said, "Take a look now Mr. Farnsworth" as she turned the makeup chair facing the mirror.

I said, "All I need is a sign that says Will Work for Beer." Agent Harrington walked into the van and asked the makeup artist lady, if I was ready? She told him that I was ready. Agent Harrington asked me to get in the car so that we can be on our way to the next location. I complied by getting into the car and he was right behind me. He started up the vehicle and we were followed by the other two vehicles. As we got onto the main road, Agent Harrington handed me a piece of paper. He said, "Read it over and you don't have to remember line for line but it is the script that you'll be using for the taping. The sheriff of Taylor county will first issue a statement saying that James Farnsworth Jr. has been found, he was picked up by a Georgia state patrolman this morning. The camera will pan from the face of the sheriff to show a complete shot of you with the state patrol standing next you. The sheriff will say something like Mr. Farnsworth has filled us in on what has happened to him. Then he'll say that Federal Bureau of Investigation is now in control of this case involving the attempted murder of Mr. Farnsworth by known mob boss Vincent Serlinni, then he'll say by issuance of the FBI a two million dollar reward will be paid to anyone, that has information to the whereabouts and the capture of Vincent Serlinni. He'll give a number to call and then the camera focuses on you and the interviewer will ask, is there anything you would like to say Mr. Farnsworth? I then said, "First I like to tell my mother, my grandmother and my people at Red Sand Studio that I'm okay and that two million dollars goes to anyone that has information on the whereabouts and capture of Vincent Serlinni and anyone else connected to this case, then I repeat the number to contact."

I asked Agent Harrington if I could say something to the nature of also linking Serlinni to the murder of Nicole Adams? He told me that once he is apprehended there will be two more charges brought against him, the murder of Nicole Adams and another attempted murder of me. He said all of that will be brought up in court.

I told Agent Harrington, "The last time that I was heading this way. I thought I was on my way to meet my maker."

Agent Harrington said, "This time you're about to unleash the hounds of justice on Serlinni's ass."

We continued the ride until we arrived in Butler and parked at the sheriff's department. Agent Harrington told me to follow him in. He got out of the car and I followed right behind him as he walked through the doors of the sheriff's department. Agent Harrington approached the attendant at the security entrance and told the attendant that the sheriff is expecting him and showed the attendant his ID.

The attendant said, "One moment, sir, and I'll page the sheriff for you."

It wasn't long before the sheriff had come through the secured doors and invited us in plus an entourage of field agents with equipment. The sheriff took us to a room to get set up for the filmed interview. Agent Harrington asked about the state patrolman and the sheriff said that he's in the break room getting some coffee.

CHAPTER 13

Agent Harrington then asked the sheriff, "have you been practicing your line?" The sheriff replied, "I think I can pull this off, and before you ask? I have not discussed this with no one and I'm sure that the patrolman will tell you the same thing." The film crew was setting up equipment and hooking up microphone leads. The film crew field manager told me to take a seat at the other side of the table. He asked the cameraman what does the shot look like? A sound person then clipped a mini mike to my grungy shirt and asked me to speak in a normal tone for a sound check. The cameraman gave a thumbs-up signal that he was getting a good signal through his head phones. Agent Harrington asked the sheriff, "Can we get the trooper in here? We are ready to roll this." The sheriff said that he would be right back with the trooper. Within minutes the sheriff and the state trooper were in the room. The soundman clips a mini mike on the sheriff and the state trooper and ask each one of the them to speak in a normal tone for a sound check. The cameraman gives a thumbs-up for the sound check. The film crew field manager said, "Gentlemen, I don't expect for you to get this right on the first take, so just relax and be calm. If you get tongue tied or stumble a little bit that's okay. My team can edit out the screwed up sections, we just want to be out of here, so that we can edit this and have it ready for the six o'clock newscast okay. Everyone take a deep breath and blow out all of your air and inhale nice and slow. All three of us sitting at the table did the breathing exercise and was inhaling nice and slow. The field filming manager told the cameraman to pan in on the sheriff and get ready. The field film manager told the sheriff to watch the cameraman's left hand because he is going to give you a three count and then you start with your narration. The cameraman starts the count down three, two one and points at the sheriff. The sheriff says" I'm sheriff Donald Bartlett of Taylor county. Our department in collaboration with the Federal Bureau of investigation and the Georgia State Patrol have after many man hours, have found the reported missing James Farnsworth Jr. After he was interviewed by my organization and the FBI, he had informed us that he had survived a failed murder attempt upon his life. Lt. Ellis had picked him up at a convenience store this morning after being called by Mr. Farnsworth. As Mr. Farnsworth was being brought to the Taylor county facility, I had received a call from the FBI field office in Atlanta and was instructed to issue this statement. The statement is that the federal government has issued a reward for the information of the whereabouts and capture of Vincent Serlinni, a known mob boss of an organized crime family. The reward amount is 2 million dollars to anyone for the whereabouts and capture of Vincent Serlinni and anyone else connected to this case. Please call this number if you have any information, the number is 770-850-3377. You will be granted anonymity. The sheriff turned to me and asked me, "Mr. Farnsworth, do you have anything you would like to say?" I said, "I just want to let my family and my friends know that I'm okay, thanks to all of the law enforcement involved and 2 million dollars to the person that helps put Serlinni and his associates behind bars." State trooper Ellis said, "If you know anything about this you could be 2 million dollars richer, so call this number 770-850-3377. Just think if this had happened to one of your family members."

The cameraman stops filming, and the field filming manager claps his hands and says, "That was a great job, guys, and you did it in one take."

Agent Harrington said, "That was a good job now, if a news station calls you for an interview. What are you going to tell them? The sheriff and the state patrolman say in almost unison, "no comment." I say, "You will have to speak to my lawyer."

Agent Harrington then says, "Like they say in the movies that's a wrap gentlemen, thank you for your time and your collaboration." I shook hands with the sheriff and the state trooper as they got up from the table. Agent Harrington told the sheriff and the state trooper that an APB will be issued nationwide before the interview gets sent out to the television network. He said all the airports and transportation system will be alerted of Serlinni's identity. He again told the sheriff and the state trooper that he appreciated this effort. He said, "Don't forget to tell your families that you'll be on local, national, and possibly international television tonight. The media will be all over this type of stuff." The field crew was packing away their equipment and Agent Harrington got on his cell phone and walked out into the hallway. I guess, he was talking to his boss and letting him know that the ball has started rolling. He came back into the room and asked the film crew manager, "How long will it take before the video segment will be ready to review before it's ready to stream out the networks?" The film crew manager said, "It should take about 15 minutes or so to down load the film segment onto the computer, so that we'll be able to enhance or edit if you like. It will depend on how much retouch of the images is required. We may even get lucky and not have to do much to the segment." Agent Harrington told the film crew manager that he needs a two hour window before the video segment gets sent out.

The film crew manager said, "That won't be a problem, it's only 10:00 a.m. now. By 11 o'clock, my crew will have something for you to review before it's ready to send out."

I asked Agent Harrington, could I get I get out of makeup now?" The film crew manager overheard the conversation and said, "not just yet, Mr. Farnsworth. I know that it probably itches and uncomfortable. Just give us a few minutes to check the tape and if the tape looks good, I'll get Anna to remove the makeup for you okay?" I said, "Well, as far as the rest of world I'm supposed to be dead anyway, so a half hour or longer won't be too bad. Can someone tell me where the bathroom is in this place?" The sheriff happened to be within hearing range and told me to go down the hall and it's the first door on the right. I told the sheriff thanks and walked down the hall to the bathroom, before I pissed in my costume and really made it authentic looking. I went into the bathroom took a leak, washed my hands, and took a look in the mirror at the makeup artist's handiwork. I must say, she did a really good job. I could pass for your average vagrant. I walked back to the interrogation room and sat back down. The film crew and sound guy had packed all of their stuff and had left the room. I was sitting in there by myself for a little while until the sheriff walked back in and sat down across from me. He said, "Mr. Farnsworth, you are really putting yourself out there by doing this, you know this don't you." I told him that this is my idea. I said, "The feds were originally going to issue an APB for the capture of Serlinni. This way I want him to become the hunted instead of the hunter. It may come down to one his own underlings to rat him out. I know of course that Serlinni could possibly put out another hit on me. Hell, I've already got a federal agent camping out in my back yard. I had federal agents watching the business the day I was abducted. What worked for the bad guys the last time won't work for the next. I'm not laying down for this one, even if it means me losing my life in the process. After the airing of the segment tonight, the people in the music industry that are being controlled by organized crime are going on notice." The sheriff said, "I've always thought of organized crime being involved with loan sharking, racketeering and the usual illegal activities like drug and human trafficking. But now I can see where ever there is substantial money involved like in the music industry, the mob would be wanting a piece of the action." I told him that my father had told me that, some studio owners that he knew in the upper East Coast had been victims of a hostile takeover. By this time the makeup artist came in and said, "My boss said that the segment looks good. Follow me to the van and I'll get the makeup off and you can change back into your clothes. The sheriff told me that he would pray that the mobster gets brought to justice and pray for me as well. I thanked him for his help and hospitality as I left the room. I followed the makeup artist to the van, got in the makeup chair as she applied some type of cream to my face. She began wiping away her handy work and told me she was going to lean the chair back, so that she wash away the fake mud and gunk out of my hair.

The water was running, and the makeup artist whispered in my ear, "My body aches for you."

The scent of her female essence had aroused me as well. I asked her is there anyone else in the van? She said, "I'm sorry Mr. Farnsworth, I don't know what came over me. I was out of line." I leaned forward, looked at her, and told her to relax and forget it even happened. I leaned back and she got back to work cleaning me up, my stomach was growling and she said "Sounds like somebody needs some food." I told her that all that I've had this morning is coffee and could use some solid food. She told me that once she finishes, I'll look presentable again so that maybe Agent Harrington will take you to get something to eat. Within twenty minutes or so, she was finished with me, and I had put on my jogging pants and my T-shirt. Agent Harrington came into the van and asked if the crew was finished with me. The makeup artist told him that I was ready to go. She had just finished blow drying my hair and told me good luck. I got up from the chair and left the van. Agent Harrington was talking to the film crew manager and motioned for me to come on over to the car. As I was walking over to the car, I heard Agent Harrington tell the field crew manager that per the higher ups, the APB will be issued at 3:00 today and the interview material is to be issued out to the media at 4:45. As I drew closer to the vehicle, Agent Harrington unlocked the car with the remote and said, "Go ahead and get in Mr. Farnsworth and we'll go get something to eat." He then told the field crew manager to call his cell the minute that the interview material is released. He got into the car, buckled his seat belt and said, "Are you hungry James?" I replied by saying, "Do catfish have whiskers?" He looked at me and said, "I'll take that as a yes." I told him that I had forgotten that he is a city boy and doesn't know of such things. He told me that his mother had a first cousin that drown when she fell from the dock. He said, "Other family members say that the cousin probably struck her head during the fall, lost consciousness and drown. Because of that incident my mother's fear of water kept me from being exposed to fishing or swimming. I didn't learn to swim until I had to take swimming lessons before I could become an agent. It is funny how someone's fear can be inherited. But I have made sure that my kids know how to swim." I said, "Fear is a learned experience and like evil thoughts, it must be kept in check otherwise; fear and evil can overwhelm if the person allows it." Agent Harrington said, "It sounds like you've gained some wisdom during your time in the wilderness Mr. Farnsworth." I told him that it was a humbling experience once I calmed down enough after escaping near death. Stumbling through the forest at night in the rain, one totally forgets about the rattlesnakes, water moccasins, poison ivy or any of the things that can cause potential harm. Self-preservation and determination take over. I wasn't about to risk walking out from the dirt road and back on the main highway. The possibility of the bad guys of still being in the neighborhood was a factor in my mind. I stuck to the forest and kept going eastward." Agent Harrington said, "Most would have tried the road and took the risk simply because they were too afraid of what remains hidden in the forest. They would've also run the risk of being picked up by the bad guys and not survived." I told him that there are far more dangerous animals driving the highways than there are in the forest. Agent Harrington had pulled up to a fast food chain drive through and asked me what did I want? I told him two burgers and a large water. I reached for my wallet and I realized that my wallet was on the dresser at Grandmother's, the jogging pants don't have back pockets. Agent Harrington said, "Don't worry, Uncle Sam has got this." He rolled forward and placed the orders the usual way, speaking to an unseen person via an intercom system. While I was making an observation, I told Agent Harrington that in the future, it will be an electronic voice that converses with you, it tells you the total and waits until you swipe your payment card. You then move forward as your food is waiting in a pickup delivery system all robotic, no human needed, except for maintenance. There was a car in front of us, waiting at the window. that person probably had to have their food a particular way, just ketchup, no lettuce or tomato or onions. Now they are annoyed that it takes extra time to prepare it. In the future, the have it your way won't be there. The future menu will be specific on how your food will be served to you.

Therefore, more efficient, no waiting and no one to complain to. The car in front finally moves on up just a little bit then stops.

I told Agent Harrington, "Look that person is checking to see if their order is right."

We could see the guy looking through the bag and finally moves away.

Agent Harrington said, "Because there is an actual person handing out food at the drive through sets them up as a target, for some picky person to bitch them out because they didn't want mustard on their burger. Like you say if it was automated, the person in the car wouldn't have anyone to bitch at. They would take their food and drive on off and if something was jacked up about the order, they could go inside to see a manager." I then said, "That's when the poor manager gets bitched out." We pulled up to the take out window the girl at the window said, "Your order total is $8.50, sir."

Agent Harrington gave the girl his credit card, she ran the card and gave him the receipt, our drinks and she said the fries will be a few minutes, that we need to pull forward and someone will bring the food out to us. Agent Harrington looked at me and said, "We are a good ways off from automation." We chuckled about that. we didn't have to wait too long before this girl came out with a bag with our food in it. Agent Harrington thanked her and pulled over to a shady spot and we sat there in the car and ate our food. Agent Harrington reached into the bag and gave me my order and some napkins. I was so hungry, I could eat the napkins with ketchup on it. I had to control my urge to just stuff the hamburger in my mouth and consume it all in two bites. I refrained from such action and just savored each bite that I took. I looked over at Agent Harrington and he was scarfing it down at a pretty good rate, he must be hungry also. I finished my first burger and started on my second one. Before I knew it I had finished the second burger and killed all of my water. I put my trash in the bag and waited until Agent Harrington had finished. Within minutes, he too had finished and stuffed his trash in the bag. I told him to pull over to the trash can on the way out, so I can throw this away. He turned the car on, buckled his seat belt, backed out of the parking place and headed for the trash can. As he drove toward the trash can, there was a stray dog standing by the trash can. I got out to throw the trash into the can, the stray laid down and when I got back into the car, he got back up. I felt guilty because I didn't have any food to give him. Agent Harrington pulled out onto the street as I buckled my seat belt. I told him thanks for the food and I feel like I have some energy now. The coffee that I had this morning just didn't have any bulk about. We were on our way back to Byron, passing through Reynolds on our way back to Peach county. On the way back, I began to think about the statement that the messenger told me about the scenario is going to change. Also about the possibility of the existence of the Nephilim. He's talking about stuff from the book of Genesis, stuff that's mentioned in the first book in the Bible. On that thought, I asked Agent Harrington a question.

I said, "I know this is totally out of context of what I'm about to ask you, but here it goes. Do you think that someone in our government could be creating incidents in the middle east to keep the war machine going. Though the administration did pull the troops out of Iraq. the incident concerning Syria and the administration's view of Israel to give in to the Palestinians. It seems all to have the makings of a holy war, especially if Iran keeps pointing the gun barrel at Israel." Agent Harrington said, "You really came out of the blue with that one. Off the record and between you and me only. The US government can't afford to stop the war machine completely, it is creating jobs for the military and civilian sector. The current administration did indeed pull the troops from Iraq, this was a political ploy to get re-elected. By doing this, the administration left the gate open for another type of faction. It's a matter of economics and politics but, mostly politics. Let's focus on the local bad guys in the United States for now and remember this, our conversation didn't happen." While we were talking, we were just miles outside of Byron. Agent Harrington said, "We are getting close to Byron. Go ahead and recline your seat and I'll let you know when we get to your grandmother's." He then took out his phone and called the field agent that is staying in the guest house. He tells the field agent that we are on our way back and he would brief him once he gets there and ends the call. As I was reclined, I began asking Agent Harrington about the media frenzy that is going to happen.

He said, "it's going to be like sharks attracted to blood in the water. It will be a good idea to let your personal lawyer be your mouthpiece from here on out. What is your lawyers name so that I can call him and brief him?" I told him that my lawyers name is Grady Byrd and his office is in Macon. I told him once I get back to the house I will get the number for him. I could feel the car slowing down, we must be coming to the first set of traffic lights. Just two more traffic lights and it won't be far from Grandmother's house. Agent Harrington told me that it's not much farther and I'll be able to setup in the seat.

After a while of driving, Agent Harrington told me that we had turned onto Farnsworth Lane and I could return the seat in the upright position. I released the seat lever and sat back upward. Agent Harrington called my grandmother and told her to open the garage door because he was bringing me in, he told her that we would see her inside and ended the call. The garage door opened and Agent Harrington pulls the car in and the door came down. I told Agent Harrington that I would need a new cell phone since, the bad guys threw my phone out of the window. He told me that he would pick up a cell phone for me to use also I need to put a freeze on my credit card. Agent Harrington said, "You're supposed to be dead until after the airing of the footage, then you can contact the bank." We got out of the car and were greeted by my grandmother at the entrance to the house. She said, "I've been crazy with anxiety since you've been gone James, not knowing if you were coming back." Agent Harrington said, "I've been taking care of him plus a small battalion of field agents on hand looking after him also. We weren't about to let anything happen to James especially with him going to be on the news tonight." She said, "Does this mean an increase in security because of this?" Agent Harrington told her that it does, but at the same time Vincent Serlinni has been put on notice.

She said, "You two come inside and lets have something cool to drink while you fill me in on what's going on." We followed Grandmother into the main house and I went to my room and got my desk top. I went back into the kitchen, placed my laptop on the counter and turned it on. I looked through my address file and got my lawyers phone number for Agent Harrington. He took out his phone and stored the number and called him. Agent Harrington told my lawyer who he was and that, it was important that he (my lawyer) to meet him here at my grandmother's house. Evidently my lawyer told him that he couldn't break away at the moment and Agent Harrington told him, that's okay the family can retain another lawyer for a television interview that will go beyond local news.

After he said that, we heard Agent Harrington say, "That's good, I'll see you as soon as you get here." Agent Harrington looked at us and smiled. "No lawyer can resist television exposure, good or bad press."

I asked Grandmother did she have any coffee left because I was feeling like I needed a boost. She told me that she would put on a fresh pot. Agent Harrington said, "No coffee for me but how about a glass of ice tea. Coffee this late in the day will keep me awake tonight." Grandmother told him that wouldn't be a problem. I asked Agent Harrington what is going to happen, once the all-points bulletin goes out on Serlinni? He told me that this would alert all of the law enforcement agencies and those agencies that are closet to him, will start to lean on him. Probably someone that is on the take from the local agency where he's located, will more than likely alert Serlinni of the situation. It's no doubt that Serlinni will attempt to go into hiding and after the televised interview stating a 2 million dollar reward; someone will come forward because of the money. It will be like winning the lottery, but they'll ask for protection, possibly relocation into a witness protection program after the trial. There is also a possibility that Serlinni won't make it to trial because some other crime family may think that Serlinni, could start chirping like a bird about them…. he gets whacked. Regardless, your level of safety takes precedence. I'm going to have an agent at the entrance of Farnsworth lane as well as an agent in the guest house. The local sheriff department will also be patrolling the area that leads to the entrance of Farnsworth Lane." I said, "Nicole's parents will probably try to blame me because their daughter is dead due to her association with me. They'll be calling over here after they see the interview on the television."

Agent Harrington said, "Simply tell them that you don't have evidence to support it but that if this guy goes to trial, he'll be implicated in the murder of Nicole and also the first attempted murder of you, Mr. Farnsworth. Plus tell them that if you had any indication of danger, you wouldn't have allowed Nicole to go with you to Arizona to begin with. But from what you've told me about Nicole, she would not have accepted that and wanted to be with you any way, no matter what. Don't worry about that, it's something that was out of your control anyway." He then took out his cell phone and called the agent that is staying in the guest house. He picked up the glass of tea and told my grandmother that, he would bring it right back in once, he briefs the agent out back. Agent Harrington walked out the back door and this gave Grandmother and myself sometime for me to tell her what happened at the filming of the interview. I sat down at the table after I had gotten a cup of coffee. Grandmother asked me what went on during the filmed interview. I told her that before the interview started, I was put into makeup by a special FBI field makeup artist and there was an entire film crew dedicated to this effort. She was amazed at the advancement of today's technology and how it was also scary because it revealed how information can be manipulated to appear to the general public. I told her that it was a sobering event that, I too had thought about how it is possible that what we see on television can be an illusion of truth. I said that in this particular case, the technology will be used as a tool to flush out the criminal element in hopes to be brought to justice. I heard the back door open and I signaled to Grandmother that Agent Harrington is coming back in. I continued to talk about how amazing the makeup artist changed my appearance. I didn't want to just stop talking because Agent Harrington was entering the house. I didn't want him thinking that we could be keeping something secret from him. Agent Harrington sat the glass on the counter and told us that, he had made arrangements for additional security, and that they would be here in an hour from now. I said, "David at the studio needs to be aware of what's coming and knowing what to say, once a representative from a news network starts asking questions." Agent Harrington told me that once he finishes talking to my attorney, he'll talk to David on how to handle the questions. The doorbell rang and I got up to look at the security monitor. It is my attorney at the door. I pressed the intercom button and told Grady that I'll be right there. Agent Harrington said, "I'll let him in." Agent Harrington went to the door and asked my attorney to come in. Grady was astonished to see me sitting at the table with my grandmother. Agent Harrington asked him to have a seat at the table with us. Grady said, "This is a shocker, I thought you could be dead James." Agent Harrington sat across the table from Grady and said, "counselor Byrd until the news interview is shown this afternoon, James Farnsworth Jr. is presumed to be missing or dead. The reason that I've asked you to be here is, after the news interview is aired today showing that James Farnsworth is alive because he survived an attempted murder by cremation. In the news feed, he is naming the perpetrator and a reward for information leading to his arrest. There will be an onslaught of news networks wanting an interview after the taping goes viral."

Before Agent Harrington could say anything else, Grady said, "Let me guess, I'm going to be James's mouth piece and answering questions for the next interview?" Agent Harrington said, "That's correct counselor except for when the networks call and they will be directed to you. You will tell them that an interview will be granted by you on behalf of Mr. Farnsworth and that it will take place at your place of business tomorrow, let's say around 3:00 p.m. Instead of giving multiple interviews to different networks, all interested networks will be there at one time. It is no doubt in my mind that just the local networks will be there but national and possibly international networks will be represented there." Grady said, "Okay, what do you want me to say or not say in this press release? Agent Harrington said, "First before you go in front of the cameras, you'll get your secretary to tell the attending news people that you'll be reading a prepared statement and won't be taking any questions and the statement will reveal most of the answers to the questions that they may have. You might begin by telling the news people who you are, and that you're representing Mr. Farnsworth's behalf then start reading the statement." Agent Harrington took a few seconds then went into the spill of the statement. He said, "You don't have to use this word for word, but it will be pretty close. So here it goes, I'm sure everyone saw the news last night and that my client James Farnsworth had been through quite an ordeal, he had been abducted, beaten, drugged and placed in a vehicle, driven out to a remote area and the vehicle was set on fire. Luckily for Mr. Farnsworth the amount of drugs administered was not enough to keep him sedated. He was able to escape the burning vehicle before it blew up. He then trekked through more than 20 miles of forest to avoid the highway, risking being picked up again by the perpetrators. Mr. Farnsworth was overtaken by hunger and had to risk getting back to the highway after two days of being in the wilderness. He called the state patrol from a convenience store in a remote community called Geneva, Georgia. The rest you know from the interview, by Mr. Farnsworth last night about what was said by naming the person that caused his near demise. The reward is real and I repeat that it will be paid to anyone that brings about the arrest and conviction of Vincent Serlinni and anyone else that was involved. Then you'll repeat the number that can be called and that number is 770-850-3377, anonymity will be granted to whoever divulges information. Then thank the news people for showing up and that'll be the end of the interview. Like I said, you won't have to use that word for word but what I told you is close." I watched Grady's face as Agent Harrington had told him about the ordeal. I could tell he was astonished. Grady then asked me, "James, I can only imagine what was going through your mind during the abduction and then waking up in a burning car. No one ever thinks about death until it is staring them in the face."

I said, "Not only was I staring death in the face, I was getting ready to shake hands with the grim reaper himself. I'll just say for now that the Lord must have other plans for me. I wouldn't been able to get out of that car without some help." Agent Harrington said, "I trust that you will uphold your clients confidentiality until you are called?" Grady said, "I won't speak about this until I get my first call from a news station. If there isn't anything else I need to know I have to go and prepare for a court deposition and prepare a statement for tomorrow."

Agent Harrington said, "Counselor, once you've prepared your statement please e-mail me so that I may read it." Then Agent Harrington wrote down his e-mail address and gave it to my attorney. Grady told me that he would talk to me later about his retainer fee. Agent Harrington spoke up and said, "Retainer fee counselor? Your face could be going global tomorrow night, you should be paying Mr. Farnsworth."

I said, "It's okay, Agent Harrington, he won't overcharge me. He's getting some free publicity from this."

Grady said, "Don't worry about the fee. If what Agent Harrington says occurs, all the ambulance chasers within one hundred miles will be wishing that they were me."

He then told us good-bye as he walked out the door. Agent Harrington said that he had given it some thought about David at the studio. He feels that because of the traitors that did work for me, it would be best that he contact David after tonight's televised interview. I agreed with him because anything is possible. Money has a way of undermining peoples thoughts, even Judas caved for a few pieces silver. Agent Harrington then told me that he had time to go pick up a cell phone, drop by the motel and freshen up and get back here before the other agents arrive from Atlanta. I looked at the clock on the wall and it was almost 2:30. Agent Harrington saw me look at the clock and said, "In thirty minutes the word goes out for Serlinni. I'll be back shortly." He then goes to his car in the garage and I went to the security panel and opened the garage door for him. I watched as he backed out and closed it as soon as he was clear. I told Grandmother that I'm going to take a shower and put on some fresh clothes. She said, "Go right ahead, I'll see you when you get out." I went to my temporary room, got some fresh underwear, a pair of jeans and shirt. I went into the bathroom, got the water going, took off my clothes and got in the shower. as I was lathering up my hair with eyes closed. My new talent worked on the makeup artist. If I didn't have a conscious, I could have drilled her in the van. I wonder what other surprises await me. I tried to piece together what the messenger was telling about the scenario changing. Maybe that there is something in Grandfather's journal that can give me some insight. I won't be able to look at it until I go to bed because I've got a feeling that there will be a lot of activity in the house today and into the night. At least I don't have to worry about being locked up due to the full moon until next month. I finished with my shower, dried off and put on my jeans. I decided to go ahead and shave to make myself more presentable. I finished up in the bathroom, got my dirty clothes together and asked Grandmother did she have anything that needs washing. She told me not to worry about it that she would do it later. I told her that I don't mind doing it because I did it at my house.

I said, "Maybe after things have settled down a bit. I'll talk to Agent Harrington into letting your housekeeper come back in."

Grandmother said, "We are running short on some supplies, somebody will need to go to the grocery store in a day or two."

I went and looked in the clothes hamper to see how much dirty laundry there was to do. There was a good-sized load, so I sorted out the colors from the whites and threw a load in the wash. Grandmother came into the wash room and asked me what was I doing. I said, "I'm earning my keep around here, it can't be just you looking after me around here. Besides this gives me something to do to pass the time. I told her to go watch some television, I got this under control. After I got the clothes going, I went into the kitchen, emptied the clean dishes from the dishwasher and put them away. I have all of this pent up nervous energy that I have to use up. I noticed some changes in my body while I was looking in the mirror a while ago. My belly bulge was gone, the depth of my navel was shallower, even my arms look bigger. Was it because I did pull ups in the cage while I was changed? Did it cause some carry over effect? Is that why the messengers told me to tell my grandmother, that I wouldn't need to be drugged? For the time being, I'm hanging out with my grandmother. I need to take advantage of this time together because looking back on my life. There were times that I should have been with my father or grandfather, instead of being out with my friends getting high. At that time you don't think about losing someone, your so into yourself and your friends, time is passing right on by you. Grandmother is eighty three years old and gets around very well for someone of her age. She is a pillar of strength when, it comes to the power of will and adaptation. I know deep down inside that she unlike me is subject to the laws of mortal man. I wonder if the statement made by the messenger that the scenario is about change is talking about her? As I was pondering in the washroom, the doorbell rings. I went to the security monitor to see who is at the door. It is Agent Harrington, I pressed the intercom button and told him that I'd be right there. I went and opened the door but on the way, I looked in on Grandmother. She's watching television in the den. I opened the door for Agent Harrington, he handed me a plastic bag.

I said, "My new phone, I presume."

Agent Harrington nodded said that he had just received a call on his cell, the agents from Atlanta and Langley will be here shortly. He said, "As I mentioned before, the security in and out of this property is about to increase. The local sheriff department has been brief by my boss and pictures of Vincent Serlinni and some of his known capos have been splashed through the justice system network. They are about to become very popular subjects especially after the televised interview goes off all over the media. In about an hour the interviewed taping will be issued out to the media. They'll have time to make calls to the source from where the interview came from which, will be us, the federal government. Once they get the confirmation of the source, it's game on." Grandmother was standing in the doorway of the den and listening. She said, "My grandson on the television, this has been a very interesting week."

I said, "Your grandson with the makeup will look like he crawled out from under bridge after he had been mud wrestling with vagrants." Agent Harrington giggled and said, "He's right Mrs. Farnsworth but for the authenticity of the interview it had to appear that way. Serlinni will be getting some light shown on him, he'll feel like a piece of chicken under the heat lamp after this. The other crime families will view this and then realize that they too could be scrutinized. They may even turn Serlinni in for the money, just to get things quieted down again. But until then, we'll have to keep our guard up and be prepared." Agent Harrington then said, "Hold on for one minute, I have a call coming through."

He pointed to his earpiece and was talking to the agents that had just pulled into the drive. I heard him tell the agents to come inside and ended the call. He then said, "Mr. Farnsworth, I want you and your grandmother to meet the agents that are coming in, so that you'll recognize their faces and won't be alarmed when they show up on and around the property."

The doorbell rings, and Agent Harrington told us that he'll get the door. He opens the door and four men walked into the foyer. Agent Harrington introduces the four agents to Grandmother and myself. He said that it's not important that we try and remember their names but to remember their faces.

Agent Harrington said, "These field agents' sole responsibility is to keep you two safe. Not only will they be rotating shifts from the guest house but posted at the entrance of Farnsworth Lane. No one comes in or out without my agents or myself knowing about it."

He then sent the agents on their way to their appointed duties.

I said, "I'm fine with that, but there are two things that need to be taken of tomorrow. One is that, we are running low on provisions here and I'll need to go to the grocery store to keep Grandmother and myself going. Next thing is that I need to go by the studio to make sure that my business is running like it is supposed to be because I have a major contract obligation to Atlantic Records to make sure, that their product gets finished so that I get paid as well as my only remaining employee. I have to find out if David has hired a receptionist and hire an assistant to assist David at the studio." Agent Harrington said, "Okay, slow down. I realize that there are a lot of things that you need to do. Tomorrow I'll send an agent with you to the grocery store but you'll need to go earlier during the morning time so that you won't be exposed to a lot of people traffic. My agent will able to keep a handle on it. Then, once you and my agent get back here, you'll stay here. We have to take every precaution that we can. Do you remember the day you were abducted? I had an agent posted outside your studio and one of Serlinni's boys was able to slip under the radar, by using your cousin as a shield. I'm not about to let something like that happen again. You and Agent Franks were lucky to have survived that whole ordeal. Serlinni is going to be really pissed off since you are putting a bounty out on him plus he's going to be desperate. A desperate man is a dangerous man." I said, "I don't doubt one word that you are saying and I am going to comply with your security measures. But at the same time I can't afford to let my business go to hell when there is a lot at stake here." Agent Harrington said, "You know how to delegate don't you? Once you find out that things are going the way that they're supposed to, tell David to get in touch with a temp agency and hire some help. Then you are to come back here and do everything by phone and e-mail. After tonight's airing on national television everyone in America will know who you are."

I told him that I'm not trying to be difficult. It's just that my patience to get this over has worn my nerves thin. He told me to trust him and to stick to the program because he and his people are also putting their lives on the line also.

He then said, "In a matter of hours, your face and pictures of Vincent Serlinni will be cast out over the airwaves and even the internet. Once this is over your business will grow by leaps and bounds because of this."

I said, "I'm not so sure that is such a good thing. Making more money could attract another Serlinni type."

Agent Harrington said, "It may attract a legitimate buyer, if that's what you want." After he said that, he said he must go and make plans for onslaught of network TV crews that will be coming to town, security will have to heightened at this point because news hungry TV crews will try anything for an exclusive. He then said that he would check back with me after the airing of the interview and walked out. Grandmother said, "Everything will work itself out. I know it will because I had dream about you getting married last night." I asked her, "Do you remember seeing her face?" She told me that she only remembers seeing the back of her wedding dress as she stood next to you. When I woke up this morning, I felt relieved that you would find someone to take care of you, I know that I won't be here forever. I have accepted that fact but because of your particular situation; you'll need someone that is strong enough to handle this. I feel that the person that was in the dream, will be strong enough plus some." I said, "Was there a messenger involved in this dream?" She told me that my grandfather had a messenger with him. I said, "I'm not ready for you go to go anywhere yet." She said that it wasn't up for me to decide. She said, "At least I'll get to see you married off before I go." She smiled and gave me a hug and told me, "Like I said, everything will balance itself out, not only will you have a wife that will love you no matter what, someone higher up has plans for you. That gives me great joy to know that my grandson is a part of the grand scheme of things and I had a part in it." I told her that if she is trying to cheer me up, that is the wrong way to go about it. She chuckled and I was fighting the urge of an emotional break down. I said, "I know it's early in the day, but I could use a drink, especially after what you told me."

Grandmother replied, "It's five o'clock somewhere."

She walked into the kitchen and got two glasses and put a few ice cubes in them. I followed her to the den where the liquor cabinet is. She set the glasses on the counter and told me to say when, as she poured the bourbon into the glass. The glass had about 3 shots in it, and I said when. She poured herself a much smaller amount than myself and opened up the cabinet door that housed the mini fridge, and poured ginger ale into her glass and asked me did I want ginger ale? I told her sure, even though there wasn't much room for the ginger ale from all of the alcohol taking up so much space. Grandmother held up her glass in gesture of a toast and said, "To better days ahead." We clanked our glasses together and took a drink. To say that my drink was a little strong would be an understatement. I drank it down anyway, I have time to activate my new phone, go back into my room and read some more of my grandfather's journal before the news comes on. I almost forgot about the clothes in the washing machine. As I was going down the hall way to the wash room, Grandmother told me that she had put the clothes in the drier while I was talking to Agent Harrington. I told her that I would hang them up once they get dry and that I would be in my room reading from Grandfather's journal. She said that they should be ready in about thirty minutes. I told her that I would take care of it while I was on my way to my room. I began thinking to myself, is that what the messenger meant by the scenario is going to change. I felt like I wanted to just go into my dad's old room , start crying and throw a tantrum it is no use, things are already set into motion. I'm going to check and see how much stash I have left. I know that there are those that say that drugs and alcohol are a form of escapism. well, to those that seem that make that claim, let them see how they deal with things like changing into a monster 3 nights every month, has killed people and eaten parts of them and has to be locked up to be kept under control. I bet they'd be doing more than just drinking and smoking weed. If those people I killed weren't bad people, my conscious would probably be eating at me. Since I'm supposed to be some tool against the dark one and evil that walks the streets, I'm handling it the best way I know how, to get comfortably numb. I went and checked on my stash that I had hidden. I took the small plastic bag and unrolled it. I probably have three joints at best estimation left. I'll need to roll them thin until I can replenish my supply. I heard the dryer buzzer go off, so I rehid my stash and went to take the clothes from the dryer and hang them up. I don't mind helping Grandmother, though this one time chore doesn't even measure up to the times that she has helped me. I had almost finished with the last article of clothing and Grandmother walked in. She took her clothes and thanked me for helping. She then walked down the hallway to her room to hang her clothes in the closet. I took my clothes to my room and hung them in the closet. I went to the kitchen, opened the phone container and got on the house phone and went through the motions of activating my new cell phone I stopped and listened for a moment to listen for Grandmother's location in the house. By the sound of her footsteps she had moved to the den area of the house where the television. Now, I'll be able to roll one up to get in the right frame of mind to read and the exploits of my grandfather.

CHAPTER 14

I went into the bathroom and shut the door, took out the papers, sprinkled a small of cannabis into the carefully creased paper and rolled it up. I grabbed the lighter from my shaving kit, turned on the vent fan and looked for the air freshen aerosol can. I looked under the sink and grabbed the aerosol. I lit it up and took a few long tokes. I didn't want to stay in the bathroom too long and raise suspicion, so I took a few more long tokes and held it in, slowly exhaling toward the vent fan. I wet my finger and put it out, sprayed the air freshener and flushed the toilet. I could feel the effects already, mixing with the alcohol. I should be there in a few minutes, comfortably numb. I opened the bathroom door, sprayed a little more air freshener, turned off the vent fan. I walked out into my bedroom and hid my stash. I got the journal from the top shelf of my closet and sat down at the desk. I flipped through a few pages and found where I had left off. My grandfather writes, I told my father that I had an idea of what triggered the change. The night that I was attacked in Europe was during a full moon. The nights that I was in the hospital, I didn't change until two nights ago, and it was a full moon just like last night. I've been back from Europe for almost a year, and nothing like this had happened until two nights ago. My father said, "If I remember correctly my son had a birthday two days ago and he just turned thirty-eight."

My father said, "It will be another one tonight, and I'm not going to chain you to a tree."

I told father that he can't just let me run free like a wild animal. Father told me that he is going to chain me up in the basement, that he can't run the risk of being seen by the farm help chaining his son to a tree.

I asked him, "What did you tell my mother?"

He told me that he told my mother, that her son has been chosen by God as a weapon to be used against the prince of darkness.

I said to my father, "I bet Mother told you had been in the sun too long."

Father told me that she would see tonight for herself. At first he didn't believe me, until he saw what I became.

My father said, "The hard part will be explaining to your pregnant wife."

He then said that he'll have to commission work from out of town to build a structure strong enough to contain the creature in the basement. My father said, last night he put a bullet through the creature's head hoping it would release his son from torment. The bullet had no effect on the creature. My father realized that something way out of human understanding was going on. I had a dream after I finally went to sleep and was told that my son is part of a bigger plan. After tonight, a section of the basement wall will be torn out so that the workmen will be able to move materials in for the construction.

He said, "If in fact that the full moon is the trigger for the change, you'll have to be here at the house to be contained before it happens. Will your job in Atlanta allow you to come home for three nights every month?"

I told my father that I didn't know yet. I may have to find a job in Macon, closer to home. Before I got any further into the journal, Grandmother had come to the doorway and asked me if I wanted a hot dog for dinner or tuna fish. I told her that either one would work for me. Whichever she picks will be fine by me. I looked at my digital clock, and it had 4:55 p.m., almost five o'clock. I put away Grandfather's journal, placing it on the top shelf in my closet. I went into the kitchen to where Grandmother was.

I said, "I wonder if the interview will be in the five o'clock show or the six o'clock news?"

She said, "In four minutes, it's going to be five o'clock. We'll have to watch and see. I'm excited to see what kind of makeup job they did on you. If you have your mother's safe house number, you might want to call her to tell her about it."

I went to my room and got my cell phone. I called Agent Harrington first, as to not to go against protocol. I asked him could I call her or will he relay the message to watch the news concerning the interview taping? He said that he had already called her and told her to watch the news this evening. He told me that, he was glad that I called him first instead of trying to calling the safe house because of protocol. I thanked him for calling her and asked if anything has shown up on radar yet.

He said, "After the airing of the interview, there should be some activity for sure. I'll call you and keep you in the loop." Then the call ended. I took my tumbler and refreshed my drink. Grandmother had already switched the channel on the television to a local network. She was in her favorite chair waiting to see what unfolds. I sat in a chair to the left of her, sipping my drinking, I'm still buzzing pretty good. The intro to the eye witness news at five came on. Doing the usual spilling, introducing the news anchors and the weatherman.

The lead anchor said, "Hello, everyone, and thank you for joining us tonight. The eyewitness team has not long ago been made privy to some information, concerning the disappearance of a local Central Georgia man. According to the information he has been found and we'll have more on the matter in a moment."

The anchor starts bantering with the weatherman saying, "Is there any more rain in the forecast because my garden is turning brown?"

The weatherman replies by saying, "There is some rain coming in from the west, but it will miss us and move into Atlanta and northern Georgia. I'll give you the seven-day weather breakdown in a moment."

Then a car dealership comes on trying to get people to hurry in and get a new car payment. Before he could say anything else,

Grandmother switched to the cable network news to see what they were doing. They were talking about a different group of terrorist unlike al queda moving into Iraq. She then switched it back to the local channel. I see now where I get the channel-surfing syndrome from. The lead anchor was saying, "Our news team was alerted several days ago about the disappearance of James Farnsworth Jr. , owner of Red Sand Studios in Byron by the local sheriff's department of Peach county. The camera shifts to a female anchor and she continues by saying, "The eye witness news production crew received a taped interview sent by the Federal Bureau of Investigation. I going to turn you over to our field reporter Lisa Lee Brown, that's here with us in the studio."

The camera switches onto the field reporter, and she says, "Just a few minutes ago, I called the Taylor County Sheriff's Department to confirm the authentication of the taping and they asked me where did I get the tape? I said to them that according to the e-mail download, it came from the FBI. The sheriff told me that it is authentic because he is on the tape and wouldn't answer any more questions. He told me to watch the tape and to talk to Mr. Farnsworth's lawyer for questions. So here is the taped interview of Mr. Farnsworth right after he was found by the Georgia state patrol. I said, "Here's James." I looked over at my grandmother's face as she was watching this unfold. She said, "You weren't kidding about the makeup job, they made you look like you had been through hell and back." We sat and listened to the interview until it was finished. Grandmother said, "I bet your phone at your house has been ringing off the wall." I called David on his cell phone. I made some small talk with him by telling him that I'm okay and that if any news people call, tell them to call my lawyer Grady Byrd.

David said, "Are you coming in to work tomorrow? I need some help."

I told him to call a temp service to get a receptionist and to hire an assistant for him also. I told him that I would be coming in some time tomorrow, right now I need to get some rest. I asked David, had he sent the completed work to Atlantic Records?. David replied, "I'm happy to report that Atlantic had called me and said that they were pleased. And if by the grace of God you showed back up, they have a check waiting for you, once you call the exec. at Atlantic because he wants to talk to you." I told David that it was good to hear such good news and that he would be getting a substantial raise that is, after I get the check in my hand. David expressed his gratitude by telling me thanks for believing in his abilities and would stay in constant contact with me. I replied by telling him that, I appreciated him for staying the course with all of this stuff going and I would check in with him. I ended the call.

Grandmother said, "So David has some good news?" I told her what David had said about the people at Atlantic, and the exec. at Atlantic wants to talk to me before he releases the check. She said, "I guess he wants to confirm that you are still alive and in control of the company. And if he is watching television tonight, he will be assured of both."

Some cop on the take in Serlinni's town had leaked to one of Serlinni's boys that the heat is going to be on Serlinni because the hit on Farnsworth failed. During this time Serlinni and his underling Saul were having a conversation about what happened near Columbus and the abandoned cars, that one was supposed to have my body in the trunk instead, had two unknown bodies burnt and another car with three burnt bodies. Serlinni has just seen himself and a very alive and well James Farnsworth on the news. He was raising hell at Saul because the guys he hired had fucked up.

Serlinni said, "How difficult is this job to do? The hired guy fucked up in Arizona, now this is another disappoint meant to me. Somebody better make this right, now I'm going to have to lay low since my face is on television now. "Saul replied by saying, "You're the boss and I hired the guys to do the job, they may have pissed off some gang members in a bar or something and the gang members took them out. For all I know the guys in the trunk of that car could have been gang members."

Serlinni said, "How is it that Farnsworth is still alive, that's what is driving me crazy. The guy should be dead already."

Saul said, "Give me one more chance to take this guy out, a cat only so many lives left."

Serlinni said, "I don't care how you do it, just do it. I don't care about the production company anymore, it's about revenge now. Also I want you to take Sid Pachoni with you, I don't want to hear about any more fuck ups. Saul and Sid left the room and was on their way. Little did Saul know, that his fate had already been decided before he had the conversation with his boss. Serlinni had given instructions to his soon to be capo Sid, to take care of Saul. Because in Serlinni's mind, Saul had made to many mistakes and it was time for Saul to go bye-bye. Saul and Sid had gotten into car and were heading toward the airport. Sid asked Saul where he was going. Saul told Sid that he had a locker at the airport with some spare clothes in it. Sid told Saul to stop at the nearest liquor store because he hates to fly and needs to get liquored up to fly. Sid didn't want Saul to make it to the airport. Saul pulled into a A-1 liquor store and Sid asked Saul did he want anything. Saul told him that he would wait and get one at the airport bar. Sid goes into the liquor store and comes out with a bag in his hand. Sid had already drawn his gun and was concealing it behind the bag. Sid opens the door and fires two rounds into Saul. Saul nor Sid knew that they too were being tailed by the feds. A car with two feds came up on Sid before he could get away. They told Sid to drop his weapon, instead he didn't want to go to prison, so he drew down on the federal agents. Sid did get one round into an agent, but the agents were wearing vest; bulletproof vest and Sid did not. Sid expired that day and it would be a few hours before the news would get back to Serlinni; compliments of the evening news. Serlinni's crew of henchmen has gotten smaller. The lights are on and the roaches are scrambling for cover. I didn't get too far in the journal and Grandmother called me back to the den. I put the journal down on my bed and walked to the den, to where Grandmother was glued to the TV remote.

She said, "According to the news channel in Columbus, some cars with burned bodies were found at an old industrial site."

She pointed at me, and I nodded in agreement.

She said, "Probably gang related activity, huh?"

I said, "Most probable."

She said that national news will be on and we'll see what has happened and then check out what is being said on the news cable network.

She said, "Someone from cable news in Atlanta will be clamoring for an exclusive. They'll be circling like buzzards. I wish your dad, Houston, could be here. He would be so proud of his son."

I said, "I miss him, but I wouldn't want to put him through this, in the condition he was in before he left us."

Grandmother said, "Houston is probably bragging to the angels about his son."

I sat down beside her and said, "I know you miss him, but you've got me and stop thinking about going to join him. You got to stay here with me and see how this plays out. When this blows over you'll be able to tell the housekeeper and your friends about this adventure. You'll be talking so much on the phone that I won't be able to call over here because the line will be busy." I told her that I was going to round up some snack food to bring in the den to snack on.

Grandmother said, "James there is some dip in the fridge and chips in the pantry."

I wound up sitting on the couch with Grandmother until the late night news went off. I told her to go to bed and I would clean up the remnants of our snack party. Grandmother told me good night as she slowly made her way to her room. I wished I had spent more time with her before now. I know that I can't keep her forever but tonight was golden. We were sharing the limelight together. I put away the dirty dishes in the dishwasher and wiped off the counters, so she wouldn't have to do it tomorrow. I turned off the lights in the kitchen and made my way to my temporary bedroom for now. I must admit this is intriguing stuff that is going on. I also realize that I am trapped into a different existence other than being a werewolf every month, I'm in protective custody with my family. My private life is about to explode onto media market out there. I took off my pants and laid them on a chair, put on a T-shirt, pulled the cover back on the bed, and lay down. I reached for the journal and began flipping through pages. Searching for when my grandfather told his first wife about his special condition. I found some entry dates on the pages and began reading. May, 1915, Marie asked me how my mother was doing. I told her that she had gotten to hot and may have had a light stroke. Marie told me that she and Katherine had found a house in Atlanta but it needs more work than the house her dad is loaning to us. I asked her if she would be disappointed if we didn't live in Atlanta? She asked me, "What is going on now?" I said, "Something very serious is going on and it is very dangerous. It is so dangerous and so unbelievable, that you won't believe a word, I say until you experience for yourself."

Marie said, "Gerald, what has happened while I was gone?"

I began telling her what had happened in while I was on an expedition in Germany. Then I told her what had occurred here while she was in Atlanta. She said, "You don't have to make up some fantasy story if you've changed your mind about us?" I told her that she wouldn't believe me and that she would have her proof in two weeks when the first full moon shows up. I told her that I would have to take her to my father's farm in Byron to be chained up to keep from killing the people I love. She stormed off into the bedroom and slammed the door. I let her be, and see how receptive she is tomorrow. I ate a snack and laid down on the couch and pondered about my family's future. I'll need a job in Macon, so that I'll be closer to my father's home. I remember getting very little rest that night because I dreamed that the beast had gotten loose and murdered a bunch of people I awoke in a cold sweat and didn't want to go back to sleep, in fear of replaying an awful massacre. The next day came early and I had gotten up and put on a pot of coffee and was smoking a cigarette. Marie walked into the room and said, "You didn't turn into no murdering beast last night and kill anyone?"

I told her that's because the moon wasn't full and that is what controls it. I told her that I don't know why or how but it does. I told her that no matter what happens, it doesn't change how I feel about her and the baby. I want us to be a family.

She said, "It doesn't bother me that we don't have to live in Atlanta, but can you find work in Macon?"

I told her that my dad has some influence with some colleagues he went to West Point with.

She said, "What do I tell my parents? They will want to know something?"

I said, "Father is already working on a solution and we don't need to tell them about the real reason."

Marie said, "What about this baby I'm carrying? Will the baby become a monster on a full moon and kill and eat its parents?"

I told her that I don't know if it would be affected or not. She then told me that she read in the paper about the black farmer and his livestock were slaughtered but the paper said, it was speculating a panther did it. Then something occurred to me that I had forgotten.

I said, "Do you remember seeing the terrible scars that you used to tend to while I was in the army hospital?"

Marie said, "Yes, of course I do."

I removed my shirt and let her look at my chest and my back. I saw the look in her face, the look of shock.

"Gerald, how is this possible?" she asked.

I told her the scar disappeared after I changed the first time. I could see that the look of shock had changed to a look of fear. She walked up and felt with her hands in disbelief. She said, "There isn't any evidence of deep tissue scarring either and I've seen my share of horrific wounds. I don't have a rational explanation to what is going on. This stuff is bordering on magic or some sort of sorcery. The modern medicine that I know of, has no way of reproducing this kind of rapid regeneration of new skin." She sat down at the table with me and said, "Okay, I want you to tell me everything that you can remember about what the thing looked like that attacked you in Germany. And tell me what you saw of yourself when you changed?" I told her all that I could remember about the incident in Germany and what I saw of myself in the mirror. She sat there and was glued to my every word. I read the journal until my eyes got too heavy to stay open. I folded the corner of the page down, turned off the lamp and went to sleep. I went into a dream state of consciousness. I found myself to what appeared to be the family farm, but it doesn't look the same. I walk around the house and I could see there are workmen on the property. I see old vintage trucks with bags of cement, concrete blocks, and bundles of steel bars loaded in the cargo area. Men are loading wheelbarrows of material, and I can hear the sound of carpenters banging away on the inside of the house.

I hear a familiar voice say, "Hello, grandson!"

I turned, and it was my grandfather.

He said, "Your great-grandfather, went to great lengths to make this happen for us. You'll see him walking around surveying the work but he won't see us."

I said, "I'm dreaming this aren't I?"

My grandfather said, "You are seeing images of what has already happened and I'm allowed to witness this with you through the help of the messengers. I know you've seen photos of your great-grandfather and how you bear a resemblance to him. You and he share a sense of regard for your family and whatever it takes to keep that family safe and secure, no matter the cost."

I said, "How did he fund this? The farm can't be taking in this kind of money to fund such an undertaking."

Grandfather said, "My dad, Sam Houston Farnsworth, had sold a considerable amount of land that was once a sugar plantation near Savannah, land that he had inherited from his family before him that had made a lot of money from the sugar plantation during and after the civil war. Luckily the plantation wasn't in the path of Sherman's army. Your great-grandfather had the foresight to invest in a new chemical called petroleum. He had gotten in on the ground floor so to speak."

I followed my grandfather and listened to him, watching as things were transpiring in front of us.

Grandfather said, "Look, here she comes."

I looked, and I asked him, "Is that your first wife, Marie?"

Grandfather nodded his head, trying to maintain his composure.

I said, "She is a natural beauty like your journal said."

"That she is," exclaimed my grandfather.

I stopped, and I realized what was coming next.

I said, "She's here to see you change for the first time, isn't she?"

Grandfather said, "Yes, and witnessing it caused her to make a fatal mistake." She had already been exposed to cases of women that tried forced miscarriages of unwanted babies, by use of barbaric practices like coat hangers and poisonous plants. She didn't want her child to be a monster that I claimed to be. She will see tonight and make her decision. A decision, that she didn't discuss with me at all. I had no idea what she was going to do. I said, "Why didn't the messengers do something?" Grandfather said, "The messengers said that her death wasn't suicidal and was accidental, that it was predestined to happen this way." The scenery changed and I see that my grandfather was chained and bound in the basement. He's writhing in pain as his body goes through the metamorphosis from man to beast. I watch as both great grandparents with Marie watch in horror as a loved on turns into a ravenous beast. The beast growls and tells them to release him and when they don't comply, the beast gets angry. Twisting and trashing about to remove his chains but to no avail, the efforts are useless. Great-grandfather tells the women to go upstairs and he would be up there in a moment. Great-grandfather pushes a bowl of water over to the beast with a broom and says, "I'll be back to unchain my son in the morning when the beast is gone."

The beast growls, "Father!" I awaken by the sounds coming from the kitchen. I look at the digital clock by my bed and it had 6:00 a.m. on it. I could smell the aroma of fresh coffee brewing and the sound of Grandmother's slippers shuffling against the tile floor. I got up and relieved myself, washed my face and slipped on a pair of shorts.

I made my way into the kitchen, and Grandmother said, "I thought I was being quiet enough not to wake you."

I said, "The noise didn't wake me, it was the smell of fresh coffee that did it. Besides, why are you up so early for anyway?"

She said that it's her normal routine that she's been doing for years plus she said that she wanted to see the morning news. She hands me a cup and I walk over to the coffee machine and poured.

Grandmother said, "I wonder what happened behind the scenes while we were sleeping? I told her that a lot of people were on the move, good guys and bad guys alike.

I said, "It won't be long before the phones start ringing and we'll let the answering machine do the work for us."

Grandmother said, "Aren't you just a bit excited about the possibility of being interviewed by a television personality?" I told her that it would be fun to do it just once, but after the hype is gone, I'll still just be another face in the crowd.

Grandmother said, "No, you'll be remembered for standing up against organized crime. You are making a stand pointing your finger in their face. Not many people would have the courage to go through this. They would rather let the FBI handle the whole thing and remain hidden until the trial happens."

I said, "If I didn't have an extra ace up my sleeve, I wouldn't have put myself out there like this."

Grandmother looked at me with puzzlement and realized what I was talking about. She nodded in agreement and whispered, "Invincible."

I walked to the fridge and could tell that provisions were low.

Grandmother said, "There's some waffles in the freezer. I know the fridge looks bare as well as the cabinets and pantry. We are gonna need provisions today."

I said, "I'll ask Agent Harrington about our situation, I'm sure he'll come up with a solution. Today would be a good time of the week to go it's Wednesday morning, not too much should be going on in the big city of Byron this early in the day."

Grandmother poured more coffee in her cup and walked to the den, where the television is. I told her that I'll be right there once I get something to eat. As I was taking the package of waffles from the freezer, the phone began to ring. I walked over and looked at the caller ID, and it had unknown number. The ringing stopped and the answering machine began its work. I opened the package and removed two waffles, placed them in the toaster. I could see the message light blinking on the answering machine. While I was waiting on the toaster to finish, curiosity had gotten the best of me. I mashed the button and listened to the message.

The recording said, "This is reporter Anthony Simms from Eleven Alive from Atlanta. I would like to interview Mr. Farnsworth, and if you wish to contact me, here's my number, 404-535-6565. I'm looking forward to meeting with you."

Grandmother had walked out into the hallway, so that she could hear the message.

She looked at me and said, "There goes the first one of the day."

The waffles pop up from the toaster. I grabbed a plate from the cabinet and plated them. I put syrup on them and took it to Grandmother. She told me to go ahead and eat them because she's not hungry yet. I finished them off so fast, I didn't take the time to taste them. I slugged down some coffee and refilled the cup. I walked back into the den to see if there is any new developing news. Grandmother had switched from the local channel to the news network channel. There weren't any new developments, only repeats of what was televised last night. I told Grandmother that I bet Grady didn't sleep a wink last night, just thinking about today's events in front of the cameras. Grandmother chuckled and said, "He probably spent some considerable mirror time last night."

I said, "I might as well go take a shower and shave to get ready in case I get to go to the store. Agent Harrington will be showing up this morning. I went and took a shower, shaved and put on a pair of faded jeans and a button up shirt. My thoughts drifted back to the dream about seeing Grandfather's first wife, Marie. I saw the pain in Grandfather's face when he was with me in the dream. It was ripping his heart out to see those images replay in front of him. Not only the loss of Marie but losing his parents to natural causes. I also felt loss because it reminded me of what is to come, the people that I will outlive. Grandfather experienced loss on many levels, loss of family, friends, and an entire generation of people just gone. Yet he remains. Luckily, record keeping wasn't as technologically advanced as it is today or someone may have discovered Grandfather's true age. I started thinking at some point in my life, I'll have to move and change my identity because of the ramifications of staying in one location, living past one hundred and thirty years would draw unwanted attention. I was putting on my socks when I heard the doorbell ring. I heard Grandmother talking on the intercom, saying, "I'll be right there, Agent Harrington."

I put on my sneakers and walked into the front room to greet Agent Harrington.

"Good morning, Agent Harrington," I said. "How about a cup of coffee?"

Agent Harrington replied by telling me the usual that, he had already had his fill of coffee this morning. He said, "You mentioned that your provisions are low and need restocking. I'm going to send two agents with you. One to drive you to the store and another will be following closely behind. I want you to be there when the store opens so there will be less people to come in contact with. It's almost 7:30 and most businesses open at eight. I'm going to round up my agents to get ready. I suggest you and your grandmother put together a grocery list so you can go in and get out with taking too much time." Grandmother walked over to the kitchen counter and produced a piece of paper. She said, "I tried to plan out two weeks' worth of meals to cover all the bases so there wouldn't be a need to be running back to the store." Now that I had my list and it was going to be a buggy full. Agent Harrington said, "Okay Mr. Farnsworth, I have an agent waiting in the garage for you. I want you to go out the garage door exit and come back into the garage door access when you get back. Make sure you have your cell phone with you before you leave. I went to my room to get my wallet and my cell phone. Grandmother tried to give me her credit card and I told her that I've got it. I got my checkbook when I went to my house. Agent Harrington said that he would fill me in to what has already happened last night, once I get back from the store. I opened the door to the garage and an agent was waiting in the car. I got in on the passenger side and buckled up. The automatic door opened up and the agent backed out and into the driveway.

On the way out of the drive down Farnsworth Lane, the agent said, "Good morning, Mr. Farnsworth, I'm Agent Brown taking over for Agent Franks until he gets well. I said, Agent Brown, I will do my best not to get you shot. I am deeply bothered that Agent Franks took a bullet because of me and I don't want anyone else getting hurt except for the bad guys."

Agent Brown said, "Just go in the grocery store, don't make small talk with anyone, get the groceries and we can be out of there before people start showing up." We arrived in town and the car I was riding in had dark tinted windows so no one could see me. As we passed the Waffle house I could see police cars and TV crew vans with different network logos on them. The TV hounds are already out and in force. Agent Brown pulled into the Giant Food parking lot and parked up front of the entrance. I put on a pair of sunglasses and a ball cap that I had brought from the house. I walked into the main entrance, grabbed a shopping cart and noticed there wasn't anyone at the register up front. I thought nothing of it and made my way to the fresh produce aisle.

CHAPTER 15

I grabbed a head of lettuce, carrots, squash, onions, and a bag of russet potatoes. I crossed off the fresh vegies from the list and pulled into the next aisle, which was the canned-goods section. I grabbed a couple cans of lima beans, squash, pinto beans for chili, chili powder, and a box of brown rice. I grabbed up spaghetti sauce, noodles, macaroni and cheese sauce. I turned into the next aisle, and I heard footsteps behind me. I turned around and it was a black guy with a gun pointed at me. I had just taken my cell phone out of my pocket.

The robber said, "That's right, motherfucker, you better put that phone down, or you will be checking out the hard way. Come on and join the party in the back."

As the robber was following behind me, I turned my head to glance behind me.

The robber said, "Turn around and keep walking."

Right then and there, I executed a perfect roundhouse kick. I connected with the robber's hand that held the gun, knocking over boxes of cereal. The robber then took out a knife and came at me with it. He thrust at me, and I grabbed his knife hand and at the same time kicked him in the gut. He dropped the knife, and I kicked it out of reach. As the robber was collapsed on the floor, I got the gun from the floor and was pointing it at him.

I said, "Where is your partner at?"

The robber said, "Fuck you, I ain't got to tell you shit."

I kicked him square in the nuts and said, "Now that I have your attention, where is your partner and the people that work here?"

He said, "They are in the stockroom, tied up."

I grabbed the robber's left hand and twisted it behind his back. He was going to be my shield as we walk into the stockroom.

As we go through the door, the robber's partner said "Stop right there and put your gun down, or I'm going to shoot the manager."

I changed my gun position from the robber in front of me to the robber pointing a gun at the store manager. I pushed the accomplice down, so the other robber would point the gun at me. Before the robber holding the gun could react, I squeezed the trigger, and the bullet found its target in the head of the gun-wielding robber.

I said to the dead robber's accomplice, "If you want to join your partner, do something stupid."

The manager recognized me and said, "Thank you, Mr. Farnsworth."

I asked if everyone was okay and took my cell phone out with my free hand and gave it to the manager. I told him to dial the number and you tell the guy that answers who you are. The store manager was so nervous and shaking that he untied a cashier and gave her the phone to dial the number. The nervous cashier asked me the number again, she dialed the number and said, Hello, this is Kim Simmons and I was instructed to call you by Mr. Farnsworth, to tell you to send an agent into the grocery store because Mr. Farnsworth has shot a robber and has another one at gun point." Then I heard the cashier say, "Okay, I'll tell him and thank you." She closed the phone and said, "The man on the phone said that he is going to send the agent in and said for you to try and not to shoot the second robber." I said, "I need for someone to go up front and show the agent where to go. The manager was busy untying the remaining employees, as I held the gun on the live robber. The cashier that made the call said that she would go up front. There were two other cashiers in the store room, an older lady in her sixties and a young girl probably fresh out of high school, the meat cutter and the manager.

I said, "I didn't have a choice because they didn't need any witnesses to a robbery, and if I had given up the gun, I would be just one more body left in the store room."

The manager said, "Mr. Farnsworth, don't worry, you made the right choice and I'm glad that your aim was true. Besides whatever occurred out in the store is on camera, every one of my employees will stand behind you." It wasn't long before the agent came in and put the cuffs on the robber.

The agent said, "You can put your gun down now Mr. Farnsworth."

I replied, "It's not my gun "and I explained to him what had happened. The agent got on the phone and called Agent Harrington and was instructed to call the local police to come, pick up the robber and take statements plus remove the dead gunman after the crime scene is processed.

I said, "Well, it looks like I may be here a while." I took out my cell phone and called Agent Harrington and asked him if he would be arriving on scene? He told me that he was on his way and couldn't believe what a simple task by going to the grocery store had turned into. I told him that Agent Brown and I will be here. It wasn't too long before the local police had arrived on scene. The sheriff and his deputies filed in and took custody of the robber. Agent Brown asked one of the deputies to cuff the robber and return his cuffs back to him. The deputy obliged by changing out the cuffs and grabbed the robbers arm, pulling him to the squad car parked outside. A couple of women were still crying and shook up from what had happened. I sat down on a box of canned peaches and waited to see what was to happen next. Agent Harrington walked in and flashed his ID badge to the sheriff. The sheriff was talking to the store manager about what had happened. Agent Harrington was listening and looked over at Agent Brown. Agent Brown looked over at me like, it wasn't me it was James Farnsworth. The sheriff asked the store manager did he have a surveillance camera capturing what happened. The manager was still shaking and a nervous wreck. He asked the sheriff could the employees go back to work? The sheriff said that he wanted everyone out of the stockroom where the dead body was except for me and the FBI agents.

The sheriff said, "I want the lead agent to go with me to view the surveillance tape and we'll return to take a statement from Mr. Farnsworth.

As the sheriff and Agent Harrington walked up front with the manager, Agent Brown said, "Agent Harrington will smooth this over by letting the locals take this, rather than let it be known that the FBI was on scene at all. It will make the local law enforcement look good and it looks like you'll be in the limelight for a different reason."

I told Agent Brown that I didn't exactly plan for this to happen.

Agent Brown said, "If I was a religious man, I would say that the hand of God placed you here this morning to save innocent lives. But since I'm not a religious man, and being connected to what has happened to you before this morning, I may need to consider the possibility of reading the book about the big picture." I told him that I don't know if it is luck or divine intervention? But either way, we are both alive and let's say by the grace of providence. We have been given the good sense not to try and over analyze something that we don't have control over, like the weather. Agent Brown said, "Not only are you a marksman but a sage. I am growing wiser in your presence."

I told him, "Stop this crazy talk. I'm going to have to go to court for killing that man that's leaking blood on the floor over there."

Agent Brown said, "You'll go court but you won't be charged. You made a judgement call that saved people's lives including your own. The whole time I've been an agent, I've never been in the situation that you were in today. It makes me think about, what would've I'd done in that instant?" I told him to stop analyzing the situation and I told him because of his training; there wouldn't be a second of hesitation. Agent Harrington came into the stockroom with the sheriff and the coroner. A deputy was also there taking pictures of the crime scene.

The sheriff said, "Mr. Farnsworth, you made a huge bet today and lady luck smiled on you. The guy laying over there lost a bet. I have one question. When you pulled the trigger, were you hoping that your aim was true or did you know that your aim was true? I said, "Sheriff, it happened so fast all I can tell you is, I aimed and fired without thinking about. I had no time to think about it and I wasn't about to drop the gun like the robber wanted." The sheriff shook my hand and told me not to worry about it. My job now is to protect the town hero. Every gun dealer and pawn shop should be sending you a commission check for every gun sold. Because when this goes public, people are going to be buying hand guns if they don't already own one. You are free to go Mr. Farnsworth, I'll get my people to type up a statement and bring it to your grandmother's for you to sign. You can have your attorney read it first if you like before you sign it and call me and I'll have a deputy pick it up." I followed Agent Harrington and Agent Brown back out into the store. The store manager stopped me and said, Mr. Farnsworth, hand me your grocery list and I'll get the things you need and bring them to you." I told him that I want to pay for it. He said, "You did pay for it, you bought me and my employees some more time. Now get out of here before you get me teary eyed. I'll bring the groceries myself if it is okay with Agent Harrington.

Agent Harrington nodded in approval and said, "Agent Brown, take Mr. Farnsworth straight to his grandmother's house, and I'll be there shortly, Mr. Farnsworth."

I followed Agent Brown to the parking lot that now contained many police cars, state patrol and couple of news vans. Agent Brown hurried me to the car before someone recognized me and we left the scene behind us. On the way back, neither Agent Brown or myself said anything. I guess we were both digesting this morning's event in our heads. We made it through town and Agent Brown turned onto Farnsworth Lane. I called Grandmother and told her to open the garage door for us. Agent Brown pulled into the garage and Grandmother closed it with the remote switch. I got out of the car and Agent Brown followed me into the house.

Agent Brown said, "If David calls you today? You should only talk business and assure him everything is okay and get him to e-mail you, if some documentation needs to be reviewed by you. Keep your conversation strictly business and short, okay? I'm going to check with the agent in the guest house, then I'll be posted at the entrance in my car. Get some rest, you deserve it after this morning's event. See you later, Mrs. Farnsworth."

He walked to the kitchen, unlocked the back door, opened it, locked it back, and closed it. Grandmother was standing by the table with the look of puzzlement on her face. I said, "Is it too early in the day for a drink?" Grandmother said, "It's five o'clock somewhere, now tell me what happened? Where is the groceries? I told her that I will fix me drink and tell her all about what happened. I went to the liquor cabinet, grabbed a whiskey glass and poured about three shots into and got an ice cube from the ice dispenser. I sat down at the table across from Grandmother, took a big gulp from the glass. Grandmother said, "It must have been some kind of morning for that big gulp of whiskey? I told her play-by-play what had happened at the grocery store. After I finished with all the details she said, "You are an instrument of God. You are like the surgeon's scalpel that cuts away the cancer. I'm glad your mother isn't here to hear this, she's not ready for any of this. But you need someone to talk to beside me concerning today's event. Why don't you give Jessica a call. I saw how she looked at you when we left, she cares for you. I'm sure that she would love to hear about today's story plus the abduction." I said, "I don't know if I can do that, it might get both of us into trouble. She already knows about the abduction from the televised interview. I'll call her on the landline and tell her about the grocery store. It would be good to hear her voice again. I looked at my watch to see what time it was, and it had 10:45 a.m. I grabbed my cell phone and realized her number isn't in this new phone. I asked grandmother did she have Jessica's number? Grandmother retrieved her purse and took out a business card. I thanked her and walked over to the phone in the kitchen and began dialing out. I could hear the phone ringing, it rang twice and I hear, "Hello, to whom am I speaking to?" I replied by saying, "Hello Jessica, I hope I didn't call you too early in the morning?" Jessica said, "I'm getting ready to go to work, let me call you once, I get to work. I assume you are calling from a landline?" I told her that I am and she told me that she would call my landline number later. The connection was terminated an I only heard a dial tone. Grandmother said,

307

"That was a short conversation." I told Grandmother that Jessica was getting ready to go to work and that she would call on a secure land-line, once she gets the chance. Grandmother commented by saying that my televised interview probably prompted some happenings in Arizona as well. Grandmother said, "She'll call because you reached out to her and she's probably been thinking about calling you any-way. My female intuition is never wrong" Grandmother asked me did I get to see the video footage in the grocery store? I told her that Agent Harrington, the sheriff and the store manager were the ones that viewed it so far. Grandmother said if the footage gets out, you will be a home grown hero for sure. I told her that Agent Harrington will be on his way to fill us in. No sooner than I had gotten the words out of my mouth, the doorbell rang. I walked over to the monitor to see who is on the front porch. It is Agent Harrington, I pressed the intercom button and told the agent that I was on my way to let him in. I walked to the front door and invited Agent Harrington in. I led him into the kitchen and we sat down at the table with Grandmother. Grandmother asked Agent Harrington would he like something to drink?

Agent Harrington said, "I'll probably need a drink after I explain to my boss what happened at the grocery store this morning."

I said, "I didn't mean to get you in trouble."

Agent Harrington said, "I should've sent Agent Brown inside the store with you."

I told Agent Harrington, "There is no sense in trying to rehash something that was unforeseen to begin with. Young Agent Brown could have been killed and I wouldn't want another person taking a bullet because of me." Agent Harrington said, "I saw the footage of how you handled the accomplice. When did you take martial arts?" I told him that I took it when I was a kid and did a refresher course while in college. I was lying of course but he didn't need to know how I learned it. Agent Harrington said, "You took a very dangerous risk today and it is apparent to me that I'm going to have to put you on a very short leash. Under no circumstances are you to leave this house unless I'm escorting you myself. Never in my years has someone under protective custody under my watch, has disabled a robber, took his gun and shot his accomplice in the head while, the accomplice was taking aim at you. The odds of that occurring while FBI agents are sitting in the parking lot, across the road from the local police station is astronomical. I'm astounded by the fact that the reflex action to squeeze the trigger by the robber didn't occur when you shot him in the head."

Grandmother said, "Agent Harrington let me get you a shot of something to calm your nerves. You are among friends here."

Agent Harrington said, "I appreciate the hospitality, but I cannot risk the other agents that are here smelling alcohol on me plus I'm on the clock. I can assure you, once I get to my hotel room, there will be alcohol consumption going on later."

Grandmother said, "By the grace of God, the bullet hit its intended target and innocent people didn't die today, Agent Harrington." Agent Harrington said, "I will have to agree with you on that Mrs. Farnsworth. Now, from my sources they have reported that two of Serlinni's men have been taken out of the equation by some field agents that were tailing them. Serlinni has no doubt gone underground and won't be using major airlines, trains or buses to try and leave the country. "I said, "Have your people been able to get any information out of my ex receptionist?" Agent Harrington told us that they had gotten Serlinni's cell phone number from her phone but he didn't answer the call. He probably figured that we have her. She is playing dumb, but she is still being held for being an accomplice in conspiring to commit murder and the murder of Nicole Adams. She'll be going to a women's prison whether she cooperates or not." Mr. Farnsworth, your lawyer Mr. Byrd will be giving a brief prepared statement to the press today at 3 o'clock to the news crews attending." I said, "What is the possibility of the news crew finding out about what happened this morning?" Agent Harrington said, "I think that a news crew has already interviewed an employee of the store. I figured that it would be impossible to suppress the incident because of the number of people that witnessed it. I will have to talk to Mr. Byrd on that issue before he goes live today." I said, "What about the footage, what's keeping it form going viral on the internet?" Agent Harrington said, "I hope that the sheriff confiscated it for evidence. As far as going viral on media trail, who knows? A copy could get made and the rest, you know the answer to." I said, "Has anything popped up on the radar about the possibility of my sole employee, David being involved with Serlinni?" Agent Harrington told me that there is no evidence gathered from bugging the studio or and cell phone traffic from him to suggest his involvement with Serlinni, but that doesn't mean we can let our guard down. We still have to treat this as if, he is a possible link replied Agent Harrington. He then said, "Don't volunteer any information about Serlinni at all, let him bring it up. Talk to David only about the day to day concerns of the business and nothing more. Now I'll be on my way, I'll be busy filing a report to my boss about today's incident. If you need to contact me, you have my cell phone number. Don't be talking to reporters on the phone, let your attorney handle everything."

As Agent Harrington was getting up from the table, he had received a message in his earpiece from Agent Brown. Agent Brown said the grocery store manager is here at the end of the drive. Agent Harrington told him to check the vehicle to make sure that no one else is hiding in the car before you send him through.

Agent Brown complied by saying, "Copy that."

Agent Harrington said, "Your groceries are on the way in, Mr. Farnsworth. You are to stay inside. I'll get the agent from the guest house to unload the groceries."

Agent Harrington pressed a button on his belt and told the agent in the guest house to meet him out front of the house. Agent Harrington told us that we would be calling to check on us later and he walked out the front door. Shortly after he left, the doorbell rang. I check the surveillance monitor and the grocery store manager was at the door with the agent from the guest house. I told them that I would be there via the intercom. I opened the door for the men to enter with bags of groceries and Grandmother told them to follow her to the kitchen. I told the grocery store manager that I would like to be able to unload the groceries from your car but I've been given strict orders, not to leave the house period. The store manager said, "By the way Mr. Farnsworth, Since I didn't get to introduce myself at the store during all the chaos. My name is Toby Jones and don't try and offer to pay for this like I told you at the store. I owe you a lot more than the price of these bags of groceries. You made it possible for my children not to grow up without a father. Now let me get these groceries unloaded, so I can get back to the store. You wouldn't believe the amount of business that has happened since this morning" He walked back out of the door with the agent and continued bringing bags of groceries in the house until the last bag was brought. The store manager held out his hand and I shook it. The manager said, "Thank you again Mr. Farnsworth and I thank God for sending you to save us." I told the manager that we appreciate his gratitude and wished he would accept payment. The manager said, "By this afternoon, once more people hear what happened at the store, the merchandise sales will more than cover, what I brought to you and your grandmother." He waved good-bye to us and walked out of the front door with the agent.

I helped Grandmother put away the groceries and Grandmother said, "See there, Toby acknowledges the fact that God sent you there for a purpose."

I said, "Yeah, the purpose to get us something to eat because we were running out of food."

Grandmother said, "There is more stuff here than what was on the grocery list. The store manager realizes that this merchandise is a small token of payment to what you did today. The man is glad to be alive for his family and knows how close to death he came. You'll be remembered more about this than being remembered about the Serlinni involvement. The reason being is that, the store manager wasn't the only one there you saved. Those other people will be telling their family and friends about today's incident for a while to come. You put yourself in harm's way for those people and to them, you are now more than just the owner of Red Sand Studio."

The Carbono Family

A captain in the Carbono family has been given the okay to find and knock off Vincent Serlinni. An emergency sit down with the main crime family bosses happened last night after the first airing of the televised interview offering a bounty on Serlinni's head. The problem is, that no one knows where Serlinni is that's outside of his inner circle. The hired hit men that disappeared that night in Columbus, were soldiers from the Carbono crime family. The Carbono family has a stake in this and they aren't about to forget about losing their men because of a failed hit, that they blame Serlinni for. Now that there will be more light shown on the dealings of the mob because of the televised footage, the urgency to find Serlinni and take care of him has taken a precedent. The Carbono and other crime families have heard about Serlinni's exploits through the underworld network before this blew up in their face. This wasn't the first time that Serlinni had brought bad press to the forefront. The crime scene at the vacant factory outside Columbus where those men's burned bodies were discovered is the second time that one of Serlinni's exploits went bad. The Carbono family had given Serlinni a task to complete for them. The task was to get rid of a Columbian drug dealer that had been moving product too close to their base of operations, so to speak. Serlinni sent his men to get rid of the problem but the Carbono family didn't know that the DEA had been watching this particular Columbian for some time. Serlinni sent his underlings to arrange for a meeting with this Columbian to fake a buy. The Columbian was too smart to go himself, so he sent one of his underlings. The DEA was watching. They had set up camp in a building across and down the street from the Columbian's hang out. A location was chosen, an out-of-the-way secluded area outside the metro area of Memphis. The Columbian cartel had been smuggling cocaine in barges that travel up and down the Mississippi. The location was a marshy area near the big muddy. The two vehicles arrive there for the meet and only one vehicle leaves. The Columbian underling was dead, lying on the ground by his car. Serlinni's guys were picked up by the DEA that had tailed them. Only one of Serlinni's boys survived the gun battle between them and the FEDS. The Columbian target managed to skirt the DEA and Serlinni failed to get rid of the Columbian cartel connection in Memphis. The Carbono family wasn't too happy about the first botched mission, and now too much attention is being put on the mob. Serlinni is a marked man in more ways than one.

I said, "It's good to have some food back in the house again. Let me fix you something, Grandmother. What do you want to eat?"

She told me a ham sandwich with a little mayo and some potato chips would be just fine. I fixed both of us some sandwiches and we had can Cokes to drink. I told her that I would boil up some tea after we eat, since we have tea and sugar in the house now. It's funny how you miss the little pleasures in life when you don't have access to it. We sat at the table, Grandmother said grace, and we made small talk as we ate the sandwiches. The house phone rang, I went to glance at the incoming i.d.. It was the Az. Bureau of investigation. on the ID. I picked up the phone and answered it.

I said, "Hello, to whom am I speaking to?"

A familiar voice said, "It's agent Jessica Carnes, I was running a bit late when you called. By the way, you looked great on TV last night." She chuckled.

I said, "The makeup artist did a real job on me. So how are you doing?"

She said, "On our end, we've been trying to find out who the shooter was at your hotel. We have some leads and hopefully they will pan out. How have you been holding up?"

I said, "Speaking of a holdup, an agent took me to the grocery store this morning, and I got caught up in a robbery and killed one robber and bruised up the other."

She said, "James, you didn't get hurt, did you? And what do you mean 'killed one robber and bruised up the other'?"

I told her what had happened, and she said, "This is going to sound crazy but I dreamed that you saved some people. I don't remember the whole dream but I do remember that you saved several lives. I bet if there was surveillance on you in the store, it will hit the media." I told her that I haven't seen the tape and only the sheriff and Agent Harrington have viewed the tape. I guess I'll get to see it once the case goes to court.

Jessica said, "You're a hometown hero twice now."

I asked her when will she have some vacation time? She told me that it would be in a couple of weeks.

She said, "Are you inviting me to come to Ga?"

I said, "Grandmother and I would love to have you come a stay with us." Jessica said, "I'll be counting down the weeks, I'll be e-mailing you and staying in touch. Stay in the house and do what the agents tell you so I won't have to worry about you, okay." I promised her that I would do as the agents say and told her to take care of herself. She said, "You're in my prayers every night James Farnsworth, I've got go." Before I could say anything, there was only a dial tone.

I hung up the phone, and Grandmother said, "How is Jessica doing, did she see you on television?"

I told Grandmother that she is okay and she did see me on television.

Grandmother said, "What did she say when you told her about the robbery?"

I told her that Jessica suggested I stay inside and listen to the agents instruction. Grandmother said, when will she be coming to Georgia?" I told her that her vacation time comes up in 3 weeks, and if she'll let me, I'll pay for her trip out here. Grandmother said, "She's already connected to you James. She is drawn to you like a moth to a flame. She can't help herself and it's because of your condition. Before the cycle starts, the animal magnetism works its magic on the opposite sex. I feel better about the situation now in case the Lord pulls my time card.

I said, "What are you talking about? You ain't going nowhere?"

Grandmother said, "When he says it's time to go, there ain't no 'Wait a minute, I can't go yet because I haven't hit the lottery yet.' I've seen and done more than most, but I hope I get to stay long enough to see you and Jessica get married."

I said, "Aren't you putting the wagon in front of the horse here?"

Grandmother said, "I was young once, and I fell hard for your grandfather. Like Jessica, I couldn't help myself.

I'm glad I didn't mention anything about what Jessica told me about her dream. Grandmother said, Your grandfather and I didn't understand why your dad didn't inherit the curse until he was diagnosed with lung cancer. He caught colds, the flu, chicken pox and was a normal child. We didn't know why he didn't inherit your grandfather's condition until he was diagnosed with lung cancer—a by-product from my side of the family. But when you were born, your grandfather and I watched you grow up. You never got sick even when your mom exposed you to the neighborhood kids that had chicken pox. You never showed any signs of sickness. The only time you've had shots was to enter school and that is a prerequisite. We watched you literally outpace the other kids your same age. You excelled in everything that you wanted to do. You were great in baseball until the music bug bit you. You did inherit one strong trait from your father, an ear for music."

I asked Grandmother, "What is a Nephilim?"

She told me that her only knowledge of such is a reference in the Bible in the book of Genesis. She said, "The purpose of the flood was supposed to be about two things. The first was to purge the wickedness that was going on and to destroy the offspring of the Nephilim. What brought about that subject?"

I told her that the messengers had made a comment about the Nephilim. I said, "Per the messengers, there could be Nephilim or offspring walking around disguised as humans."

Grandmother commented that the dark one is planning something. She and I had talked for hours until I looked at the clock in the kitchen. It had 11:55 a.m.

I said, "The midday news is about to come on. Let's go to the den and see what unfolds on the screen. The TV was going through the tail end of an ED commercial, and now the opening theme music for the local midday news was coming on. The announcer was announcing the different anchors names and the weather woman's name and then said this is eyewitness 14 news team. The lead anchor began by saying that the top story of the day so far, is about a man that happened to be at the right place and at the right time for some employees at a Giant Foods Store in Byron. The lead anchor turned to the reporter that was on a monitor and he said, "We're live on location with Lisa Lee Brown. What can you tell us Lisa, What happened at the Giant Foods Store in Byron?" Lisa Lee said, "well it turns out Steve, a local man named James Farnsworth Jr. The one in same man that was on our broadcast last night, walked in on a robbery, disarmed one of the robbers, took his gun and shot the other robber that was holding a gun to the store managers head. I have here the store manager, Mr. Toby Jones. Mr. Jones is what I just said pretty much sums up what happened this morning? Toby Jones said, Thanks to Jesus and James Farnsworth, those two kept me and my employees from dying today. The final score Jesus and James 1 and the robbers zero.

The anchor, Steve, said, "Any word from Mr. Farnsworth?"

Lisa Lee said, "Mr. Farnsworth's attorney, Grady Byrd, will have a news conference today at 3:00 p.m., but it will mostly concern the Serlinni incident and doubt anything to do with this morning's thwarted robbery."

The anchor said, "Okay, Lisa Lee, we'll check in with you later. Now here's our own weather expert to tell us what we have in store for us."

The camera switched to weather girl Jane Gilmore.

Grandmother turned to me and said, "Jesus and James, what a team, huh! I'm glad the store manager gave props to Jesus first."

I said, "Where did you hear that slang word *props* from?"

Grandmother said, "I heard it on some movie I was watching."

We continued watching the news and Grandmother said, "It is good to that we get to spend some time together like this. I know my time here will be reaching an end. I know because I dreamed about it. and I'm okay with it because I can go knowing that someone will be taking care of you." I said, "Stop that crazy talk and I'm not okay with it. I'm tired of losing people that are close to me." Grandmother said, "Death is part of the package deal for the majority of us. It just happens sooner for some and later for others but eventually it happens. Your grandfather witnessed many people die off for 135 years. Because he loved you so much and knew that you would need that room in the basement, he drank the colloidal silver to end his suffering. He told me that he didn't want to outlive another wife and was in hopes that Nicole was to be your wife. He too dreamed of your marriage, but in the dream he told me he never saw the face of the bride and only assumed that it was Nicole." I said, "Didn't the messengers give him any clue? "She told me that the messengers gave him vague answers about the future, but they did tell him that an heir would deliver a great blow to the evil one to come. I said, "You're talking about the Antichrist from Revelation, aren't you? Am I the one to do battle in the end of days?"

Grandmother said, "It may not be you but the one you'll be training." I said, "Let's not talk about this, my mind is still trying to cope with having to shoot that man in the head today. In the Bible, it says thou shall not kill and I'm not sure I'll be forgiven for killing?"

Grandmother said, "I've already told you that you are a tool from God's toolbox and as long as you don't let the dark one sway you, you won't have anything to worry about from the heavenly host."

I suddenly realized something that Jessica will be here in three weeks, just in time for the first full moon of the month.

I said, "Grandmother, Jessica will be here in three weeks, just in time for the first full moon of the month. What am I going to do?"

Grandmother said, Jessica won't turn and run. She already loves you no matter what may come. Jessica is a strong-willed woman and reminds me a lot about myself at her age—headstrong and ready to take on any situation that got in my way. Even though I had to take time off from veterinary medicine to have your dad, your grandfather paid for my tuition to finish, and I got my degree. I did have a practice for a couple of years, but I found that my child was growing up without me, and I was missing it, so I went to being a part-time vet to stopping the practice until your dad became a teenager. I eventually had to get back into it because the supply of animal tranquilizer that I had been stockpiling was becoming low. I had to take a refresher course to retain my license in order to buy medication and see animal patience. I used the guest house as an office, and I did minor treatments to animals like shots, minor surgery, and occasionally go out to farm location to help horses and cows that were in trouble. Doing it gave me the feeling that I was contributing to something, that kept my mind off of what your grandfather had to go through every month. Even the sedatives stopped working him, I guess his metabolism became immune to it. I wound up mixing two different types together in order to get it to work. He had grown tired of the pain during the transitions. He would rather stay sedated." I looked at the clock on the wall and it had 2:45. I said, "Grady will be on in fifteen minutes." Grandmother with remote in hand switched channels to a local station in Macon. I said, "Grandfather had more or less was burned out, wasn't he?" Grandmother told me that he was tired and had enough. We focused on the television, waiting to see what was going to happen next.

The theme music for *Channel 14 Eyewitness News* had begun after a commercial and led into the anchor saying, "We have some live breaking news from Byron with Lisa Lee Brown at the office of Grady Byrd, Mr. James Farnworth Jr.'s lawyer."

The scene changed to Lisa on location.

Lisa said, "Steve, we are waiting with other networks for Grady Byrd to come out, and here he comes. Let's hear what he has to say."

Grady approached a podium that was set up in front of his office.

He said, "I want to thank all of you for coming, and I know you have questions, but I'm not here to answer questions but to make a statement in behalf of Mr. Farnsworth."

CHAPTER 16

"Mr. Farnsworth and his family are in protective custody for their own protection, and as the video that was shown stated, there is a reward for the person that provides the whereabouts of Vincent Serlinni and anyone connected to the kidnapping and attempted murder of Mr. Farnsworth. Originally the reward amount was one million and now two. For those with information that leads to the arrest of Vincent Serlinni, the number to contact is 770-850-3377, and the FBI will see to it that the person or persons will remain anonymous and will be paid two million dollars when Vincent Serlinni and anyone connected to this crime are apprehended. I thank you for coming today, and I hope that Mr. Farnsworth's life returns to normal once Serlinni is behind bars. Thank you."

Before Grady could make a clean getaway, Lisa Lee said, "Mr. Byrd, can you comment on this morning's thwarted robbery by Mr. Farnsworth and the killing of one of the robbers?"

Grady responded by saying, "The local police consider this an open investigation, and the Peach County Sheriff's Department would be the ones to ask such a question."

Grady waved bye to the crowd and walked back into his office.

Lisa Lee said, "There you have it, Steve, we'll have to see if we can get a statement from the sheriff's department on the robbery issue. So maybe with some luck, I'll have some information for the six o'clock broadcast. Back to you, Steve."

Steve said, "That concludes the special report, and we'll see you at six on *Eyewitness News*."

Then it switched to the regularly scheduled program, *Dr. Bill.* Grandmother quickly changed the channel to the history channel.

I said, "Grady pulled it off pretty good, don't you think?"

Grandmother said, "I bet Grady had to take a big shot of liquid courage before getting behind the podium, especially seeing several networks being represented right in front of his office." I said, "He probably took another shot after he finished to calm his nerves." We both chuckled about our comments. Grandmother said, "How long do you think we'll be under house arrest?"

I told her that I have no idea because I've never gone through anything like this before.

I said, "The irony of this is, Serlinni is out and about moving around while we are under house arrest so to speak. At least, the hunter has now become the hunted. I think he'll probably get gunned down by somebody trying to capture him alive. If he's smart, he'll probably go underground because he won't be able to trust his own people because of the money involved. I seriously doubt that he would try anything now, especially with the spotlight on him now."

As we were talking, the phone began to ring. I let the answering machine take the call and I would check the message after the caller finished. I checked the caller ID, and it was my cousin Chris's cell number. I pressed the button to play the message. It was Chris's wife, Terri.

She said, "James, call me once you get this message. I'm at the end of my rope with Chris. He has barricaded himself in the house and won't let the kids out of the house. I had to fight with him to let me go to work so I wouldn't lose my job at the bank. I'm afraid he could lose his job if he doesn't snap out this. Please call me."

Grandmother was listening and said, "Sounds like Chris is feeling guilty about what happened to you and is frightened to the point that he knows nothing but to protect his family. You need to talk to Agent Harrington and get his agent to take you to Chris's house. You have a gift use it, make Chris understand that it wasn't his fault and he doesn't need to live in fear anymore."

I called Agent Harrington and explained the situation to him and he said to let him think about it and he would call me back with a plan. An hour goes by and my cell phone began to ring. I looked at the caller ID, and it was Agent Harrington.

I answered the phone and said, "Hello, Agent Harrington, what do you have on your mind? He said, "I thought about going over there myself but he doesn't know if I'm a good guy or a bad guy. As much as I am reluctant to do this, we don't have any other choice than you going over there with two agents with you. The agents would stay in the cars so that your cousin Chris doesn't take shots at them. Your cousin does have firearms in the house doesn't he? I told him yes.

Agent Harrington said, "I'm going to arrange for Agent Brown to drive you over there and I'll have another agent follow. I want you to call Chris and tell him that you are coming over to talk to him and that you'll have two FBI agents with you. After you call him, I'll have Agent Brown take you there and I want you to return back to your grandmother's, period. Is that understood?"

I told him yes. He told me to call him and he hung up. I called Chris's house, the phone rang three times before, someone finally answered. It was Chris's little girl Tanya. I said, "Hello Tanya, it's your cousin James Farnsworth, can you put your daddy on the phone? In her little girl voice, I heard her yell. "Daddy it's your cousin on the phone, he wants to talk to you." I heard Chris's voice in the background say which cousin is it? Tanya said, "Your cousin that was on television, James." There was a hesitation and Chris answered the phone."

He said, "James, I'm sorry I let you down, but they told me that they would kill my family, if I didn't do what they asked me to do." I said, "It's okay Chris, I would've done the same thing if I had been in your shoes. Can I come over and talk to you, Terri is worried about you and I don't want you to lose your job because of this. I'll have two FBI agents with me and they will stay in the cars and I'll be the only one that comes in the house." Chris said, "I'm sitting here with a

243 in my hand and I've had very little sleep since that day I thought you were killed. You make sure those guys stay in the cars and they won't get shot. You are the only one I trust." I assured Chris that the agents would stay in the cars and I would be the only one coming in and would be there in a little while. I told him don't worry and I'll see you soon and hung up the phone. I called Agent Harrington and told him the situation, Agent Harrington told me that he had made the arrangements and the agent in the guest house will swap with Agent Brown at the drive entrance, Agent Brown will be taking you to Chris's house and he will be tailed. Agent Harrington told me to go ahead and open the garage door so that Agent Brown can pick you up. I told Agent Harrington thanks and hung up. Grandmother said, "When you talk to Chris make sure that you are making eye contact with him and be stern with him and after you finish with him, you'll have to use some type of trigger to disconnect from the session, and invoke amnesia to what occurred. You'll have to do the same thing to his kids to let them know that everything is okay. They don't need to be traumatized by this event that could affect them later."

She told me that she will never forget the first time that she saw my grandfather use his powers of persuasion on someone.

She said, "When you get back I'll tell you what happened after you return and tell me the results." I went and opened the garage door with the remote and watched the monitor while waiting for Agent Brown to pull into the garage. Only a few minutes pass before Agent Brown's car pulls into the garage. I closed the door and told Grandmother to open it once I get into the car. I walked out the side entrance into the garage and got into the car with Agent Brown. I buckled up my seat belt and the garage door opened.

Agent Brown said, "You're not going to going to get us into trouble today, are you, Mr. Farnsworth?"

I told Agent Brown that I didn't plan on yesterday's incident either, but it happened." Agent Brown told me as he was backing out of the garage, "Mr. Farnsworth, I know you didn't plan it and I didn't get into trouble, only a slight reprimand for not walking with you into the store. But from what I hear, you took care of things on your own." I told him that I got lucky that things worked out the way they did."

We made small talk on our way to Chris's house and I could see in my rearview mirror that a vehicle was following us. I made the comment to Agent Brown that I hoped that it is Agent Harrington following us. Agent Brown replied by telling me that it is Agent Harrington.

Agent Brown said, "You are going to have to tell me where to go since I'm not from around here." I told him that we would be going about six mile from here I would show him where to turn. We continued west on 49 towards Ft. valley and I told Agent Brown to slow down that we would be turning at the next right. Agent Brown turned on his turn signal to alert Agent Harrington that we would be turning up ahead. Once we turned, I told Agent Brown that we would be turning right at the fourth house just ahead. We were in a subdivision of homes and we pulled up into Chris's driveway. I looked up at the second story window and a gun barrel was sticking out. I saw that it was Chris holding the gun. I got out of the car leaving the door open. I asked agent brown to call agent Harrington and tell him to stay in the car. I began walking towards the house and told Chris to put the gun down or these federal agents are going to shoot you.

Chris yelled out the window, "How do I know that they are federal boys."

I said, "Don't be stupid. If they were the bad guys, they wouldn't be bringing me here, I would be dead. Now put the gun down and open the door."

Chris withdrew the gun barrel from the window and said, "Okay, you can come in."

I told the agents to stand down and I would be right back out and told them that only Chris and his kids are inside. I walked to the front door, and I heard the door unlock. A frightened little girl slowly opened the door, it was Chris's eldest daughter Brittney. I said, "It's okay Brittney, no one is going to get hurt today. Just take me to your father okay." Brittney grabbed me and hugged me and said, "Daddy hasn't been himself since we thought you were dead." I assured her that things would be straightened before I leave here. She led me upstairs and I slowly opened the door. By the looks of Chris, he was a man on the edge of sanity. Chris's youngest daughter, Tanya was in the room with him and I told her to wait in the hall way while I talked to her daddy. She complied and I told Chris to relax and put the gun on the floor. Chris was hesitant and told him, "Chris look at me and put the gun on the floor." He complied and gingerly place the rifle on the floor. I sat down on the bed, maintaining eye contact with Chris. I told him to relax and said, "Chris, the crisis is over for you and your family. From this day forward, I want you to go about your normal life by going to work, and taking care of your family and put this bad experience behind you. I want you tell me what you're going to do?"

Chris said, "I'm going to take care of my family by going back to work and put this bad experience behind me." I said, "That is good and when I walk out and you hear the door close, you will feel at ease, you'll remember we had a good positive talk. I want you to call your boss and tell him that you will be to work tomorrow okay." Chris nodded as he stared blankly forward. I got up from the bed, opened the door and closed it behind me. I waited and listened, I heard Chris pick up the phone and mashing buttons. I asked Tanya to show me her room as her sister Brittney was standing in the hall with the look of puzzlement in her face. I followed Tanya to her room and told her to sit down on the bed as I closed the door. I made eye contact with her and told her that I want her to forget about this bad situation and that her and her family is in no danger and I want her to concentrate on being a normal six years old little girl. I asked her, "Do you understand Tanya?"

She nodded her head with a blank stare, and I said, "When you hear the door close to your room, you will forget all the bad stuff and feel happy." I opened the door and closed it. Her sister Brittney had been listening to what happened and said, "What is going on, this is crazy." Before she could say anything else, I grabbed her by the shoulders and made direct eye contact with her and said, "It's okay Brittney, just relax and I released her and I could see that she is complying. I told her to show me her room. She walked down the hallway and opened her door. I told her to sit down on her bed as I gently closed the door. I squatted down in front of her, maintaining eye contact and went through the same procedure as I did with the other members of her family. I got up and closed the door of her room and Tanya and her dad were in the hallway.

Before either of them said anything, I said, "I want both of you to give your cousin James a hug before I go, okay!"

They both hugged me, and I began to talk to them in a normal tone, stating everything is okay and as I walked toward the door, I told Chris to tell his wife Terri to come by my grandmother's house once she gets off from work today. Chris said, "Sure thing cousin and I opened the door and walked out to Agent Brown's car. Chris and his daughter's waved good-bye to me as I got in the agents car. Agent Brown said, "I'm glad you were able diffuse the situation" as he turned the key over to crank the car. I put on my seat belt and I told him that they were pretty traumatized and I'll get them some counseling set up. Agent Brown backed out the driveway and we headed back to my grandmother's with Agent Harrington following behind us. I sat there and was amazed at what happened. I didn't realize the strength of my ability beyond, of what occurred by accident with Agent Harrington. I had pulled it off like a trained hypnotist. If I had this ability while I was in school, I could've had every girl I knew, taking their clothes off for me and never remember doing it. I guess it is a good thing that I couldn't, I would've abused the ability. Since I'm older, a little wiser and still learning things about myself. I also have to be careful at the same time. I don't need to subconsciously use it on someone. It wasn't too long that we had turned onto Farnsworth Lane, I called Grandmother to tell her to open the garage door. As we drew closer to the house, the garage door slowly opened as we approached. Agent Brown pulled into the garage, and Grandmother closed the garage door.

I shook Agent Brown's hand and said, "At least no body died or got shot today. Though I did have a gun aimed at us, it turned out okay. Thanks for the backup. I almost forgot to mention that Chris's wife Terri is going to drop by here today when she gets off of work today. So when she shows up at the end of the drive today, it's okay to let her pass after you've checked her ID. Agent Brown said, "No problem Mr. Farnsworth." I got out of the car, walked inside and opened the garage door for Agent Brown to make his exit. I watched Agent Brown as he backed out of the garage and closed it. Grandmother said, "Well, how did it go?" I told her that I diffused the situation and did as you suggested by treating them individually. I almost had a problem with the oldest daughter. She had been listening while I had her father and her little sister in session. I brought her around to my way of thinking and I told Chris to call his wife and tell her to come by here when she gets off of work today. I figured I might as well treat the whole family and get the programming reset." Grandmother said, "That is very noble of you James Farnsworth. You will and have already done great things in a short span of time. You won't go unrewarded for this act of kindness. But at the same time you'll have exercise caution and be mindful of your actions. You don't want to mistakenly force your will power onto someone by accident, especially while your angry. People can say things while they are angry and regret saying them later. You on the other hand can cause things to happen by the use of words and the powers of persuasion." I said, "I'll have to remember that and control myself." I told Grandmother that I wanted Terri to stop by here first before she went home. She would not be able to understand the dramatic change in her family." Grandmother said, "That was good thinking on your part, she doesn't need to experience a role reversal like the movie *The Stepford Wives*. She would think her family was replaced by some overtly happy robots."

My cell phone began to ring. I took it from my pocket and saw that it was Agent Harrington calling.

I answered, "Hello, Agent Harrington, what's up?"

He said that he had gotten would word from his boss that Serlinni's family, had been spotted at Chicago's O'Hare Airport. He said, "His wife and kids had booked a flight to Aruba. A team of agents will follow her to Aruba, to see if Serlinni shows up in Aruba. Serlinni no doubt told her to get out of town before the Carbono family got to them. I thought you should know and I'll keep you updated as things develop." I told him thanks for letting me go to my cousins house today, he had gone through a very traumatic experience and his family was suffering because of me. I told my cousin Chris to tell his wife to come by here today if it's okay with you, before she goes home from work?"

Agent Harrington said, "That's okay as long as she checks in at the entrance with Agent Brown. I'll be talking to you later, stay inside and out of trouble okay!" I'll be good, I replied and closed the phone. I looked at the clock on the wall, and it had 4:30 p.m. Terri will be in a little while. I need to think about how to handle the situation. I used the closing of the door as a trigger to erase, what had happened during the reprogramming so to speak, and it came to me, what to do. Grandmother asked me did I have a plan mapped out in my head. I told her that I think I have a possible scenario that will work. I already know that Terri is going to be aggressive towards me and I'll have to calm her down to begin with. Grandmother said, "Yes, she's going to be cocked and loaded for bear. You'll have to hit her with full force right away and make sure you keep full eye contact on her. She's going to be like a lit stick of dynamite ready to blow. Maybe by me being in the room, she might not be as volatile. Then again, she may not give a damn because in her mind she's directing her anger towards the whole Farnsworth family in general, who knows. Just remain calm that is the key." Grandmother then said, "I'm going to fix me a drink and get ready for the floor show. You can have a drink when you finish, you'll need an unclouded mind focus to do this. You can do this without the alcohol cause you didn't need a drink before you went to Chris's house today." She Then said, "What will be the trigger to break the trance, so that she won't recall what happened here today." I told Grandmother that I used the sound of a closing door as a trigger to break the trance on Terri's family and I'll use her car door as the release trigger. As we talked about different things, time ticked on by. My cell phone rang and I looked at the caller ID. It was Agent Brown.

I picked up the phone and answered, "Hello, Agent Brown, can I help you?" Agent Brown told me that Terri Harland is on her way to the house. I told him thanks and I hung up the phone. I told Grandmother the show is about to go on. I told Grandmother that I had better answer the door, in case she pulls out a gun from her purse. The doorbell rings, and I walked to the door and invited Terri in. Terri said, "Before I got here I called the house and talked to Chris. I asked him what are the girls doing and he said they are outside playing. This morning the house was on total lockdown, and he wouldn't even let the girls look out the windows, much less go out in the yard and play. What did you tell Chris to change his demeanor, he's gone from paranoia to the normal Chris that I knew before this shit happened. "She saw Grandmother sitting at the table and apologized for her language. I said, "Terri come sit down at the table, I've got something to tell you." Terri said, "I don't need to sit down, you tell me what the hell is going on." I grabbed her by the forearms and made eye contact her and said, "Terri, sit down at the table and relax." Terri walked over to the breakfast table and sat down. I sat down across from her and began the session. I said, "Terri, when you get home everything will be as it was before Chris's encounter with the bad men, you and your family are safe, Chris will continue to work and the girls are fine. I want you to repeat by saying that everyone is fine and everyone is safe." Terri complied by repeating the phrase. I said, "Terri, When you get up to go to your car and get in, once you hear the car door close, you will be at peace knowing that your family will be safe and all is back to normal, you'll remember that we had a good conversation and you will feel happy about the outcome and remember nothing else. Do you understand, Terri?"

Terri replied by saying yes.

I said, "Terri I'm going to walk you to the door, you can stand and walk with me." I took her hand and led her to the door and opened it and told her to go and get in her car. I eased the door closed and ran to the surveillance monitor to watch. I watched Terri walk to her car, she opened the door, got in and closed the door. She put on her sunglasses, cranked up her car, turned the car around and headed out the drive.

I told Grandmother, "It seems to have worked, I'll give her time to get home and settled in and call to check in on them." Grandmother said, "If I had been looking at you instead of Terri, I would have been hypnotized also. You are a natural kid. Sigmund

Freud is second fiddle compared to you. It feels good to help someone in distress doesn't it?" I said, "I'll feel better after I talk to her in
an hour. I want to make sure that the technique worked. Now, I'll
have that drink that you promised." Grandmother said, "I'm really
floored on how fast you have evolved and how quickly you have
learned to use the newly acquired skills. There is no telling what else
there is, until you stumble across it." I was pouring myself a vodka
on ice and said, "I found out I have a connection with canines. I had
one talk to me, I could hear him in my mind. The day my car got
shot up, the same day I was to leave out for Arizona. As I was getting
ready to leave and get into the car, a dog was barking loudly on the
passenger side of the car. I walked to the other side and that's when
I heard it speak.

"The dog said, 'You're not going crazy. I am talking to you, and
those bad men that are causing you trouble will wish they never F'd
with you.' Before I could say anything, he and his companions disappeared behind the dumpster and into the woods."

Grandmother said, "Your dad wanted to get you a dog but we
discouraged it for the same reason we didn't get him one. We told
him that we didn't want to see him get his heart broken when the
dog would get ran over in traffic. But that wasn't the real reason
because of your grandfather's condition and now yours. Any breed of
dog would show its absolute loyalty to the point of the unnatural to
outsiders. You nor Grandfather didn't need to draw the attention." I
told her that I could see why now. Not meaning to change the subject, but I have been meaning to ask about the precision, involved
with the hidden staircase construction. Grandmother told me that
my grandfather had it done shortly after my father's first birthday.
She said, "By having a locked door, would only pique the interest of
a growing boy in the house. We didn't need the risk because we knew
early on, he didn't inherit the curse. We almost lost him to bronchitis." I said, "What a twist of fate, his lungs were in a predestined state
when he got here. At least he wasn't plagued with what I have."

After I finished the drink, I felt a little tired and washed out. I
told Grandmother that I feel kind of tired, mentally tired. I said,
"After I call Terri to check on her, I'm going to lie down for a while."

Grandmother said, "You've probably over did it today, since you used it for the first time. An hour or so passes and I picked up the phone and dialed Chris's house. The phone rang twice and I heard a small angelic voice say, "This is the Harland residence, can I help you?" I said, "Hello Tanya, this is James Farnsworth. Is your mom or dad close by so that I can talk to them?" She told me to hold on for a minute and she would get her mom. A minute or so passes then Terri picks up the phone and said, Hello James, I want to thank you for getting Chris out of this crisis. I don't know how you did it and it doesn't matter how. I seems my family is on an even keel and I couldn't be happier. If you were here right now, I would give you a kiss on the mouth. That's how glad I am, that my family is back to normal. By the way, I heard some crazy stuff today at the bank. One of the tellers good friends, works at Giant Foods as a cashier. The teller said, you, James Farnsworth, took the gun from one of the rob-bers and shot the other robber in the head while he was holding a gun to the head of the store manager. Is that true James, did you save some people's lives this morning? Terri began crying over the phone and she said, I was steaming mad at you today before I got to your grandmother's house. I was prepared to tell you and your whole fam-ily where to get off. Now after seeing my girls and my husband back to their normal selves, my feelings are just pouring out of me. We love you James Farnsworth, I have to go. I can't talk to you anymore just now. "I said, "Terri, it's okay maybe when this stuff is all over, we'll get together and take the girls out on a picnic on me okay?" Terri was still sniveling and told me that it would be okay and told be good-bye. Grandmother asked me how did the phone conversation go? I told her that I talked to Terri and she got really emotional on the phone. She was crying tears of joy that her family is back to nor-mal. Grandmother said, "She was crying because what you did was more or less released the anger she had and you reset the program." I said, "I guess in a mechanical sense, you would be right. I just need to lay down and recharge." Grandmother said, "I'll wake you up when dinner gets ready, so go ahead and take a nap. I closed the blinds in my new room, turned on the lamp next to the bed and grabbed my grandfather's journal. I thumbed through some dates that were written on the corners. I stopped on this one page and it had May 1, 1915. Marie along with my parents witnessed me change into the beast while I was shackled with chains and anchored to the floor. The beast heard my father say to Marie, "Your husband, my son will be back to normal in the morning. And since there will be two more nights of the full moon, he'll have to be chained up again for the next two nights." The beast pleaded with Marie to release him, but father told her that the beast cannot be trusted. My son cannot control the beast he becomes." The beast growls and yells in protest, father tells the women to go upstairs. He pushes a bowl of raw meat over to the beast with a broom, just out of reach of the beast. The beast is bound in a way that he cannot stand, he merely rolls over to the bowl, tips it over with his head. Dumping the contents on the concrete floor, biting and chewing the raw meat like a dog eats off the ground. The beast doesn't care, he is getting something to satiate his hunger. The morning came and my father came down to the basement. to unchain me. father said, "Hurry we have to get you out of here, the workmen will be here soon. Hopefully you won't have to be chained up to night, maybe they will finish the cage today. Come up stairs and we'll get you cleaned up." On the way up the stairs, I asked father how is Marie taking this? Father said, "She took it pretty hard last night, your mom and I finally got her to calm down and go to bed." If I had only known what Marie was planning, I could've prevented it. Later that day, Marie told me she just need some time to herself to think. She said that she is going to take a walk around the family property to clear her mind. I helped the men in the basement construct the steel cage in the basement. The men were asking me what's with the cage Mr.? I told them that father is expecting a shipping carton from Africa. Told then an wild tale that father had won a bet with J. D. Rockefeller and J. D. Rockefeller lost. The prize is a lion from the Serengeti plains of Africa. The men were intrigued by the story which, that's all it was; a story. I first thought to tell them that a bank vault will be locked inside the cage. , but they could one day return to try and rob my father. So I made up the story about the lion and I told my father to stick to the story. While all the construction work was going on, Marie was walking the hedgerows looking for a particular plant that grows wild here. The plant is called poke salad, she had heard of women eating a few of the berries to cause an abortion of the fetus. She had heard reports by physicians at the hospital in Warm Springs about women wanting to abort unwanted babies due to rape or incest. She wasn't sure what parts of the plant that were toxic, so she cut some the leaves and gathered a few of the dark berries. She came back to the house before it got too terribly hot. We all had lunch together and no one mentioned what they had witnessed last night. Marie was sitting next to me at the table and placed her hand on top of mine and said, "Gerald Houston, I love you no matter what and I want you to remember that and kissed me on the cheek. At this point, my parents and I had figured that she had accepted the fact that her husband turns into a monster 3 nights a month. We finished our lunch and I went to help the men with the construction and Marie helped mother do the dishes and put away the remaining food. She went on the front porch and sat down on the porch swing. She took the berries and leaves from her dress pocket and ate them. The next thing I know, I heard my mom yelling for me and father to come to the front porch. My Marie was gone, I saw the leaves in her hand and checked her mouth. Her mouth was stained from the berries. I said, "Father, I have to clean her up before the doctor gets here to pronounce her dead and this can't look like a suicide." I took a wet washcloth and swabbed the inside of mouth, to remove the berry stains. I rolled her on her side and noticed that her dress was soaked with blood on her back side. I told father to get on the phone and call the doctor. The doctor arrived in about thirty minutes. He came over and rolled her over on her side and noticed that there was blood on her backside and wrote the cause of death attributed to a premature aborted birth and caused her to hemorrhage. The doctor told me that he would write up the death certificate and have it ready later today. I dreaded having to call Marie's parents and tell them that their daughter and the baby are both gone. It was hard enough on me to come to grips with it, I don't know if she wanted to commit suicide or just abort the baby. I do remember what she said at the table that day, She told me that she loved me no matter what and kissed me on the cheek. I don't know if that was her way of telling me good-bye or what? My condition has caused my Marie to take her life by mistake or intentionally, I'll never know. I finally was able to get in touch with her family. Her father fell apart on the phone, I can't say I blame him. I explained that the doctor said that the pregnancy aborted and caused her to hemorrhage. I told him that she was on the front porch swing while I was helping my father do some construction work in the basement. I went upstairs to get some water and take it to her. I found her lying on the porch and she was gone. It had happened so fast because we hadn't long finished lunch." I asked her father did he want her buried in Warm Springs or do you want her buried in our family plot? I said, "Whatever you decide I will pay for the services." Her father asked me how could I pay for the services if I just started a new job? I told him that My father had a trust fund put away for me while I was in college, before I was inducted into Army special intelligence. Don't worry about the arrangements, discuss it with your wife and I gave him my parents phone number." This is very hard for me to do Mr. Bartlett to tell you this, I lost a wife and a child all in one day. I will do whatever you want, I could get our families mortician to begin preparations because of the heat. Like I said, whatever you and your wife decides call me. Both Mr. Bartlett and I were sobbing and trying to have a conversation in between the crying. By this time, my eyes could no longer remain open and I fell asleep with the journal on my chest. Once I had fallen into a deep sleep, I was sitting by the pool in my parents back yard. As I was watching the sun glisten in the pool, up walked my grandfather. He looked about my age now and he sat down across from me at the patio table. Grandfather said, "Hey kid, you've been extremely busy haven't you. You've been a big topic on television for the past two days. Just wait until the video surfaces and gets on the internet." I said, "I don't mean to change the subject but I've been reading about Marie's death in your journal. There is a lot of connection in similarity with Nicole and Marie, they were both the only child that their parents had and they died because of us." Grandfather said, "A messenger told me that Marie's death was accidental, she didn't want her child to be a monster and took a huge risk and lost. Your Nichole was a victim of circumstance, she happened to be in the wrong place and at the wrong time. You were the intended target not Nicole. But I'm not here to rehash a past that neither of us can change. I'm here because you, unlike myself, have demonstrated that our condition can be used for good. The higher ups are very pleased with your actions and I'm here to provide moral support and guide you as far as the messengers will permit me. I'm so very proud of you. It is a shame that your father isn't here to see what you've done. I asked him, "How come my father won't know about this in heaven?"

Grandfather said, "Your father has been reborn as a new person and so has Nicole and Marie. Marie has probably been born twice because of the long time span from when I lost her." I said, "In other words, God is recycling people?" Grandfather said, "Recycling isn't the correct term the messengers use. They say that the soul has reentered service on earth. Only the people that haven't screwed up get to return. Like I told you before, what you do also determines my fate as well as yours. Continue to use your gift wisely because change is coming and there is nothing you or I can do about it." Before I could ask him what kind of change, Grandmother gently place her hand on my chest and woke me up. Grandmother said, "That must have been some dream, you were just mumbling away." I told her I was reliving what happened to me when I got abducted. I didn't want to tell her that I had been talking to my grandfather in my dreams. She's already telling me that she's ready to go to the other side. I don't need that right now. She said that she had some dinner ready. I told her that I would be there after I rinsed my face and wake up. She walked back to the kitchen and I went into the bathroom and turned on the cold water. I let it run for a few seconds and splashed it on my face. I felt like I either slept really hard or I had been under the influence of some pharmaceuticals, I felt groggy for some reason. I was trying to wake up and make some sense of what Grandfather had told me. I wiped my face with a towel to dry it and I slipped on a pair of sandals. Grandmother said, "Hurry up and fix your plate, so we can watch TV in the den, the evening news will be on in a minute."

I followed my nose to the kitchen. Grandmother had baked some chicken thighs, green beans and biscuits. I grabbed a plate and started shoveling food on my plate, grabbed some eating utensils, couple of paper towels and my glass of tea. I headed into the den and sat on the couch, placed my tea glass on a coaster. I said grace before we ate and the theme music for the local evening news had begun. As I was tearing into the chicken thighs, the usual introductions of the key people on the news team. The lead anchor said, "Hello, everyone, this is eyewitness news and I'm Steve Walker. Earlier today an attempted robbery occurred in Byron at the Giant Food store. We have footage with Lisa Lee Brown, interviewing the store manager." The scene changed to the taped interview with the store owner that we saw at lunch. The scene changed back to the anchor Steve Walker and he said, On concerning Mr. Farnsworth, a press release was held with Mr. Farnsworth's attorney, Grady Byrd, at three o'clock today and Lisa Lee Brown was there also." The scene changed showing the partial interview of Grady and Lisa Lee Brown quizzing Grady about the thwarted robbery. The scene went back to Steve Walker and he said, "We have yet to get an interview with Mr. Farnsworth and when we do, you'll see it here first on Eyewitness News. Now let's get a check on our weather situation with our chief meteorologist Cliff Harris. The scene changed to the weather lady telling us that we may get a slight chance of rain tonight and right after the commercial break I give you the seven day outlook. While some usual car dealership was trying to get people to buy his cars and trucks, Grandmother winked at me and said, "How much do want to bet, that someone from the sheriff's office leaks the video footage onto the internet within the next day or so?" I said, "I would like to see it myself." While we were eating and watching the TV, the house phone began to ring. I told Grandmother that I would go and check the caller ID. I hurried to the kitchen and glanced at the caller ID; it was Agent Brown.

I picked up the phone and said, "Hello, What's going on Agent Brown? He told me that the Peach county Sheriff Terrance Hartley is on his way to the house to bring you a statement concerning the robbery and shooting this morning. He informed me not to sign it until Agent Harrington or my attorney looks at. I told him that I won't sign it until I get it checked out. I thanked him and hung up the phone. It was a matter of minutes and the doorbell was chiming. I looked at the surveillance monitor to make sure that it was indeed the sheriff and I pressed the intercom button. I'll be right there sheriff, I said. I walked to the door, unlocked it and invited the sheriff in. I said, "Come on in Sheriff, would you like something cold to drink?" The sheriff said, "I'm fine Mr. Farnsworth, I'm dropping off this statement as I told you I would. Have your lawyer look it over if you like, before you sign the affidavit describing the events at Giant Foods this morning. I've got to tell you Mr. Farnsworth, you have really put Byron on the map this week. You are the towns first genuine hero that I've actually witnessed in action via video tape." Grandmother had walked into the hallway and said, "Hello Sheriff Hartley." Good afternoon Mrs. Farnsworth, replied the sheriff. The sheriff said, "Mrs. Farnsworth, your grandson did a miraculous thing this morning. With the crimes occurring in the surrounding towns that border our community, your grandson gave the ordinary citizen a glimmer of hope that, there are people out there like James that refuse to be a victim. I'm not advocating taking the law into your own hands but sometimes, like the case of James; He didn't have time think, only to go into survival mode. Though there will be a court case, James won't have to worry about any legal repercussion to his actions. Once the judge views the tape, the case will more likely be self-defense of others in a hostage situation." I asked the sheriff what was the likelihood of me getting to see the tape? The sheriff said, "For the moment, it is locked in the evidence room and when the case comes up you'll get to see it. I must repeat myself again James, you took a big chance this morning and lady luck or someone upstairs smiled in your favor. You've been lucky more than once this week, so please do me a favor and stay indoors and out of harm's way okay. I can take only so much action in one week." The sheriff reached out and shook my hand and said, "Call me once the affidavit is signed and I'll come pick it up. Remember, it's not just the federal boys that are looking after you." "I realize that sheriff, and I appreciate it, "I replied. The sheriff told us good-bye as he walked out of the door. Grandmother said, "I hope they don't wait too long before they have the trial. You know what happens in three weeks from now." I said, "The citizens of Byron wouldn't take to kindly if their hometown hero changed in the courthouse. They would be like the villagers in the old Frankenstein movie except they wouldn't be carrying torches." Grandmother said, "There are forces at work that wouldn't allow that happen, you and I both know this. The messengers wouldn't leave you high and dry unless you fell under the influence of the dark one. Your grandfather told me about his encounter with the dark one once. The dark one told your grandfather he could increase his wealth and women beyond his wildest dreams if he would worship him, and your grandfather told him that if he couldn't remove the curse; the conversation is over plus there is only one God."

I said, "Did the dark one appear to Grandfather while he was changed?"

Grandmother said, "It was after his first wife died and at a time when your grandfather was at low point in his life. He went to a local bar to drink his sorrows away and was driving back home in the wee hours of the morning. He said that a man standing by the road waved him down. Your grandfather stopped and picked him up. He said that he should've known something wasn't right because of the way the man was dressed. He said that the man was wearing a three piece black suit and standing by the edge of a deserted dirt road back then. As they were going down the road, your grandfather asked the man in the black suit where did he need a ride to? The man in the black suit told him that he was waiting for your grandfather to drive by. Like I said, your grandfather was at a low point and vulnerable and the prince of lies and deceit knows when to take advantage of us. He has been watching the human condition for several millennia. So don't ever think that you are alone in this because you're not, you've been chosen to be an instrument of God."

I told Grandmother that I had seen the dark one in my dreams and messengers showed up twice. In both times that it happened I was shot up with narcotics while in the hospital and the night I changed here and the meat was tainted with narcotics. The messengers warned me to stay away from the pharmaceuticals, it made me vulnerable." Grandmother said, "I only did it to keep you quiet with the feds camping out in the back yard." I know, I replied. We finished eating our dinner and I took Grandmother's and my plate to the kitchen, scraped the food remnants into the garbage disposal. I rinsed the plates and eating utensils and put them in the dishwasher. I then returned to the den, where Grandmother was channel searching. I asked her did she need anything before I go to my room and check my e-mail. She said that she was fine and told me not to worry. As I walked to my room, I kept thinking about what Grandfather said in my dream that change was coming and there is nothing he or I can do to change it. I opened up my laptop and checked on my incoming messages. I had one from David at the studio. He said that he had hired a secretary from a temp agency to handle the phones and that he had received word from the execs at Atlantic, they were very happy with the finished product and glad that I was alive. He went on to say when would it be possible for them to wire the money to the company account? I replied back to David saying that I would call them personally and arrange for the transfer of funds and I told David to expect to get a change of pay grade and he'll have to start interviewing someone to take his place because he would be taking Tim's old position, if he is up to it. I hit send and there is a message from Jessica. I opened it up and she said in the e-mail, Well, Mr. Farnsworth you have been busy and it's just the middle of the week. Please stay out of the limelight, you already have your face on national TV with the Serlinni situation as it is. Just stay in the house and listen to Agent Harrington. Looking forward to vacay time and ttyl. I had to go on the internet to see what the abbreviation meant and in the texting world it means, talk to you later. I have texting capability on my phone but I don't use it. If I want to communicate with someone, I call them. That's the whole purpose of the cell phone, to use as a phone and not as a typing keyboard. That additional option is going to cause many deaths on the road because some moron is paying more attention to the phone than what is happening on the road. If I wasn't immortal, I'd be more apt to get killed on the interstate by some one of these new generation of kids texting than I would die of natural causes. I noticed Jessica was real short and to the point, she must figure that the feds are monitoring e-mail traffic as well as cell phone traffic. It will be a couple of weeks before I see her and I don't know how I'm going to handle it, especially with the arrival of the first full moon of the month.

CHAPTER 17

Is she part of the change that is coming that my grandfather talked about? It could mean another attempt on my life by Serlinni. Until then, I guess Grandmother and I will be keeping each other company. I turned off my laptop and was closing it and heard Grandmother in a labored voice say, "James." I rushed to the den, and she was collapsed on the couch. I felt her neck for a pulse, and there was none. I began giving her CPR chest compressions and calling her name. After about two minutes of chest compressions, she gasped for breath.

She asked me, "What happened, James?"

I told her that she had blacked out. I didn't want to tell her that she had died and cause her to panic. I sat her up straight and went into the other room and called 911 and requested an ambulance at our location. The operator said that an ambulance will be on its way. I then walked back into the den to check on Grandmother to see if she was all right. She was all right enough to start raising hell about me calling an ambulance. I told her that it was a safety precaution and she needs to get checked out. I then called Agent Harrington as I walked out into the hallway and in a low voice told him what had happened and an ambulance will be on its way to the house. I finished the call and went back to sit with Grandmother on the couch.

I felt of her forehead to see if she had a fever. I asked Grandmother if she had any aspirin in her medicine cabinet.

She said, "I was gone, wasn't I?"

I told her that she had only blacked out and had a faint pulse.

She said, "You did chest compressions on me. I know this because I was watching you do it. Let's say it was my first out-of-body experience. I'm sorry if I got snappy with you about calling the ambulance. I know you love your grandmother, but please realize I have a no-resuscitation clause in my living will. I don't want to put you and your mom through the agony of watching me being kept alive by some damn machine."

I had already begun to feel the tears well up in my eyes. I said, "Grandmother, stop all this crazy talk. I'm going to get you an aspirin."

I hurried down the hall to Grandmother's bathroom, checked her medicine cabinet for some aspirin. I found a small bottle of Bayer aspirin. I grabbed it, hurried to the kitchen, got a glass of water, and took it to the den. Grandmother was watching television, and I held out the aspirin, and she took it. I gave her the glass of water to wash it down.

Grandmother said, "They won't let you ride in the ambulance with me, just so you know."

I told her, "One of the agents will be driving right behind you."

The doorbell rings, and I ran to the kitchen to check the monitor. It's the EMTs. I pressed the button on the intercom and told them that I would be right there. I rushed to the front door and the EMTs came in with a gurney. I showed them where Grandmother was. They followed me, and with some coaxing, they finally got Grandmother to agree to go with them. One of the EMTs asked me my hospital preference. I told them to take her to the medical center in Macon.

Grandmother said, "All the medical and insurance documents are in the bottom drawer of the dresser in my room."

I told her that I would take care of it and would be right behind her. The EMTs carted her off and into the back of the ambulance. Agent Brown and Agent Harrington were standing at the edge of the porch as this was happening. I told the agents that I would be right with them as soon as I get her paperwork and her ID. I had to slip on my sneakers because I was barefoot, grabbed my wallet, cell phone, and keys to the house. I went to Grandmother's room and found her insurance policy and medical records. Then I thought about Grandfather's journal. I went to my room and stuck the journal between the mattresses of my bed, sped to the door, set the alarm, and locked the door.

I asked, "Which of you guys are going to take me to the hospital?"

Agent Harrington said, "I'll be driving you, and Agent Brown will be following. Agent Williams will be watching the house. Let's go, my car is right there."

I jumped into the passenger seat, put on my seat belt, and by the time the seat belt clicked, Agent Harrington had already cranked the car, and we were speeding down the driveway. In no time, we were on the ambulance's tail. I closed my eyes and said a prayer in my mind, "Lord, please don't take her now. Please restore her to good health again. In thy mighty name, Jesus of Nazareth, amen.

I opened my eyes, and Agent Harrington said, "My driving hasn't scared you enough to close your eyes, has it?"

I told him no and that I was asking for a favor from the man upstairs.

Agent Harrington said, "She'll make it, she's a fighter!"

"I hope you are right," I said.

It wasn't long before the ambulance reached its destination, the emergency room at the medical center. Agent Harrington found a place to park the car. As the car stopped, I opened the door, and Agent Harrington grabbed my arm.

He said, "Hold on, wait until Agent Brown comes to the car. We still have to protect you, James. There are televisions in the waiting area. Your face has been on it a lot, and we don't need to draw attention."

He reached in the backseat and gave me an Atlanta Braves baseball cap to put on. It was the real deal, a fitted ball cap, and it fit perfectly. Agent Harrington told me that he wants it back because it

341

has a signature on it. I took it off and looked at it under light of the street lamps; it was signed by John Smoltz.

Agent Harrington looked at me and said, "Agents do have lives outside the bureau."

I put the cap back on, and I could see Agent Brown approaching the car.

Agent Harrington got out of the car and said, "Agent Brown, go ahead of us, go to the main desk, show the person your ID, and request the head of hospital security. I'll get the hospital security to take us to a more secure place than the waiting room."

Agent Brown went ahead of us, and we waited for a few minutes before we started towards the entrance. We go through the automatic doors, and the waiting room was semifull of people. As we walked towards the desk, a security guard was approaching.

Agent Harrington said, "Sir, this man is in my protective custody, and the ambulance just brought his grandmother in. Can you take us to a more secure location?"

Agent Harrington had shown the guard his badge, and the guard said, "Come with me."

We followed him through a series of doors, and he put us in a room.

I said, "How am I going to give the person in admissions the information on my grandmother?"

The hospital security guard suddenly realizes who I am and says, "Hey, you are the guy from Byron that they have been talking about on television, aren't you?"

I nodded my head and replied "Yes, it's me."

The security guard said, "I can get you someone from admissions, bring her here, and she'll take the information and enter it on the computer at the nurses' station, which is just around the corner from this room, if it is okay with you, federal guys."

Agent Harrington looked at the guard's name tag and said, "That would be fine, Officer Jones, as long as no one else knows. The admission person must stay quiet about it also."

Security Guard Jones said, "We will keep this played down, okay?"

The security guard left the room, and I am shut off from Grandmother, not knowing anything about her condition. Agent Harrington told Agent Brown to post outside the door for safety precaution.

As Agent Brown opened the door, an electronic voice came over the intercom system in the hallway saying, "Code blue."

I said to Agent Harrington, "She's gone."

Agent Harrington said, "It doesn't mean the code blue was your grandmother, it could be anyone."

I know different. I felt something just before the code blue was announced. I didn't tell Agent Harrington that. I kept it to myself. I pray that it isn't my grandmother. I have no choice but to wait. The guard came back with a lady from admissions. I gave her all the paperwork, and she told me that she would be right back with my grandmother's current condition. She and the guard left the room, and I've never felt this alone except when I was abducted, shot in the head, and thrown in the trunk of a car. As the minutes ticked away, I sat with my head in my hands.

I then heard a whisper in my right ear say, "It's okay, James, I'll never stop loving you."

I sat up in the chair and told Agent Harrington that something's wrong and I know it. I want someone to take me to her.

Agent Harrington said, "I have no control over doctors, and I'm responsible for you. The doctors are doing what they are trained to do. We'll know something shortly, be patient"

The minutes ticked away, and a different person came into the room. By their dress, it was a doctor in scrubs.

The doctor made eye contact with me and said, "Mr. Farnsworth, I have some bad news. Your grandmother has passed away. She had a second massive heart attack caused by an aortic embolism. An embolism is a clot that stopped the flow of blood to a main artery to the heart. I'm sorry, Mr. Farnsworth."

I asked the doctor if he could take me to her so that I could see her.

The doctor said, "Sure, Mr. Farnsworth, follow me."

Agent Harrington followed but hung back a ways to give me a private moment. The doctor took me to a room, and there were two nurses cleaning her up and removing IVs.

The doctor said, "Nurses, could you step out for a moment so Mr. Farnsworth can have a moment with his grandmother."

I walked over to her, and I could see that the blood had begun to drain from her face. Her expression looked like she was at peace. I picked up her left hand as the tears began streaming down my cheek. Her hand squeezed my hand one last time. I don't know if it was a muscle reaction or she had just enough spark left in her to do that. I stayed there with her for a moment and reflected on what she had told me in correlation with what my grandfather said in my dream. Change is coming, and there is nothing I can do about it. I gently put her hand at her side and kissed her on the cheek and said, "Save a seat for me. I love you." I walked back out into the hallway with Agent Harrington and Brown waiting on me.

The doctor walked up and said, "You can wait and call the mortician tomorrow. I'm giving you some medication so you can get some rest tonight. Eat some food before you take it. It could make you nauseous if you don't." He handed me a bottle that contained a few pills. "I thought you should know this, but while we were working on her before her catastrophic heart attack, she told us to stop what we were doing because she was ready to go. You grandmother was a strong-willed woman right to the end." The doctor shook my hand and said something surprising. "Keep fighting the good fight and stay vigilant."

He turned and walked down the hall. The lady from admissions brought me some paperwork to sign.

She said, "I'm deeply sorry for your loss, Mr. Farnsworth."

I thanked her and asked her if she could lead us to the emergency lobby. She told us to follow her, and we went through a maze of corridors until we were back in the lobby. Agent Brown was behind me and Agent Harrington in front of me. Agent Harrington headed out the exit, and we followed right on his heels until we had gotten to his car. He unlocked the car, and we got in.

Before Agent Harrington cranked the car, he said, "James, I'm deeply sorry about your grandmother. You've been through quite a lot in a short period of time. I wish I could tell you something profound and meaningful, but I can't imagine having to go through the things that you've experienced firsthand."

Agent Harrington cranked the car, and as he was pulling on to the street, he continued telling me about what had happened to him when he was a child.

He said, "I had spent many summers at my grandparents' house as a kid. My father was a hard man. The word *strict* isn't even close. But when I got to spend time with my grandparents, I could be a kid. One summer night, my grandfather and I were watching this old horror movie, and Grandfather gripped my arm and started convulsing. I didn't know what to do except to call for my grandmother. She came into the room and saw what was happening. She told me to call the ambulance right away. Grandmother and I were helpless to help him. I watched as the light in my grandfather's eyes went out. By the time the ambulance got there, he was beyond resuscitating. I know how it feels to be absolutely powerless to do anything."

I said, "It is an empty feeling. I guess it's a way that the master of the universe shows us just how fragile we are as human beings, and we have limited control."

Agent Harrington asked me if I wanted him to call the safe house where Mom is staying. I told him to wait until tomorrow.

"Mom doesn't handle things like this too well since my father's death plus my abduction. She isn't as strong a woman as my grandmother was. Grandmother was cut from a totally different cloth than my mother. When I get back to the house, I'll call Lawrence Stoddard, the mortician, and tell him that Grandmother's body is at the medical center. He'll have someone pick her up in the morning, and I'll call my attorney to see if Grandmother had any final wishes drawn up. Right now, I could use a drink."

Agent Harrington said, "I'll have you home in a minute, and you can fix you a drink."

I looked at my watch, and it was already 11:00 p.m. It's too late to call anyone at this hour of the night. I might as well wait until morning to call anyone. I told Agent Harrington that I didn't realize that it was this late, and I might as well wait until tomorrow to call the funeral home director and my lawyer.

He said, "You need to get as much rest as you can, James, because the next few days are going to be hectic. Do you want me or one of my agents to camp out on the couch so you won't be alone in the house?"

I told him that I appreciate the concern but that I would be okay. Our exit was coming up to get off the interstate and head for the house. I thought to myself, *The house—a big empty house that contained a century's worth of memories.* We got off at the Byron exit and headed east on highway forty nine towards Farnsworth Lane. A few more miles and we'll be turning onto Farnsworth Lane. There are only two people left that have the Farnsworth name, my mother and myself. I know now what my grandfather meant by being a witness to death as death passes you by. Agent Harrington called ahead to alert the agent posted just inside the entrance of the drive. Agent Harrington turned into the drive and stopped beside the agent's car.

He asked Agent Williams if everything is okay. Agent Williams told Agent Harrington that there hasn't been any traffic in or out since we left. Agent Harrington told Agent Williams that he would be relieved by Agent Brown in a couple of hours then drove towards the house. On the way down the drive, Agent Harrington told me to stay in the car. He asked for the house key and the alarm code.

Agent Harrington said, "I'm going to park in front of the garage and walk to the house, and once inside, I'll open the garage door, then you drive the car in, okay? I don't want to run the risk of one of Serlinni's guy's with a night scope taking a shot at you from the tree line."

Agent Harrington stopped the car in front of the garage door, got out, and went into the house. I slid over into the driver's seat, and the garage door opened. I drove the car into the garage and waited for the garage door to close before I turned off the car and got out. I made my way to the side entrance to the house from the garage. I could hear Agent Harrington talking to Agent Williams with his earpiece. I heard him saying to be on his toes tonight, that someone may have noticed some action at the house due to the ambulance entering and leaving.

I walked into the kitchen and said, "Sounds like you have put some thought to this."

Agent Harrington said, "One has to think like a criminal to beat the criminal. If I were watching the house and waiting on an opportunity, I would take the moment that is least expected and take the shot. Serlinni already knows that the feds are here, and he doesn't care. We found that out when he abducted you. We can't leave you exposed for someone with a high-powered rifle. I have already been thinking ahead on how to provide protection for you during the funeral of your grandmother. I'll talk to you about it tomorrow. Tonight has been a tough night for you, and I want you to get some rest because tomorrow will be here before you know it. I want you to call me tomorrow after you have talked to the mortician and your attorney. I'll call your mother at the safe house in the morning after you call me once you find out the particulars from the mortician."

I said, "My mom will want to come and stay with me, but like I told you before, she'll be an emotional train wreck. The only way that I could handle her here is to have a doctor prescribe her some medication to keep her calm."

Agent Harrington said, "If it comes to that, I can have the family doctor come in."

I told Agent Harrington thanks for being here in this time of crisis, and I shook his hand. I told him that I would open the garage door for him as he made his way to the side door to the garage. I went to the surveillance monitor and watched as he got into his car. I hit the switch to open the garage door and watched him back out. I closed the door and locked the front door and reset the alarm system. It's midnight, and that would make it around nine in Arizona. I got on the landline and called Jessica.

Her phone rang twice before she answered, "Hello, Mr. Farnsworth, you should be in bed instead of calling me this time of night. What is happening?"

I told her, "My grandmother passed away a few hours ago, and she told me to tell you that she liked you the moment that she met you. I thought you should know since you left a lasting impression on all of us."

There was a considerable pause before Jessica said anything, then she said, "James, what happened to her?"

I told her what happened at the house and at the hospital and how Grandmother argued with me about calling an ambulance.

I said, "She wanted to die at home, and I wasn't ready to let her go. I guess the man upstairs disregarded my terms and used his."

Jessica said, "Call me once you find out the funeral arrangements, and I'll see if my boss will let me use my vacation time a little early."

I told her that I'm to talk to the mortician tomorrow morning and get an idea when the funeral is to take place, and I offered to pay for her airfare round-trip if she would permit me to.

She said, "James, call me tomorrow, okay, and get some sleep. You'll be in my prayers."

I told her thanks and I would call her tomorrow.

She said, "Good night, James"

And the phone conversation was over. She wanted to say more but didn't want to run the risk of being monitored by the feds. The house is lot bigger now since it's just me here now. I went into the den and sat down where she was sitting when she died the first time and wept. I lost track of time after I cried all that I could and passed out on the couch from exhaustion.

I had fallen asleep, and while I was dreaming, a young woman approached me. She looked familiar, and I realized who she was from the photographs in the family album. The young woman was my grandmother, and she said, "My dear James, I don't have long, so listen up." She said all the information I need is in the wall safe and gave me the combination. She told me not to worry, that everything is going to be fine.

She said, "James, always remember that I will love you forever."

I reached for her, and she just faded away.

A messenger stepped forward, and said, "Not many people get to share their final good-byes. I had to pull some strings because your grandmother wouldn't cross over until she got her message to you.

You inherited your strong will from her, and it will be useful to control the beast when the moon is full again. James, your grandmother was right about what she said about you being an instrument of God. Those that you killed were destined for hell. You just hurried them along the way."

I said, "What about the commandment 'Thou shall not kill'?"

The messenger replied by saying, "While Joshua was on his way to the promised land, God instructed him to wipe out everything in Jericho once the walls fell. Moses killed an Egyptian because he was beating a Hebrew, yet Moses found favor in God's eye. James, in this time of sorrow, you are being prepared for what is to come."

Just as I was about to ask what he was talking about, my cell phone began to ring, waking me from my dream. I looked at the clock on the wall, it had 6:30 a.m. on it. I grabbed the phone from the coffee table and looked at the incoming call.

. It was my newly appointed assistant manager, David.

I opened the phone and said, "Hello, David, what is wrong?"

In a frantic voice, David said, "It's either Serlinni or one his men that's been leaning on me to flip me to their side or else. I'm afraid, James. I may not survive an abduction like you did."

I told David, "Calm down. I will see to it that you and your family are protected. Serlinni is desperate now, and he is bent on revenge against me for putting out a bounty on his head. What did he tell you to do, David?"

There was a pause, and before David could answer, I said, "He offered you a lot of money to kill me, didn't he?"

David replied by saying, "Yes, a million dollars."

I told David that once he got the briefcase in his hand, he wouldn't make it to the bank or airport.

"Someone would be following you, pull up next to your car, blow your brains out, and get the briefcase. By the way, where are you?"

"I'm at home," he replied.

I told him, "I'm going to send an agent to talk to you. The agent is going to call you on your cell phone to let you know that he is in your driveway. Don't go to the door to let anyone in until you get the call, okay?"

David said, "Okay, James."

I told him to hang tight and help will be on its way and hung up the phone. I called Agent Harrington's cell number. It rang twice before he answered.

"Hello, James, what's going on?"

I filled him in on the conversation that I just had from David.

Agent Harrington said, "This could be genuine or a way to remove some of your protection at the house. I'm going to send a spare agent to his house and get a statement from him, then the agent is going to call me back to give me his assessment of the meeting."

I said, "I told David not to let anyone in the house and that an agent would call his cell and let him know that he is in his driveway."

Agent Harrington said, "That's good thinking for this early in the morning. Now what is David's number so that I can give it to the agent? Don't forget to call me after you've found out the particulars from the mortician."

I told him that I would call him just as soon as I find out something, and I hung up the phone. First things first, I need a couple of cups of coffee in me. I put on a pair of shorts and walked into the kitchen. Under normal circumstances, Grandmother would already have a pot of coffee ready. I only wished last night was a bad dream and that I could hear Grandmother's bedroom slippers shuffling across the floor as she walked into the kitchen to greet me. Then it occurred to me that she gave me the combination to the wall safe. I went to the wall safe that's hidden behind the refrigerator, pulled the fridge forward to allow myself room. I began to recall the series of numbers that she called out to me. I turned the dial to the indicated numbers, gripped the handle, and twisted it. I heard the lock release, and I pulled the door open. Before I began going through the documents inside, I got a piece of paper and wrote down the combination and placed it in my grandfather's journal. I then placed the journal between the mattresses of my bed for now until I can put it in a better location. I went back to the safe and began to look at what was contained inside.

There was an envelope that had last will and testament on it. There were some bank CDs, property deed, and a thick envelope full of cash. I took out the last will and testament, left the rest in the safe, and closed the safe back up, pushing the fridge back in front of the safe. I placed the envelope on the counter so that my lawyer can open it. I already have an idea whom the beneficiary is anyway, so to keep things legal, I'll let my lawyer be the first to open it. Now, I'm dreading the most difficult task that I've ever had to do. That is calling the mortician and reporting that I have lost a valuable family member.

The coffeemaker that I started is finished, and I need a cup of coffee urgently. I took a cup from the cabinet and poured a cup of straight black, no creamer today. I need to face the world in high gear today. I grabbed the cup from the counter and headed for the phone book. I got the phone book and flipped through the pages. I found the number I was looking for, and I dialed it. The phone rang a couple of times before someone picked up.

A male voice said, "Stoddard's Mortuary, George Stoddard speaking. Can I help you?"

I said, "George, is your father around? This is James Farnsworth."

George said, "Wow, it isn't every day I get to speak to a real live hero. Mr. Farnsworth, my father is ill and is at the medical center in Macon. What can I help you with, Mr. Farnsworth?"

I said, "I'm sorry to hear your father is ill, but the reason I'm calling is that my grandmother passed away last night. Her body is at the medical center in Macon. I would like Stoddard Mortuary take care of the funeral arrangements and notify me when we can finalize the circumstance. I won't be able to come to your place of business to finalize the proceedings. I'm under protective security."

George said, "Mr. Farnsworth, I'm deeply sorry to hear about your grandmother, and Stoddard Mortuary will be glad to take care of her. I will call you and bring out the necessary documents, a brochure of casket types and colors, and handle whatever wishes she may have made plans for."

I told him that I would be home all day and to call me at my grandmother's home.

"If it is possible, could you give me some idea of how soon she could be ready?"

George said, "If everything goes like clockwork, I could have her ready for the family viewing tomorrow night."

I said, "I'm not trying to rush things, but since I'm under the protection of the FBI, security is of utmost importance. Is it possible to keep her death announcement out of the paper? If this were under normal circumstances, it would be okay to notify the paper. Right now we need to avoid a media circus and keep this within the family and a few close friends only."

George said, "Yes, of course, Mr. Farnsworth, there will be no death announcement, and we can keep it under wraps, so to speak."

I told George, "An Agent Harrington will be contacting you about security protocol. He'll ask you a couple of questions, so don't be nervous. Agent Harrington is a good and bright individual, so feel free to call me. Thank you, George, and I pray that your father recovers and can come home."

George thanked me and said that he would be calling later today. The phone conversation ended, and I got on my cell and called Agent Harrington to brief him on what George Stoddard told me. I also told him that I suggested that the death announcement would be kept out of the papers to avoid a media circus.

Agent Harrington said, "We definitely want to keep this strictly within the immediate family and a few close friends. I will visit Mr. Stoddard and check out the layout of his business."

I said, "I told George Stoddard that you would probably visit him today because this is a security issue."

Agent Harrington said, "I'll also have to coordinate with the local sheriff's department for extra men on the day of the family viewing and the day of the funeral. Thanks for the information, Mr. Farnsworth, I mean, James. I will be in contact with you later today, so stay inside, and I'll break the news to your mother at the safe house. So again, stay inside and call your immediate family and a few friends. Keep track of the people's names that will be attending. They will have to show their identification to enter. I'll talk to you later."

The phone conversation ended, and I called my attorney, Grady Byrd, to tell him to come to the house.

Grady asked me, "What's happened now, James?"

I told him, "Grandmother passed away last night, and I want you to come over and open the envelope containing the last will and testament. I will alert the agents that you will be coming over. What time shall I expect you?"

Grady told me that he could be over right after he opens up the office and gets his secretary to begin working on a court deposition. He estimated that he could be here around eight forty-five. I told him that I would see him then. I need to fix myself some breakfast to keep my energy level up. Under certain stressed times, I would fire one up. Now, I'm not even in the mood for that. I guess to keep my mind occupied, I can get a pen and paper and make a list of close family and friends to contact. This shouldn't take long as far as family members. I could contact Grandmother's sister Helen's kids that I haven't seen since my father's funeral. It is a shame that the only time that families get together anymore is when someone passes. I wrote down their names. No sense in calling them until this afternoon because, like everyone else at this time of day, they're at work. I wrote down some more names of relatives and friends of the family, and by the looks of it, it will be a small group.

I'm sure there would be a bigger crowd if the death announcement went out, but I think Grandmother would prefer a small, serene setting for the send-off. But I really don't know what her wishes are until the lawyer comes over and checks out the last will and testament. Speaking of the lawyer, Grady should be ringing the doorbell any minute now. There is so much going on, it is hard to focus on any one particular thing. I'm now worried about my newly appointed studio manager, David, after he called me and told me about the threat coming from Serlinni or one of his capos. In a matter of just weeks from now, the monthly full moon phase starts, and I don't have anyone to lock me up and let me out. Then there's the possibility that the feds will want to move my mom in with me.

Like Grandmother commented once, saying that my mother wouldn't be able to mentally handle that her son changes into a monster three to four nights a month, she would probably take a handful of sleeping pills and never wake up. I had a hard time with her while Father was in the hospital, and she almost went off the deep end when he died. I had to take her to a shrink to get her on some good shit because she was talking suicidal stuff. I've got to talk to the exec at Atlantic, which will have to wait a couple of hours since he is in the West Coast. It's still too early to call Jessica because I still don't know all of the details about the funeral arrangements yet. Something just occurred to me out of the blue. I know now why my grandfather wrote in his journal instead of just internalizing all of his thoughts and feelings. I'm sure he did talk to Grandmother about a lot of stuff but not everything. I can understand fully what he must have gone through—that feeling of overwhelming loneliness, having to contain all of this in one's mind without going insane.

The doorbell rang and brought me back to reality. I went to the monitor and saw that it was Grady. I pressed the voice button and told Grady that I would be right there. I said to myself, I'll have someone to talk to for a little while anyway. I went and unlocked the door to let Grady in.

Grady held out his hand and said, "James, I'm deeply sorry to hear about your grandmother passing. Boy, with all this stuff happening to you, you need to start going to church with me and my family."

I said, "I wished I could, but it would be a security risk on innocent people near me."

Grady then said, "From what I hear, your escapade at the grocery store, you've already got some divine intervention going on. Now what do you want me to look at while I'm here?"

I asked him if he wanted any coffee, and he told me yes, and as I went into the kitchen to get a cup, I said the envelope is on the table. I grabbed a cup from the cabinet and asked Grady how he liked his coffee.

Grady replied by saying, "Two sugars and a splash of milk please."

I put two teaspoons and a splash of milk in his cup and poured myself a straight black, and I poured a dash of Kahlua in the cup. I walked over to the table, and Grady had opened the envelope and was looking it over. I put his cup down in front of him and asked him what the document said.

Grady said, "Well, James, it appears that you've inherited the property, bank CDs, and whatever is in the checking and savings account."

I said, "I'm not interested in the money or property parts. Does she mention any last request concerning her funeral?"

Grady said, "Let me finish reading to that part. Your grandmother's request is that she is buried in a red coffin and wear a red dress because red has always been her favorite color. She wants to be buried next to your grandfather and have a graveside service, no music. She said to get some preacher to read from Ecclesiastes 11. She also put up a trust for your firstborn child, and the child will receive the trust fund upon completion of high school and is to be used to go to college or technical trade. She then said, 'My grandson James will be the executor over the trust fund.' And in the final sentence she says, 'James, follow your heart instead of your thoughts. Thoughts can be corrupted but not the heart. The heart is the first organ that forms in the womb. It already knows what to do before the brain even forms.' Grady looked up. "Wow, your grandmother laid down some deep subject matter. Where is your Bible? I want to read what Ecclesiastes 11 says."

I went to my grandmother's room and got the Bible from the nightstand by her bed. I took it to the dining room, placed it on the table, and began flipping through the pages until I found Ecclesiastes 11. I read over it and slid the Bible over to Grady for him to read it. After he read it, he commented that she picked a very fitting and profound passage.

Grady said, "I wish I could've spent some quality time with my grandmother like you did, James. In a strange twist of fate, you were forced to be with her. Just think, if the Serlinni situation hadn't happened at all, more than likely you wouldn't have been here for her when it was her time to go. No one should have to die alone, and she didn't."

Grady began to tear up and told me that he was at a fraternity party the night his grandmother died.

He said tearfully, "I should have been with her instead of thinking of only myself, and she wouldn't have died alone."

I told Grady to stop, that he's making it harder on me as it is. He told me that he was sorry about losing his composure. I told Grady that he shouldn't blame himself for not being there. He had no way of knowing that it was her time to go. No one knows when that time will come. Grady told me that he would take care of the legalities and get it set up with the judge to get this all finalized. I said, I almost forgot, I need you to read this statement from the sheriff's dept. before I sign. It's about what occurred at the grocery store." Grady took the document and read it through. Grady told me that is standard operating procedure and that I am in the clear. I signed the statement and asked Grady would he mind dropping it off at the sheriff's office? Grady replied by saying that it wouldn't be a problem.

Grady said, "James, call me to let me know about the funeral arrangements once you find out something from the mortician. The wife and I would like to pay our respects."

I told him that I will add him and his wife to the list. I explained to him the security protocol that will be in effect, and ID will be required. Grady understood the seriousness of the situation and told me that he and his wife will be there regardless. I told Grady that I appreciated his friendship as well as our business collaboration. As Grady was going out of the door, he said that he would pray for a swift end to the Serlinni situation. I told him thanks, and he walked out.

I locked the door behind him, and I looked at the clock on the wall. The clock had 9:30 a.m. I hear my cell phone ringing. I dashed to the kitchen and got it from the counter. I looked at the incoming call, and it was a 404 Atlanta area code. I took the chance that it could be my mom calling.

I answered the phone, "Hello, this is James Farnsworth."

Then a familiar voice said, "It's me, your mother. I'm sorry you had to go through the ordeal with your grandmother alone, and I wish I could be there for you."

I could hear her voice begin to start quivering, and I knew the crying was coming. I told Mom that I was glad to be here because, under normal circumstances, Grandmother would be in the house by herself. By this time Mom was really sobbing on the phone, and I told her to calm down, and I explained to her that the graveside service would be limited to a small group of people due to the security issue. I also told her that the mortician said that Grandmother could be ready for the family viewing tomorrow night. Mom had calmed down enough to ask if Grandmother left any last instructions about her funeral. I told her that she wants to be buried in a red coffin and in a red dress because red has always been her favorite color. Mom told me that there could possibly be nice red dress in her closet that I could give to the mortician to use. I told her that I would check it out once I got off the phone because I have more calls to make, like to Grandmother's sister's kids in Flint, Michigan, to let them know what has happened and to tell them I could have the funeral on Saturday or Sunday, which would give them a chance to arrange a flight.

I said, "I really don't know their situation because if they have seen me on television, talking about the bounty, they may not want to come and risk being in the same vicinity of me, which I wouldn't blame them if they come up with an excuse stating that they can't make it. They have their own families to worry about without adding this complication to the mix."

My phone began signaling that I had an incoming call coming. I saw that it was Jessica trying to get through. I told Mom that I've got a call coming through, and I would keep her aware of what is happening, told her that I love her, and ended the call.

I caught the third ring and answered, "Hello, Jessica, you must be getting ready to go to work."

Jessica said, "Any word about funeral arrangements yet?"

I told her that the mortician could have her ready for a family viewing tomorrow night, and I kind of got the impression that the family could set the funeral date.

Jessica said, "I'm going to ask my boss this morning if I can use my vacation time early for this occasion."

I told her to call me after she finds out something, and I would pay for the round-trip tickets on my company card.

Jessica said, "You will not have to do that, James. I've got money saved up. Plus it will get me out of this desert heat for a little while. How's your mom taking this?"

I said, "She's not taking this well at all because, so much has happened to this family in a short period of time."

Jessica said, "She has every right to be torn up because you are all that she has left. Well, I've got to finish getting dressed and go in to work. I'll call you around my lunchtime. Got to go, James. Stay inside and out of trouble."

The phone conversation ended, and before my mind started thinking about a half-dressed Jessica, I refocused on the burial clothes. I went into Grandmother's room. I could still smell remnants of her in the room. I went to her closet and leaned forward to smell her clothes. I closed my eyes, and I could almost see her in the room just by the picture that my keen sense of smell had painted. I opened my eyes and looked through her wardrobe. She had a lot of pastel-colored dresses, and what caught my eye were a couple of garment bags. I pulled one garment bag after another. Though they did have the color red on them, the right dress hasn't been found yet. I got the last unopened garment bag from the rack and unzipped it. Inside the garment bag was a shimmering red silk dress. She must have been saving it for this. I'll have to get the mortician to send someone for the dress since I'm under protective custody.

My stomach is growling for food. I took the garment bag with me to the kitchen and laid it gently across the back of a chair. I opted for a big bowl of cereal. I wasn't in the mood for bacon or eggs. The bowl of cereal was like an easy convenience to ease my hunger pains. If only the cereal could heal the sorrow. I gobbled up the bowl of cereal and drank the milk from the bowl. I then placed the bowl in the dishwasher and grabbed Grandmother's address book. I found my cousin Jake's number, the one who lives in Flint, Michigan. He is my grandmother's sister's son. He is about my dad's age, if dad had lived. I called him and told him that his aunt Lorraine was gone. Right off the bat, he told me that he had seen me on television.

Jake said, "How's the investigation, and are the feds any closer to catching Serlinni?"

I told him that I'm under protective custody, and a few of Serlinni's men are now Satan's bitches. Jake is or was an ordained minister the last time that I had talked to him. I went on the defensive, sarcastic mode when he didn't even ask how his aunt died. He was more interested in what is going on with the mob thing.

Jake said, "Nobody is going to heaven or hell without judgement."

He shouldn't have gone there.

I said, "Those men had already signed up for season tickets when they joined the organization, just like the robber that I put to sleep few days ago when I walked in on a robbery. I sent his ass on his way to the sauna."

Jake said, "What are you talking about?"

I told him, "I'm sorry for the anger I'm feeling right now. I called you to see if you and your family wanted to come to the funeral, which will probably be Saturday. If you guys can't make it, I understand. I reached out to you to let you know because you are family."

Jake started backpedaling and told me that his wife is sick, and under the circumstances, they can't make it. He said that he would pray that this ordeal would be over soon, and he will certainly miss his aunt Lorraine. I told him that I would pray that his wife gets better. I wanted to tell him so bad that I have seen the face of evil, the source of all that is bad in the world, and to tell him that I had seen where the end of the road actually goes, the left side, the middle, and right; but I didn't. I told him that he needs to try to get down here one of these days when things have calmed down, and I told him good-bye. Damn, I need to get my hands on some weed to calm this anger tendency down. I poured myself another cup of coffee, and I called Terri at her job at the bank.

I said, "Hello, Terri, it's me, James Farnsworth. Grandmother passed away last night. She had two heart attacks, one here at the house and another at the hospital. George Stoddard said he would have her ready for a family viewing tomorrow night."

Terri said, "Have you called Chris and told him?"

I told her that I haven't, and I would appreciate it if she would tell him for me. I told her that it would be a small graveside service with family and a few friends.

I said, "Because of security reasons, don't say anything to anyone outside the family. The FBI said that we have to keep this as low profile as possible."

Terri said, "James, you want me to cook you some dinner tonight?"

I told her that it wouldn't be necessary, that I had plenty of food here, and I appreciated her generosity.

Terri said, "We love you, James, and you would be surprised about what people have said about you in and out of this bank. You have given these people a reason to be proud to be from Byron, that's because of you. I know you'll miss your grandmother. She will be missed by all that have come in contact with her. I wished you'd let me bring you some dinner, especially after you got my family back to normal. I don't know how you did it. I just know that you have God on your side. I've got to go now. A customer needs my attention, and I'll tell Chris at lunch. Talk to you later, James."

She ended the call. I then called Stoddard Mortuary and talked to George about the dress for Grandmother and to order a bright red coffin. I told him that it is my grandmother's final wishes; red is her favorite color. George told me that he would be coming to the house today. He said that he would bring some photo examples of what is available.

George then said, "I'll need a current photo of your grandmother. I'll need a beautician to fix her hair the way that she wore it. I want her appearance to be a great memory for her family."

I said, "I trust you, George, just like my family members before me have. The Farnsworth and Stoddard family have a long history in this town."

George said that he has come from a long line of morticians, and he has a standard that he has to live up to.

I said, "Your family's quality of work is of undisputable craftsmanship. Just call me ahead of time so that I can alert my guardian angel at the end of the drive."

George said he would call first, and he would see me later today. The phone conversation ended, and the next thing was to call the Atlantic exec Hank Stevens. I looked at the clock on the wall; it had ten thirty. That would put the time on the West Coast at seven thirty, still too early to call Hank. If Hank fits the stereotype of high-level executives, he won't be in at eight, more like nine.

Just when I was about to slide into a feeling of deep sadness, I caught a whiff of Grandmother's perfume that she wore. Either my mind was playing tricks on me or I just got a signal, a small hint, that she's still with me. I strained my ears to listen. I even stopped breathing so I could listen. I only heard the ticking of the clock that's in the den. I started back breathing again, and I guess my mind is playing tricks on me. I guess no one really leaves you as long as you have a memory of them. My mind is still trying to hold on to the last vestiges of her very essence, not wanting to let go. I walked over to the counter and grabbed my cell phone. I called Agent Harrington.

Agent Harrington answered, "Hello, Mr. Farnsworth, I mean James. What can I do for you?"

I asked him what he is going to do about David's situation. Agent Harrington told me that David was honest enough to come forward with Serlinni's proposition, and he's afraid.

I said, "Are you going to post an agent with him for protection?"

Agent Harrington said, "Serlinni is either getting close to running out of options or he is planning on David as a means of redirecting our attention. No matter the situation, security of the person that can put Serlinni away, which is you, James, is paramount."

I said, "Last night while I was unable to get to sleep, even with the sedative the doctor gave me, an idea came to me. Instead of having the family viewing at the funeral home, I'll find out from Mr. Stoddard if her body can be brought here. This is her home, and it's more secure than the location in town."

Agent Harrington said, "Securitywise, that wouldn't be a bad idea. You'll probably have to turn the air conditioner on a much cooler setting. Do you think you can handle something like that?"

I said, "People used to bring their dead home and have a wake for their loved ones. In this case, it would be fitting for her to spend one last time in her house. If my mom has a problem with it, I'll just get the family doctor to give her some calming medicine."

"James, as you know, with the funeral happening, you and other innocent bystanders will be out in the open. I know I can talk to the sheriff's department and get as many uniforms that he can afford, maybe even get the state patrol to spare some support, but even that might not be enough. I'm going to be as straightforward as possible with you. In the event that Serlinni has a hired gun with a 700 mag. Rifle, people can still die, and you wearing body armor still isn't a guarantee. The very best that I can do is secure a perimeter within the range of a high powered rifle, depending on the layout of the real estate. I'm going to need to know exactly where the cemetery is and the family plot location."

I said, "There's a field road that runs just behind the guest house. It goes back past a pine thicket that opens up to an open pasture. Just across the other side of the pasture is the family plot, where my great-grandparents, my grandfather, my father are laid to rest and are waiting for my grandmother to join them."

Agent Harrington breathed a sigh of relief and said, "One way in and one way out, am I correct on this assumption?

"Yes," I replied.

Agent Harrington said, "If you don't mind, I would like to drive back there and survey the surroundings."

I told him that I didn't mind, and I reminded him that the field road could be a little grown up.

I said, "A local farmer has been leasing the open pasture to grow crops to feed his cows. Let me know the condition of the field road once you get back. I may have to get the farmer to bring his tractor with the bush hog to cut some of the brush down to make it look more presentable."

Agent Harrington said, "Which side of the house should I access the field road?"

I told him that at the end of the row of pecan trees, on the left side of the house, the field road starts and winds around to the back of the property. Agent Harrington told me that he would be right back as he headed for the door.

He opens the front door and turns to me and says, "Stay inside and call me on my cell phone if you need me."

I gave him a thumbs-up sign as he exited the house. I looked at the clock on the wall; it's almost lunchtime. I don't even have an appetite. I got to thinking about Grandmother being in this huge house by herself. If this weird stuff wasn't going on in my life, she could've passed away, and no one would have known about it until someone checked in on her. I consider myself blessed for being with her during this very brief amount of time that we had a chance to reconnect with each other. After much hesitation, I mustered up enough courage to call Nicole's parents house, luckily her father answered. I said," Mr. Adams, I calling to let know that my grandmother loved Nicole like she was her own. Now grandmother is with Nicole, she passed away last night." Mr. Adams said, "hold on son, so I can the mobile phone and go outside." A minute or 2 goes by and Mr. Adams said, "Are you still there James?" I replied, "yes sir." Then, Mr. Adams said," James, I felt a lot of anger losing my only child and after seeing on the television, what you've been through with the abduction, then you saving those peoples lives in the grocery store and now Ms. Lorraine is gone. I really don't know what I feel now other than absolute shock. If my wife and I weren't in such a state, we would be glad to attend Ms. Lorraine's funeral but right now, she nor I could take it. Honestly son, I don't understand how you've been able make through those extreme trials by fire, survive it and lose so much because of it. James, I'll tell my wife about Ms. Lorraine in a few days and tell her that I talked to you also. One thing I'm going to do for you is pray that somehow you manage to come out of this, and from an outsiders view looking at this, it appears that the Lord has plans for you. Just know my wife and I still think highly of you James and I've got to go now. We love you son." I told Mr. Adams that I loved he and Mrs. Adams and bid him a goodbye. I broke down, that man poured his soul out to me on the phone. I was expecting something else altogether different.I don't blame them for their scorn.

After I was able to pull myself together I went to the bathroom and shaved to make myself presentable. The undertaker will be visiting here sometime day. I need to convey some type of integrity to the situation. There's no telling who else may show up today. I put on a casual shirt, some dress slacks, and my dress shoes. By the time I had left my room, I could hear my cell phone going off. I ran to the kitchen and retrieved it from the counter. I saw the incoming call was Agent Harrington's number.

"Hello, Agent Harrington, what do you think about the lay of the land?"

He told me his only concern was the pine thicket. He said, "Someone with a high-powered rifle could set up a vantage point and be able to fire at the target in the family plot. That is, only if they know about where the burial takes place. My question to you is, who knows about the family plot other than the immediate family?"

I sat down at the kitchen counter and thought for a second. I told him the funeral home director knows, for one, because he buried my grandfather and my father there. There are also the people who attended both of their funerals.

Agent Harrington said, "I'm going to call the sheriff and see how many men he can spare. If any bad guys are watching the entrance, the chance to enter would be when the line of cars start filing in for the funeral at graveside. An attendance list would have to be made, of the people that you anticipate showing up."

I asked him if the field road was in need of bush-hogging. Agent Harrington told me that it could stand trimming.

I said, "I'll call Mr. Register. He is the farmer that has been leasing the pasture from Grandmother. I'm sure he wouldn't mind bringing his equipment over."

Agent Harrington reminded me that Mr. Register is to call me in advance before he comes over. I assured Agent Harrington that I would follow protocol, and I would be making a list of the people that would possibly be attending the service. He ended the conversation by saying that he would be at the end of his cell phone if I needed him.

I called Mr. Register and asked him if he was busy.

He said, "James Farnsworth, is that you?"

I answered by saying, "Yes, Mr. Register, it's James Farnsworth. The reason I'm calling you is, I am prepared to pay you to bush-hog the field road that leads to the family burial plot. My grandmother has passed away, and I need your expertise with a tractor."

Mr. Register then said, "That's nonsense, son. My grandson and myself will be glad to do it for free. Your grandparents have been good to me and my family for many years. I'm saddened to hear that Mrs. Lorraine is gone. I hope she didn't suffer on her way out."

I told him the whole circumstance and to not to mention it to anyone. I said, "Because of the security risk, I'm having to create a list of people that will be attending graveside services. You, your wife, and grandson are invited if you want to attend. I'll understand if you decline because of the circumstances."

Mr. Register said, "We can come armed to teeth if need be, son."

I told him about the security that is already in place, and it would best if he didn't have weapons in sight when he comes over. The FBI could mistake his intentions. Mr. Register told me that he would be here in about two hours. He'll need to load the tractor on a trailer and bring it over. I informed him to call me just before he arrived so I can alert the agents at the entrance to the driveway. Mr. Register told me he would comply and call before arriving. I thanked him and ended the call. I carried the cell phone with me to the den and turned on the television, and I wondered how Grandmother did it. She was in this big house alone, and the only time she needed help was when she caught the flu. My mom and grandmother's part-time housekeeper came in to wash clothes, cook for her, and kept the house going until she got well. I wonder if she really was self-reliant or it was just a front because she couldn't open up to anyone about what she had experienced with Grandfather and me. I think she had become self-absorbed into her surroundings until the time came to reveal my situation. She bore a heavy weight all these years with my grandfather and then me. I can fully understand why she drank now. She didn't have anyone to confide in except for me, and that was a brief amount of time. Time to a normal human is an enemy because every day that he or she lives puts them one day closer to the grave.

The house phone began to rang out as I was channel-surfing through mind-killing daytime programs. I ran to view the incoming caller ID and saw that it was Stoddard Mortuary.

I picked up the phone and answered, "Hello, this is James."

The voice on the phone stated, "James, it's me, George Stoddard, calling ahead of time before I come out to see you."

I told him that I had notified the security and assured that it would be okay to come on over. George then told me that he would be on his way out. I explained to him that he would need to show his ID to the agent at the entrance to the drive.

"No problem, I'll see you in few minutes," replied George.

I told him that I would be here and hung up the phone. I looked at the clock, and it showed that it was a matter of minutes before 1:00 p.m. It's amazing how time can fly by at times, and other instances, it could just crawl by. Today, the clock seems to be at a snail's pace. I need to see if the guy who does my lawn will come to Grandmother's to trim up the yard. I'll have to run it by Agent Harrington first. I want the place to be presentable for the guests that will be attending the funeral; Grandmother would want me to. I did get in touch with Hank Stevens, Atlantic Records exec. Hank told me that he was glad to finally hear from me. I went through the whole rundown about Serlinni and Grandmother's passing. Hank told me that he wished he could attend my grandmother's funeral, but his son's wedding is this Saturday.

Hank said, "James, you and your recording technician did a terrific job on the sound track as well as the video. You guys did so well, the board of investors want me to do another project with you. Your nationwide notoriety has gained a lot of ground in the music industry. Some of my colleagues that I play golf with from Sony have been asking me if I have you on an extended contract. Of course, I told them I did so that they couldn't steal my team of talent that I have at Red Sand. Speaking of Red Sand Studio, has my accountant wired money to your company yet?"

I told Hank that I would call the bank and check. He said for me to call right back to confirm either way so he'll know that my company has been taken care of. We made some more small talk, and I told him that I would be calling him back shortly. I ended the call and called the bank, gave them the account number and security code numbers. I waited for a minute or so, and the lady at the bank said that $298,000 had been deposited from Atlantic Records. I thanked her for helping me, and then I called David at the studio. I wanted him to go and check the contract to see what the dollar amount is and call me back. It was too long before David had called me and confirmed the dollar amount. I asked David if my accountant had been issuing checks to him in my absence. David said that he has been getting paid and that the new receptionist is working out. I told him about my grandmother passing away and the final funeral arrangements haven't been finalized yet. David gave me condolences and asked me to call him with the details so that he can attend. I asked him if the FBI had been to see him. He told me that an agent has been tailing him around and parks across the street from the studio.

I said, "David, you are the only one left that I can trust, and if you stick with me, I can guarantee you a raise, plus Atlantic wants us to do another project. That means more money for both of us, and after my grandmother's funeral, I'll be coming in to the studio, and we are going to be the studio that everyone will be clamoring to get in of. I'm not going to let Serlinni come between me and my new partner. You and I will go further than Tim could ever think about. Tim was only concerned with his own selfish gains with no regard to who had to die in order for him to get what he wanted. We know what happened to him in the end. His world had collapsed onto itself, and he was facing a prison term."

David said, "I can assure you that I'm unlike Tim or Trina. I have a conscience to deal with. Those two didn't have a conscience nor any morals and deserve what they've got coming to them."

I closed the conversation saying, "David, I am counting you to hold things together at the studio, and you need to let the agents know everything because they are here to protect us."

David said, "My parents are afraid for me and want me to quit the studio. I told them that I'm not going to cave in because you need me now more than ever. I think Serlinni is grasping at straws that aren't there. He is running out of options."

I told David that I totally agree with him and that Serlinni is slowly getting backed into a corner with nowhere to go. It's only a matter of time when the rat springs the trap and is captured.

I then said, "When this is over, we'll be running at full throttle, and I want you at my side. I'll be letting you get back to work and send updates to my e-mail on things that are pending, okay? Feel free to call me day or night, and thank you. Talk to you later."

I closed my phone and thought about the conversation I had with David. I'm hoping that if David had any second thoughts about Serlinni's proposal that I built him up and gave him an incentive to want something that he can be proud of. And if that didn't work, I also added in the part that the rat would eventually spring the trap, meaning anyone can slip up and get caught in the snare. I walked into the kitchen to fix me a sandwich, just something to bide me over. I grabbed the sandwich-building materials from the fridge and took the bread from the pantry. I had just started untying the bread, and the doorbell rang. I walked over to the monitor and checked to see who was at the door. It is George Stoddard, the mortician. I pressed the intercom button and told him that I am on my way. I twisted the bag close on the bread and proceeded to open the door for George. I opened the door and invited George in. He shook my hand as he entered the house.

George said, "I got the full shakedown at the drive. The agent asked me for my ID and asked me to pop open the trunk."

I told him that it is all a precaution, and I explained how my cousin Chris was used in my abduction. George had a look of astonishment on his face.

George said, "I knew you had been abducted from the televised interview, but I never realized what transpired before the abduction. You are a very lucky man, James, to have survived two brushes with the grim reaper."

I said, "George, I was about to fix myself a sandwich when you showed up. Would you like one or something to drink?"

George said that he would like something cool to drink. I told him to sit at the table while I fixed him a glass of tea.

I said, "George, did you bring me some color samples to choose from for the casket color?"

I walked over to the table and placed the tea glass in front of him. George placed a booklet on the table and pushed it towards me. I sat down at the table across from George, and I opened the pamphlet. There was an array of colors available from the pale pastels to the shocking bright, vibrant colors. I saw a particular shade of red that closely matched the color of Grandmother's dress. I placed my finger on the color, and the color had a numbered code.

I said, "George, I think I have found her favorite color."

I got up and walked over to the chair where the garment bag was draped. I unzipped the bag and placed the color sample against the dress. There was only a shade difference in the two. George had a notepad and asked me the color number. I told him the color code is 712 red, and the interior can be white. George told me that he didn't have that color in stock but could have one brought in from Atlanta. It would be here tomorrow before the family viewing. George asked me if I knew the beautician that used to fix Grandmother's hair. I told George that I didn't have a single clue. George asked me if I had any current photos of her so that a beautician can replicate the way she normally wore her hair and makeup. I told George if he had a minute or so that I can gather up some photos to use. As I was going down the hallway, I took the picture down that has her and Grandfather in it. I told George that this picture was taken last year.

I handed him the picture, and he said, "She'll be with your grandfather now, just like in the picture."

I said, "They were together for a very long time, and I think she had been going through spells of loneliness since Grandfather's passing. George, do you need any money up front until her insurance company settles up?"

George said, "I'll call you when I get back to the office and make arrangements for the casket from Atlanta. You'll need a vault, slab, and headstone, which we can work on after the ground settles. I'm not worried about it, Mr. Farnsworth. I know you can handle the cost. Besides, what would the community think of me if Stoddard Mortuary took advantage of the hometown hero when he is at his weakest. I'll take your grandmother's dress with me and have her ready for the family tomorrow evening."

I gave George the garment bag that contained the dress and walked him to the door.

I said, "Before you go, I have a question. Is it possible to bring my grandmother's body here for the viewing due to the security risk of having it at your place of business?"

George said, "I don't see that being a problem except, due to the temperature being almost eighty degrees, the air conditioner would need to be set to at least sixty nine degrees while your grandmother is here. After the viewing is over, I'll take her back to the mortuary."

I said as I was walking him to the door, "Under normal conditions, I could've had it at your place of business. Thank you, George, and let me know how your father is doing. I'll pray that he recovers fully."

George replies by saying, "Thank you for your kind words, Mr. Farnsworth. I'll tell my dad this afternoon when I see him. He was your dad's golf partner when they had time to go."

George walked to his car and drove away. I closed the door, went to the kitchen, and finished making a sandwich. I poured myself a glass of tea and sat at the table, said grace, and began eating. If it wasn't for the faint noise of the TV from the den, the silence in the house was deafening. I never knew how important interacting with other people was until I became isolated. Even though I was alone in the wild after the abduction, I knew I would eventually make contact with someone. This is a totally different situation. The one person that knew about my unique condition that held my utmost trust is gone. I finished my sandwich, finished off my glass of tea, and placed the dishes in the dishwasher. I went to the den and crashed on the couch. I might as well channel-surf and watch television to pass the time.

I stopped on the Discovery Channel and got interested in a documentary about the Egyptian pyramids. This one scientist suggested that the pyramids were not built by the Egyptians and are much older than the Egyptian civilization. He said that the early Egyptians found these structures and placed their own markings on them, making them their own. The guy that was interviewing him asked him who did he think actually built the mega structures. The scientist commented that the culture of people responsible were the Minoans, and they could also be responsible for all the pyramid structures all over the planet. Another scientist chimed in by saying sarcastically that the Minoans must be space hybrids and chuckled. I lay there, listening to the scientist argue the point, and before I knew it, I had fallen asleep.

I found myself at an ancient site. It looks like an Aztec ruin.

A messenger walked up to me and said, "James, you are partly right. The Aztecs did live here, but the structure is much older."

I looked at the messenger with a puzzled look on my face.

The messenger said, "The scientist is only half right. It was built by a hybrid race, a hybrid race that was a mix between fallen angels and humans."

I said, "Let me guess, the Nephilim. The great flood destroyed the hybrids and left only their structures behind."

The messenger nodded and said, "James, not only were the hybrids corrupted but they were too advanced. God had to slow man's progression down considerably. Just imagine if the whole world spoke only one common language and they had access to the knowledge of the fallen ones. Man would consider himself God and forget the creator that made all this possible."

I said, "I can see that today. People have turned from God and focused on themselves. I was even guilty of such until my eyes were opened a lot wider. You mentioned the Nephilim to me before. Will they seek to destroy me because I'm in league with the good guys?"

The messenger said, "Your senses will allow you to know when evil is present. The downside to that is, you will have to recognize them before they recognize you. My brothers and I have time to train you for what is either faced by you or an heir James, you have grown more than just an individual. I know it is hard on you to lose the people you love. Your grandmother imparted to you the gift of thinking of others before yourself. You saved the people in the grocery store. You restored your cousin and his family back to normal. You have demonstrated that you can use your gift as a tool for good instead of self-gain, which is how evil takes over. You won't be alone much longer."

Just as I was about to ask the messenger a question, the house phone rang, and I woke up. I walked sprang over to the phone in the den, looked at the caller i.d., it is Jessica. I picked up the phone and answered, "Hello, Jessica, what did you find out?"

Jessica said, "My boss said that I could take an early vacation and still be on the job. He wants me to be a liaison between the two bureaus. My boss had already talked to Agent Harrington's boss, and now that extra agents are needed for the funeral, I'll be flying to Atlanta in a couple of hours."

I said, "Agent Harrington had explained to me that I would be vulnerable out in the open along with other innocent bystanders. Unless you are planning on staying at a local hotel, there are three bedrooms here, and if Grandmother was still alive, she would've loved to have you stay here."

Jessica said, "Mr. Farnsworth, I could be arriving late tonight, and I don't want to impose on you."

I told her, "I won't be getting much sleep until things return back to normal, so rent a car with a GPS and call me when you land in Atlanta. I will give you the address to the house, and it will be a nice change to have someone to talk to."

Jessica told me that she would call me once she got a rental car. I told her that it didn't matter what time of night that she called because I'll be awake.

Jessica said, "Okay, Mr. Farnsworth, I'll call you."

The phone conversation ended, and I felt better knowing Jessica would be here. Just as I was about to place the phone on the table, the phone rings. I looked at the incoming call, and it was an Atlanta area code. I took a chance that it could be my mom and answered it.

"Hello, James Farnsworth speaking," I said.

A familiar voice said, "James, it's me, your mother. The FBI is letting me come to your grandmother's house and stay until the funeral is over. I'll be there around lunch tomorrow. I have to pack up a few things and buy a dress for the funeral. How are you holding up, son? I know you miss her terribly and so do I."

I told Mom, "Don't start crying, okay. Jessica called, and she'll be taking her vacation early to be with us also. So get your things packed up, go shopping for a dress, and I'll be waiting for you. I love you and will see you tomorrow."

The phone conversation ended, and it appears I'll have two women in the house. I don't know how long that will last. At least I'll have some human contact for a little while. The one thing that concerns me most of all is, What am I to do about the first full moon coming in a few weeks from now? I need to think of a contingency plan. My resources are very limited, and I'm under protective custody by the feds. I definitely don't need to be seen in an altered state by the feds; that would be a big mistake. I shuddered at the thought of the government's black project operations finding out about me and my ability. I sat down on the couch and began channel-surfing again, I know for a fact that daytime television sucks. I had much rather be at work than to rely on the brain-killing programs that they have on daytime slots. I glanced at the clock; it was almost four thirty. Where did the time go? I might as well get used to seeing time drift by. Grandfather witnessed time pass by for 135 years. I wonder how old I'll be when I've grown tired of living. Grandfather probably hated the fact that he was dependent on Grandmother having to lock him up and unlock the cage after the night was over.

The messenger said that I wouldn't be alone much longer. I know he can't be talking about Mom; she couldn't handle the mental strain. It can't be Jessica. She's too committed to her job, and I'm assuming that she's coming out here so that the Arizona FBI division can get some face time. Being that my face and story have gone nationwide, the high-level criminal element has attracted the upper echelon of the justice system. Speaking of the justice system, I hope that the court schedule concerning the foiled robbery doesn't run parallel with the moon phase. That would be really fucked up. There is way too much stuff going on in my head right now. I don't know how Grandfather was able to maintain a sense of sanity.

The house phone rang, and I looked at the caller ID and answered it. It was Terri Harland, Chris's wife.

I said, "Hello, Terri, how are you doing?"

Terri answered back by saying, "James, me and the whole clan are at the end of the drive. I've got food for all of us. Could you tell the agent to let us pass?"

CHAPTER 18

I told Terri to hand the phone over to the agent, and I would talk to him. Terri handed the cell phone to the agent, and I talked to him. I told him to do his normal security checks like the trunk and their IDs and let them through.

The agent said, "I'll let them through once I clear them, and I'll send them through, Mr. Farnsworth."

I thanked the agent, and he handed the phone back to Terri. I told Terri to show her ID and Chris also. "The agent will check the trunk and wave you guys on in."

Terri said, "Okay, James, we'll see you in a minute."

A couple of minutes go by, and the doorbell rings. I went to the monitor, and I saw Chris, Terri, and their girls. I pressed the intercom button and told them that I am on my way to the door. I walked to the door and let them all in.

I said, "It's good to see you guys, come on in."

Chris and Terri were carrying KFC bags, and I told Terri that she didn't have to bring food. I said that they could have visited without bringing anything because they're family. I told them to follow me to the kitchen, and they set the food bags on the table.

Chris turned to me and said, "Cousin, Terri and I got off from work a little early today so that we as a family could be with you. You pulled off a miracle by helping me and my family through a crisis that I created in my head. You and your family have suffered a lot more than that brief crisis that I had. I told Terri that if we all had to be frisked to get in here, we would still do it because we are family, and you need our support more than ever."

Chris already had tears streaming down his cheeks as he was talking. Terri was crying and hugging me at the same time.

I said, "Okay, stop crying, and everyone go get washed up, and I'll get some plates and dinnerware. Let's get these girls something to eat."

Terri said, "I've got it, James. Tanya, Brittney, let go of your cousin James and go wash your hands."

I took the girls to where the bathroom is and walked back to the kitchen. It was comforting to have some different noise in the house, the sound of people interacting with each other. I walked over to the sink and washed my hands, got some glasses, and filled them with ice. I got a small tumbler to fit little Tanya's hands. I grabbed napkins while Terri placed the dinnerware and plates on the table. Terri laid out the cream potatoes, corn, gravy, and biscuits. I placed the glasses full of tea at each place setting and sat down. Brittney and Tanya picked up their plates and sat to the left and right of me. I don't understand what is going on with the girls, but it felt good to have someone drawn to me.

Terri sat beside Chris across from us, and Tanya said, "Say the blessing, Cousin James."

I placed my open palms on the table as the girls placed their small hands in mine while Chris and Terri stretched across the table to hold their daughters' hand.

I said, "Lord, thank you for this food and thank you, Lord, for my family members at this time of grief. Lord, we place all our faith in you to help us through this difficult time. In your holy name, Jesus, we pray, amen."

I asked Tanya what her favorite piece of chicken was. She told me that she likes the drumstick. I asked Brittney the same, and she said she likes the thigh. I gave the girls their favorite piece of chicken and dipped them out some cream potatoes and gravy and a biscuit. They didn't want any corn. Their mom said that they'll only eat it off the cobb. I told the girls I like it off the cob also. The grown-ups took turns doling out the fixings, and we began to eat.

While we were feeding our faces, Brittney said, "James, one of the kids in my class told me that you saved her mom by shooting a robber and beat up another at the grocery store. Is that true? Did you really do that?"

Everyone stopped chewing, and all eyes were on me.

I said, "Brittney, it is true, and I hated having to shoot the robber, but he didn't give me a choice because he had a gun aimed at the store manager's head. I couldn't let him kill an innocent person, so without thinking, I aimed and shot the robber with the gun that I took away from the other robber after I roughed him up."

Chris said, "You weren't afraid that you would miss?"

I said, "I didn't have time to be afraid or have second thoughts, just pushed the robber down so that the other robber would point his gun at me. At the same instance, I pointed and shot the other robber in the head."

Chris said, "We are sitting at the table with a genuine hero."

I said, "I don't feel like a hero. It was an instant impulse that just so happens to have a happy ending, except for the guy that I shot in the head."

Chris said, "It felt good to put a dirtbag away and get some payback in for Nicole, didn't it?"

I said, "To be truthful, I felt kind of numb after it was over. I had taken away a total stranger's snub-nosed .38 aimed at his partner that was about twenty feet or so and fired. I have never shot a snub-nosed .38 before. I felt compelled to do it. In reality, those type of guns are only accurate at very close range, ten feet max."

Terri said, "God placed you there, and that's why the bullet hit its mark. Now let's eat this food before it gets cold."

Chris said, "After we eat, I want you to tell me how you got the gun. A guy at work has a relative with the sheriff's department and said there is a video of you in action. Is that true, James?"

I answered, "Yes, but I haven't seen the footage yet."

Terri said, "Chris, let James eat first."

The fried chicken was good, and I was careful not to scarf it down like a starving animal. It was nice to sit down in a family-like atmosphere and have conversation at the table. I asked Tanya if she wanted another drumstick. She nodded, and I grabbed the bucket and took out a drumstick for her. I also asked Brittney if she was ready for another piece of chicken. She said that she would like more cream potatoes and gravy. Terri commented and said that Brittney likes cream potatoes and gravy. I said that I like potatoes and gravy also. We finished off the meal, and I helped Terri clear the table. The girls helped load the plates in the dishwasher. I put the remnants of the chicken bones down the garbage disposal and put the empty containers in the trash compactor.

I said, "Let's go into the den, and I'll tell you about the attempted robbery at Giant Foods." I asked Terri and Chris if they would like an adult beverage.

Chris said, "I could use a beer if you have any."

I said, "The grocery store manager took my grocery list and added to it. I think there is beer and wine. I'll fix myself something a little harder. I didn't sleep that much last night. I have some can drinks for the girls if they want it."

Terri said, "Let me give you a hand, James."

Terri followed me into the kitchen. I opened the refrigerator and got the girls the cans of ginger ale and a bottle of beer for Chris. I asked Terri if she liked wine, and she turned to me, holding something familiar in her hand. She placed her finger to her lips, signifying not to say anything.

She forced the bag of weed in my hand and whispered, "You need this more than Chris does."

She asked me if I had a wineglass as I shoved the bag of weed in my pocket. I told her that the wine goblets are in the cabinet above the microwave.

I said, "I'll take the girls and Chris their drinks, and I'll come back and get the wine bottle opener for you."

I took the girls and Chris their drinks; they were busy watching some action movie on TV. I went back to the kitchen, opened up the drawer that had an assortment of utensils. I found the corkscrew bottle opener, took the wire and foil from the bottle, inserted the corkscrew, and extracted the cork. Terri held out her goblet, and I filled it. I got a tumbler, poured bourbon in then ice and just enough cola to finish floating the ice.

I said while I patted the gift in my pocket, "Terri, thanks for the great dinner. That was very thoughtful of you. Let's go in the den. I've got a story to tell you."

As we were walking back to the den, Terri said, "There's a beautiful young girl at the bank that has been asking about you, James. Do you want me to set you up?"

I said, "I appreciate what you're trying to do, Terri, but my mind is so preoccupied with all this other stuff going on, it wouldn't be fair to the other person. Maybe once the funeral, the mob stuff, plus trying to get my business back on track have been taken care of, just maybe I'll be able to focus on myself."

We had walked into the den, and I sat down on the couch. Chris was in the La-Z-Boy, and the girls were on each side of me.

Terri sat on the end of the sectional sofa and said, "Okay, turn the TV down. Let's hear James tell us about his crime-fighting escapade."

Chris grabbed the remote and turned the volume down on the television.

Chris said, "Don't hold back. Give us a play-by-play of what happened."

I took a sip of my drink, and I began explaining the events that led up to the trip to the grocery store. I then proceeded to give them a play-by-play account of what happened in the grocery store. They all sat glued to my every word, as if captivated with my words.

I concluded the event by saying, "The sheriff took a statement from me. I haven't gotten the chance to view the footage myself, but I'll probably get a chance once I have to appear in the hearing."

Chris said, "A hearing? You saved those people, plus it was self-defense. Why do you have to be there?"

I explained to him that I won't be on trial, just a piece of the case to convict the surviving robber.

Chris said, "When did you take any martial arts classes?"

I told him that I took a few courses while in college.

Chris said, "Why didn't you use it that day you got abducted?"

I said, "I didn't want to risk you getting shot. I would rather it be me than you, cousin. You've got a family to take care of."

Terri said, "That's amazing, isn't it, girls, just like in the movies, except your cousin James actually saved innocent people from the bad guys. I can't wait to tell my friends at the bank that I got a firsthand account from the hometown hero himself. I'll have all the single girls pining for you, James."

Chris said, "I want to see the video. I'm surprised someone hasn't put it on YouTube yet."

I told him that the tape is being held for evidence at the sheriff's office.

Terri said, "James, what time is the viewing tomorrow?"

I told her that the viewing will be here, and a time hasn't been set. I explained about the security issues, and I would let them know.

I then said, "I want to thank you for sharing your food with me and conversation. I wished Grandmother was here. She loved when company came over. She loved to talk. That's what I'm going to miss the most. She always had an upbeat personality no matter how tough things got."

Chris said, "We'll miss her also, James. Just remember, we'll always be there for you. Just call me, okay."

They all gave me a hug as I walked them to the door.

I said, "Maybe when all of this is over, you all can come over, and we can make use of the swimming pool in the back."

Chris waved and told me that he would see me tomorrow. I closed the door and watched them from the front window as they got in their car and wheeled down the driveway. Terri really surprised me today in more ways than one. I guess in the past she used to think that the only reason in her mind that I hung around my cousin Chris was because he always had weed. Chris and I used to play together as kids. The only difference was Chris went to public school, and I went to a private school. Chris could've gone to private school, but his grades weren't up to par with private-school standards. To think about it, his parents getting a divorce in the crucial years of his development could've caused his decline in achievement. I guess there was some mental instability inherent between sisters, Chris's mom and my mom. But Chris is doing all right for himself. Actually, he's doing more than just all right. In my eyes, he's one very lucky man. He's got a wife and kids that love him, and that can't be bought from any store.

Yes, Terri really dropped her guard today. I don't know if it has anything to do with the hypnosis session or she really felt compelled to do what she did today. Whatever the reason, I'm glad that they all came to see me. It took a lot of guts knowing that I'm a marked man as far as Serlinni's concerned, yet they came anyway regardless. I am especially grateful for the happy sack she gave me. I wonder if it was Chris's idea or she took Chris's stash.

I looked at the clock on the wall in the kitchen, and it was almost seven o'clock. If Grandmother was here, I would have to build one and smoke it my bathroom with the fan on. I went to my room and found my rolling papers and took the bag from my pocket. I opened the bag and automatically knew it was primo. I took a bud and pulled the leafy matter from the stem and loosely placed it in a prepared paper. I didn't roll a big one because it could be a while before I get any more. I rolled it up and took it into the kitchen. There I could turn the exhaust fan on over the stove, plus I'll be able to spray some Lysol in case the doorbell rings. I turned the burner on high until the coil turned red, touched the chronic to the glowing red coil, took a couple of puffs, and turned off the burner. It tasted good as I inhaled it, holding it in to get maximum results. I exhaled the spent smoke into the exhaust fan. I still felt like a teenager hiding from my parents, having to mask my activity. I took a couple more hits and put it out to see if the effects are what I'm looking for. I sprayed some Lysol just in case and took the half of a joint to my room and placed it in one of my grandfather's old ashtrays and slid it under the bed. I put the bag and papers between the mattresses and walked into the den. I grabbed my glass, poured myself another drink, and sat down.

I began thinking about what the messenger said about what is to come and the involvement of my offspring. I wonder how far down the road that will be. I began flipping through channels, looking for something of interest. I began to feel the effects of the cannabis, and it feels good. I remember my Nicole liked to share this moment with me when we were an item. At least she is free from being held prisoner like I am. I sat there drinking my drink, watching some documentary about heaven and hell. They are way off base considering what I've seen. They just don't realize who is pulling the strings. I've seen the man behind the curtain. I don't mean the wizard of Oz either. The dark one can appear in any form that he chooses or, should I say, that fits the occasion that he is trying to manipulate. He is the cause of the majority of chaos that occurs. I haven't met the big man yet, but I've met his messengers, the agents of heaven. They seem to think there will be redemption for me down the road as long as I don't stray from the program—whatever the program is. But like my grandfather told me, my actions also can have an impact on his final outcome. I don't want to be responsible for sending him to left side of town, the highway to hell.

I changed the channel and started watching the local news. Maybe there's something good happening around middle Georgia that isn't gloom and doom as compared to the rest of the world. Just happened there is. I heard the news anchor say there is a new development concerning the attempted robbery at the Giant Foods Store in Byron.

The anchor said, "We have a surveillance video that was leaked on YouTube by an unknown source. Channel 14 was called by an anonymous caller about the video. Lisa Lee Brown is on scene with the Peach County Sheriff's Department. What did you find out about the video's origin, Lisa?"

The field reporter said, "The sheriff's department isn't commenting on the video, but I did ask the store manager did he have a copy. The store manager told me that the police confiscated the only tape he had. Evidently, the video was leaked out from an unknown source and now is on YouTube. So far it has gone viral with the amount of hits that the video has achieved in a brief amount of time. I've seen it on my personal computer, and Mr. Farnsworth is someone I would want to take shopping with me."

The news anchor said, "Thank you, Lisa Lee, and here is the video that is now on YouTube. We must warn you that the scene you're about to see is graphic."

I was glued to the TV, watching the footage of me pushing a grocery buggy down the aisle and the gunman showing up. I left the buggy as the gunman walked behind me, and I looked back at him, slowed down, and *wham*, the roundhouse kick. I knocked the gun from his hand, and he produced the knife, and I knocked that out of his hand and kicked him in the nuts. As the robber was rolling on the floor, I grabbed the gun from the floor. I twisted the robber's hand behind his back, and the gun stuck to his head. The footage showed me walking into the storage room, and a different camera picked up the scene where the other gunman had a gun to the manager's head. I could see the gunman's mouth moving; that's when he told me to drop my weapon. I pushed the robber in front of me away and, at the same instant, fired at the head of the other robber. The local news censored the shot, but I bet YouTube didn't.

The news anchor said, "I'm sure that the store manager and the other employees of Giant Foods were glad that Mr. Farnsworth went shopping that fateful morning. Now a change of venue. Let's find out what the weather is going to be like the rest of the week."

The weather girl said, "I agree with Lisa Lee. I need Mr. Farnsworth, especially during last-minute shopping for Christmas. It can get pretty brutal out there."

The house phone began to ring. I went over to the table and looked at the caller ID, and it was CBS News. I let the answering machine take the message. I wished Grandmother had lived long enough to see her grandson in action. But I got a feeling she knows all about it and is probably bragging about her grandson on the other side. I was feeling pretty low. I really needed that boost. My cell phone rang, and it was Agent Harrington.

I answered it, "Let me guess, you just saw the YouTube footage, and you don't want me to answer phones and I should let my attorney handle the press."

Agent Harrington said, "Yes, you are partly right about the reason I'm calling you. I will have to get more men on the grounds to keep the media hounds away. I also talked to a colleague of mine from Homeland Security about using some of their resources. The Homeland Security guy said that Serlinni has been on their radar for some time for drug trafficking internationally, and they want to team up with the ATF with the bait-and-trap plan. I'll tell you more about it when the plans get finalized, but for now I need to get the security around the house beefed up."

I went ahead and told him, "Jessica Carnes from the Arizona bureau is flying in for the funeral, and I offered her a spare room here, if that's okay with you."

Agent Harrington said, "I can use all the extra help keeping you safe. What time will she be in?"

I told him, "She will be arriving later on tonight, depending on what time her flight is scheduled. I told her to call me when she got a rental car in Atlanta, and I would give her directions to Byron. I would then alert the guys on post to her arrival."

Agent Harrington said, "Mr. Farnsworth, because of the video, you have become a national and possibly international phenomenon. People are going to be coming out of the woodwork to get an exclusive interview. Under ordinary conditions, it wouldn't be a problem, but this is a security nightmare now. Luckily, there is one way in and one way out, and I'll have to get some men to cover the adjoining property as well. This extra press could be a blessing because Serlinni knows that the security will be beefed up even more."

I said, "I hope you are right. I don't want any more innocent people to get killed because of me."

Agent Harrington asked me to call him once Jessica gets to Macon so that he can alert the sentry at the drive. Agent Harrington then said, "By the way, Agent Franks is at post at the drive. It's his first day back on the job."

I said, "If I was him, I would want another assignment."

Agent Harrington said, "Agent Franks could've requested another assignment. He's had a taste of what most agents never experience. He's one up on me. I've never been in a real gunfight like he has. He's wearing that bullet-hole scar like a combat medal. The rookie agents are wanting a chance to get some trigger time, but they are too anxious. Being too anxious could get yourself or someone else killed."

I told Agent Harrington to tell Agent Franks that I would like to meet him and shake his hand.

Agent Harrington said, "You'll get your chance to do just that. He'll be your shadow during the funeral. I'll be going now. I have a lot of arranging to do with the local law enforcement. Talk to you later."

I told him, "Later, Agent Harrington."

I closed my phone, and the house phone began ringing. I checked the caller ID, and it was my cousin Chris Harland.

I picked up the phone and answered it, "Hello, Chris, what's up?"

Chris said, "We just saw the footage that you told us about. Terri and I were shocked being that we only heard you tell us the account a half hour ago, and now it's on TV. James, this is too much of a coincidence. You said the police had the footage held for evidence."

I said, "It's likely someone from the police force copied it and put it on the Net. They may get fired for it, but they may get some notoriety from it for being the first to release it."

Chris said, "James, you've gone from a news story to a full-blown media sensation. More than that, you've become an inspiration to people not to be a victim. People need to be shown that they need to man up to the situation. I can tell people I know that it was my cousin that kicked one robber's ass and put another in a box. I'm proud of you, cousin. My girls are ecstatic about it. I'll let you go, so check out the uncut version on YouTube before they take it offline."

"I will, Chris, talk to you later," I replied.

I hung up the phone, and before I ran to my laptop, I thought, *What is really going on here?* One moment I had hit rock bottom in depression, Chris and Terri show up with their kids and food, and now the footage from the attempted robbery has hit the media. I went to my room and opened my laptop. I hit a major search engine, and there it was. The title of the YouTube video is "Robbers Beatdown." I clicked on the video and watched the uncut version and stored it in my personal documents for posterity. I'll have it saved for Jessica in case she hasn't seen it yet. I checked my e-mail, and I do have an e-mail from Jessica.

I opened it, and she said, "Saw the YouTube clip. Didn't know you were a student of martial arts and so much for playing it low profile. I'm thirty minutes from landing in Atlanta. I will call you when I've rented a car. Jessica Carnes."

I looked at the time that she sent it, and it was ten minutes ago. Her boss must have let her off early. Otherwise, she would be getting here much later tonight. I turned off the laptop and walked back to the den with my cellphone in hand. I'll tune in on the syndicated news network and listen to what they have to say. I already have an idea what the news talk show is going to do. They will do just as they normally do things—run it into the ground. I am sick to my stomach with lawyers with talk shows, lawyers in congress, lawyers in the house of representatives, and a damn lawyer for president. Hell is going to have to increase its acreage just to house the lawyers and the rest of the criminals.

The news network was running the footage right after the video of the footage of me putting a bounty on Serlinni's head. I didn't even wait to see what the news talk show was going to do. I would probably get angry because they would spin it like I had it out for the black guys; that is simply not the case at all. I went back to my room and the rest of the joint and smoked the shit out of it. I needed to be calm and mellow when Jessica gets here. I turned on the kitchen exhaust fan and then sprayed some Lysol, refreshed my drink, and changed the channel on the TV to some show about refurbishing cars. That would be a neat hobby if I had the time to devote to it. Albeit the characters on the show aren't that way in real life in the shop. I bet they are real assholes to their help because of their overinflated egos. I would never treat my employees like they are beneath me because just like the case with David, he could've just as easily flipped over to Serlinni, but ever since I've always treated my employees in a professional manner on and off the job. Now the case with Tim and Trina, they just caved in to evil, plain and simple greed. Tim just took the express lane to hell because he committed suicide instead of going to prison. Trina has a possible chance at redemption, but like free will, it's all up to her which choice she makes.

The effects of the two stimulants had begun to take effect. My runaway thoughts had slowed down to an even trot. I didn't need to sit in front of the television and let my brain slowly decay. I should fire an e-mail to David to send me a file of Trailer Dolls very best song and listen to it. I did just that. I went back to my room, opened the laptop, and fired off an e-mail to David. Grandmother wouldn't want me to just mope. It would be easy to give in, but I won't let the dark one weasel his way in—no way. I can't rest on the laurels of Desert Reign. I need to continuously be ready to mold new talent into the next superstar.

I miss my grandmother deeply, and there's so much going on in my mind. I harken back to a phrase that my father told me before he died, "We've all gotta go sometime." Do I have the will to last as long as my grandfather? My dear grandmother doesn't have to carry secrets with her anymore. She is free from all of this—everything. She deserves the rest. My cell phone goes off in my pocket, and I almost jumped out of my skin. I looked at the incoming caller, and it is Jessica.

I answered the phone. "Are you almost in Macon?"

Jessica said jokingly, "Are you kidding? If these people in front of me drove five miles an hour faster, I might make it by Christmas. I'm leaving the airport and getting on 75 South."

I said, "Call me when you see the 475 split when you get close to Macon. I don't want you talking on the cellphone while you are driving in Atlanta traffic. Take your time, watch the exit signs, and be careful. I'll be waiting to talk you in once you get to the 75/475 split."

"I'll call you in a little while, bye," replied Jessica.

It won't be long and I'll have someone here to talk to instead of just having a conversation with myself in my head. I need some different material to process. I'm tired of the movie that is playing now in my head. I began thinking about the two encounters with Jessica. I wondered if her feelings for me are genuine, or is it because of my condition? I guess I'll find out when she puts her guard down.

I can't do anything but wait now. I'm forced to give in to the television. I went back to the den and channel-surfed until I stopped on the retro channel that shows movie classics. One of my favorites was playing, Gary Cooper in *Sergeant York*. I had missed half the movie, so I settled back into the couch and watched. In my grandfather's diary, he had been in Europe before the United States entered in 1917, and like Alvin York, he was put into a dangerous situation with a different outcome—an inheritance stained with blood that I now carry. I watched Alvin's exploits until my eyelids became heavy.

I slipped off into a dreamlike state. I found myself sitting on the back porch of my grandparents' house. I heard footsteps coming from behind me. I turned around, and it was my grandfather.

He sat down beside me and said, "I remember seeing that movie when it was a fresh release. That was ancient history compared to now. You need not worry, my dearest grandson. Someone is coming that loves you unconditionally. In fact, a messenger told me that she was destined to be with you. Don't think that she is drawn to you because of the animal that is inside. It is you that she now knows in her heart, that she can't live without. Your grandmother knew that you would be taken care of. She was ready to go. I want to be able to see her and perhaps my first wife one day, but it all depends on you."

CHAPTER 19

Before I could get a word in, the phone rang in the den and startled me awake. I looked at the caller i.d.. It was Jessica. I answered the phone.

"Where are you now besides in the car?"

Jessica chuckled and said, "I'm supposed to get off on Exit 149 and take a right?"

I said, "Yes, take a right on Highway 49."

Before I could tell her anything else, she told me where my location was.

She said, "Remember, being an agent provides me access to public and private records. Agent Harrington and I have already had a talk about the increased security, and I'll be there once I'm cleared at the checkpoint."

I said, "Okay, just stay on the phone since you're close. After you're cleared with Agent Franks, proceed straight down the drive, and I'll open the garage door for you."

"Okay, Mr. Farnsworth, I'm nearing the entrance of Farnsworth Lane. Hold on for a moment."

I listened to the background noise of the electric motor whirring as her window went down. I heard her speaking to Agent Franks as well as Agent Franks asking for her identification and opening the trunk. I continued to listen, and I heard Agent Franks give her the okay.

Agent Franks said, "I'll call Mr. Farnsworth to let him know that you're on your way."

Jessica handed her cell to Agent Franks and said, "Mr. Farnsworth is on my cell phone now. You can tell him."

"Agent Carnes is clear and on her way, Mr. Farnsworth."

I thanked him and told him that I hated that he took a bullet for me.

"It's my job, Mr. Farnworth. Just stay inside and open the garage door for Agent Carnes," replied Agent Franks.

I pressed the remote switch for the garage door to open. I'm anxious to see her; this house is too big for one person anyway. I then rushed to my bathroom, brushed my teeth, combed my hair, and splashed on some cologne. I then sprinted back to the surveillance monitor and waited for Jessica to pull into the garage. I watched for the oncoming glare of the headlights.

A few minutes go by, and she rolls into the garage. I closed the garage door and opened the side entry door to the garage. I waited until she got out and walked toward the car.

I said, "Can I help you with your luggage, ma'am?"

She looked at me and smiled. "Yes, you can help me, Mr. Farnsworth," she replied.

I heard the trunk lid pop, and I walked around the back and took out three pieces of luggage. I closed the trunk and grabbed the bags and told her to follow me. She had a small bag and her purse and followed me into house. I took her bags to another guest room and set them down.

Jessica said, "Is your mother here?"

I said, "She'll be here tomorrow for the family viewing. Other than that, it's just you and me. Oh, I forgot, the agent in the guest house out back, and you met Agent Franks at the entrance. Take your shoes off and relax while I fix you a drink."

As she was slipping off her shoes, she said, "How about a glass of real sweet tea?"

I told her that I would fix her right up. While I was washing my hands, I watched her look around at the surroundings.

She walked into the kitchen and said, "I'm sorry about your grandmother. She was a nice person for the short time I was around her."

As I was putting ice and pouring the tea into the glass, she walked up to me and put her right arm around my waist and took the glass with her left.

She took a heavy swallow of tea and said, "That's what proper iced tea is supposed to taste like." Then she set the glass down on the counter. "Hold on a second, I brought you something from Arizona."

Jessica went into the other guest room and came back with a small plastic case. She held her finger to her lips, gesturing to be quiet. She opened the small case and took out a piece of electronic equipment. She placed an earpiece in her ear and turned the device on. She walked over to the house phone and pointed the device at the phone. She looked at me and mouthed the word *bug.*

She walked around to other areas of the house and came back and said, "Only the phones are bugged, and I didn't detect any other bugging devices. I want to be sure that our conversations aren't being listened in on. Now, have you had something to eat?"

I told her that my cousin brought his wife and kids and Kentucky fried chicken over. I asked her if she had anything to eat. She said that she had a burger and a Coke at the airport in Arizona. I told her that I had plenty of food here, compliments of the grocery store manager.

Jessica said, "By the way, James, did you feel any way unusual before you walked into that store that morning?"

I said, "I felt weird when I didn't see people in their normal locations, like at the cash register or someone in the manager's office. I grabbed a cart and began gathering items that were on the grocery list compiled by Grandmother. Everything changed once I turned down the next aisle. That's when the robber came up behind me with a gun. If you've seen the video, you know the rest of the story except for the audio."

Jessica said, "James, I dreamed you would save some people the night before it happened."

I sat down because I had a feeling she was about to tell me more to this.

I said, "Before you go any further, let me get you something to eat. How about if I scramble you some eggs and grits with toast? It's too late to eat anything really heavy."

I got up and told her to get her some comfortable clothes on while I fix this up. I told her that her room was the next room on the right. She walked up to me and cupped her hands around my face and kissed me. Then she walked down the hall to the guest room, carrying the bug detection case with her. I got out a boiler, filled it to midlevel with water and put in a cup of grits. I turned on the stove as the coils heated up. I grabbed a couple of eggs and scrambled them and put some butter in a frying pan. I turned on the stove and waited until the butter began to melt, sprinkled salt and pepper on the eggs, stirred, and poured them in the fryer. I turned down the heat, grabbed a couple pieces of bread, and stuck them in the toaster.

I see the grits have started to bubble. I plopped a bit of butter in and stirred. I stopped for a moment because I could feel someone was watching me. I turned around, and Jessica was watching me from the hallway. She was wearing a T-shirt and pink pajama bottoms.

Jessica said, "I was trying to be as quiet as possible and watch you, but you heard me, didn't you?"

I was stirring the grits and nodded yes to her question.

Jessica said, "What do you have going, Chef James?"

I asked Jessica if she knew how to cook. She said she used to cook until her work schedule didn't give her ample time to cook a meal. She said she would invite her mom over and cook for her. I was taking the scrambled eggs up and putting them in a bowl. The grits have a few more minutes and they'll be ready.

I said, "If you would, push the button on the side of the toaster for me please."

Jessica pressed the button down and started the toaster. A few more stirs and I can turn the heat down on the grits.

Jessica sat down on a stool at the bar and said, "James, I haven't stopped thinking about you since you left Arizona."

I said, "I was hoping that you would be able to get on the plane with us that day, but you are here now. Let me get some plates, forks, and we can get some food into you."

Jessica asked where the plates were, and she retrieved them. The toast was ready, and I buttered them, placed them on a saucer, and grabbed the bowl of eggs. I placed them on the table and went back for the grits and spooned out the grits on our plates. I grabbed my glass and poured some tea in where alcohol once was.

I sat down beside Jessica and said, "Do they have grits in Arizona?"

Jessica said that her mom introduced her to grits when she was a child. I placed my open hand on the table, and Jessica gently placed her hand in mine.

I said, "Lord, thank for your many blessings. Thank you for bringing Jessica safely to me, and take care of my grandmother for me. Amen."

Jessica kissed me on my check and said, "I love you, James Farnsworth."

My chest was bursting with joy, and I told her, "I know you do, and I feel the same way about you. Now, let's eat before this stuff gets cold."

I'm happier than a kid in a lunchroom with the prettiest girl in school sitting next to me. Jessica was scooping in the food; she must be hungry. I asked her if my cooking was that good or if she was that hungry. Jessica almost spit food out her mouth trying to laugh.

She said, "It is good, your grandmother trained you well." She took a swallow of iced tea. "James, a man is going to try and kill you the day of the funeral, but he won't even make it to the gravesite."

I said, "Let me guess, this came to you in a dream."

Jessica told me these people came to her and said the shooter would be taken out at the checkpoint, only one way in and one way out to the family gravesite. I stopped eating and put my fork down.

I said, "Jessica, you just described the gravesite location like you have been there before. Tell me what else these people are telling you."

Jessica told me to finish eating because I'm going to need my strength, and we would talk more later. Usually I'm the first one to finish eating, but Jessica had shoveled it in and was rubbing on my inner thigh as I was putting the last of the grits and eggs in my mouth. Something was going on beyond my reasoning, but I had been in far worse predicaments. I grabbed the plates, the grits boiler, and placed them in the sink with some hot soapy water.

Jessica said, "I'll put those in the dishwasher in the morning. Could you get me a paper towel so I can wipe off the table."

I got a paper towel, wet it, and gave it to her. I told her that I was going to brush my teeth. I went into the bathroom. The scent of her perfume clung to the inside of my nose. I grabbed my toothbrush, squeezed out some toothpaste, and commenced to brush my teeth. I finished brushing, got a washcloth and soap on my face. I washed off the butter residue from cooking and rinsed my face. I was almost finished when Jessica walked in behind me. She had her toothbrush in her hand and asked me if she could borrow some toothpaste. I squeezed the paste from the tube onto her brush.

She winked at me and said, "Thanks, baby."

I sat down on the toilet and watched her breasts jiggle as she brushed her teeth. Her nipples were sticking outward, and I was getting excited myself. I reached out and gently caressed her curvaceous ass.

Jessica said, "Do like what you see, my dear James?"

I said, "I've been dreaming of the moment when I could be with you again."

Jessica spit out the toothpaste and wiped her face with my washcloth.

She said, "I don't think your bed is going to be big enough for both of us."

I told her, "My temporary room used to be my dad's room when he lived here. Your bed is a queen-size bed. If you want, I could sleep in there with you."

Jessica said, "You don't think I flew all the way from Arizona just to sleep by myself, do you?"

I told her that I would go and turn down her bed. I sniffed to make sure the sheets weren't musty from lack of use. I went to the kitchen and got a can of air freshener and sprayed the covers to freshen up the room. Jessica walked in and asked me if I had been entertaining any loose women in here.

I said, "Are you kidding? With the FBI and while Grandmother was here, bringing anybody in here was out of the question."

She said, "I know, just kidding. I know your grandmother wouldn't let just anyone get close to her grandson."

I said, "I'll be right back. I've got to set the alarms for the front of the house and cut off the lights in the den and the kitchen."

I stopped by my room and looked in my shaving kit for a condom—only one left. I stuck it in my pocket and walked to Jessica's room. She had turned off the lights except for the lamp by the bed. She had already taken off her clothes and was sitting up in the bed, leaning against a couple of pillows. I sat down at the edge of the bed and began to unbutton my shirt. I slipped off my shoes, socks, and slipped off my pants.

I said, "Jessica, these people in your dreams, did they tell you why they are contacting you?"

I took the condom and laid it on the nightstand. I slid under the covers next to her as she turned the lamp off. My nostrils already detected the wetness from her excited vagina.

Jessica said, "We've got plenty of time to talk about that later. I came here to be with you. My body has been aching for you, James, and I won't feel complete until you are inside me—where you belong."

She was fondling me, and I was nearly hard already.

I said, "Do you want me to get the condom?"

She said, "It isn't necessary."

She climbed on top of me, gently guiding me inside her warm, wet vagina. Her whole body just quivered for a moment, and she started to grind against me. I caressed her firm breasts in my hands and told her to slow down a little bit.

She said, "I'm planning on fucking you at least three more times before the sun comes up."

"You are that confident, are we?" I said.

Jessica said, "Confident? I'm absolutely sure."

She continued to grind and pump as we both exploded with ecstasy.

I said, "Damn, I should've gotten a towel."

Jessica said, "You mean one of these?"

She had gotten a towel and pulled it from beneath the pillows. We both got up and went into the bathroom and cleaned ourselves up. Jessica asked what time my mom was going to be here tomorrow. I told her she could be here in the morning or around lunch. I didn't know for sure.

Jessica said, "We'll have everything clean before she gets here. We'll sleep in our own rooms until she goes to sleep, and then the fucking starts."

While I was cleaning off the love juice, I said, "Jessica, when I mentioned the condom and you said that it wasn't necessary, what did you mean by that?"

Jessica said, "My love, I'm already carrying your seed, and it's growing inside me."

ABOUT THE AUTHOR

L. Edward has always been a rabid fan of all genres of the supernatural. His first brush with the world of fantastic tales of the things
that go bump in the night, all started with comic books in the early
1970's. L. Edward is a patented inventor and does freelance work
from his part-time home business. When he isn't writing, he is reading blueprints, quoting jobs or creating CAD drawings in his full
time job, in the industrial manufacturing industry.

L. Edward and his girlfriend call central Georgia their home.

CPSIA information can be obtained
at www.ICGtesting.com
Printed in the USA
BVHW071158180219
540524BV00001B/94/P